THE SAFEST PLACE

"You should have waited for me to help you down," he said, though there was no heat in his words as he untangled her skirt from her heel.

"I didn't want to be a burden." But she'd become one anyway, and my, didn't it feel wonderful to be in his arms.

Before she could extract herself from a position that was far too cozy and too comfortable, he turned her to face him. She looked up at him, expecting a lecture on being impetuous to follow.

He cupped the side of her face in one palm, and the glide of his thumb over her hot cheek sent a delicious shiver coursing through her.

"Beautiful, independent Maggie," he said. "What am I going to do with you?"

"What do you want to do?" she asked, a bit shocked by her own boldness.

A low sound rumbled from his chest, but she scarcely heard it over the hammering of her heart. And then he did just what she'd dreamed he'd do.

He lowered his head and captured her lips with his. This wasn't the tentative peck that she'd expected.

He kissed her with bold intent. He kissed her as if he wanted only her.

She felt safe, desired. She felt his need in his touch and the change in his body, and an answering want zinged along her nerves. She was startled by her own electrifying response.

Books by Janette Kenny

One Real Cowboy

One Real Man

A Cowboy Christmas

In a Cowboy's Arms

In a Cowboy's Arms

Janette Kenny

ZEBRA BOOKS
KENSINGTON PUBLISHING CORP.

Chapter 1

Colorado—1895

It wasn't yet ten in the morning, and Dade Logan was already bored clean out of his mind. Other than locking the town drunk up every Friday night when he got a snootful, there wasn't much in the way of law to enforce in Placid, Colorado.

Not that he was anxious for trouble to come to this sleepy town that rested in the valley east of the Sangre de Cristo Mountains. Nope, he'd been waiting all winter for one person to return, and if she didn't show up soon he didn't know what the hell he would do.

The hiss of the locomotive and clang of the rail cars pulling out echoed up the main street of Placid. Two folks had boarded the Denver & Rio Grande, heading east to Pueblo. He hadn't seen anyone get off.

Maybe she'd arrive on the afternoon train. As the racket from steel wheels on rails grew faint, he heard his name being called out.

"Sheriff Logan! Sheriff Logan!"

Dade smiled. Raymond Tenfeather was pounding down the boardwalk somewhere between the stable and the jail, hollering out his name like he did every day about this time.

When the liveryman's younger son wasn't trailing his elder brother Duane around town, he had taken to following Dade on the pretext of helping him look for lawbreakers. Dade had gently explained that wasn't necessary, but the boy took it on himself to be the town spy. God only knew what Raymond had seen this time.

Dade rocked back in his chair and stacked his crossed boots on the edge of his desk, awaiting the boy's imminent arrival. As always, his gaze narrowed on the wanted posters tacked on the wall.

Dammit all if the three outlaws staring back at him weren't smirking. His pa and uncles would find it amusing that Dade had taken an oath to uphold the laws that Clete, Brice, and Seth Logan had been hell-bent on breaking all their lives.

It'd been twenty years since he'd seen any of them, though their wanted posters had haunted him most of his life. There sure as hell wasn't any love lost between him and his kin.

Yet one question nagged at him right after they pinned a tin star on his chest. If his pa and uncles came to town, could he draw on them?

Part of him said yes. His pa had had no qualms about deserting him and his little sister. Yet when all was said and done, he wasn't sure he could turn on his blood. Hell, unlike Reid Barclay, he couldn't have turned on either of his foster brothers either.

"Sheriff Logan!" Raymond burst into the jail, his dark skin glistening with sweat and his scrawny chest heaving from his run. "I saw her."

"Just who'd you see?" Dade asked.

"The lady you been waiting for," Raymond said.

"Daisy?" he asked.

The boy nodded. "She got off the train, just like you was hoping she'd do."

Now how the hell had he missed seeing her?

Dade's heart took off galloping at the thought that sticking around here had paid off. His missing sister had finally come back like everyone in town said she would.

For the first time in months he visited that dream of buying a nice little farm for them to call home. He could run a few head of cattle. Do a bit of farming. Hell, he could find his brother Trey and bring him into the deal.

It was a damn sight better thing to dwell on than the idea of going back to the Crown Seven and having it out with Reid, the foster brother who'd sold them out when they needed him the most.

First things first. He'd waited twenty years to find his sister. He wasn't about to waste a second forestalling their reunion.

"Where is she?" he asked, heading for the door as he spoke.

"Mrs. Gant's boardinghouse," Raymond said, hot on his heels.

The place where Daisy and her crippled traveling companion had stayed before. Mrs. Gant had told him about their visit to Placid. How Daisy had caught the young sheriff's eye. How she'd promised to come back last fall and marry Lester.

But the sheriff was dead, spring was in full bloom, and nobody in town had any idea where Daisy Logan and her lady friend hailed from.

Dade figured she'd heard about Lester's murder and wasn't coming back to Placid. He feared he'd lost her again.

"Thanks, Raymond." Dade flipped the boy a silver dollar and headed out the door.

Long determined strides carried him across the dusty

street. He wondered how much Daisy had changed. Would she recognize him? Would she be as glad to be reunited with her family as he was?

He'd find out damn soon, he thought, as he cut down the street between Hein's Grocery and Doc Franklin's house.

Mrs. Gant's boardinghouse sat the next street over, but the elevation made the walk seem farther. He bounded up the steps then paused at the door to steady his breath.

The climb was nothing, but the excitement pounding inside him made it hard to draw a decent breath. He blew out the air trapped in his chest, inhaled deeply, and stepped inside.

Mrs. Gant was in the parlor, serving tea to a lady seated on the stiff Victorian sofa. Neither seemed to have heard him come in.

That was fine by him, for it gave him time to study his sister. Her golden hair had darkened to a rich honey. Her features were still delicate and refined, but she didn't resemble their mother or father.

She wasn't a cute little pixie anymore. Nope, she'd grown into a beautiful woman with all the curves in all the right places. But it was the odd combination of grief and fear in her eyes that gave him pause.

"I am so sorry to be the one to tell you that Lester has passed over," Mrs. Gant said, verifying what Dade suspected had caused his sister's distress. "I didn't know where you'd gone, but when you didn't come back last fall like you said you would, I thought maybe you'd heard."

"No, I had no idea," Daisy said. "What happened?"

"It was just awful," Mrs. Gant said. "This ruffian came to town, intent on robbing the bank. Lester was there, and before he could turn and confront this no-account, the ruffian shot him dead."

Daisy pressed a hand to her mouth, clearly horrified by

the news. Mrs. Gant's version was close enough to the truth that Dade didn't see the need to comment.

"I tell you truly," Mrs. Gant said, "I shudder to think what would've happened if Dade Logan hadn't stepped in like he did and ended the robber's reign of terror on our town. No telling who else would've been gunned down if not for your brother's courage."

Dade winced. The townsfolk had taken to embellishing the events of that day to the point Dade cringed every time he heard it. Now was surely no exception, for Daisy's face had leached of color at the mention of his name.

"W-what?" Daisy said in a voice that was way too high.

"Yes, indeed, your brother is a hero." Mrs. Gant launched into telling Daisy the details.

This surely wasn't the reunion he'd had in mind. A sound of disgust must've slipped from him for Mrs. Gant glanced his way and smiled.

Daisy, on the other hand, looked ready to bolt as her head snapped up and her gaze clashed with his. Instead of recognition lighting her eyes, they narrowed with suspicion and something bordering on dread.

Mrs. Gant patted Daisy's hand. "It'll be all right now, dear. You have family to help you through this difficult time."

Daisy shook her head. "No! I'm an orphan."

Dade scrubbed a hand across his nape, frustrated and more than a mite worried about his sister's increased distress. He wasn't surprised that Daisy hadn't recognized him after twenty years, but forgetting that he existed signaled something else entirely.

"You saying you don't remember me?" Dade asked.

She shook her head, her gaze focusing on his tin star before lifting to his face. He hadn't thought she could get any paler but he'd been wrong.

"Don't you remember that Pa left us at the Guardian Angel's Orphan Asylum?"

She shook her head and stared at him with troubled eyes.

"You recall being in the orphanage?" he asked.

She frowned. "Some. Mostly I was scared."

So was Dade, but it did him no good then or now to admit it. How could her memory be that bad?

She'd cried and screamed for Dade after their pa had dumped them there, and put up more of a ruckus when they'd been separated—boys in one wing of the drafty old building and girls in the other.

They'd seen each other precious little after that, but she hadn't forgotten him then. She'd pitched a fit when they took her away on the orphan train, to the point that they'd had to restrain him from going after her.

As the wagon pulled away, he'd vowed he'd find her and keep them together as family. But he hadn't been able to keep his promise.

"Reid, Trey, and I tried to find you," he said, but though they'd run away from the orphanage a few months later, they'd failed to pick up the trail of the orphan train that Daisy had taken west.

He'd failed his sister.

"Reid and Trey. Are they family?"

"They're as close as brothers to me." Or were. "But they aren't blood kin like we are."

Daisy didn't look the least bit relieved. In fact, she acted more leery than before as she turned to Mrs. Gant.

"Is he really my brother?" she asked the older woman.

Her trust in a stranger was a gut punch to Dade. It didn't ease his mind none that Mrs. Gant was giving him a long assessing look either. He knew trouble was coming before she voiced an opinion, which the lady always had on everything.

"Well, he says he is. But all we have is his word." Mrs.

Gant pinned him with a squinty stare. "You have any kin in these parts?"

He hoped to hell not. The last thing he needed was for his outlaw pa and uncles to show their faces. He'd be lucky to get out of town without getting shot.

"No kin left but me and Daisy," he said, and he reasoned that could be true. Any day he expected to get word that his old man and renegade uncles had been gunned down.

He swore under his breath, damning his pa again for abandoning his family. Daisy had only been four years old when they'd arrived at the Guardian Angel's Orphan Asylum. She'd just turned five when she'd been put on the orphan train.

"Forgive me for being skeptical." Daisy swallowed hard and looked up at him. "But I was told that I had no family."

"That's a lie," Dade said. "You've got me."

Daisy grimaced and seemed not the least bit repentant about her aversion to him. "If you're telling the truth."

Dade scrubbed a hand over his mouth to smother a curse that ached to burst free. What the hell could he do to convince his sister of the truth?

"Well, this is quite an interesting turn of events," Mrs. Gant said. "You don't favor each other at all. Pity you don't have a photograph of when you were children. We'd likely be able to put all doubts to rest then."

Truer words were never spoken. "There was one," he said, barely recalling the day it'd been taken but knowing it had happened all the same. "Ma kept it in her locket."

Daisy was clearly uncomfortable with his recollections for her cheeks turned pink, and she began fidgeting with something at her throat. He gave a passing glance at the blue cameo broach pinned to her bodice, then just gaped at the locket.

"That's it, handed down to her by her ma." He could've

sworn pure panic flared in Daisy's eyes. "Before Pa left us at the orphanage, he pinned that to your dress."

Her lower lip quivered as she turned to Mrs. Gant. "I don't know what to believe."

"Well, let's have a look inside that locket," Mrs. Gant said, taking the words right out of Dade's mouth.

Daisy squirmed, as if nervous over finding the proof of his claim. Finally she unclasped the cameo from her bodice, hesitated a moment, and then handed it to Mrs. Gant.

"My hands are shaking too badly to search for the clasp," Daisy said.

Not so for Mrs. Gant. The lady found and opened it before Daisy finished talking.

"There's nothing inside it," Mrs. Gant said.

Dade should've figured that'd be the case. And did Daisy just let out a sob? Or was that a sigh of relief?

The older woman closed the broach and pressed it back into Daisy's hand, then enfolded her in her arms. "There, there. You've been through too much, what with just hearing that your beau passed on. And now all this about having a lost brother."

"What happened to the photographs?" he asked his sister.

"I have no idea," Daisy said. "I didn't even know this was a locket until just now."

He snorted at that. How could she not know?

Mrs. Gant chastised him with a look that would've done a schoolmarm proud. But he wasn't backing down. Not now.

"Look at the back of the broach," he said, then stubbornly waited until she did as he said. "The inscription reads, 'Be true to yourself.' The initials *TL* are struck below it."

A frown marred Daisy's smooth brow. "Who's *TL*?"

"Our mother. Tessa Logan."

Her narrow shoulders slumped as she tightened her fingers around the broach in her hand. "That's it exactly. I guess that means you're telling the truth."

"It does. I've been looking for you for years," he said.

"Well now you've found me." She didn't sound particularly happy about it.

Dade couldn't fault her for that. He couldn't even grumble much about her hesitation now.

They were strangers. She'd lived a life apart from everything she'd known, just like him. She'd obviously lost her heart to Sheriff Emery and had intended to marry him. Or had she?

"Why didn't you come back last fall?" he asked.

"I couldn't decide if marrying Lester was the right thing to do," Daisy said, and avoided meeting his eyes. "By the time I knew what I wanted, winter hit and snowed me in."

That sounded fine on the surface, for he'd been stranded here as well. She'd gone back to wherever she'd called home, thought things over, and then returned to marry her beau. But Lester was dead, shot down by a young outlaw who was trigger-happy.

He reckoned it was better it happened now than after they'd married, leaving Daisy a young widow, perhaps with a baby. Yet Daisy didn't seem all that brokenhearted over Lester's death. In fact, she appeared more worried than anything.

"You never did say where you were raised," Dade said to break the awful silence.

Daisy fidgeted just enough to make him think she was uncomfortable talking about that. "A mining town west of the divide."

"This town have a name?" he asked.

She looked away. Swallowed. "Burland."

He'd heard of it. A couple of men had swindled claims

out of many a miner, ending up rich while the rest of the miners went broke. Considering the way she was dressed, he had a feeling she'd been raised in one of the rich households.

So why marry a poor small town sheriff when she could likely have her pick of gentlemen? Now that Lester Emery was gone, why stay here with a brother she didn't remember?

"Will you return to Burland now?" Mrs. Gant asked.

Daisy's narrow shoulders went stiff. "There's nothing left for me there."

Mrs. Gant tsked. "Then you should stay right here with your brother. That'll give you both time to get to know each other again."

"Thank you," Daisy said, her smile as thin as Dade's waning patience.

He ground his teeth. She wasn't sticking around because she wanted to get close to her brother again. Nope, she had nowhere else to go. That wasn't a kick in the shins but it came damned close.

His little sister had been a delicate, fragile child who'd clung to him. She'd been unbelievably shy and prone to tears. But the Daisy before him seemed to have developed the grit to take off on her own across the Great Divide.

She also possessed an alluring womanly charm that called to some need deep inside him. Hell, if he wasn't her brother he'd have been drawn to her.

He shook off those disquieting thoughts and focused on the problem at hand. He still didn't know what type of folks had taken in his sister and raised her.

Not that it mattered. She had him to protect her now, just like he'd sworn he'd do twenty odd years ago.

If she'd let him. Right now that didn't seem too likely.

Dade blew out a weary breath. For damn sure he had his work cut out for him gaining her trust.

* * *

Maggie Sutten read the determination in Dade Logan's brown eyes and knew with a sinking heart that she had landed smack dab between a rock and a hard place.

She'd had no idea that Daisy had a brother. A brother who was waiting here in Placid for her to return. A brother who'd spent years trying to find his sister.

Heavens to Betsy! Now he believed he'd done just that. Could things get any worse?

They surely would if Whit Ramsey found her.

However, for now she'd do well to play along with Dade Logan. That was the best way she could hide from Whit until she decided what to do next.

Yes, Whit would turn over every rock in Colorado looking for Maggie Sutten. He'd never dream she'd assumed another name and be living with a man.

And there was the advantage that Dade was a lawman. Though in truth she didn't think that would stop Whit from taking her.

A chill passed through her at the thought.

"Are you cold, dear?" Mrs. Gant asked.

"Just a case of nerves," she said. "It's a lot to take in at once."

Dade tucked his hands under his armpits and eyed her, and for an instant she feared he could look clean through her and see she was spinning a mile-long yarn. "You end up with a good family?"

Painful memories of the first family who'd taken her in threatened to torment her, so she blocked them from her mind and focused on the Nowells instead. "They treated me well enough, though it was clear I was just the companion to their crippled daughter."

As soon as the words left her mouth, she realized

Mrs. Gant had put two and two together. "I had no idea that Eloisa Reynard was your foster sister."

Maggie forced a smile, for nobody here knew that Eloisa was in fact Caroline Nowell, the "Silver King's" daughter. "We thought of ourselves as best friends."

"You were fortunate," Dade said.

If only he knew the truth! But that was a secret she had to keep. Just like she had to keep up the pretense of being Daisy Logan.

"Eloisa was a delight, and that made living there enjoyable," she said, and that was the honest-to-God truth.

The hell didn't come into play until her foster father had to pay up what he owed, and Whit Ramsey refused to honor the agreement of taking Harlan Nowell's crippled daughter's hand in marriage.

According to him, Whit Ramsey wanted Maggie.

If Whit had been a decent man and courted her, she might have considered his suit. But he was an overbearing snob and a lothario to boot.

She refused to marry him, but Harlan Nowell informed her she had no choice. She owed him for taking her in.

Maggie detested Nowell, and she didn't have much more regard for his wife. But she loved her foster sister and had hesitated over abandoning her.

"You can't marry him," Caroline had said after the last argument Maggie had had with Harlan Nowell. "Leave. Go far from here and never look back."

"I'm afraid what will happen to you," Maggie had said.

Caroline had laughed. "I'll grow old alone. No man wants to get saddled with a cripple."

"Never say never."

The long winter had proved true Maggie's suspicions about Whit Ramsey. He came to visit often though he usually ended up secluded in the library with Nowell, but even on those rare occasions when he stayed for supper he paid Caroline no attention at all. In fact, he'd often make some excuse and leave the room when she entered in her wheelchair.

So Maggie and Caroline planned out what she should do. Which, given the fact she'd told Lester she'd return to Placid, pretty much set the stage.

In the meantime, she went along with Harlan Nowell's plans for a big wedding this spring and suffered Whit's attentions.

The second the weather cleared and she found a chance, she ran away—ran here to Lester. Even then she'd back-tracked and paid a painted lady to use her real name and take the train west. For if Whit got wind that Maggie Sutten was here, he'd come after her.

"You said there was nothing left for you in Burland," Dade said, bracing a shoulder against the doorjamb. He gave the impression that he was relaxing and exchanging idle chitchat, but Maggie wasn't fooled.

He was fishing.

"That's right," she said, and summoned up a sniffle.

"What happened to your foster family?" Dade asked.

"They came down sick with a fever over the winter," Maggie said, thinking that was the easiest way to keep her lies from getting too tangled. "Father survived it. Mother didn't."

Mrs. Gant made appropriate sounds of distress. "Did dear Eloisa pass over too?"

"No!" The thought of Caroline dying made Maggie sick, though as it had turned out she'd lost the only friend she'd had anyway. "No, her father sent her east to live with an aunt and receive treatment at a hospital."

Another lie, but again it'd divert attention away from Burland, the Nowells, and Whit Ramsey.

Mrs. Gant embraced her in a smothering hug again, and

Maggie was just too weary to resist. "You poor dear, losing most of your foster family and your beau."

"It's been a trial," she said, and felt tears sting her eyes over Lester's death.

She'd genuinely liked him. But on the train ride here she'd finally decided she couldn't marry a man she didn't love. Not Lester Emery. And surely not Whit Ramsey.

"Now then I'm going upstairs and get your old room ready." Mrs. Gant smiled at them, and Maggie noted the moisture in the older woman's eyes. "For the first time in years this house will have a real family living in it."

Maggie forced a smile and hated that she lied to this kind woman who seemed hungry for family. As for Dade . . . Well, if lying sent a person to hell she was halfway there.

"I'd about given up hope of finding you," Dade said after Mrs. Gant took herself off, his voice going rough with emotion.

Maggie squirmed, truly bitten by guilt. "I'm sorry I don't remember you."

Sorry she didn't know what had happened to Daisy. And sorry that she was going to destroy his dream of a family without any explanation. But she couldn't keep up this charade.

She couldn't get too close to Dade Logan either.

The man was simply too big and too discerning for her peace of mind. And if she was honest, he stirred feelings in her that were best left sleeping. Feelings a woman would never feel for her brother. Feelings that would surely give her lie away.

No, she didn't dare get too close or too comfortable around Dade Logan.

As much as she wished otherwise, she couldn't remain here long either. Harlan Nowell would come looking for her, and he might do worse than drag her back to Burland and marry her to Whit Ramsey.

A chill tripped down her spine at the thought of being sold off like cattle. There had to be a trustworthy man she could confide in, a man who'd help her escape Whit Ramsey for good.

Her gaze flicked to the tall imposing man beside her. Dade Logan?

Those clear brown eyes of his had seen a world of trouble. According to Mrs. Gant's tale, he knew how to use that gun strapped low on his hip.

Yes, he was the type of man who'd risk his life to save his sister. But she wasn't his kin. She couldn't intentionally make him a target for Harlan Nowell's wrath.

For a few days she'd be safe here in Mrs. Gant's boardinghouse. She could plan what to do. After she'd gained Dade Logan's trust and he let down his guard, she'd make her escape.

It was the only way. She knew Harlan Nowell was in a bind. He needed her to satisfy a debt, and he'd move heaven and hell to bring her back.

Or silence her.

Chapter 2

Dade sat at his desk, crossed boots stacked on the edge and fingers twined at his nape. He'd left the boarding-house an hour ago so Daisy could settle in and he could make his rounds. Now he had nothing to do but watch time crawl by, hope trouble didn't gallop into town, and think about Daisy.

He pinched the bridge of his nose and heaved a groan. Finding his sister should've eased the worry that had nagged him for years. Instead, he was more restless than before.

The door swung open, and his gaze shot to the door. Damn, he'd been so lost in thought he hadn't heard footsteps on the boardwalk.

Nor would he have, he realized as the former U.S. Army scout stepped inside the jail and closed the door without making a sound. Dade still couldn't believe Duane Tenfeather could move like smoke and catch him by surprise every time.

"How is your sister?" Duane asked, likely having heard about Daisy's arrival from Raymond.

"She doesn't remember me."

Duane straddled a chair and crossed his arms on the

back. "You told me she was very young when she was taken away."

He snorted. "I can remember back that far." And he wished to hell he didn't, for that brought to life dark memories of his pa abusing his ma that he'd just as soon forget.

"So she will come to know you in time, and maybe then her memory will return."

"Maybe." But he wasn't holding out much hope that Daisy would mellow toward him anytime soon.

"You will stay here as sheriff then?" Duane asked.

Dade shrugged. "Reckon so."

He didn't have the money to buy a farm. Didn't have a home to take Daisy to anymore, thanks to his foster brother selling him and Trey out.

"What about that ranch in Wyoming?" Duane asked.

He rolled his shoulders where the old tension tended to pull tighter than bowstrings. "I've no claim on it now."

If he'd gone to the Crown Seven before last Christmas, he could've claimed his rightful shares and had it out with Reid Barclay once and for all. But he'd stayed here too long waiting for Daisy to arrive and ended up snowed in.

"You could fight for your shares," Duane said.

His mouth quirked to one side. "It'd be that all right."

But he wasn't about to drag Daisy along with him, and he wasn't willing to leave her here while he headed off to Wyoming.

It wasn't that he thought she needed protecting. But she had that jumpy look about her like she was running from something.

Yep, if he left her to her wiles now, he feared she'd skedaddle and he'd have the Devil's time finding her again. It was just dumb luck that he'd stayed put long enough for her path to cross his this time.

"You are going to give up on it then?" Duane asked, his one good eye fixed on him.

Dade rocked forward, boots hitting the floor and fore-arms slapping the desktop. "You trying to get rid of me?"

Duane smiled, his teeth stark white against his dark copper skin. "I know you don't want to be the sheriff."

"And you do?"

Duane rolled his muscular shoulders. "It beats working in my father's livery."

"Is this what you had in mind to do when you mustered out of the cavalry?"

"Yes." He downed his head. "I'd lost an eye in battle and the desire to keep fighting my own people. I wanted to come home to heal. Find a good woman and raise children."

Dade wanted the same someday, but that dream just kept getting pushed farther away for him. A good woman wouldn't want to hitch her wagon to a man who didn't have a pot to pee in or a window to throw it out of. A man whose kin were notorious outlaws.

Staying in this sleepy town was his best bet right now. Daisy and he could live comfortably in Mrs. Gant's board-inghouse. He could remain on as sheriff, watching over the town and his sister. And if Daisy refused to stay here?

Well, he just might follow her because there was nothing to hold him here but his promise to protect this town. Duane could take over the job. If he could still handle a gun.

"How's your aim?" he asked.

"I haven't tested myself since I was wounded," Duane said.

"Let's make a point to do that one day," he said, and Duane gave him a broader smile and a nod in answer.

Duane got to his feet and towered over the room. "Give your sister time to get used to having a brother, and don't be too bossy with her. Siblings don't like it."

"I'll bear that in mind."

The door swung open and a wooly haired boy poked his head inside. "Sheriff Logan! I bought a bag of penny candy—" The boy gaped at his big brother. "Duane, I didn't know you were here."

"I was just fixing to leave," he said. "How did you afford candy?"

Raymond gulped. "The sheriff gave me a reward for finding the pretty lady named Daisy."

"Well, now, that's good work, little brother."

Raymond smiled nervously as he moved toward Duane. "Are you going to tell pa?"

He ruffled Raymond's mop of curly hair and dredged a smile from the boy. "Nope. That's for you to do. Don't bother Dade too long now, you hear?" Duane said as he headed out the door.

"I won't stay long," Raymond promised, and Dade knew he'd be good to his word.

Raymond took a few shuffling steps toward his desk, his gaze fixed on Dade. "She's sure a pretty lady."

"That she is."

"You sweet on her?"

"Not like you're thinking," Dade said, refusing to acknowledge that odd pull he'd felt for Daisy when he first saw her. "She's my sister."

Raymond's eyes went wide. "She is?"

"Yep."

The boy leaned on Dade's desk and stared up at him. "I got a sister too. And a brother. You got a brother?"

He hid a wince. "Two of them."

"Are they with your ma and pa?"

Dade shook his head, not wanting to go into the details of his sorry life with the boy, but looking into those wide dark eyes told him he'd have to say something. "Our ma died when Daisy was a baby."

The boy frowned like he was deep in thought. "Did you cry?"

"Yeah." Dade scrubbed his knuckles along his jaw, having admitted that to two people in his life—Reid and Trey.

"I would've too. I can't imagine not having Ma around," Raymond said.

Neither had Dade been able to imagine it. In fact, the world he'd known ended the day his ma died.

Not long after his pa had brought a woman into the house to tend to Daisy and him—their new ma, his pa had told him. But she hadn't taken care of the house or them like his ma had. Pa started spending less time on the farm chores and more time alone with the woman.

Dade never knew if they'd tied the knot, but she held sway over his pa all the same. He'd never forget the day he overheard the woman suggest that his pa get rid of the brats and head out west.

Lying in the loft on his cot, Dade hadn't believed his pa would do such a thing. But he had without batting an eye.

"What about your pa?" Raymond asked.

He flicked a quick glance at the wanted posters and felt that old slow burn in his gut flare to life. "Don't rightly know what happened to him." Didn't rightly care either.

At the time, Dade had hated his pa for putting him in the orphanage, and hated those in charge for taking Daisy away. But he had fared better in the long run.

Reid, Trey, and he had formed a bond tighter than brothers. But the saving grace came to their lives when Kirby Morris took them in and made men out of them. He'd been a good father figure. He'd made them a family.

He'd given them a home, and though Reid had ultimately betrayed them, Dade wouldn't trade those early memories for anything.

A flash of deep blue across the street caught his eye. He

took a better look at the woman on the other side of the street and scowled.

The feathers on her hat shielded her face, but he remembered that dress and that eye-popping figure. Daisy.

She was walking at a good clip down the boardwalk, head high, firm breasts thrust forward, and hips swaying to a beat that pounded in his blood.

He wasn't the least bit surprised that male heads were turning her way. But the sudden jealousy that tightened his balls took him by surprise.

Hell's fire, what was wrong with him? She was his sister, for God's sake. But what he was feeling for her right now wasn't the least bit fraternal.

He expected her to slip into the general store, the dress shop, or the milliner's nook. But she breezed past them and headed for the little house tucked between the bank and the meat market.

Now why in the hell was she visiting Dr. Franklin? Was she sickly?

Worry had him pushing out of his chair. If something was ailing Daisy, he needed to know about it.

Maggie stared at the kindly physician who'd cared for Caroline Nowell for years as well as assumed the duty of company doctor before he'd fallen into ill favor with Harlan Nowell and been dismissed. It was reported he'd left the county, but down deep Maggie had feared he'd suffered a deadly fate.

So when she and Caroline stayed in Placid the last time, they'd been surprised and delighted to discover the doctor had taken up practice here. He'd laughed when they'd told him they were traveling under aliases, but agreed to go along with it.

Now it was imperative that he keep her identity secret.

"Well if it isn't Maggie Sutten," Dr. Franklin said, giving her a thorough once over. "Is Miss Nowell with you again?"

She gave the room a quick scrutiny and heaved a sigh to discover they were alone. "Caroline stayed in Burland. Do you recall how she liked to pull spoofs on folks?"

He laughed, a deep rumble of sound that brought a smile to her face. "That I do. If a sense of humor could cure a person, she'd be pain free and walking on her own."

She couldn't argue with that—Caroline had such a wonderful attitude, even on those days she was beset with pain. "She thought it would be fun if we assumed different names each time we left the springs. So last time I picked my friend's name."

"I remember," he said, and she nodded. "The sheriff was mighty smitten with you as I recall."

"He asked for my hand in marriage."

"So I heard. When you left without enlightening him about your identity, I assumed you weren't coming back."

"I promised I would, and here I am."

His expression turned somber. "You've heard about Lester."

"Mrs. Gant told me everything." She blinked back the sudden sting of tears over Lester dying far too soon. "Lester was a good man—I'd never met anyone quite like him before, so honest and so sweet. The day we left Placid he proposed marriage, and I almost told him my real name then."

"He didn't know?" Doc Franklin asked.

"I couldn't tell him the truth then, but I intended to do so this time." Before she told Lester that she couldn't go through with the wedding. Before she surely broke his heart.

Doc scrubbed a hand over his grizzled face. For all the care he dispensed with compassion, he looked more outlaw than gentleman. But she knew the heart of the man was pure, and she knew about some of the demons that drove him.

"What'll you do now?" Doc asked. "Return to Burland?"

"No! I'm never going back there." At least not willingly.

One bushy gray eyebrow squiggled over a discerning hazel eye. "Who are you running from, Maggie?"

"Whit Ramsey."

"Harlan Nowell's partner?"

"One and the same," she said.

"Why? What did he do to you? Or should I ask what have you done to him?"

She smiled at that. Doc was one of the few who knew about and applauded her spunk.

"It's a long story."

"I've got time. You want coffee?"

"Please."

She followed the stoop-shouldered man to the kitchen in the back of the house. He poured two cups of strong coffee and added a generous splash of whiskey to his own.

"Don't have any milk but there's sugar if you're so inclined."

Maggie added one lump and took a chair across from the doctor. She wasn't entirely sure where to begin.

"How is Caroline?" he asked.

A sad smile tugged at her mouth. "She had a bad winter, in pain more than not. But she didn't complain."

He attempted to flex the gnarled fingers on one hand. "Like me, she's learned that complaining doesn't make the arthritis any better or worse."

Maggie felt the same about the mess she was in. Complaining solved nothing.

"Now tell me why you are running from Whit Ramsey."

She took a sip of coffee and welcomed the jolt to her senses. "Did you know that when silver prices plummeted in the early seventies, Whit's father was the man who stepped in and kept Harlan Nowell from going bankrupt?"

"I knew, but it was an uneasy partnership from the start."

She suspected as much. "Whit's father and Harlan made a verbal agreement to blend the families in marriage."

"I'd heard rumors," Doc said. "I hoped Nowell would come to his senses and find a way to break the agreement."

"He did," Maggie said. "At Christmas, Harlan told Whit that Caroline's condition was worsening and that the doctor said she'd never be able to bear a child."

Doc whistled. "Extreme and I trust a lie, but Caroline deserves a man who'll care for her instead of being part of a business arrangement."

Maggie felt the same, but her foster sister had seemed hurt when Whit bowed to her father's wishes. "According to Harlan Nowell, Whit was more than glad to be released from that obligation."

"Interesting that Whit didn't put up a fuss over breaking the contract that would bind the families."

Her gaze locked on Doc's questioning eyes. "Oh, he fussed plenty. Instead of Whit having to marry Caroline, Harlan offered me to him instead."

Doc grimaced before taking a sip of his coffee. "You refused, I hope."

"Staunchly, so Harlan kept me under lock and key and made it clear I would marry Whit Ramsey."

Doc stared at her, as if he couldn't believe what she'd just said. "He intended to force you to marry this man?"

"Yes." Maggie was sure he'd have stopped at nothing to get her compliance. And if that failed, he'd have resorted to other unsavory means.

Doc smacked both gnarled hands on the table. "That's goddamned barbaric! When is the wedding supposed to take place?"

"Last Saturday, and before you ask, I escaped before dawn that day."

She sucked in a shaky breath, reliving the fear and anxiety that dogged her as Caroline helped her make her escape while it was still dark. She'd been on the run since, traveling from one small town to another to get here.

"Well now, I imagine that caused quite a stir when the bride disappeared on him," Doc said.

"That's what I'm afraid of and the reason why I assumed an alias," she said. "A lot depended on that marriage going through. He'll come after me."

"The change of name will slow him down." But the look Doc passed her way warned that it wouldn't stop Whit Ramsey. "Did you know that Logan is the name of the new sheriff?"

"We've met." She sighed, wondering if she'd ever be free to relax again. "It's such a muddle. Daisy was my friend on the orphan train, the one who couldn't remember anything of her past. They said she was like me, without kin. Not so. I was shocked to learn that the new sheriff is her brother."

"Damn. So Logan knows you're not his sister."

"Actually he thinks I am." She swallowed hard. "Though it's wrong to let him go on believing it, I couldn't tell him the truth. I can't dare to let anyone know." At least not now. Maybe not ever.

Doc made a face. "Because of Nowell?"

She nodded. "Any sage advice on how to disappear?"

"Depends on what you're willing to do."

Deceit didn't set well with her. But she so wanted to be free. To live her life. But would that ever be possible?

"You said I had a talent for nursing," she said, and he nodded in agreement. "I thought maybe you'd know of a hospital that would hire me."

Doc frowned at that, and she held her breath for fear he'd

changed his mind. "Don't know for sure, but Mullanphy Hospital in St. Louis is always looking for good workers. I might be able to get you started there as an apprentice nurse."

"Oh, thank you so much."

She grasped the doctor's hands that were stiff and bent with arthritis. He'd shared this with her foster sister. He knew what lay in store for a young woman suffering with the crippling malady.

Caroline. God, how she missed her. Was her pain great or tolerable today? Had her father found a suitable companion to assist her?

"You sure that's what you want to do?" Doc asked.

"It's a good career," she said honestly. "Besides, Whit wouldn't dream of looking for me in a hospital."

He bobbed his shaggy head. "All right, Maggie, I'll—"

"Daisy," she interjected, as the doctor's front door opened.

"Daisy?" Dade Logan asked. "I saw you come in here some time back. You all right?"

She lifted widened eyes to Doc, praying he'd go along with her lie in front of Dade. "Yes, I'm fine."

"Come on back to the kitchen, sheriff," Doc said, though the invite was unnecessary because the tall handsome lawman filled the doorway a heartbeat later. "Help yourself to coffee."

Dade stayed where he was and looked from the doctor to her. The concern in his warm brown eyes stirred awake the guilt she'd tried to ignore. What she would give to have kin that cared that much about her . . .

But she was totally alone.

Guilt was an emotion she couldn't afford to foster. Not for abandoning Caroline. Not for lying to this man.

She simply couldn't risk telling him the truth. No, that was something she'd let Doc do once she'd left here.

The sooner that could happen the better for her. Hopefully one day Dade would find his sister.

Dade pushed from the doorway and helped himself to coffee, his blue cambric shirt going tight across his shoulders as he did the simple task.

A tingle of awareness went through her. She'd be beside herself with joy if she had a man who cared for her instead of one who simply wanted to use her as a brood mare.

Doc shifted in the chair and winced. "I guess I'm the slow one in town, for I never connected Daisy here with the sister you've been looking for."

Dade hiked one shoulder. "Logan is a common enough name."

"That it is." Doc pushed back in his chair. "So where's your family from?"

"West Virginia," Dade said. "I barely remember it outside of it being real green."

"Pretty country. You got any kin back there?"

"None that I know of." Dade paid undo attention to his coffee. "Only family I have is Daisy."

Which of course made her feel worse for deceiving him. But then his being a lawman might goad him to get word to Whit.

The experience she'd had with men of late hadn't been good, outside of the friendship she'd formed with Doc Franklin and Lester. Any ties to family were just as questionable, beginning with her own family.

She'd been told that when her grandmother died, her aunt wouldn't take her in. She barely remembered the cross woman. What had happened to her mother? What kind of person would turn out a child? And what were the chances of a child finding two such families?

Maggie hoped that was a rarity, for she wouldn't wish her own kin on her enemy, nor would she give a sterling recommendation to the first family that had taken her in.

They'd treated her well enough before their daughter's death, but afterward . . .

Well, they had shuttled her back to the orphanage without any explanation. She'd gone from feeling loved to despised.

At least she'd known where she'd stood with the Nowells from the start. They'd made it clear that she wouldn't be a part of their family. She was Caroline's companion.

And yet Harlan Nowell decided that she would take Caroline's place and marry Whit Ramsey.

"Forgive me for my rudeness but I need to send off a telegram today," Doc said, slipping her a telling look.

She got to her feet immediately. The sooner he contacted the hospital in St. Louis, the sooner she'd be on her way there and to a new life.

"Thank you for seeing me," she said.

Doc nodded, his expression dutifully solemn. They'd said all that needed to be said before Dade Logan arrived.

She left Doc Franklin's house, very much aware that Dade was beside her. That was a new experience in itself. She'd never been this close to such a big, powerful man before but she took note of his smallest details.

She'd been in Dade's company for only an hour or so, yet she was aware of so many little things about him. The breadth of his shoulders covered in soft cambric. The measured surety of his long-legged gait.

The unique blend of strong soap and spice that was Dade's scent enveloped her. That slow tingle of awareness of him as a man left her skin pebbled.

She'd love to take a stroll with this man and let her senses soar. But there was risk in being out in the open where Harlan Nowell or Whit could happen upon her.

"Come over to the jail so we can talk in private," he said.

Spending time alone with him would be expected of

reunited siblings, but it was the worst thing she could do because she was drawn to Dade. And goodness, hadn't they said all that had to be said this morning? What more could he want to talk about?

She dreaded to guess. Had he seen through her ruse so soon? If that was the case, it was better if she found out now so she could make her escape.

"This sounds serious," she said and planted on a smile meant to put them both at ease.

He didn't return the gesture. "It is, but it's something you have to hear from me."

Worry settled into her bones as he escorted her across the hard-packed street. Her instincts bade her to run, but she knew she'd not get far from Dade Logan.

No, he was as dangerous as a loaded gun with a hair trigger. He had to be handled very carefully.

He opened the door with "Jail" painted on the upper glass pane and motioned her inside. A shiver zinged between her shoulder blades as she complied, bringing back the fear and desperation that had consumed her whenever Harlan Nowell locked her in her room.

That man had been so sure a locked door would hold her when she'd balked at marrying Whit. If not for Caroline, she'd likely be Whit's unwilling wife right now.

The door shut with a firm click, and the sense of being trapped nearly had her trembling.

"There's coffee on the stove," Dade said, his boot heels rapping out a slow steady cadence as he crossed to his desk.

He dropped his wide brimmed black hat on the worn surface, took a seat in the oak chair, and leaned back, the chair creaking in protest. He threaded his fingers through his wealth of warm brown hair and stacked his boot heels on the desk at the same time, the movement so masculinely arousing that she could do nothing but stare. He was the most assured man she'd ever met.

A man's man who made his way in this world by his own cunning and courage. A man who wouldn't force his will or his attentions on a woman.

He lifted discerning brown eyes to hers. "Something wrong?"

Yes, she was attracted to him and didn't know how to slam the door on those feelings. Certainly a sister shouldn't be looking at a brother the way she feared she was doing.

"I'm just a bit weary from my trip. Maybe we should put off our talk until later," she said.

"This can't wait."

"Then I suggest you speak your mind," she said, and dropped onto the lone chair with as much grace as she could muster.

He scrubbed a hand over his mouth, and she sensed he was as uncomfortable as she felt. But was he unnerved because of being alone with her, or was he uneasy about this urgent matter he felt compelled to discuss with her right now?

"You really don't remember our family?" he asked.

"Not at all."

He dipped the firm set of his chin and pointed to the wall. "Take a look then."

Frowning, she focused on the array of wanted posters as unease tied her stomach in knots. None of the sketches or photographs were familiar. Just what was he trying to tell her?

On the second pass scanning the posters, she caught the name that stiffened her in her chair. Not just on one poster. No, her assumed surname was on three of them.

She turned to Dade, and the disgust hardening his features

confirmed her fear. Still she asked, "The Logan Gang are our relatives?"

"Clete is our pa. His brothers Brice and Seth are our uncles and the only living kin I know of."

Good heavens. She'd never suspected she'd tie herself to outlaws by using her friend's name. She looked from the posters to the tin star pinned on Dade Logan's broad chest.

"Do the folks around here know?" she asked.

He shook his head. "Hell no, and I aim to keep it that way. But I'll be honest with you. I'm worried they'll get wind that I'm the sheriff here and come calling and not in a social way."

She went still as his meaning sank in. "You're afraid they'll attempt to rob the bank?"

"Yep. Considering the disregard our kin showed us as children, I don't see them treating either of us with any kindness now." His eyes held a desire for retribution that made her go cold inside. "It'd be like them to challenge me—see if blood is thicker than water."

"Is it?" she asked in all sincerity, because her own kin had turned their backs on her when she was just a child, and she couldn't imagine giving them the time of day should she meet them again.

But then she doubted they'd even acknowledge her, which was fine with her. She wanted nothing to do with the family who'd deemed her unworthy and sent her to an orphanage.

"Hell if I know. But I'd just as soon not find out."

Chapter 3

Disapproval flashed in Daisy's eyes, at odds with the curious emotion he'd glimpsed and tried to name a moment before. "You want to confront your father."

"Far from it," he said as he twined his fingers and cupped his aching head. "I don't rightly care if I ever lay eyes on our pa again."

She stared at him a long hard moment, as if gauging the truth in his words. "Then why did you take the job as sheriff, knowing you'd stand a greater chance to have to face off against your outlaw relatives?"

"I got roped into it." He swore when her delicate brows lifted in question.

"You shot the man who killed Lester, so the town offered you the job of sheriff," she said, and he nodded because that summed it up. "You could have declined."

"I needed a job, Daisy," he said. "This was the last town I trailed you to, and I wasn't about to leave and risk missing you again."

She blinked, and pressed her fingers to her lips. "So you stayed here all winter waiting for me to return."

"Yep, and I'm glad I listened to my instincts."

She didn't say anything to that. But then she hadn't

given any indication that she was pleased about reuniting with him.

He blew out a frustrated breath. "So what do you want to do?" he said. "Stay here or move on?"

She dropped her gaze to her lap, her brow pulled in a frown. "I don't know what I'd do here."

Maybe that independent streak was a common thread among orphans. Whatever caused it, he wasn't sure what to do with this beautiful woman with veins of grit.

Damn if he knew what to tell her. Most women her age were looking for a husband instead of a job. They'd marry. Raise children. Keep house.

But the fact remained that pickings in this town were slim. He couldn't think of one man he'd like to see married to Daisy. Hell, just thinking of her with another man annoyed him.

"Do you plan to remain sheriff then?" she asked.

"It's a decent job." He slid her a quick glance and caught her staring at him and not with sisterly curiosity either.

And damn it all if her boldness didn't get his blood heating.

He dropped his feet on the floor and sat up straight, as annoyed with her as he was with himself. "Anyway, we could continue living at Mrs. Gant's until I could buy us a place. Maybe a farm so we could run some cattle—"

"I don't want to stay here," she said.

Well, that answered that question. But the fact remained that he didn't care to stay here either, at least not for the rest of his life.

"You got some place in mind where you'd like to live?" he asked.

"East, west. I don't know. Just far from here."

That sounded like running away to him. But from what?

Maybe it was too painful for her to think of staying here now that Lester was gone.

By her own words, there was nothing left for her in Burland. He suspected she felt the same here now. He dreaded that she couldn't see them forming a deep family bond either.

"How'd you come to spend time here in Placid?" he asked.

She stared out the lone window, and for a moment he wondered if she was thinking up some story to tell him, for the truth ought to be easy enough to explain. But it was mighty clear she didn't trust him.

But then that was not a commodity he handed out often either. At least they had something in common. He just hoped she hadn't inherited their pa's lying cheating ways.

"My foster sister and I passed through here last summer," she said at last. "We were returning from Manitou Springs when she took sick, so we were obliged to stay until she was fit to travel."

"You two were traveling alone?"

She nodded. "Yes. Car—" She broke off and pursed her lips, and he wondered what she'd started to say and why she'd changed her mind. "Actually, Eloisa's mother had tired of making the monthly journey with us to the springs some time back, so we were used to traveling without a chaperone."

"A mite risky for two women to go traipsing through the mountains alone," he said.

"E-Eloisa would be the first to tell you that folks tend to ignore a person in a wheelchair," she said.

Again she stumbled over her foster sister's name. "What was wrong with her?"

"Arthritis. She was in the habit of taking the waters there." Her brow creased, and a sadness came over her again. "She refused to give up hope that she'd be able to walk without pain."

Now that had to take a lot of fortitude. "Did it help?"

"For a little while, but the crippling pain would return. Last winter was her worst yet." She shook her head, clearly concerned over her foster sister's health. "When her mother died, her father decided to stop her sojourns to the springs."

"Is that best?"

Her fingers tightened on the handbag she clutched. "No, not when the waters eased her pain for a spell."

No doubt this was a sore subject for her, but knowing how she lived, how she cared for a foster sister told him a lot about her. She had a good heart to battle for another's care.

"A shame that you couldn't convince her pa that the waters were a benefit for his daughter."

"He never listened to me," she said. "This time was no different."

"But you tried to get him to see reason anyway and got on his wrong side."

Her narrow shoulders racked tight, a clear sign he'd hit a nerve. Had she been asked to leave the home she'd known when she'd disagreed with her foster father? Had he turned her out cold?

Or had that been the out she'd been looking for all along? She was surely of an age to have a life of her own now. Is that why she'd come here alone to Placid, knowing Lester would marry her?

"You locking horns with your foster father have a bearing on why you left Burland?" he asked.

"Yes." She stood and faced him, and the fury sparking in her eyes took him aback.

He had a hunch she hadn't just had a set-to with the senior Reynard. She'd had an all out battle with the man who'd taken her in.

"What happened, Daisy?"

"He had made arrangements to send Eloisa to a relative, and since I was basically her companion, there was no reason for me to stay there." She downed her head, hiding her face from him, hiding her emotions. "Even if he'd wanted me to."

The last said it all. His own anger kindled to life over what she'd been put through. Being cast out again.

"Did he know about Lester Emery?" he asked.

She shook her head. "Eloisa knew, but neither of us felt the inclination to mention him or our time in Placid."

A secret well kept between friends who were as close as siblings. He understood that trust well. Or had at one time.

"The journey here was more taxing than I recalled." She moved to the door in a flurry of skirts. "I'm going to return to Mrs. Gant's and take the powder Dr. Franklin gave me for the misery in my head."

He rose, annoyed that she was closing him out again even though he had a better understanding of why she was slow to trust. "We're family, Daisy," he said, and that had her stopping in the doorway. "Think about what you want to do. Where you want us to live."

She didn't look at him, but she nodded. "I will."

Then she was gone, and Dade was left to wonder if he'd ever be able to form that close bond with Daisy again.

Of all the things Dade disliked about being sheriff, the long stretches of having nothing to do but think wore on him. He'd spent the last twenty years on the Crown Seven working every job from rounding up cattle and mustangs to putting in the first fence that wide open Wyoming range had ever seen.

Though he'd often complained of having to fight the elements, he missed filling his lungs with clean air. Missed working from sunup to sundown and the pride that came with owning land and cattle.

He missed Kirby Morris and his sage advice.

He missed his brothers.

His jaw tensed. Reid's betrayal had destroyed that bond. That year he was away in England with Kirby's cheating cousin had been hard on all of them.

But the worst was yet to come.

When Kirby passed over, Dade and Trey had been forced off the Crown Seven. They'd taken jobs working from ranch to ranch in order to survive. Sleeping in bunkhouses or out on the range left him miserable and antsy.

By the time he'd learned that Reid had sold them out instead of securing the ranch for them as Kirby had intended, Trey had hired on with an outfit out of Texas and was long gone. Dade had lost touch with the man he'd considered a younger brother for the past twenty years.

The same anger and sense of abandonment that he'd felt when his pa dumped him and Daisy at the door of the Guardian Angel's Orphan Asylum had engulfed him again. Only this time he was truly alone.

He'd lost his trust in Reid, the elder brother he'd looked up to. He'd lost track of Trey, the younger brother he'd taken under his wing in the orphanage. He'd lost his home and sense of place for the second time in his life.

Thanks to getting stranded here last winter waiting for Daisy to return, he had lost his second chance to reclaim his shares of the Crown Seven. He'd hoped that Trey had swallowed his pride and anger and showed up to confront Reid.

He hoped he had a stake in the ranch through Trey, if only to call it home. But he knew the chances were great that Trey had never returned to the Crown Seven. That

Reid had screwed them over again, sold the whole damn ranch and moved on.

It shouldn't matter. He'd made the choice to risk his stake in the ranch when he'd picked up Daisy's trail. He'd counted himself damn lucky when he'd found her. But the close family bond he'd hoped to regain with Daisy seemed a lifetime away right now.

Dammit, family should stick together, even if they simply lived in the same town. But she might want to move east, and the home he'd hope to have one day was in the West.

Home. He longed for one so damned bad. Would he ever have a place to call his own?

The slow steady drum of footsteps on the boardwalk caught his attention a heartbeat before the front door opened. Dade shoved his worries to the back of his mind and whispered his Colt Peacemaker from the holster just as the stranger stepped inside the jail.

"Sheriff Logan?" the man asked.

"That's me," Dade said, sensing this stranger had all the charm of a rattler and was just as dangerous. "Something I can do for you?"

The man closed the door, and Dade got a glimpse of a pearl-handled revolver tucked in a tooled holster. Yet there was no star or badge pinned on his vest.

From his experience, men who sported flashy weapons were either outlaws or hired guns. Often it was difficult to distinguish between the two.

"I'm looking for a woman," the stranger said, answering the question of why he was here. "She's probably traveling alone."

Like Daisy. "This woman have a name?"

The stranger dipped his chin. "Margaret Sutten, though she tends to go by Maggie."

Dade shook his head. "Haven't heard the name. What's she look like?"

"Light brown hair, blue eyes. Taller than average and on the thin side. Mighty fetching."

"That description would match a lot of women." *Including his sister.* "Are you a lawman or a bounty hunter?"

"I prefer the term private detective," the stranger said.

Dade just bet he would. "Afraid I didn't catch your name."

A couple of beats of silence drummed the air. "Carson. Allis Carson."

Dade had heard the name mentioned and not kindly either. Allis Carson was a hired gun. A bounty hunter who tracked the worst outlaws and hauled them into the law, usually slung over a saddle dead to the world.

"What did this Sutten woman do?" he asked.

"She stole money and jewelry from her employer."

"Must have been worth a lot for him to send a detective after her. What was she? A domestic?"

The bounty hunter shook his head. "Orphan. Family took her in as the companion and helper for their crippled daughter."

Same as Daisy and her foster sister Eloisa? Had to be a coincidence. Yet the niggling unease that chaffed Dade's nerves told him there was a connection he wasn't going to like hearing.

"Sounds like she tired of being the nursemaid. How much did she make off with?"

Carson dipped his chin. "Several hundred dollars."

Why would anyone hire a brutal bounty hunter to find Margaret Sutten if she was no more than a petty thief? Unless there was more to this story than Carson was telling.

The bounty hunter strode over to the posters on the wall, seeming to take his time staring at each in turn. Dade had the feeling the man did this often, looking for those outlaws who'd warrant the biggest rewards.

Like the Logan Gang.

Good thing he looked nothing like his pa and uncles. His surname was common enough that nobody should instantly think he was related to the Logan Gang. But the way Carson studied the posters made him uneasy.

"Who are you working for?" Dade asked.

A mocking smile curled the bounty hunter's grim mouth. "Harlan Nowell. He hired me to find Margaret Sutten and bring her back to Burland and justice."

Burland? The same place Daisy had been living? Ah, hell! Who was he to believe? Daisy or the bounty hunter?

He feared the latter, for Carson watched him like a hawk sighting prey. But Dade had learned at a young age to hide what was on his mind for his pa never hesitated to take the razor strap to him.

Those in the Guardian Angel's Orphan Asylum weren't any more lenient. He had the scars to prove it.

"You said this woman stole jewelry too?" Dade asked.

The bounty hunter faced him again. "The daughter's blue cameo broach. According to Nowell, it wasn't costly but it was a family piece that their daughter treasured."

The words slammed into Dade like a gut-punch. He stared at the scuffed floorboards, feeling sick inside as he thought back to the broach Daisy wore. She'd not known it was a locket. Not realized that it'd been their ma's.

Now he knew why her memory was so bad. Why she hadn't recognized him—hell, why she hadn't remembered she had a brother. She'd lied to him about her name. About her foster family.

She wasn't Daisy Logan.

But the broach was his ma's. He was sure of it. So why was the Silver King of Burland claiming it belonged to his family? What connection did Daisy have with Nowell and Margaret Sutten?

"Bound to be a good many cameo broaches around," Dade said. "How will you recognize the stolen one?"

The bounty hunter's cold dark eyes glittered with malice. "Because this one is inscribed, and I doubt there are two blue cameos with the same quote. Once I find it, I'll know I have the right woman."

A feeling of dread settled over Dade, as biting as a winter northwester off the Rockies. "What's the inscription?"

"'Be true to yourself.'"

The stab of betrayal sank into Dade's heart. Logic said his sister must have lost the broach somewhere in her travels. Margaret Sutten had found it.

Yep, that made sense.

He'd found his ma's locket, but Daisy was still lost to him.

"Good words to live by." But were there initials under it?

Hell, was *TL* struck below the saying on Margaret Sutten's broach? He only had her word, and he was doubting that now.

Dade blew out a deep slow breath when he longed to cuss like a trooper. Dammit all, he'd been conned good. But it explained why he'd had less than brotherly feelings toward the woman posing as his sister.

The woman who stirred his lust was Margaret Sutten. Thief. Liar. God knows what else he could tag onto that.

Annoyance vibrated along his nerves like a mirage shimmering over the dry high plains of Wyoming. He'd spent six months here for nothing.

"You sure you haven't seen her or the blue cameo?" Carson shifted his tense form almost in a show of defiance, and again Dade caught a glimpse of the pearl handle on his sidearm.

He thought of Carson hauling Margaret Sutten back to Burland, Colorado, and cringed.

She'd be answerable to Carson. She'd be a victim to his rules and to his baser desires. She'd get no mercy from this man.

Not that Dade should give a damn one way or the other. She'd stolen Daisy's broach and her identity.

But he couldn't turn her over to Carson now.

"Afraid not," Dade said.

She might be the only clue to finding Daisy. But how could he get to the truth of what happened to his sister when a ruthless bounty hunter was on the Sutten woman's trail?

Only one way he could see. He'd have to continue to pretend that Margaret Sutten was his long lost sister.

Instead of upholding the law, he was bending it badly in hopes of finding out how this woman came by the broach and what she knew about Daisy Logan.

"Reckon I'll ask around town." The bounty hunter left without another word.

Not that there was anything more to be said.

Silence thundered in the room and set Dade's nerves to twanging. This must be how the old miners felt when they hauled a load of nitroglycerin up a mountain trail. One wrong move, and they'd blow themselves to hell and back.

Dammit, he hoped nobody in town connected Daisy Logan with the imposter Carson was trailing. Hoped Carson would decide Margaret Sutten wasn't here and move on.

He hoped he could get over to Mrs. Gant's and tell Margaret she'd best stay hidden. But as soon as he left the jail he'd likely draw the bounty hunter's attention.

So he damned sure couldn't head right to the boardinghouse. Nope, he'd have to make it look like he was taking his rounds. Had to go slow and talk to folks and shoot the shit with Duane when every instinct in him screamed to run over there.

Then it'd be a wait and see game.

Dade thumbed his Peacemaker's hammer to half cock and rotated the cylinder, ignoring the tightening of his gut and the sweat tickling his nape. Six chambers, six bullets, same as the last time he'd checked it.

Hell, he couldn't remember when he'd last fired a shot. Couldn't remember why.

Dade clicked the cylinder back in place and carefully released the hammer. The boiling inside him eased to a simmer as he stood and slid his revolver into the holster.

He knew Carson would kill anyone who got between him and Margaret Sutten. Knew too that nothing short of a bullet would stop Carson from taking her back to Burland.

Dade couldn't let that happen, not now. Maybe not ever. He glanced at the outlaws on the wall, certain their smug grins were just for him. They'd be damned proud he was set on protecting a thief.

"Go to hell," he told his kin, then stepped out the door like he'd done every day since he'd taken on this job.

He moved with slow determination down the boardwalk, noting the town looked the same as always with nobody in any hurry to do anything. It was a peaceful town.

A shotgun blast split the air, driving that thought from his mind. His blood ran cold. Trouble had come knocking again.

Chapter 4

Dade whipped his revolver from the holster, trying to pinpoint where the shot came from. His gaze honed in on the bank down the street. Not one horse was tied in front.

The clerk peered out the window, seeming as curious as Dade. The bounty hunter stood beside the banker in the open doorway. Both men were looking down the street as well.

The trouble wasn't at the bank. Didn't involve the bounty hunter either. But was Margaret safe?

He longed to run to the boardinghouse to check but he didn't dare. Not with Carson watching him.

The bounty hunter crossed his arms, as if letting Dade know he'd get no help from him. Fine by him. Dade didn't want Carson's brand of swift justice.

Dade glanced south toward the livery. Duane Tenfeather had closed one stable door and stood just outside its twin, staring uptown. Duane's pa was just inside the open door with his big hands clamped on Raymond's scrawny shoulders. No doubt the boy was straining to get a look out.

Dade inclined his head marginally in a silent message for Duane to stay put and keep watch. He started up the boardwalk. His heart had settled into a steady gallop, and his senses were honed razor sharp.

He needed a calm head, for he didn't want to die this day because some fool had gotten trigger-happy. When Dade was halfway between the grocer and the butcher shop, another shotgun blast exploded.

This time he knew the source. He took off at a lope toward the lone saloon at the edge of town.

Two men burst out the door and took a tumble into the street, scarcely landing in a puff of dust before they scrambled under the boardwalk.

One man was the town drunk who'd spent every Friday night in the jail. The other was a young cowboy who'd gotten a job sweeping the saloon floors over the winter and still hadn't found an outfit that'd hire him on.

Dade ran across the street and slammed his back against the saloon's rough log wall in the alley, hoping to hear what the hell was going on inside. It was too damned quiet.

He hurried to the side door and turned the knob, careful not to make a sound. The bartender should be talking sense to whoever had fired that shotgun. But instead of talk or cussing, all he could make out was a whimper.

Shit, that wasn't the sort of noise he'd ever heard in a saloon before. Had somebody plugged the bartender? Had the shooter left the saloon already?

He took a fortifying breath and stepped into the narrow back room that was used for storage. The calico cat hunched atop the crates gave him a quick look before resuming her vigilant stare at the doorway leading into the saloon.

"Stop your damned whimpering, boy," came a gruff voice tinged with disgust.

"I c-c-can't as long as you're p-p-pointing that shotgun at m-m-me," a young man said, his tone unnaturally high and strained.

The responding curse was low and guttural, summing up the first man's regard for the younger one. "Already told you I ain't gonna shoot you dead unless you decide to hightail it, though I'd prefer that to having you kinned up with me."

Dade slid his Colt back in the holster, finally recognizing the gruff voice as well as the situation at hand. Mac-Garren had a small ranch ten miles or so outside of town and kept a handful of cowboys on full time.

Word around Placid was that MacGarren was overprotective of his two daughters, both shameless flirts who were likely itching to find a young man. One of them had run off with a soldier from Fort Carson last year.

From the sounds of it, the other one had found herself a cowpoke to warm her bed. Now there'd be a shotgun wedding, which was a damn site better than a funeral.

Dade eased into the saloon, snaring the bartender's and MacGarren's attention. "Shooting your firearm off in town carries a fine."

The rancher worked his mouth into a knot. "It was worth it to run this no-account to ground."

"I thought you was aiming to kill me," the younger man said, keeping a white-knuckle grip on the back of the chair he was straddling.

He didn't appear to be much older than eighteen if he was a day.

Thank God the cowboy hadn't taken a shot at MacGarren or he likely never would have lived to see nineteen.

MacGarren had been an army scout and had true aim. If he'd wanted this boy dead, he'd have gotten the job done with one shot.

"Now that you got him cornered, I suggest you put your shotgun back in its saddle scabbard," Dade said.

The older man snorted. "I'll do that once he's behind bars."

"The boy broken some law?" Dade asked.

"He stole a horse."

Now that was a damn serious crime and one that could get him strung up in most places. "You want him tried for rustling?"

"Nope, just keep him under lock and key until I can fetch the preacher," the older man said.

Dade looked at the boy and saw he was eager to flee. No doubt he'd do just that after the vows were exchanged. But at least the girl would be married and the child would have a name.

"Let's go then." Dade motioned for the cowboy to get a move on.

He was on his feet and out the door, but had the good sense not to run. Dade reckoned part of the reason was that MacGarren was right on his tail.

The trio proceeded across the street under the curious stares of those who'd ventured out of their shops as well as those watching from behind the relative protection of closed doors.

The banker was still on the boardwalk but Carson was nowhere to be seen. Panic knifed through Dade. Where the hell had the bounty hunter gone?

He hoped to hell he hadn't decided to visit the boardinghouse. If he caught Margaret there, he'd haul her out of Placid before Dade could stop him.

Dade hustled the boy into the jail with MacGarren trailing him. Damn these people for causing a ruckus at the same time the bounty hunter was searching for Margaret.

"If all goes as planned," MacGarren said as Dade closed the cell door with a resounding click, "we'll hold the wedding tomorrow."

The cowboy stared at MacGarren with more courage than he'd shown so far. But then he was where the older man couldn't get his hands on him.

"Is Charlene all right?" the cowboy asked.

MacGarren swore. "She'd be better off if I'd never hired you on, but what's done is done. I'll be back tomorrow."

"Tell her I asked about her," the cowboy said, earning a curse in reply.

"You going through with it?" Dade asked.

The cowboy puffed out his scrawny chest. "Yes, sir. Ain't no secret that I'm sweet on Charlene."

Ain't no secret that the boy was leg-shackled good and proper, even before the vows were said.

Dade had misjudged him. The cowboy would stay married to her, produce a passel of kids, and maybe one day earn his father-in-law's respect if he busted his ass hard enough to provide for MacGarren's daughter and the children they'd likely bring into this world.

Damn the cowpoke and MacGarren for causing this brouhaha. But at least having a prisoner gave Dade reason to head to the boardinghouse.

Mrs. Gant provided a cooked meal when Dade had a prisoner. Another reason why he figured the town drunk made certain to spend at least one night in the jail each week.

"You hungry?" Dade asked.

The cowboy scratched his belly and grinned. "I could eat."

"I'll be back in a spell then."

Dade stepped out of the jail and scanned the street. Every thing seemed back to normal from one end of town to the other. Folks here just expected him to settle things like he'd done the moment he'd ridden in last fall.

He set off for the boardinghouse, mulling over what he'd say to Margaret Sutten. If he confronted her now, she might make like a wild hare and run off again. He couldn't risk that.

Fact was he didn't want Mrs. Gant to know the truth yet either. So that left him waiting to get Margaret Sutten alone. And where in the hell was he going to do that with Allis Carson in town?

Have to be at the boardinghouse, maybe when Mrs. Gant went to town. Or deep into the night when the lady was asleep.

And dammit all if the thought of getting Margaret alone in a bedroom didn't rouse other urges in him, ones that he was free to feel for her now. If he was fool enough to.

All he wanted from the pretty thief was information about Daisy. Margaret—no, Carson said she went by Maggie.

That name surely fit the cunning woman who had grit to steal from the richest man in Colorado. Who had convinced everyone in Placid, including him, that she was his sister.

He couldn't trust her behind a broom stray with both eyes on her. She was trouble he couldn't afford to have, and yet he couldn't let her go.

He found Mrs. Gant in the kitchen, busy shaping dough into loaves. "What was the shooting about?" she asked before he could get a word out.

"A rancher and his impending son-in-law had a disagreement." He gave the lady a brief version of what had happened.

She tsked as she slid the pans of bread into the oven. "I'll fix a plate then and take it down to the jail."

"Thanks." That would give him time alone with Margaret.

Mrs. Gant wiped her hands, her gaze reaching down the hall before coming back to him. "Is Daisy still visiting with Doc Franklin?"

The simple question had anger and frustration colliding in him. "Not that I know of. Last I heard she said she was coming back here."

"I guess she changed her mind."

Or somebody changed it for her. Somebody like Allis Carson. Shit!

Dade hiked back across town to Doc Franklin's, but the sign on the door proclaimed he'd left on a call and wouldn't return until early evening.

He checked the stores in case Maggie Sutten had decided to do a bit of shopping. He ventured inside the church in case she had gone there to ask forgiveness for the mountain of lies she'd told. He stopped at the depot to see if she was waiting for the next train.

But she was nowhere to be found. Neither was Carson.

Worry settled over him like a cold wet blanket. What had happened to Maggie Sutten?

"A bounty hunter came by today to ask about a woman," Duane Tenfeather said, his stealth startling Dade.

"What did you tell him?"

"I had never seen or heard of her before."

That was a relief. "Daisy's missing."

"Ah, you didn't know," Duane said. "Your sister left this afternoon with Doc."

Damn! Was the woman totally fearless? Or was it just recklessness? "When did they leave? Where'd they go?"

"To the Orshlin farm. They left town about thirty minutes before the bounty hunter rode into the livery," he said, and Dade heaved another relieved breath.

Maggie was gone before Carson arrived. She should be safe unless someone in town put two and two together like he had.

"The oldest Orshlin boy came to town to get Doc because his mother is near to birthing," Duane went on.

Of course Maggie went with him. Dade wanted to be angry that she hadn't consulted him. Wanted to be pissed that Doc hadn't sent word over either.

But the fact was they were in a place where Carson would likely never look. She was safe.

"What about the bounty hunter?" Dade asked. "See him around lately?"

The usually stoic half-breed tensed, his anger so hot Dade felt the burn. "He rode west, taking the trail up to the mines."

The opposite direction from the Orshlin farm. "He must have picked up somebody's trail."

Duane looked to the mountains. "God help them."

Silently, Dade offered up another prayer for his sister, himself, and Maggie Sutten.

Maggie was sure she'd just seen a miracle as Doc Franklin brought the Orshlin twins into the world. There were several tense moments when the doctor had to guide one baby into the proper position, and that just awed Maggie. Even then, the afternoon had given way to dusk before both twins were delivered into Doc's gnarled hands.

As Maggie cleaned up the tiny, squirming, crying bundles of joy, she felt as if she'd finally done something worthwhile in her life. The strong tug in her heart also confirmed that she wanted children of her own. At least three, though she'd take more or less, God willing.

If she could finish her nurse schooling and find a good man to love and marry, she'd be happy beyond belief. Dade Logan's handsome face came to mind right off, and the ache in her heart shot straight to her womb.

She shook off that fanciful dream with a bone deep shiver. Until she was sure that Whit Ramsey wasn't out for revenge, she couldn't think about marrying any man. Considering how much he had lost financially by not marrying her, the "adopted" daughter of the Silver King, made her fear he wouldn't forgive or forget her anytime soon.

But even if he did and there was a way she could have

a romance with Daisy's brother, he'd likely never forgive her when he found out what she'd done.

She didn't kid herself into believing he'd remain ignorant of her deception for long. Doc Franklin knew her identity. All it would take would be one slip of the tongue for Dade to get suspicious.

No, she'd have to tell him the truth—at least that she wasn't his sister. She didn't dare reveal her true name to him or tell him she was on the run from a man.

"How are they?" Mrs. Orshlin asked after the doc had finished tending to her.

"They seem perfect," Maggie said. And tiny and so vulnerable.

How could any woman not love her baby? Not want to keep it?

She caught Doc's nod and pushed those questions that had tormented her all her life aside. Carefully she transferred both babies to their waiting mother. Tears filled the woman's eyes, but her smile attested that they were happy tears.

"Thank you both for coming so quickly," she said.

"That's my job," Doc said.

Maggie glanced past the curtain that separated the bedroom from the main part of the cabin. The other children were seated at the table, and the oldest boy—the one who'd ridden alone into town to get Doc Franklin—was feeding his siblings.

The boy was capable, but he never would've been able to deliver both babies alive.

"When's your husband due back?" Doc asked.

"Five days from now, maybe more," Mrs. Orshlin said on a yawn, confirming her exhaustion. "Please, help yourself to supper. You know you're welcome to spend the night."

"Considering the hour, we'll take you up on that offer,"

Doc said. "Let's get those babies in the cradle, and you take a nap."

She gave a weary smile. "All right. But just a short nap."

Doc nodded to Maggie. She removed the sleeping babies to the wicker basket and snuggled them tightly in blankets. They barely stirred.

"Are we really staying the night?" Maggie asked as they slipped out of the alcove that served as a bedroom.

Doc gave the children a quick glance then nodded to the door. "I'd just as soon."

He and Maggie stepped onto the stoop and closed the door. A stiff breeze had kicked up, carrying with it the smell of rain.

Maggie bundled her heavy wrapper around her. "You're worried about her."

"Yep. She tore inside. I'm afraid the packing won't hold and she'll start bleeding." Doc frowned up at the dark clouds scudding across the sky.

She shivered at the thought. "When will she be out of danger?"

"If the bleeding stays through the night, she should do fine." She caught his barely perceptible wince and could only guess at the pain such exercise cost him. Yet he hadn't given up his vocation. Dedicated to the soul.

"It was the most wonderful thing to witness," she said.

"That it is, but it can be a challenge too." He made a face. "Before long my own infirmities will force me to retire. Don't know what folks will do then without a doctor."

The same thought had crossed Maggie's mind when she saw how badly Doc's hands had been affected by arthritis. If he hadn't been here to guide these twins into the world, would they have survived?

Surely another doctor would come along to take his

place. Doc must have connections to the fine medical school in St. Louis. He should be able to persuade a young doctor to come here and take over his practice.

"What did they do before you came here?" she asked.

"Prayed for the best, since doctoring was left to the barber and an old woman who served as midwife."

That combination of Wild West doctoring saved some and buried far too many. Even good nurses were nigh impossible to find.

That was part of the reason that her foster parents had chosen her off the orphan train. She was a tall sturdy girl. They believed she'd be able to "assist" their crippled daughter in her daily tasks.

She tipped her head back and drank in the wild beauty around her. Even during the years she'd lived with Harlan Nowell, she could look out a window anytime and enjoy the mountain vista.

"It's a fact I'll miss living in the mountains." But to stay would place her at great risk.

She'd made enemies of two powerful men. Both had the reputation of leveling swift retribution on their adversaries.

A wry smile played over the old doctor's mouth. "You'll be a great asset to the profession. Why I'd hire you right off, though I couldn't afford to pay you near what you'd earn in a hospital."

She'd be happy being his nurse. "If I thought Whit would give up looking for me, I'd take you up on your offer."

Doc scowled at his gnarled fingers. "Maybe he will in time."

She doubted it. From all she'd heard over the years, Whit didn't forgive easily. She knew Harlan Nowell was the type to carry a grudge to the grave. By running off, she'd not just ruined Whit's plans for a partnership with Nowell, she'd cost Whit a small fortune.

Whit would want to ruin her. Nowell would likely want to see her dead, and would level the same punishment on anyone who dared to help her. That's why she couldn't stay here and bring trouble on Doc Franklin.

"I should see to supper," Maggie said, and Doc Franklin gave a weary nod.

"You go on. I'll be in directly," he said.

Maggie watched him amble off toward the barn before she turned and slipped into the cabin. The eldest Orshlin girl, nearly eight years old by Maggie's estimation, had placed a strange array of food on the table and had begun peeling potatoes.

"What are you making?" she asked the girl.

Boney shoulders lifted in a shrug. "Stew, I reckon. Ma usually puts in what she has on hand."

Maggie doubted the woman added dried apples and raisins to the mix. "May I help you?"

The little girl glanced from the alcove to Maggie, clearly torn between doing as she'd been told and welcoming a helping hand. Maggie understood the dilemma.

"I assure you I make a very good stew," Maggie said. "But I could use a helper."

That was all it took to get the girl's capitulation. She nodded her head. "I help Ma all the time."

"Well then tonight you'll be my helper," Maggie said, and set to work preparing a goodly portion of food that would last the family through tomorrow.

By then Mrs. Orshlin should be able to oversee her daughter's culinary attempts. Hopefully Mr. Orshlin would return by then.

If not . . .

Then Maggie might volunteer to spend another night here to help the family. It'd keep her hidden from anyone Whit would send looking for her, and she'd get away from Dade Logan and his discerning brown eyes.

For she wasn't sure how long she'd be able to hide her secret from him.

Maggie pressed a hand to the small of her back and stifled a groan. It'd been some time since she'd functioned on so little sleep, and longer still since she'd dragged out of bed and set to work at a stove.

Her body was mightily protesting the short hours and the hard cot where she'd grabbed a few hours rest. It didn't help that thoughts of Dade Logan had invaded what sleep she'd managed, leaving her more restless.

He wouldn't be happy that she'd left Placid without telling him her plans, but she wasn't about to begin accounting for her every move to another man. And if she was honest, she'd had to put distance between them because she was afraid she'd make a mistake around him last night, one that would prove she wasn't his sister.

Why oh why did Daisy have to have a brother? Especially one who was too handsome and too discerning by half? Who'd spent the entire winter here waiting for her return?

"Is the baby going to be all right?" the eldest Orshlin child asked Maggie as she spooned oatmeal into bowls.

She prayed that would be so, but she'd caught the worry on Doc's face in the wee hours. Something was amiss with the second born twin, and whatever it was could take the child's life.

A wave of helplessness washed over Maggie the likes of which she'd never felt before. Yes, she was helping the family by caring for the younger children and lending Doc a hand when needed. But it didn't feel like near enough.

A deeper yearning swelled in her to help the baby who had fallen into a death-like sleep three times now. According to Doc, there was no cure for the ailment.

She'd heard the same thing of Caroline years before. There was little to ease the pain and nothing to stop the debilitating twisting of her limbs as she aged. And in her case she aged quickly.

Laudanum for pain. A wheelchair allowed her some range of movement when the pain was too great for her to hobble.

Maggie hated that her foster sister's world was confined to her spacious suite at the mansion. That watching others enjoy a life was likely all she'd ever have.

She shook off the memories that troubled her still and bent to the cooking task at hand. The fragile baby needed a nurse for the next week, and she'd volunteered to stay and help the family any way she could. She hadn't hesitated to take on the job. Not only would she be able to provide much needed help, but staying here would keep her out of Dade Logan's company.

That man had commanded far too much of her thoughts since just meeting him yesterday. Heaven knew how much more she'd catch herself thinking of him—his eyes, his impossibly broad shoulders—if she was in his company more.

"Do you have children?" the oldest daughter asked her as she added the last ingredient to the medicinal recipe Doc Franklin had given her to ease Mrs. Orshlin's condition.

"No, but then I'm not married either."

The little girl nodded, taking that in. "Are you going to?"

"Going to what?" she asked, confused.

The little girl let loose an impatient huff. "Get married and have babies."

The question caught her totally off guard. There'd been a time when she'd dreamed along with Caroline about winning the heart of a good man and having a family. But now that she had defied Whit and Harlan Nowell, that dream seemed a lifetime away.

"Maybe some day," she told the little girl as Doc exited the alcove.

His smile, though tired, relieved her. "She's resting and both babies are stable. How's the formula coming?"

Maggie gave the thick broth a stir. "It's about finished."

Doc helped himself to a taste and nodded approval. "You'll need to feed this to the mother twice a day for the first four days to rebuild her blood. After that she can resume her regular meals."

"What should I do for the baby and this death sleep that threatened him before?"

"Enlist the help of the children and keep a close watch. If either stops breathing, just wake him or her up." Doc picked up his black bag, looking far too worried and tired. "I've done all I can, so I'll head back now. If you need me, send the boy into town, and I'll come back."

"I will."

But as she followed him outside to his waiting buggy, she prayed all would go well. That Mrs. Orshlin would regain her strength with the aid of the meat broth and the precious babies would thrive.

And after that?

Maggie watched the doctor's buggy disappear around the bend, momentarily tempted to pick up her skirts and run after him. She wanted to stay here for this was where she was needed. Hopefully it wouldn't be long until Doc had secured a position for her at the St. Louis hospital. As Daisy Logan?

Maggie frowned, questioning the wisdom of continuing to use her childhood friend's name. If she remained Daisy, then she'd forever be Dade's sister. She'd be subject to surprise visits from him. She'd have to continue leading him to believe that he'd finally found his sister. That they were family.

If she hadn't been attracted to him, then maybe she could continue that ruse. But even if that were so, continuing this deception wasn't fair to him or to Daisy. Brother and sister deserved to be reunited.

How could she tell him the truth?

She couldn't. It was too risky to contemplate. He was a lawman, and he'd not rest until he knew her real name. Telling him would just be another loose thread for Whit to pick up on.

No, she'd have to choose a new identity. She'd have to disappear in St. Louis and hope Dade Logan never found her again.

Dade perked up when Doc's buggy passed the jail, but his relief vanished when he realized that Maggie Sutten wasn't with Doc. He tossed a disgruntled glance at his snoring prisoner before heading out the door.

He looked over at the general store. He doubted Doc had dropped her off there before continuing on to the livery. Hell, he wondered if she'd even come back to Placid.

Anger boiled in his gut as he strode down the street, his long legs eating up the distance in minutes. Running off was just what he'd expect of a thief. If she had gotten away, he'd likely never set eyes on her again.

Unless he went after her right now.

Doc climbed from the buggy with effort, then reached back to retrieve his black bag. He turned toward the street just as Dade reached the livery.

Before he could fire off a question, Doc raised a hand to stop him. "Daisy stayed with the Orshlins to help the new mother and babies. She'll likely be there a few more days. Maybe a week."

So she hadn't run off. "That her idea or yours?"

"Mine. She's needed there, and she wanted to help." Doc grabbed his cane and started across the street, his gait as shaky as Dade's thoughts.

He couldn't fault her for that. Going to the aid of a stranger proved Maggie Sutten had a good heart, even if she was a thief and a liar.

"Yesterday, a bounty hunter came to Placid looking for a woman," Dade said when he caught up with the doctor. "Margaret Sutten is her name."

Doc stared at him, his expression conveying annoyance. "Don't recall hearing the name around town."

"That's what I told him," Dade said, certain if Doc knew Margaret Sutten, his next remark would dredge a confession from him. "What's interesting is that the woman he described matches Daisy to a T."

Doc huffed a sigh, or maybe it was a muffled curse. "This bounty hunter move on?"

"Yep, but not far," Dade said.

"What'd you tell him?" This time, Doc Franklin's expression was burdened with worry.

"That I hadn't seen her," Dade admitted.

Doc didn't say anything, but Dade caught the slight flaring of his eyes. He thought back to yesterday when Maggie had stolen over to the doc's. They'd been deep in conversation when he walked in.

How well did Doc know her? Was he helping to protect her?

"Well, go on," Doc said, seeming more annoyed than interested.

"He said Miss Sutten had stolen money and a family heirloom. Harlan Nowell hired him to bring her back to stand trial."

"Damn!" Doc resumed limping down the boardwalk.

Dade kept pace beside him, more certain than before that Doc was protecting her. But why was he being loyal to a thief?

"How long have you known Miss Sutten?" he asked, tired of pussyfooting around the truth.

"Since she was a child," Doc said, not bothering to concoct a story and surely not inclined to apologize for helping to pull the wool over Dade's eyes. "I was the company doctor at Nowell Mines."

He wanted to be angry at Doc. But he couldn't.

The man wouldn't lie unless there was reason. Dade damned sure wanted to know it all, starting from the beginning.

"I want the truth," Dade said as he followed Doc into his house.

The old man's shoulders bowed a fraction. But Dade didn't draw a breath until Doc Franklin nodded.

"As well you should," Doc said. "Sit down and I'll tell you what I know."

Chapter 5

Doc fussed around the stove putting on coffee and stretching Dade's patience to the breaking point. "What do you want to know?"

"How did Margaret Sutten come to live with Harlan Nowell?"

"Maggie—that's what she's always gone by—was one of the last girls on the orphan train that summer that passed through Denver," Doc said. "Harlan Nowell selected her."

"As a companion for his crippled daughter," he said, repeating what Maggie and the bounty hunter had told him.

"Yes." Doc flexed his gnarled fingers and winced. "Caroline Nowell was afflicted with crippling arthritis. The family consulted me about easing her pain."

"So you were treating the daughter before Maggie arrived."

"I was."

No wonder Maggie had run right to Doc's place when she got here. He was the closest person she had to a friend. And when she found out her beau had been shot dead, she needed someone to talk to.

"Tell me more about Caroline Nowell," Dade said, getting right to the heart of the thing nagging him.

Doc frowned. "I thought you wanted to know about Maggie?"

"I do. But right now I'm concerned about finding Daisy."

"Your sister. Of course," Doc said. "I can't see what she has to do with Caroline Nowell though."

Dade watched Doc closely. "The bounty hunter accused Maggie of stealing Caroline's cameo, but I know for a fact that the one Maggie was wearing belonged to my sister."

"I wouldn't know anything about that."

That didn't surprise him. If Nowell had taken the cameo from Maggie, Doc had likely never seen her wear it until now.

"Are you sure Caroline is Harlan Nowell's real daughter?"

Doc bobbed his head. "Without a doubt. I delivered the child myself soon after moving to Burland. She favored her mother, right down to her coal black hair and dark eyes."

Dark hair, dark eyes. Definitely not Daisy then. If Doc could be believed, and Dade did believe him.

He scrubbed a hand over his mouth and swore silently. He was back to square one looking for Daisy, not knowing what the hell happened to her after she boarded that orphan train. Or was he?

"I need to find out how Maggie came by that broach," Dade said. "Why did she decide to use my sister's name? Did she know Daisy? Can she tell me what happened to her?"

"I can't answer those questions," Doc said. "Talk to Maggie. If she knows anything about your sister, it's up to her to tell you."

He thought that over and knew Doc was right. Maggie held the key to so much.

"You doctored there for a good many years then?" Dade asked.

"Close to twenty years." Doc leaned back in his chair and cradled his coffee cup that was surely empty now. "Reckon you're curious why I left Burland."

Dade nodded. "Twenty years in one place sounds like home to me." It sure had been for him growing up on the Crown Seven.

"It was a good place to live at the time, and since I served as the company doctor as well as doctor for the town of Burland, I was always busy."

"Why'd you leave it?"

Doc downed his head, shoulders rounding enough to tell Dade the reasons pained the older man. "There was an accident at the mine. Some men were trapped deep in it. Some of them that got out needed medical attention immediately or they'd lose a limb."

Dade didn't have to be told that being reduced to a cripple would threaten a man's livelihood. The majority would likely prefer death to being lame.

"I set up a makeshift infirmary on the site and got to work," Doc said. "Harlan Nowell ordered me to stop. Seems his brother had suffered a minor injury, and he wanted him seen first. I refused."

"Harlan Nowell fired you over that?"

Doc laughed, though the sound held no humor. "He did one better than that. He brought in another doctor and threatened my life if I didn't leave town."

Dade studied Doc and knew the man was being honest with him. Harlan Nowell had everyone under his thumb in his town, and woe to anyone who crossed him. Including an orphan?

What had it been like for Maggie living there?

She was likely nothing more than a servant to Nowell.

The big house wasn't a home for her but a place of employment.

"Why'd Maggie leave there?"

"Again, that's up to her to tell you, but suffice to say she had damned good reason to run." Doc braced both arms on the table and leaned forward. "No matter what you think of her now, you can't turn her over to that bounty hunter."

Dade couldn't fault the man for being protective of Maggie. Hell, he'd bet there were things about Harlan Nowell that Doc was keeping to himself.

"Never intended to." Dade pushed to his feet. "Thanks for the coffee and information. I'll head out to the Orshlins' and have a talk with Maggie."

"Don't," Doc warned. "You'll lead that bounty hunter right to their door, and those folks don't need trouble or upset."

Patience wasn't Dade's long suit, especially when he'd been searching for years for his sister and Maggie could hold the key to her whereabouts. But he understood the doctor's concern too for the Orshlins and for Maggie.

He was certain Allis Carson would go to any lengths to capture Maggie. All his earlier concerns about that happening rushed forward to needle him again.

"All right then. I'll stay away from the Orshlin farm until the bounty hunter tires of Placid and vamooses."

"Even then watch your back," Doc said.

Dade dipped his chin and left. Yep, Allis Carson would surely kill anyone who stood in his way of taking Maggie into custody.

There was more to this story than what Carson had told him. More than what Doc had said. What the hell had Maggie done to warrant Harlan Nowell hiring a bounty hunter to haul her back?

Anger snapped along Dade's nerves as he returned to

the jail to bide his time until Carson moved on. It was going to be the longest damn week of his life.

Maggie hung the last of the laundry and bent to retrieve her basket. A flash of light from the grove of aspens to her right stilled her.

She stared hard at the place, chills rippling over her skin. The sun had to have reflected off metal. Nothing else made that kind of arc of light.

Someone was out there. Someone was watching her.

She hurried back into the cabin and closed the door, heart hammering too loudly. Had Whit sent someone to find her?

"Mighty fine flapjacks," Mr. Orshlin said.

"Thank you." It was a recipe she'd gotten from the cook at Harlan Nowell's mansion, back in the day when she was thinking ahead to getting married and cooking for her own family.

That was before she realized the depth of deceit Harlan Nowell dipped to when he took her—an orphan—into his home. Though she'd never felt unwanted there, she'd never felt any kindness either.

She was hired help, no different from the cook or the housekeeper or the troop of guards Harlan Nowell employed. Though for her, he had a more devious end in mind. She was to take the place of his crippled daughter in a marriage merger that would be a prison sentence for her.

She turned to the family she'd enjoyed helping out this week. The greatest danger was over for the babies and the new mother.

Now that Mr. Orshlin was home, Maggie was no longer needed. In fact, she could be a danger to these kind folks if she stayed here longer.

Mrs. Orshlin emerged from the alcove with the youngest baby cradled in her arms. Her smile was wide and genuine.

"He is thriving now," she said, smiling down at the baby she'd come close to losing. "Won't be no time and he'll catch up to his twin. I can't thank you enough."

Maggie held up a hand. "I've enjoyed every minute."

Simon, the youngest boy before the babies came along, wrinkled his nose. "Even the times you had to change Samuel's and Em's diaper?"

She laughed, the moment of fear forgotten in the wide-eyed excitement of a child. "Even then."

"You have been a godsend," Mrs. Orshlin said. "I dread to think what would have happened if you hadn't been here."

So did Maggie. "I'm sure Doc would have stayed or found a lady from town who'd have done just as good a job."

"Whether that would have been the case or not," Mr. Orshlin began as the clatter of an approaching buggy grew louder, "we shall be eternally grateful to you."

It had been a very long time since Maggie had felt such warmth and love of family. She certainly hadn't had even a smidgeon of that growing up in Harlan Nowell's palatial house. She couldn't remember her own family well— just an aunt who had made it plain she didn't want her.

"Can you come back?" Simon asked, tugging on her skirt to get her attention.

"I'll surely try." But she wondered if she'd ever be free to visit with friends.

Friends. That was another thing she'd been in short supply of. She'd had that with Caroline Nowell, but as Caroline's health had worsened, she'd even lost that to a degree.

Not for the first time she wondered how Caroline was faring. Had they found another person to care for her daily needs? Was that person as understanding and gentle with her?

The creak of the buggy stopped just outside, and Maggie quelled the urge to hide. She peered out the window. Doc had returned for her.

"Doc is here." Maggie moved to the door, paused to steady her nerves, then opened it.

The children rushed out the door and clustered around the buggy, all talking to Doc at once. All sharing a snippet of the week with the new babies with him.

She marveled at his patience with the children, then applauded his grit as he moved toward the cabin. His limp was much more pronounced.

To her surprise, Dade Logan had come along with Doc, following on horseback. Dade didn't look to be in good temper. Still, just the sight of his broad shoulders and handsome face sent a delicious shiver rippling through her.

She didn't want to be attracted to him, especially while she was pretending to be his sister. But try as she might, she couldn't stop it either.

Yes, she had to be careful around him, for at times she was certain he could see right to her soul. He'd surely see the lie if he looked too deeply.

"How is everyone?" Doc asked her.

Maggie tore her gaze from Dade's probing one and smiled at Doc. "Fine. The babies are growing like weeds."

She stepped back to admit the doc. Dade stayed outside by the buggy, staring at her.

"I didn't expect you to drive out with Doc," she said, planting a welcoming smile on her face like she supposed his sister would do.

He didn't return the gesture. In fact, his expression hardened.

"I need a word with you," he said.

She didn't like that grave tone at all. Something was wrong, and that something must concern her.

"Of course. We'll talk when we get back to town."

"This needs to be settled now."

Settled? She didn't like the sound of that at all. She was tempted to put him off, to make an excuse and avoid the confrontation she sensed was coming.

But there was something in his eyes that stilled her. Some desperation that she understood all too well.

"Very well," she said, damning the fact that her voice cracked. "What is so important that you couldn't wait until I returned to town?"

He stared at her so long that a fine sheen of sweat slicked her skin. Then his gaze shifted to her throat, and his mouth pulled into a grim line.

She'd been the subject of dismissing or derisive looks all her life. But she'd never had anyone look at her with such open hostility before.

"That broach was my ma's," he said.

She nodded agreement, then what he'd said slammed into her. He'd said his mother. Not theirs. *His.*

He knew the truth. She was almost relieved that she wouldn't have to continue this charade. Almost.

"I've always loved it," she said, and lifted trembling fingers to the only thing that did matter to her.

"Is that why you stole it, Maggie?"

Her mouth went dry, and her heart sank to her toes, but there was no sense denying the truth when he knew her name.

"I didn't steal it. Daisy lost it."

"Likely story." Before she could think of a pithy reply, he asked, "How did you know Daisy?"

She hadn't prepared herself to explain this part of her past, not that she needed to rehearse it. Those days in the foundling home had been hard. But they were also one of the best memories she'd had because she'd bonded with Daisy.

"Well?" he asked when she got lost in memories.

"Daisy and I became friends in the foundling home when she became too sick to travel on the orphan train."

Maggie had vowed never to get close to anyone after the first family who'd adopted her brought her back. They blamed her for their daughter Becka's death, and Maggie blamed herself as well. That was a heartache she never wanted to relive again.

But something about Daisy had called to her. An aching loneliness that she understood all too well.

"How long were you there?" he asked.

"Close to two months," she said, though it had seemed longer.

His narrowed eyes told her that he didn't believe her. "Two months, yet Daisy never told you she had a brother?"

She sighed, realizing she should have expected this question. "Daisy suffered a mishap shortly before arriving at the foundling home."

"What kind of mishap?"

"I was told she took a bad fall off the wagon." Maggie could remember the large bump on the girl's head that took a week to go down. "The doctor who came to treat her said her memory had been damaged."

"Convenient that she couldn't remember her family."

Maggie sent him a sad smile, taking no offense at his biting sarcasm. It was deserved in this. "Daisy didn't even remember her name. The matron had to remind her who she was."

Daisy had begun feeling poorly after the first two weeks, and Maggie had appointed herself the older sister to look out for the little girl with the too-big eyes. As soon as Daisy recovered, they put her back on the orphan train.

But this time they placed Maggie on it too for she'd been adopted once and returned to the foundling home.

It was time for her to move on where she'd stand a better chance of finding a home. She'd hoped it would be with Daisy.

She always thought part of Daisy's illness was a broken heart, for the child was horribly sad. Now she understood why. She'd been separated from her brother and sent to the West among strangers.

"How did you figure out my charade?" she asked.

"Had an interesting talk with a bounty hunter from up round Burland," Dade said, his gaze probing hers with an intensity that made her shiver. "He's looking for Margaret Sutten."

She pinched her eyes shut a blessed moment. So Whit had hired someone to find her. He was more than angry too if he resorted to hiring a bounty hunter.

She tried to tamp down the panic erupting within her, but she couldn't. A cold tremor skated through her veins, for if she hadn't gone with Doc, she'd have been in Placid when the bounty hunter arrived.

She could be well and truly caught by now.

"Did this bounty hunter tell you why I was wanted back in Burland?" she asked.

"Yep. He said you'd stolen money from Harlan Nowell's crippled daughter, and a family heirloom."

"I never stole a red cent," she said. "Caroline gave that money to me."

Again his gaze dropped to the broach pinned at her throat. "Did you steal my ma's broach from my sister?"

"No. Daisy lost it the day she was taken off the orphan train."

He stared at the ground, but the muscle pounding along his jaw was proof he was holding a tight rein on his temper. "Doc fessed up to knowing you when Harlan Nowell adopted you."

That was a laugh. "They took me in as a companion for their crippled daughter, though I ended up being more of Caroline's personal servant."

"That's what Doc said." He pinned her with eyes shining hard with steely determination. "What happened to Daisy?"

She cringed, unsure how to answer that. He'd see through any denial she'd voice, and what was the use of lying to him?

"I don't know," she said. "But I hope the family who took her in gave her a good home." Unlike what she'd endured all her life in Harlan Nowell's home.

Dade grabbed her upper arms and pulled her close. "Where was Daisy adopted? What was the name of the town?"

She shook her head, involuntarily shivering at the memory of the desolate place where the train had stopped. "We were in Kansas. But there was no signpost. Just cattle pens, a trading post, and a big white house up on a hill . . ."

"You sure?"

"Positive."

"What about the towns before or after it?" he asked. "Do you remember either of them?"

She thought hard to bring the trip to mind again, but in truth they hadn't been paying much attention. "We stopped at Wakeeney but I'm not sure if it was the last stop before they took Daisy. I can't remember the name of the one after either."

She'd been too distraught over Daisy to pay any mind to her surroundings. "I don't think it was a scheduled stop because there wasn't a crowd gathered when the matron trotted us girls out onto the platform."

The skin beneath his eyes and around his mouth paled. "Just the girls?"

She nodded. "The matron told us to smile because the gentleman was looking for a pretty little girl."

Maggie had known then that she'd not be chosen, for she was too tall and too hardy to be considered a pretty little girl. Even now she'd call herself average looking.

"This man. He just picked Daisy and went on?"

"Pretty much so." She closed her eyes, bringing that moment to mind. "It was cold that day, the wind feeling like it blew right through us. But the matron made us stand side by side so the gentleman could get a good look at us. When Daisy clung to me the matron pulled her away from me. That's when Daisy started crying."

The skin around Dade's pursed mouth paled even further. "She was always prone to tears."

"Only when she was afraid."

That made him scowl, but she couldn't tell if he was disagreeing with her or if he'd never realized that fear was what made Daisy whimper. Not that it mattered now.

"The matron dragged Daisy to the end of the platform and shook her. Told her to hush," she went on. "That drew the gentleman's attention. He pushed the matron aside and pulled Daisy to him."

"Bet she howled then," Dade said.

"She kicked up a fuss and broke free, but she was too close to the edge. She fell hard and didn't move." Maggie blinked and swiped at the sudden moisture in her eyes, surprised she still had tears to shed. "He picked Daisy up, put her in a buggy, and drove up to that big house. I never saw or heard from her again."

Dade's jaw looked anvil hard. "Would you know him if you saw him again?"

"Without a doubt." She'd never forgotten the calculating look on the man's face when he got his hands on Daisy.

"But I wouldn't know where to begin looking for her now. I don't even know if she's still alive."

Dade was silent for a long beat. She wondered at his thoughts, if he had any idea how to find his sister.

"How'd you come by her broach?" he asked, a note of suspicion back in his voice.

Her hand went to the piece of jewelry that tied her to the timid girl who'd befriended her. "I found it on the ground after the man left with Daisy. The clasp had broken."

He just looked at her, as if trying to determine if she was joshing him. Finally he nodded, letting her think he believed her in this. And it was the truth.

Afterward, the lie about the broach being a family heirloom began, for it was the only suitable reason why Harlan Nowell would let her keep such a cheap piece of jewelry. Even then she was only allowed to wear it when they had visitors.

She could still remember the fuss Mrs. Nowell made over their ward's "family trinket." Few folks knew that as soon as company left, Maggie had to hand over the broach that gave her comfort.

If not for Caroline Nowell, she never would've been able to retrieve it from the safe the day she escaped.

"I've given it a lot of thought," she said, her voice breaking the tense silence. "The gentleman had to have had money to convince the matron to stop the train in the middle of nowhere."

"Maybe it wasn't really nowhere." Dade scowled off into the distance. "You said there were cattle pens? It must've been the railhead for shipping cattle east." He rubbed a hand over his chin, his eyes darkening to match the intense expression on his face.

"You think that this could have been on the gentleman's property? That he lived in that white house?"

"There's a chance he did," Dade said. "I'll follow the

tracks until I find a big ranch west of Wakeeney. If I can find some old-timers along the way, they might remember the location of such a big spread."

For the first time in years, she felt a smidgen of hope. "If you can do that, we might be able to find Daisy."

Dade shrugged, not showing the same enthusiasm that she felt. "Do you remember anything distinctive about this man?"

Maggie thought on that sad moment in her life. She'd begged to be taken too, but the gentleman hadn't spared her a glance.

He'd had his eyes set on Daisy from the start, and he'd gotten her. But why?

The question had worried her for years. Daisy was such a fragile girl, and the man who'd taken her had seemed so cold and demanding.

"He was a bossy man. He told the matron, 'I'll take that pretty blonde hiding behind the gawky girl.'" Meaning her, the tall girl nobody wanted in his home unless it was to lend a hand. She could still hear his voice as if it'd just happened. "He was dressed well, and his buggy was a fancy one."

Dade scrubbed a hand across his nape, as if reminded of what a daunting task it'd be to find one gentleman among so many. "Anything else you recall about him?"

"He commanded respect, like he was somebody important," she said. Like he was a man who expected to be obeyed without question. Like Harlan Nowell.

"I need more to go on if I'm going to find her," he said, though she sensed he was talking more to himself than to her.

Her heart went out to him then when she realized just how desperately he wanted to find his sister. She wished she knew more, for she'd like nothing better than to find her long lost childhood friend again.

Oddly enough, that bond between her and him touched something deep in her. She'd not had that with another soul for so long. If only she wasn't being hunted by Whit. If only he'd let her go.

But she was afraid to take the chance. Afraid that getting close to another man could cost that man his life.

"This bounty hunter who's looking for me," she said, drawing Dade's shrewd gaze back up to hers. "Is he still in Placid?"

He shook his head. "Duane saw him heading up into the mountains with a packhorse. With any luck he won't come back for some time, if ever."

So she had time to gather her thoughts and few possessions before moving on again. Hopefully Doc had found a place for her to hide in St. Louis. If not, where would she go?

Chapter 6

Dade trailed Doc Franklin's buggy back to town, his senses attuned to trouble while his mind spun off with all he'd discovered. Finding the gentleman who'd taken Daisy off the orphan train was going to be like looking for a needle in a damned haystack.

Rich gentlemen tended to be demanding—at least the ones he'd had dealings with. His best bet was finding this big ranch in Kansas.

He wasn't familiar with that state, but there couldn't be that many big ranches past Wakeeney that were close to the railroad and had their own cattle holding pens to boot. The trading post nearby should help narrow it.

Problem he might face was if any of it was still standing. The prairie had changed a lot in twenty or so years. Prairie fires, tornadoes, bankruptcy. Any of it could've happened and erased what had once been there.

Yep, the way it was shaping up, unless he recognized his sister right off, he might never find her unless someone pointed her or the gentleman who adopted her out to him. He didn't hold much hope of either happening.

I'd never forget his face, Maggie had said.

Was it true? Could Maggie Sutten recognize the man

who'd taken his sister? Would she recognize the big white house? Would she know Daisy?

As for Maggie's explanation about Daisy's lost memory due to an accident, well, if she was telling the truth, then that explained a lot. He'd always wondered why his sister had never tried to find him. Why he'd never heard mention of her these past twenty years until six months back.

He'd been just about certain that whoever had taken Daisy in had changed her name when he'd picked up Maggie's trail. That's when he'd decided to wait for her to return to Placid.

If there was even the slightest chance that Maggie would know Daisy on sight, then he had to convince her to go east with him. He didn't expect it'd be easy to get her to agree, but there was the very real threat of the bounty hunter looking high and low for her.

As long as she was with him, he'd protect her from Carson. They could travel as brother and sister. Or husband and wife?

Nope, that was a bad idea. As it was, he couldn't stop the very male feelings she roused in him. But he could damn well keep his hands to himself.

Yep, he needed someone who'd seen this gentleman. Who might have a better memory of what his sister looked like at that age. He needed Maggie Sutten's help.

Above them at this point in the road lay a rocky outcropping that stacked into the foothills. Up there a person had a bird's eye view of Placid, but down here on the road the town was hidden until they rounded the bend.

The road headed straight into the town that had remained a stopping off point to the minefields west of here back when the silver era was in full swing. Even the train had been used more by miners than anyone else in the area.

At any rate, folks tended to buy their supplies here and move on. Few stayed in Placid.

Dade suspected most of the good citizens liked it that way. Right now, a handful of them were clustered on the boardwalk in front of the mercantile as if they'd just had a meeting.

Nothing unusual about that. Yet as the anxious faces of the townsfolk turned to them, Dade sensed trouble.

Damn, had Carson returned and prattled about Maggie's description? Were they riding into a trap of sorts?

Doc must have realized something was off too, for he stopped the buggy in front of the mercantile instead of driving Maggie on to the boardinghouse.

Mayor Willis strode to the steps and took a stand while the townsfolk fanned around Doc Franklin's buggy. All of them were staring at Dade.

"Sheriff Logan, your absence from your duty came at a most inopportune time," the mayor said.

"How so?" Dade asked, his sense of trouble ballooning.

"A band of outlaws descended on our fair town about an hour past," Willis said.

"They robbed the bank." This from someone in the crowd, and that was all it took to open the floodgates.

Everyone commenced talking at once, and Dade could scarce make head or tails of what had happened.

"Hush up! All of you," Dade said, but the gathered crowd didn't stop chattering until he pulled his sidearm and pointed it heavenward.

They hushed without him having to fire off a round. "Now then, one at a time, tell me what happened."

"Take a look at the jail," Duane said. "They rode in and shot out the windows first. Good thing we didn't have any prisoners at the time."

"They who?" Dade asked.

"The Logan Gang," Willis said. "Lionel was a victim of theirs long ago and recognized them right off."

The banker? *Hell!* His worst fear had come knocking at his door.

"Anyone hurt?" Dade asked.

"By the grace of God, we all escaped injury," Willis said.

Murmurs of agreement echoed through the crowd. Dade silently gave up his thanks. There were enough tales circulating about the Logan Gang to know they didn't hesitate to shoot anyone blocking their escape.

"What are you going to do about this travesty, sheriff?" Willis asked.

"A question I'm curious about as well, Sheriff *Logan*." Lionel Payne stepped from the crowd, putting undue inflection on Dade's surname. "Mighty interesting that you share the same name with the outlaws who ran roughshod over the town and my bank while you were off doing whatever it was that you was off doing."

"Just what are you implying?" Dade asked, knowing full well what Payne was getting at.

The banker puffed his barrel chest out. "Are you related to the Logan Gang?"

An uneasy silence whispered around them, but it was the looks folks cast Dade's way that left him on edge. He'd bet his last sawbuck that they were second-guessing themselves for not thinking to ask if the outlaw gang was his kin before they swore him in as their sheriff.

Payne fixed a dark accusatory glare on Dade, and he knew from that look that the banker was speculating if Dade's leaving town today was planned so he wouldn't have to face his family as they made an illegal withdrawal from the bank. He'd likely shared that suspicion with the townsfolk.

Nothing could be farther from the truth. But Dade had a feeling they wouldn't believe him.

"It shames me to admit I'm related to the Logan Gang," Dade said in all honesty.

"You had no right to keep that from us," Payne said to a chorus of assenting murmurs.

"I had every right." Dade stared Payne down. "All I shared with the Logan Gang is a surname. All I know about them is what I've read on wanted posters or heard as hearsay."

Payne was shaking his head long before Dade even finished. "You expect us to believe that you're estranged from your family?"

The old anger that had simmered in Dade for years fired up a notch. It wasn't the first time he'd been judged unfairly because of his thieving kin.

The truth had never exonerated him. Didn't matter that his pa had abandoned him and Daisy when they were children after their ma had died. It didn't matter that Clete Logan never made any attempt to find his children in twenty odd years.

"It's the truth, but I don't rightly give a damn what you believe," Dade said, earning him nods of understanding and scowls of disapproval.

Mayor Willis turned his attention to Maggie. "What have you got to say about your family descending on the town, Miss Logan?"

Maggie sat straighter beside Doc, and Dade expected her to deny being any relation to him now. "I'm appalled by their actions, but truthfully, I wouldn't know my father if I passed him on the street."

A commiserating chord twanged in Dade. He suspected there was a good dose of truth to that statement, for Maggie had been an orphan just the same as Daisy and he.

For the first time he didn't see Maggie Sutten as a cunning imposter or manipulative liar, but as a lonely little girl nobody wanted. She certainly hadn't had it easy being the companion to Harlan Nowell's daughter.

Hell, Maggie clearly preferred being linked to an outlaw gang to fessing up to her identity. She was that desperate to hide from Nowell and the bounty hunter he'd hired to track her down.

"Nobody is suspecting you of subterfuge," Mayor Willis said to her, earning a disapproving glower from Lionel Payne. "You were with Doc lending aid to those in need. Your brother is another matter."

"He wouldn't do anything underhanded," Maggie said, surprising the hell out of him.

"Of course you'd say that about your brother," Payne said, his expression as unyielding as the granite mountains rising around them.

"I wouldn't defend him if he was as crooked as the Logan Gang," she said. "I tell you truly they are strangers to us."

Payne scoffed. "I am not convinced, Miss Logan. You came here six months ago and stole our sheriff's affection. A few months later he was gunned down the day before your brother came to town."

The townsfolk muttered among themselves. One good hard look at them screamed their suspicion that this could all be more than happenstance. And hell, it did look mighty fishy.

"Have you forgotten that Dade single-handedly routed the ruffian who'd gunned down our sheriff?" Mayor Willis asked. "Has it slipped your minds that we asked him to take over the job of sheriff?"

Begged was more like it, but Dade wasn't about to point that out. At least a few folks seemed to be mulling over what Mayor Willis said. Not so for Payne.

The banker had come out the loser here, for it was his bank that the Logan Gang had robbed.

The hell of it was, Dade couldn't be sure if his pa and uncles knew he was the sheriff in Placid. If they did, it'd be like them to keep watch then strike when he left town. It sure put him in a prickly situation.

"How much did they make off with?" Dade asked.

"Fifteen thousand dollars," the banker said. "What do you intend to do?"

Dade took a bracing breath. "Not much I can do now but send a wire to the U.S. Marshal in Denver, then round up a posse and try to find their trail."

"That could take days," Payne said. "Weeks, maybe."

"If I'm lucky." And for Dade, luck would mean he didn't have to hunt down his kin.

"I dislike the notion of your leaving the town unguarded again," Mayor Willis said. "I wouldn't want to see lightning strike us twice."

The townsfolk muttered the same fear.

"We need to hire a deputy so we always have a lawman in town," Doc said, drawing everyone's attention back to the buggy where he and Daisy sat.

"Good idea," Dade said, and the surprised look on Lionel Payne's fleshy face proved he hadn't expected Dade to readily agree.

There wasn't enough commotion in town to keep one lawman busy, much less two. But the fact remained that Dade would be moving on soon in his quest to find Daisy.

If the town had a deputy, he wouldn't feel like he was leaving them in the lurch. Though looking at their faces now, he guessed a good many would just as soon see him light out of town and take trouble with him.

Mayor Willis stepped up on the boardwalk and looked down on the throng. "Anyone know of a man who'd be interested in the job of deputy sheriff?"

"I could do it," said the town drunk, which earned a

medley of laughs and curses. "Hell, I spend most my time in jail anyhow."

Out of the corner of his eye, Dade saw Duane Tenfeather square his broad shoulders and knew that he was going to volunteer. "I'd be interested in being deputy."

That statement from the liveryman's son had everyone staring at him, and some not too favorably. Sad fact was that while folks abided Indians and Negroes in certain types of work, they disliked their being in charge.

Didn't matter that Duane had been a scout with the U.S. Army. That he'd been honorably discharged after being wounded in battle and even decorated for his service.

Men cursed by prejudice, like Payne, hated to give a half-breed a position of authority. Dade just hoped the banker's venom didn't poison the rest of the town against Duane.

Folks scanned the crowd as if expecting someone else would step forward. But nobody did.

Dade smiled. Duane wasn't quite as thick in the shoulders and chest as his pa, but he seemed to stand a mite taller and hold his chin a bit higher as time stretched out.

That steely quality in his bearing bellowed confidence that even a blind man could see. If Duane could still handle a gun, he'd be the perfect man for the job.

"I can't think of a better man to work with than Duane," Dade said.

That got folks mumbling amongst themselves. Duane stood stock still, not showing any reaction to the scrutiny.

"His pa is the most trustworthy man I know," the grocer said. "Reckon Duane is of the same bent so I say we hire him."

One by one folks chimed in, adding more agreement than reservation. But they hushed when a woman asked, "Are you serious, Duane?"

Dade saw the telling and nearly imperceptible jerk of

Duane's stance as he stared at Serena, the Mexican widow who ran Placid's lone restaurant. It was enough to tell him that this woman was important to Duane.

"I'm sure," he said.

Serena pressed a hand to her mouth and stepped back into the crowd. Dade wondered if Duane would take that hint of disapproval and change his mind about being the deputy. But Duane squared his shoulders and held his head high. Proud.

"Duane's got my vote," Dade said.

Mayor Willis held his hands up in a call for silence when folks started jabbering at once. "This holdup has drawn out the good citizens of Placid, so I suggest we decide right here and now if we want to hire Duane Tenfeather as deputy. All in favor say aye."

A chorus of ayes followed, some more enthusiastic than others. But the majority of those gathered stepped forward to support the hometown boy.

That settled it. Duane Tenfeather was the deputy, whether he could shoot straight or not. He was a trusted member of the community. And right now, they were more interested in having someone at the jail who could keep an eye on Dade Logan.

"Sheriff Logan," Benjamin Willis began, "I trust you will swear in the new deputy and apprise him of his duties."

Dade dipped his chin. "Yes, sir. No time like the present."

"Duane, raise your right hand and repeat what I say," Dade ordered him as he said the vow he'd taken when he'd been sworn in.

The former army scout snapped to attention and did just that, saying his vow to uphold the law with his life if necessary in a clear loud voice. The man surely didn't lack bravado.

"Congratulations, Deputy Tenfeather," Dade said. "You're

now an official officer of the law in Placid. Come by the jail and we'll hunt you up a star."

"Yes, sir, Sheriff Logan," Duane said, then strode off looking proud as all get out.

Some of the townsfolk clapped. Some merely nodded approval before they turned and went on about their business.

Doc set off in his buggy as well, and Dade silently groused that Maggie didn't pay him a passing glance. He watched them disappear for too long before the lone man on the boardwalk caught his attention.

Saying the man wanted retribution didn't do justice to the look Lionel Payne fixed on him. "I'll be watching you."

"You'll be bored then."

He whirled his chestnut gelding around and headed toward the livery. If nothing else, today's events convinced him that his time here was over.

Foremost on his mind, he'd never find Daisy staying here. Now that he had an idea where Daisy had been claimed by a family, he was chomping at the bit to head to Kansas.

Though he'd been pissed to high heaven when he found out Maggie was pretending to be his sister, he was glad now that she'd done so. Hell, she was the first person he'd met who remembered Daisy.

Nope, if not for her, he'd be tramping from town to town, trying to find a hint of where Daisy had disappeared to. He wasn't at all sure he'd have had any success.

Even so, it still wasn't going to be easy to find her.

Dade left his gelding at the livery and headed down the boardwalk. Hard to believe that several hours ago there'd been a holdup here. But then the town had looked much the same the day he rode in six months past.

Of course folks were hiding then after the murder of their sheriff. Now? Now they believed they were safe with a new sheriff and a deputy. Never mind that the deputy was green as grass and Dade was kin to outlaws.

He poked his head in the saloon. A trio of cowpokes were playing poker at a back table. Another was standing at the bar with a shot glass of whiskey in his hand.

The bartender looked his way and nodded. "Ready to wet your whistle?"

"I'll pass for now," Dade said. "That bounty hunter who came through a few days ago. You see him around?"

"Nope. Far as I know he headed out for good."

He sure as hell hoped so. "If he comes back, let me know."

"Sure enough."

Dade headed across the street toward the jail. Not surprisingly, Duane Tenfeather stood outside the door. Seeing as he'd been a soldier, he knew the dangers he'd face upholding the law in Placid. He stopped before the man whose Adam's apple seemed to be working double time in his dark bronzed throat. "How's your gun hand?"

Duane lifted his right hand and flexed the fingers slowly. Too slowly. "I still got a good eye with a rifle."

"What about sidearms? Have you been practicing?"

Duane's skin darkened, looking more coppery than black. "No, sir, I surely ain't."

Just what Dade feared. "Then let's head out to the bluff and see how you do."

The last thing he wanted was to feel responsible for Duane getting killed. Nope, before he left this town, he wanted to believe Duane could hold his own against anyone. Including the Logan Gang.

Doc parked the buggy before the boardinghouse, and Maggie restrained herself from leaping out and sprinting to the front door. When he started to get out to assist her, she laid a hand atop Doc's gnarled one.

"Don't bother helping me down," she said. "I can manage well on my own."

"My bad knees appreciate your independence, Maggie."

She smiled despite the worry nagging at her. "Thank you for seeing me to the house."

"It was the least I could do after all the help you lent the Orshlins this week," Doc said. "I fear things would have turned out badly if not for you."

"I was glad to help." She fidgeted with her handbag, hesitant to leave. "How much longer do you think it'll be before you hear from your friend in St. Louis?"

"Wish I knew." He slid her a questioning look. "You're worried about this bounty hunter."

"He could return any time. I'm afraid to venture out on the street now." Afraid that she'd get caught and dragged back to Burland. God only knew what fate would await her then.

Doc fisted the reins on his knee and swore softly. "I'll send another wire to the hospital."

"Thank you."

"Get some rest," he said.

She climbed out and removed her small satchel. "I suggest you take your own advice. It won't do if you fall under the weather."

He laughed at that. "Point taken. Now go on with you."

Maggie sprinted up the front steps, anxious to get inside. Yes, she was weary, but rest could wait. The desire for a bath throbbed in her veins, and she was determined to answer that call.

Mrs. Gant looked up from dusting the front room. "I hear you would have done Florence Nightingale proud with all the help you gave at the Orshlin farm."

"The birthing was the most wondrous thing to witness," Maggie said. "But caring for the babies the first few days was worrisome."

"Doc certainly sang your praises." She flicked Maggie a sad smile. "I know it's wrong of me, but I couldn't help thinking how wonderful it would've been if Lester hadn't met such a deadly fate, and you and he married."

Maggie smiled, hating the lie she'd woven here. Hating that she still didn't dare draw Mrs. Gant into her confidence.

Deceit didn't sit well with her, but she'd been afraid to trust. She was still afraid of revealing all.

She'd never dreamed when she concocted this plan to escape Nowell that she'd come to hurt those she liked so well. And she would hurt them when she left, for Doc or Dade would surely tell these kind folks the truth.

"Listen to me rambling on," Mrs. Gant said. "You are surely exhausted and wish to rest."

"Actually I long for a good bath." She'd managed to work up a good sweat the week she was at the Orshlins' farm.

Unfortunately their bathing facilities were a tin tub set up before the fireplace once a week and shared by all. Bath day was Sunday—today—so she'd missed out on that tradition.

Not that she was complaining, for she'd had no desire to join the family in their weekly ritual. "Availing myself of the washstand had to suffice during my stay."

"Then a bath is what you shall have. I'll get the water heated and start sending buckets up to you in the dumb-waiter."

"Thank you."

She climbed the stairs and deposited her satchel in her room. Having lived most of her life in Harlan Nowell's mansion, she'd forgotten that most folks had adequate bathing facilities at best. Why, besides the company of her foster sister, the bathing chamber she shared with Caroline was what she missed the most.

While Mrs. Gant didn't have a boiler in her cellar or pipes to feed into the claw foot tub, she did have a good substitute to provide her guests.

She slipped into the bathing chamber with a fresh change of clothes and gave the velvet cord a tug. A faint bell could be heard below.

Before long, the pulley inside the dumbwaiter began squealing as buckets were hauled up. While she took the buckets from the lift, Mrs. Gant chattered on.

"Why, I told Mayor Willis at the grocery store that you'd been orphaned when you was just a baby and didn't remember your family at all," Mrs. Gant said.

"That is true." Even if they were talking about a different family, the end result had been the same.

"And your poor brother," she went on. "Why, I was just thunderstruck when Lionel accused Dade of being kin to that gang and Dade said it was so. I imagine it shamed your brother and you to know family had robbed the town that he'd vowed to protect."

From the glimpse she'd gotten of Dade, that much was true. Not that Lionel Payne believed it.

"He was upset by it all." As was Maggie with this town for assuming the worst of Dade. "The liveryman's son is taking on the job of deputy," she said as she took the last bucket from the lift and poured the hot water into the tub.

"Duane? Why, he'll do the town proud."

"That's what Doc said."

She stripped to the skin and climbed into the tub scented with lilacs and rose oil. An aphrodisiac for the senses. She leaned back and welcomed the lap of water over her tired body.

She'd been sure that getting away from Dade Logan for

a few days would temper these yearnings she had for him. Instead she caught herself thinking about him at odd times.

While she was dreaming fanciful thoughts about them that could never be, he was discovering her lie. But she wasn't sorry that had happened. If he'd not ridden out to the Orshlins when he did, he'd have been in town when the Logan Gang road in.

Chills feathered over her heart at the thought of that happening. She barely knew Dade, yet she was sure he would have taken a stand against his father. He could have ended up like Lester, gunned down.

"I plumb forgot to tell you about the man that came round," Mrs. Gant said, her voice carrying well up the shaft to intrude on Maggie's musings. "He said he was one of those private detectives, but he was a rough character."

Maggie gripped the smooth cool edge of the tub as cold hard reality destroyed her respite. "Dade mentioned that a bounty hunter came to town, looking for a thief." For her.

Pots and pans rattled in the kitchen below. "When this man told me what this Sutten woman had done, I just couldn't believe my ears. She stole from the kind folks who'd trusted her to care for their crippled daughter."

"How horrid!" If Mrs. Gant only knew the truth.

"Right off I thought of you and Eloisa and how close you'd been," Mrs. Gant said. "Of course, you was adopted into that family."

Maggie pinched her eyes shut, dreading to know what Mrs. Gant had said. "What all did you tell this bounty hunter about me?"

"He wasn't one for conversation. So I only told him the truth, that nobody but the sheriff and his sister lived here." Mrs. Gant tsked. "My land, it surely tells you what kind of person this Sutten woman is to bite the hand that's been feeding her for years."

"So true," Maggie managed to get out.

Maggie's enjoyable soak was forgotten. If the bounty hunter had been the friendly sort, Mrs. Gant would have told him all about Daisy Logan's and Eloisa Reynard's stays here. He would have found out that Eloisa was a cripple, and he surely would have figured out their true identities.

Clearly using Daisy's name any longer would be too risky now. If the bounty hunter dug deep enough in Manitou Springs, he might find someone else who remembered that Daisy Logan and a crippled friend had taken the waters there—and figure out that they used false names. That would have him coming right back here to Placid.

Maggie toweled off and quickly dressed, her body tensing once again. It was simply too dangerous for her to stay here much longer.

She'd have to come up with a new name and disappear. And she'd have to do it soon.

Chapter 7

A mile outside town, the steady pop from Dade's Peace-maker echoed off the canyon walls. He pitched the last can out from behind the boulder that shielded him, and before it began its downward arc, a bullet caught it and sent the tin spinning back into the air.

Worry had crouched on his shoulders over Duane Ten-feather's ability to handle a gun again, but it had lifted as the deputy continued to hit the target.

Duane's accuracy was dead on, but his lack of speed with a sidearm was a concern. His injured hand just couldn't draw in a blink, which would leave Duane vulnerable in a showdown.

However the speed with which he handled a rifle more than made up for it. Dade was duly impressed with Duane's inborn patience, his ability to wait out the best opportunity to fire.

Maybe that came from his Indian blood. Maybe he'd developed it from watching his pa pounding hot iron into shape at the livery. Whatever it was, that trait would be a benefit to him in this job.

He already stood back from folks and observed—something that likely came from his being a breed in a town that was mostly white. Patience could save his life if he got holed up in a standoff and risked running out of ammunition.

"Who taught you to shoot like that?" Dade asked.

"My pa." Duane showed sense and respect as he handed the Colt to Dade. "He fought in the Civil War for the Union Army, helping them track renegades and bushwhackers. Come to find out the sergeant in my cavalry unit had ridden with him."

A far nobler service than that of Dade's pa, who abandoned his family farm after his wife died giving birth to a baby that died with her. Clete Logan had taken Dade and Daisy to an orphanage soon afterward, telling Dade that he and his uncles Brice and Seth were heading west to work on the railroad.

It wasn't until Daisy was put on the orphan train that Dade learned the truth. Clete, Brice, and Seth Logan had thrown in with a band of outlaws who were terrorizing the west.

By the time Dade, Reid, and Trey escaped the orphanage, Dade had heard that the Logan brothers had formed their own outlaw gang. But while Dade longed to find Daisy, he had no desire to ever see his pa or uncles again.

He'd forged a new family with Reid and Trey. The foster brothers had formed a pact to stick together through thick and thin. That became easy after Kirby Morris took them in.

"Your pa know you volunteered to be the new deputy?" Dade asked.

Duane nodded. "He thought it was a good thing to do, but my ma and my intended ain't so sure."

"Didn't know it had gotten that serious with you and Serena." But he should have suspected as much when he saw the disappointed look on Serena's face when Duane volunteered. "The women will worry about the danger you're putting yourself in."

"Way I see it, being a deputy is a damn site safer job than being an army scout," Duane said. "And I sure as hell don't want to take over Pa's livery some day."

Dade didn't blame him none for shunning a job he hadn't wanted. Dade had hated having his life planned out for him as well, which was one of the reasons why he banded together with Reid and Trey and escaped the Guardian Angel's Orphan Asylum.

He wasn't about to be railroaded into becoming a steel-worker or taking on some other trade in Pittsburgh, Penn-sylvania. He wanted to live his own life. He wanted to find his sister, and damn anyone who stood in his way.

"Why'd you leave the army when it's obvious you can still handle a gun?" Dade asked.

"I was tired of the killing. Tired of always watching my back. Tired of owning nothing but what was in my knapsack." Duane looked at him. "I missed my family and home."

"Yep, I know what you mean." Hell, he missed the Crown Seven. Missed his brothers, even the one who had betrayed him.

"Nosiree," Duane said. "Ain't a bit sorry I mustered out."

Dade smiled, hoping his deputy felt the same a year from now. "Would you want to be sheriff some day?"

A dull flush crept up Duane's neck. "I ain't trying to force you out, sheriff."

"I never thought you was, Duane," Dade said. "Fact is that I plan to move on. So do you want to be the town sheriff?"

"Yes, sir, I do."

Dade nodded, appreciating Duane's honesty. "Then I'd best take pains instructing you on the ins and outs of being sheriff."

"Like an apprentice?" Duane asked, the pitch in his voice betraying his excitement.

"Yep, like an apprentice." And wasn't that just a hoot.

Dade had had nobody to show him the ropes of this job when he took it on six months past. He'd just known that a sheriff had to have eyes in the back of his head.

He felt certain Duane had already honed that same trait. Yep, when he moved on, which seemed to be sooner than later now, it'd be with a clearer conscience.

"That bounty hunter that came through last week," Duane said. "I swore I saw him this morning riding just north of town."

That was the last thing Dade wanted to hear. "Did he seem to be moving on?"

"Hard to tell. At first I thought he was setting up camp above town, but when I looked up on the ridge an hour later, he was gone."

But where to?

Dade had a hunch it wasn't far. Allis Carson was probably looking for a place to watch the town unobserved. Like a sniper, he needed a location that gave a good view of the town so when Maggie stepped into the open, he'd know where to find her. He'd be able to figure out the best place to catch her off guard and make off with her.

"About what time did you see him?" Dade asked.

"Right before the bank was robbed."

Dade swiped a hand over his mouth, mulling that over. He'd assumed Carson had returned to town in the hopes he'd spy Maggie. But it was just as likely that he was trying to pick up the trail of the Logan Gang.

"You remember what ledge you saw him on?" Dade asked.

"I sure do," Duane said.

"Then show me."

They mounted up and headed out with the new deputy leading the way. Twenty minutes later they stood on a wide natural ledge of granite.

Dade squatted by the fire pit that had been covered over. He looked south. This location gave an unobtrusive view of the bank, but when he shifted a bit to the side, the livery, the boardinghouse, and Doc's office were visible.

"You said you noticed he left after the bank was robbed?" Dade asked.

"Sure did." The deputy toed the stub of a brown cheroot that'd been stomped out, and Dade noted it was one of many the bounty hunter had smoked while he was up here. "You think he went after the Logan Gang?"

Dade shrugged. "Hard to say."

Whether Carson recognized the outlaws or not, he could be trailing them if he'd witnessed the robbery. The reward on them would be mighty tempting to most men, and if this bounty hunter had run into a dead end searching for Maggie Sutten, he might invest the time necessary to round up the Logan Gang.

The outlaws and Carson could be miles from here by now. No matter how much he wished that to be the case, he suspected Carson would come back. Maybe not today. Maybe not tomorrow. But when Dade and Maggie least expected it, the bounty hunter would show his face.

Carson had been hired to find Margaret Sutten, and he imagined Harlan Nowell was paying a handsome fee to find her. The man damned sure wouldn't give up the chance of making easy money—and tracking a woman was considered just that.

"Carson will come back," Dade said.

"What makes you think so?" the deputy asked. "The woman he seeks isn't in Placid."

It wasn't in Dade's nature to lie, but he had done it many times when he was protecting his sister. Though he had no idea where to find her, Maggie was his strongest tie to Daisy. He wasn't about to just hand her over to this bounty hunter now.

"He thinks she is. You tell me if you've seen her." Dade repeated the description Carson had given.

The deputy went white around the mouth. "That sounds like the mayor's wife."

Now there was a bonus Dade hadn't anticipated. "It also sounds like my sister, but I have my doubts that this bounty hunter would take the time to figure out which one was Margaret Sutten."

"You think he'd just grab any woman who came close to that description and hightail it?"

"It's a possibility we can't dismiss."

"We damned sure ain't gonna stand for that."

Just what Dade wanted to hear.

He got to his feet and scanned the canyon walls that curved around the mountain town like protective arms. The serenity was deceptive, as those who'd recently been robbed could attest.

Yep, the town lay before him from this angle. He wasn't fool enough to think this was the only spot. If Allis Carson had found one place to observe the comings and goings down below, he had likely found another hidey-hole.

The bounty hunter could know Maggie had returned to the boardinghouse. He could be planning how to grab her at this moment.

Duane scanned the area with sharp eyes, looking more like a lawman than Dade could have imagined. "Just what the hell did this Sutten woman do anyway?"

"Stole a couple of hundred dollars from the man she worked for, plus an old broach."

"Seems a waste to send a hired gun after her for just that."

Dade couldn't agree more. How much of what Maggie told him was fiction?

She swore Harlan Nowell's daughter had given her money to escape, yet Harlan Nowell claimed Maggie had stolen it. If that was not the truth, then why was Harlan Nowell hounding her?

He had a hunch that Maggie had done something far more serious to rile the rich man. Something that he wasn't willing to forgive or forget.

"Let's head back," Dade said. "We've got a town to protect."

Dade had to have another long talk with Maggie. If he was to protect her, he had to know the whole story.

Even then he knew it wasn't going to be easy to keep her safe. What he wasn't sure of yet was if he should even try.

Maggie paced her room at the boardinghouse, pausing at intervals to gaze out the window. Her bath had refreshed her, but tension continued to hold her prisoner.

How long would it take for the bounty hunter to find out that she and Caroline had stayed in Placid after visiting the baths in Manitou Springs? How much longer would Maggie be safe here?

At the time it had seemed like such a grand adventure to pretend to be someone else as they rode the narrow gauge rail from Colorado Springs to Burland. She and Caroline had both wanted to escape the lives they had, so dreaming up new names and pasts had been innocent fun that they could enjoy if only for a little while.

But on three occasions they'd taken their journey a step further by taking the southern route out of Pueblo instead of the western one that wound toward Burland. That's how they found Placid. That's where they'd had a taste of true freedom.

If Maggie had known what Nowell had in store for her then, she would've boarded a train and disappeared. She wouldn't have returned to Burland. But she hadn't any inkling of his plans.

Just like she hadn't had any idea that Daisy Logan had a brother. That he was here in Placid waiting for his sister to return. Now that the truth was out, escaping him might be more difficult than eluding the bounty hunter Nowell had hired.

Maggie could change her name again, but she couldn't change her appearance that much. She had no idea how many people the bounty hunter had questioned about her, but she knew staying in Colorado was far too dangerous now.

But unless Doc could secure a safe place for her in St. Louis, she'd be afraid to stay in any town too long. She could end up being on the run for the rest of her life.

She left the quiet of her room and hurried down the steps, wishing that she was once again that little orphan that nobody wanted. She could be herself then. She could do what she wanted to do.

If she didn't have the threat of facing Nowell's wrath, she could entertain thoughts of having a normal life. She could marry. Have a family.

Now she'd be lucky to have a brief romance. The thought had her thinking of Dade again. Dare she encourage him that way? Would he even be interested in getting cozy with the woman who'd deceived him?

"Ah, you look refreshed," Mrs. Gant said, catching her before she could dart through the parlor.

"I feel more like myself." A truth on several levels.

She was beset with that old fear of having to run and never look back. Of never fitting in. Of never having anything permanent in her life. Heavens, would she ever find peace?

"You never did say exactly where Eloisa was living now," Mrs. Gant said.

"Sss"—Maggie caught herself before blurting out St. Louis—"Cincinnati."

That kind of slip of the tongue could mean the end of her freedom, for it would draw the bounty hunter to the place she'd hoped to disappear.

Mrs. Gant went about dusting the parlor, seeming not to have noticed her near blunder. "I've never been there."

Neither had Maggie, nor would she ever go there now that she'd claimed that Eloisa was there. "I hear it's quite cold in the winter."

"Poor dear. That won't be easy on her," Mrs. Gant said. "I hope this new hospital helps her condition."

"As do I."

If only it were so. If only Caroline was getting the help she needed.

It angered her that Nowell had denied Caroline the healing benefits of the waters after his wife died. That he'd likely keep his own daughter a prisoner in that emotionally cold house. That he might just decide to ship her off to a private sanitarium anyway.

But if he did, at least she'd be able to take the waters again. She'd be pain free, and free of her father's interference.

If only Maggie could be so lucky.

"Well, if you get back that way to visit Eloisa, do tell her I'm thinking fondly of her," Mrs. Gant said.

"I'll surely do that should I make the journey there, though I don't imagine it'll be any time in the near future."

Yes, for all the money that Harlan Nowell possessed, she and Caroline were equals in one regard. Both had been unwanted by their parents.

"How terrible that you're so far apart," Mrs. Gant said. "Have you any family other than your brother?"

"None."

She had a vague memory of an older woman singing to

her and holding her close. She couldn't bring the woman's face to mind, but she remembered feeling safe.

Another memory triggered a lightning flash of ice-cold fear. There'd been another woman too—one who was much younger and who terrified Maggie. Her aunt perhaps? The one who hadn't wanted her?

"What about friends?" Mrs. Gant asked.

Maggie shook off the unpleasant memory of her own life. "Eloisa is the closest I have to family or friends."

The truth, and just knowing she'd likely never see her again brought sudden tears to her eyes. There was no one out there for her. There never had been.

Mrs. Gant enveloped her in a hug, and Maggie resisted her natural urge to pull away. "Now, now, don't fret, child. Eloisa might have a miraculous recovery at this new hospital and make a trip here to see you."

"That would be nice."

She'd like nothing better than to one day hear that Caroline was cured and had slipped free from her father's hold. But she also knew it wouldn't be easy for either of them to escape the life planned for them.

If Caroline returned here, Maggie would be long gone.

She gently extracted herself from Mrs. Gant and flushed at the compassion the woman directed at her. She wasn't used to anyone fussing over her.

Heavens, she could count on one hand the times someone had coddled her or hugged her. She hadn't known how to take their kindness then, and she still hadn't learned.

"Forgive me for prying," Mrs. Gant began, putting Maggie on alert that she was in for another probing question. "But how old were you when the Reynards adopted you?"

"Eight years old," Maggie said, clearly remembering that cold day.

"Oh, my! Judging by the close bond you and Eloisa

had, I was sure you'd been taken in by them when you were a baby."

Maggie merely smiled, for she wasn't quite sure what to say to that. But Mrs. Gant didn't appear to take her silence as an insult. No, she took it as an excuse to ask more questions.

"Dade never said, but had you been in the orphanage long?" she asked, staring at Maggie with such pity that she wanted to scream.

"Too long . . ."

The longest months of her life, for the foundling home had felt like a prison sentence. But she surely couldn't tell Mrs. Gant about the first family who'd adopted her, only to return her to the home nearly two years later.

She'd tried to fit in with them, to win their affection, to form a sisterly bond with their beautiful daughter, Becka. And maybe that would have happened if not for the accident.

To think how different her life would have been if she'd been able to stay with them. She surely wouldn't be on the run now. Nor would she have met Dade Logan.

"Such a long time for a child to be cooped up in an orphanage," Mrs. Gant said. "Am I to assume you and Dade lost your parents? That you had no other family to take you in?"

Maggie nodded woodenly, for she didn't wish to say anything that would contradict what Dade might have said. Nor did she care to go into the painful details of her own life.

"Such a shame that the Reynards didn't take you and Dade both into their home," Mrs. Gant said.

"Very true." Having remembered how alone Daisy had been, and knowing how hard Dade had tried to find her, she thought it a crime that the siblings had been separated.

Mrs. Gant heaved a sigh. "But good fortune reigned when you found each other again."

"I suspect that is a rarity among separated siblings."

"And how sad that you had forgotten you had a brother," she said, and Maggie got the first inkling that Mrs. Gant was piecing things together to see if there was a hole in the Logan family story.

She couldn't blame the woman. After all it was two tales and both were centered on lies and half-truths.

Maggie thought back to what Dade had told her and factored in what she remembered about Daisy's mishap. "My brother and I were separated when I was just five years old. I was told I took a spill from a wagon, but I don't remember it. I don't remember anything much before age seven."

"For one so young, you have certainly led a tumultuous life." Mrs. Gant looked genuinely worried. "There are those in town who fret about you and the sheriff being the outlaw's children."

Maggie thought back to what Dade had told her. "As Dade said, our father lost all rights to call us his children when he dumped us on the steps of an orphanage."

"I believe you, dear. Truly I do. But I'm not the one who is determined to stir a pot best left to cool."

"The banker?"

Mrs. Gant nodded. "Lionel Payne is not a nice man."

Maggie already knew that after that scene in the street today when Payne flung those accusations at Dade. "He tried to get folks to suspect that Dade purposely left the town unguarded today when he was simply riding out to the Orshlin homestead to see how I was doing."

Not the truth, but only she and Dade knew the truth.

"I know you went with Doc to help him, and that Dade rode out with Doc to bring you home." Mrs. Gant gave the room a quick scan, but still lowered her voice as if fearing they'd be overheard. "Lionel Payne has had dealings with that evil man in the past."

"How do you know that?"

"I was friends with Lionel Payne's wife. She'd married him at the urging of her family and hoped in time she'd come to love him. But it never happened. She was miserable with him and begged him to agree to a divorce," Mrs. Gant said. "Lionel was violently opposed to it and told her flat out there was only one way they'd part. Death."

Maggie shivered, thinking that would be her fate as well if she was forced to marry Whit Ramsey. "A pity the poor woman was trapped in a loveless marriage."

"Oh, she left him." The older woman looked away as if suddenly troubled. "I knew she was going to run away from him, and I knew he'd be furious. But I never thought he'd hire a bounty hunter to track her down like she was a criminal."

Maggie could certainly understand how the woman must have felt. "Did he find her?"

"That depends on who you ask," Mrs. Gant said. "According to Lionel Payne, his wife was set upon by a ruffian while she was traveling by train to Omaha on a visit to her sister. In the struggle, she fell off to her death."

"You don't think that happened," Maggie said.

Mrs. Gant worried her hands together and frowned. "Oh, I think she was attacked all right. But I believe it was arranged by Lionel Payne."

"You think the bounty hunter pushed her off the train?"

"Or threw her off. Payne met with him the day after his wife disappeared. Two days after that Lionel announced his loss to the town."

Maggie's stomach heaved. If Payne couldn't have his wife, then he'd see that nobody else would either. Just how she expected Whit Ramsey to be. And since she'd jilted him at the altar, he'd have reason to want her dead as well.

A new worry seeped into Maggie's bones. All along she'd been worried that the bounty hunter would drag her back to Burland. That she'd be forced to marry Whit Ramsey, the man she'd publicly jilted.

Now she wondered if this bounty hunter had been hired to eliminate her. Yes, it made sense. Harlan Nowell had accused her of stealing, and few folks would question anything bad befalling a thief.

Maggie laid a hand on the older woman's and started at the tremors she felt racing through her. "You're sure the man who came here looking for Margaret Sutten is the same bounty hunter that Lionel Payne hired?"

"Yes. It's been years since I'd seen him, but I know it was him." The older woman grasped her hand, her eyes wide with fear. "That poor Sutten woman. I dread to think what will happen to her if that bounty hunter finds her."

It was Maggie's fear as well, and that trepidation exploded in her as she stared into the older woman's eyes and saw that her concern was directed toward Maggie. My God! Mrs. Gant knew, or suspected the truth.

Dare Maggie trust her? She wanted to, but trust wasn't something she gave easily.

"Maybe Miss Sutten will outwit him," she said.

Mrs. Gant just stared at her, like a parent would to a child who'd just told a whopping lie. "If she's got any sense, Margaret Sutten will run far from here and never look back."

Chapter 8

The Denver & Rio Grande came through Burland twice a day on the narrow gauge line and occasionally it arrived on time. Today the morning train was late by nearly two hours, prompting many in town to speculate whether it had been held up along the way.

The train was the only means to ship silver from the mines to the smelters, which made it a temptation to those looking to fatten their pockets without laboring. Those narrow mountain passes made an ambush an easier feat for those inclined to live by their guns.

Nobody mentioned the Logan Gang were the likely villains, but Dade knew that was on the townsfolk's minds. Hell, it was on his as well.

He shrugged his shoulders against the unease he'd been unable to shake since coming back from yesterday's trek with Duane and strode down the boardwalk toward the small depot at the edge of town. He tipped his hat to the few ladies who were out this crisp spring day and dipped his chin to the gents. Some folks smiled. Some stared. More than a few turned their heads.

Yep, it was clear that he was about as wanted here as ants at a picnic. Good thing they had a deputy who could shoot straight, though Dade worried how Duane would fare in a draw.

Most lawmen knew that their lives depended on how fast they could clear leather. Duane's injury was a hindrance.

Dade stepped inside the cramped depot and gave the room a quick glance. It was empty save for the regular loungers. A few old men met here every day to swap lies.

"That'll be fifty cents," the ticket agent said to the woman standing at the window.

"Mighty expensive for no more than I had to say," she said.

"That it is, but a telegram is still faster than the mail."

"I'll wait for a reply." She bustled to the bench against the wall and eased down to do just that, earning her a grunt from the agent.

Dade offered her a brief smile. She turned her head and denied him the same.

He snorted and glanced back at the train. If not for Maggie, he'd be tempted to hop on and put this town behind him.

Soon. Once the deputy was settled in, he'd head east and begin his search for Daisy all over again.

He didn't doubt that Maggie Sutten had been on the orphan train with Daisy. But had they been as close as Maggie claimed?

Maggie wasn't a scatterwit. If she'd befriended Daisy like she claimed to have done, his sister would've shared her fears and memories with her friend.

To convince him that she was his sister, Maggie would have trotted out a memory or two. But she'd been stunned to learn that Daisy had a brother.

If Maggie was telling the truth, then his sister lost all her memory of her family. How the hell long would something like that last? He'd have to ask Doc Franklin.

Surely Daisy's memory had returned over time. Surely she knew who she was now. And if she didn't?

His reasons for enlisting Maggie's help solidified in his head. He couldn't let her go. Not now.

Dade stepped up to the window. "Anybody get off?"

"Nary a one." The railroad agent looked around the deserted platform. "Don't look like anyone is leaving either."

"Nothing unusual about that."

Life moved at a snail's pace here, and that's just the way most folks liked it. The main reason the train stopped here at all was to deliver the mail and freight.

"Got a telegram that just came for Doc," the agent said. "Would you mind dropping it off at his place?"

"Sure thing. Going right by there." Dade took the note and caught Daisy's name midway down it. "What do I owe you?"

"Not a thing. Never take a red cent from the doc," the agent said. "Never know when I'll need his help."

One back scratching the other.

He left the depot and started back through town. The telegram was private, yet catching mention of Daisy made it his business. Never mind that the Daisy Logan Doc Franklin was referring to was Miss Margaret Sutten.

Still and all it was to his advantage to pay attention to what that woman was fixing to do.

He paused in the alley and gave the telegram a quick read. His temper erupted in a slow boil.

The headmaster at the John Sealy Training School for Nurses in Galveston was responding to Doc's telegram. They could enroll Daisy Logan in their late summer session and provide a room for her while she worked in the hospital and took classes.

Hell, Dade would bet if he hadn't seen this telegram, he'd have had no idea what Maggie was fixing to do with

Doc's help. He'd have just woken up one morning, and she'd have been gone.

He barged into Doc's without knocking. "You busy?"

"Nope," Doc said. "Come on back to the kitchen."

He strode right there and came up short in the doorway. Maggie sat at the square table with Doc, a cup of coffee before her.

"Were you going to tell me about this nurses' school?" Dade asked by way of greeting.

Her lips parted but no sound emerged. Good. At least he'd gotten an honest reaction from her for a change.

"The more folks know her plans, the less safe she's going to be," Doc said.

Dammit all but Dade couldn't find fault with that logic. But he was still the law in this town, duty bound to protect everyone in it. He couldn't do that if he was kept in the dark.

He handed Doc Franklin the telegram and noted the letter lying between him and Maggie. "How many of these hospitals have you contacted?"

"Just three," Doc said. "One in Denver, one in Galveston, and one in St. Louis."

"Which other one have you heard from?" he asked.

Doc glanced at the new telegram. "All of them. But Maggie feels that Denver is too close to Burland."

She wasn't just fixing to get out of town. She was planning to leave the state.

"What's this one say?" she asked Doc.

Tension hummed in the air as Doc read the telegram. He passed it to her and heaved a sigh. "They'll take you too, but their next class doesn't start until late summer."

"I can't wait that long."

Dade helped himself to coffee in hopes he'd calm down a spell. The thought of Maggie heading south or east didn't sit well with him.

Which was stupid when he thought on it.

She wasn't his kin or his responsibility beyond the fact that she was a lone woman living in Placid. He should be glad to see her go, for she'd be more hindrance than help as he set off in search of his sister.

"When are you fixing to leave?" Dade asked her point blank. He had the satisfaction of watching her cheeks turn a dusty pink.

"I'm not sure." She toyed with the letter and frowned. "The school in St. Louis can promise me a place in the upcoming class, but I'm not fond of the wait or their rules."

"Didn't know you was a rebel," Dade said.

Doc muffled a laugh. "Can't say as I blame her for being hesitant about the school. It's run by the Sisters of Charity. She'll work and learn nursing around the clock seven days a week."

Hell, even cowboying gave a man time off to relax some. "They give students rooms there too?"

"A ward, just like the other, though I'd imagine this is going to feel more like being in a nunnery." He caught the nearly perceptible shift of her shoulders and guessed this was a hot topic.

Not the most inviting situation. Even Maggie's excitement seemed to dim. Or was that simply worry he was reading on her face?

Doc tapped the second paragraph on the letter. "I know it sounds like a prison sentence to you and all, but you'll be safer at the Mullanphy Hospital under the nuns' tutelage."

"The problem is remaining safe while I wait for the time that I can enroll," she said, flicking Dade an uncertain glance that had him questioning her thoughts.

Doc bobbed his head in agreement. "I could ask a friend in St. Louis to put you up in his home until that time comes. I'm sure he and his wife would welcome the company."

Dade wasn't surprised that Doc knew of someone who'd take her in. But they'd likely get more than they bargained for if Allis Carson picked up her trail.

"I don't know." Maggie chewed her lower lip, and he wondered if the same thought had crossed her mind. "It's a risk no matter what I do. Staying here surely isn't an option. It's a fact that trouble could follow me to St. Louis, so unless I can get right in the school, I'd be better off if I kept moving."

The curling of Doc's fingers was the only evidence that he disliked the idea of Maggie traipsing from town to town on her own in an attempt to stay one step ahead of the bounty hunter. Carson was no fool. He'd figure out where she was heading and beat her there, catching her when she got off the train.

"You'll never give Carson the slip if you travel by rail or stage," Dade said.

"What other choice do I have?" she asked.

Dade took another gander at the plan that had formed on his walk over here. Maggie had a month-long wait and needed protection. He needed her to identify the man who took Daisy.

The way he saw it, his way satisfied both wants. As long as he didn't think about those times when just the two of them would be alone God-knows-where, they'd be fine.

"Well, spit it out, boy," Doc said at last.

"I'm heading east in search of my sister, thinking the best way for me to find out what happened to her is by visiting the last place Maggie saw her." Dade caught and held Maggie's steady gaze with his own. "Come with me, Maggie."

"You think we'll just happen on the man who took Daisy?" she asked, the incredulity in her voice loud and clear.

"It's a long shot, but you've got a month to stay one step ahead of Allis Carson," he said. "Being on the move will work to your advantage. And yep, if we're lucky, we'll find out who took Daisy off that orphan train."

"You'd leave the town in the new deputy's care?" Doc asked.

"In a heartbeat. Only reason I took on the job was because most folks believed my sister would come back here." He flicked Maggie a look that made her squirm, but he derived no pleasure from her discomfort. "As far as folks around here need to know, my sister and I have headed on."

"I dislike the idea of us traveling together as siblings," she said, not mincing words. "It will be too easy for the bounty hunter to follow us."

Dade nodded, having already deduced the same. "We'll leave here as siblings. Didn't say we'd stay that way for long."

But he didn't intend to advertise they were traveling as husband and wife unless it became necessary. Better to let folks draw their own conclusions; that way he wouldn't be obliged to carry on an act twenty-four hours a day.

As for their nights together . . . Just thinking of sleeping with Maggie stirred him below the belt and promised he'd get damn little rest.

Her eyes held a mixture of innocence and anticipation that let him know she understood his plan. He held his breath, expecting another objection more forceful than the first.

Doc was the one to speak up. "You're planning to pose as husband and wife."

"When we have to," Dade said.

As long as he kept his hands to himself around her, he could get through it. If he gave in to his urges, he'd likely be rewarded with pleasure and untold grief.

"I suppose that's the wisest course to take," she said.

The lady was scared out of her wits for good reason, yet she'd never moaned or cried about it. She used her head to find a means to escape Harlan Nowell. Would she do the same to him?

"Then it's settled," he said.

Dade could begin getting supplies together for their journey. He just hoped it wouldn't be a quick escape with Allis Carson hot on their trail.

"You do know how to ride?" he asked.

That nervous shifting in her chair didn't bode well. "I've been on a horse a time or two."

Dammit, her inexperience in riding would cost them time.

"That will be an arduous journey for someone unused to the saddle," Doc said, voicing what was Dade's worry as well.

"Never said it'd be easy," Dade said. "But taking the train or stage leaves a trail a blind man could follow. Besides that, it's easier to hide if we stay off the beaten trail for the most part."

She didn't flinch or bitch about taking off on horseback and being isolated for the most part with him. He acknowledged another trait he admired in her. Fortitude.

"I trust that you are right," she said.

So did Dade. He didn't relish getting ambushed by the bounty hunter, which meant he'd best stay ahead of him at all times.

"Reckon a few lessons on a horse are in order," he said, and she relaxed some at that. "You know how to handle a gun?"

That got her tensing back up again. She shook her head, and he tried to ignore the way the sunlight gilded strands of her hair a rich gold.

"No, but I'm willing to learn that too."

He smiled at the determination ringing in her voice.

But it was the jolt of awareness that licked through him like fire when their gazes met that warned him this journey would be a challenge for him as well. Traveling from town to town with her was asking for trouble on several levels.

Foremost was the fact that she was a desirable woman. It would surely shred his patience to remain in close company with her on a journey and keep his hands to himself.

Though they could pass themselves off as siblings for a spell, there would still be some places where they'd be obliged to spend the night together out of necessity and safety.

God's truth, that'd test his honor as a gentleman.

Yep, he'd likely be buying into trouble when he left town with Maggie Sutten. But it was the only choice to make.

He needed her to identify this man who'd taken Daisy, and he needed to protect her from Allis Carson. That could prove a bigger challenge than he'd first thought.

Maggie had secrets he suspected that even Doc Franklin didn't know. He just hoped to hell they didn't land in a fix that he couldn't get them out of.

Yep, once they found Daisy, he'd take Maggie to St. Louis and see she was enrolled in her nursing school. She'd have what she wanted and so would he.

Family. He'd do anything to make that a reality. He'd made his sister a promise that he'd find her. That they'd be reunited as a family one day.

He damn sure wasn't going to let her down again.

"We'll start you on riding this afternoon." He looked into Maggie's wide eyes and felt his gut lurch. "I want you comfortable in the saddle."

There wasn't a bit of trust reflected in her eyes—just wary resignation. "I'm sure I'll manage."

More likely she'd suffer in quiet when her backside was

too tender to touch. The image that conjured up reminded him of the dangerous game he was playing with Margaret Sutten.

For more times than he cared to count, he wondered if there was another way. As before, none came to mind. With the bounty hunter breathing down their necks, their only chance was to stay off the beaten path.

He fished the pocket watch from his vest pocket, absently pausing to rub his thumb over the inscription on the back. Family. Would he forever lose those he cared for?

"Meet me at the livery in an hour," he said. "We'll start with a short ride."

After he talked with his deputy. If Duane had found more signs of Allis Carson today, the ride would have to wait.

Maggie got to her feet, looking proud yet vulnerable. "I'll be ready."

Dade returned his watch to his pocket and tamped down the wild urge to take her in his arms and hold her close. She brought out his protective side all right, but she also stirred his baser wants more than any woman he'd met in a long time.

Best keep your grub hooks to yourself, cowboy.

He hightailed it out of Doc Franklin's house, fixing his mind on all that had to be done in short order instead of the inviting bow of her mouth. He had to get her ready to ride hard and fast when the time came.

The folks he passed on the boardwalk seemed in no hurry as they went about their business. Nothing looked out of the ordinary, and he wasn't beset with the feeling that something was wrong.

Even the welcoming quiet of the saloon was unusual in the West, proving the town lived up to its name. But like all watering holes, men who gathered to drink tended to talk, whether it was to boast or bitch.

That fact made the bartender the eyes and ears of the town.

Dade stepped inside the room that smelled of smoke and liquor and gave his eyes a moment to adjust to the dim interior. A good scrubbing of the window glass would admit more light, but the accumulation of grime on the panes was proof that the owner didn't feel so inclined.

Two Mexicans sat at a round table in the back playing poker, garbed like cowpokes but acting like drifters. The lamp suspended above them encompassed them in light, though their wide brimmed hats kept their faces in shadow.

Cy Shepard leaned on the bar with a bottle of rotgut before him, the knees and seat of his dungarees so worn they were nearly threadbare. The old prospector had been a Saturday regular since the spring thaw, exchanging what dust he'd gleaned at the assay office then ambling to the saloon to drink it away.

This was the first time Dade had seen Shepard in town during the week. He appeared to be in the process of getting seriously drunk.

Dade guessed he'd hit a vein and was celebrating, or he'd realized that his piece of the mountain was panned out. Either way Dade suspected before the day was done he'd have to lock the old man up for the night, if for no other reason than to give him a place to sleep it off.

He strode to the bar and motioned for two fingers of whiskey. If anything unusual had happened north of here, the old man would have heard about it.

One look at the fear on Shepard's face told him something was dead wrong. Hell, even his hand shook as he poured whiskey in a glass.

"What brings you to town?" Dade asked.

Shepard paused with the glass clutched in one shaky hand. "Too damned many varmints in the hills."

"I'm guessing they're of the two-legged variety?" he asked as the bartender placed a shot glass full of whiskey before him.

"Yep." Shepard tossed back his liquor like it was water and promptly poured another. "You remember Myron Zule who lived up the mountain from me?"

"Sure do. I enjoyed listening to his stories about the old days."

Unlike this old man, Zule came to town once a month. But where Shepard panned the streams, Zule had a placer mine in the mountains that meted out enough silver for him to keep hoping he'd strike a vein.

He'd been in frail health when Dade first met him a month or so before winter hit. Come spring, he'd learned that Shepard had found him dead shortly after that and buried him.

"Turns out a gang of outlaws holed up in his mine over the winter," Shepard said.

The whiskey blazed in Dade's gut. Damn, could the gang be his kin? His fingers curled around the heavy glass, holding on to it like he'd held on to his memories all these years.

"How'd you find out they were there?"

The old man swallowed hard. "I caught a whiff of bacon frying a couple of days ago. Figured somebody had claimed Zule's mine, so I went up there to say howdy. I spotted three men standing outside the mineshaft."

"They see you?"

"Yep. I recognized those fellers right off. The Logan Gang."

Just what Dade feared. The outlaws had been holed up

in that mine all winter, likely venturing out to keep a watch on the town, likely watching Dade.

"You're damned lucky you didn't get shot."

"Came close to it." Shepard's ruddy skin paled, and his bleary eyes went wide. "I lit out and just about reached the tree line when I heard shots. My danged feet got all tangled up, and I fell. Didn't stop to see if I took a bullet until I crawled in the bushes."

"I'm surprised they didn't come after you." Even more surprised that a Logan had missed an old man whose idea of running was more of a shuffle.

"Hell, they weren't after me at all." The old man splashed more whiskey in a glass and gulped it down, his whole body shaking now. "I ain't never seen shooting like that before."

"From the outlaws?"

"Nope, from a lone man. He was as fast with a sidearm as he was with a rifle," Shepard said.

"You got a good look at this man?" he asked, suspecting a lawman had tracked down the gang. At the old man's nod, he said, "Describe him."

Shepard scrunched up his leathery face. "On the lean side. Long dark hair. Wasn't nothing memorable about him 'cept he had the fortitude to stare down a rattler."

It was an apt description of Allis Carson. He poured whiskey in the old man's glass. "Tell me the rest."

Shepard finished off the whiskey first, then reeled back and swiped a hand over his mouth. "I tell you that feller put a bullet right betwixt the eyes of one of them outlaws before the other could pull leather."

Dade went still as death, feeling oddly distressed to know that one of his relatives had been gunned down. It was bound to happen. When a man lived by the gun, he tended to die by it.

All these years he'd told himself he wouldn't give a shit if his uncles or pa died the way they'd lived. He hadn't expected to feel this sense of loss. Which one had died? Brice or Seth? Or Clete?

"What happened to the other two outlaws?" he asked.

"That bounty hunter shot one of them in the leg as he was running to his horse. God almighty that man screamed something awful," Shepard said, and Dade swore over the fact that he winced. "The outlaw wasn't about to go down easy though. He pulled his gun, but the bounty hunter was faster."

Dade swallowed hard and hated himself for that hesitation. He was a Logan by birth, but he damn sure didn't have their thieving, murdering bent.

"Kill him?"

Shepard snorted. "Nope. He was still hollering when the bounty hunter hogtied him then tossed him over the saddle. Did the same with the dead man, though he didn't complain."

"Which direction did he head?" Dade asked.

"North," the old man said. "Didn't seem in any hurry either. He mounted up, smoked a cigarette, and rode off."

Dade went still. His hunch had been right. The bounty hunter hired out to whomever would pay his wages. In between, he wasn't opposed to making a little extra on the side by hauling in outlaws.

Anger sluiced through him like water flooding a millstream. If Carson got his hands on Maggie, God knew what he'd do to her when they were alone.

The bounty hunter had likely hauled the two outlaws in to the U.S. Marshal in Colorado Springs. That was the only place close where he could collect his reward off the Logan Gang, dead or alive.

"What about the third outlaw?" Dade asked.

The old man shrugged. "He got away. Heard him ride off, so he must have dodged them bullets somehow."

So one of his relatives survived. Which one?

A sense of unease curled in Dade. No, he couldn't feel deep grief over his kins' death and arrest, but he didn't like the heavy-handed way Allis Carson acted either.

He'd been hiding on a ledge above town, watching and smoking those cigarillos. He'd returned in hopes of finding Margaret Sutten.

"I gotta take a leak." Shepard scowled at the barkeep and hiccuped. "I'm coming back, so don't go messing with my bottle."

"It'll be where you left it," the bartender said.

Dade paid the old man little heed. It'd take Allis Carson two days to ride to Colorado Springs. Longer if he had to go into Denver. It'd maybe cost him another day to get his reward.

Would he go after the remaining Logan brother? Only if he could do that and pursue Maggie.

The bounty hunter would be back. Dade maybe had a week to get Maggie ready to ride and light out of here. Maybe less.

If the surviving outlaw was able, he'd likely be gunning for Allis Carson, who had done what no man had been able to do for nigh on twenty years. He'd be back with blood in his eyes.

"You gonna drink that whiskey or stare it to death," the bartender asked Dade as he wiped down the bar.

Dade toyed with the shot glass glistening with the amber firewater. Instead of answering, he said, "If you hear of anyone seeing that bounty hunter near here, let me know."

The bartender continued wiping down the bar, his expression deadpan. "I'm guessing by the time anyone knows this bounty hunter is around, he'll have moved on or found who he's looking for."

That was Dade's fear as well. Yep, no doubt about it. He had to get out of town as soon as he could.

Maggie's riding lesson would tell him how soon they could disappear. He hoped they could go before it was too late.

Chapter 9

Maggie thought horses were the most beautiful creatures God put on this earth. But she had an unnatural fear of getting on one of them.

The one time she'd ridden sidesaddle, she'd suffered the experience in quiet agony and vowed never to do it again. It'd brought back the horrific memory of her and another little girl riding ponies.

Her foster sister Becka had been fearless on a horse. She'd taunted Maggie to race with her.

Though Maggie had been afraid, she'd given in to her new sister's challenge. The greater fear of being left out, of being unwanted, goaded her to do whatever her new family expected of her.

Becka had laughed at her frightful attempt to ride and raced off. Maggie had clung to her pony in terror, unable to get the animal to obey, and finally bearly able to see Becka, who'd outdistanced her.

"I hate you," she'd screamed at her foster sister, simmering with all the anger a seven-year-old could feel.

Becka, older than Maggie by two years, laughed harder, but not for long. Right before Maggie caught up with her, Becka's pony suddenly shied.

Maggie had watched in horror as her foster sister's pony reared and pitched her off. Becka had just laid there unmoving while the pony stomped over her body before galloping away.

Her foster mother screamed. "Do something you stupid girl!"

Even if Maggie had been able to get off the pony, she was too young and too scared to be of use. So she clung to the pony while tears streamed down her face.

Becka's father rushed to his daughter's side. One of the men who worked on the horse farm grabbed the reins on Maggie's restless pony while another pulled her from the saddle. And all the while Becka's mother was screaming and blaming Maggie for the accident.

Maggie had never seen a man cry, but Becka's father did as he rose with his daughter in his arms. "She's dead."

Her foster mother had glared at Maggie with such hatred that she flinched as if slapped. "Take her away."

"No! Please let me stay. Please," Maggie had said.

But her plea had been ignored. Everyone stared at her, condemning her with their eyes.

The same man who'd lifted Maggie off the pony took her by the hand and led her away. She'd been numb with the sense of being unwanted yet again, as she was taken back to the foundling home with just the clothes on her back.

For the second time in her life she'd been stripped of everything that she'd possessed. This time she lost something that couldn't be replaced. Trust.

From that day forward she never tried to be friendly and cute when folks came in search of a child. If she was never chosen, she'd never have to suffer the pain of rejection again.

She lost track of the nights she'd cried herself to sleep,

secretly blaming herself because she hadn't been able to help her foster sister.

She'd stayed at the foundling home until they'd tired of her and decided to ship her west on the orphan train. Surely someone would have need of a strong healthy girl to help around the house. But nobody did.

Nobody showed any interest in her until Harlan Nowell gave her a second perusal. Instead of being part of his family, she ended up the companion to a crippled rich girl who was just as lonely as she had been.

This time, as she learned eventually, she was expected to honor the arrangement Nowell had made years ago and willingly take the place of the crippled daughter in the marriage bed. All because Caroline wasn't whole enough to be a rich man's wife.

Maggie knew that deep down Caroline was bitter about Whit Ramsey's rejection. As Caroline aptly put it, Maggie was the sacrificial lamb.

But where Caroline's health prevented her from escaping her fate, Maggie was capable of running away.

Now she was ready to run again. She tried to view the one-month wait to enter the nursing school as a good thing. After all, she'd now have Dade to escort her there.

If she could get over her fear of horses.

She ran shaky hands down her skirt and left the boardinghouse. The walk toward the livery seemed to take ages.

She could do this. She had to.

As promised, Dade was waiting inside the shadowy interior. He was adjusting the saddle on a small black horse whose head lifted the moment Maggie entered.

The horse stared at her with big inquisitive eyes, and Maggie wondered if the animal could sense her fear.

Dade gave her a brief critical look. He dropped his gaze to her feet and started that slow meandering perusal that made her skin tingle and had heat pooling between her legs.

"Don't you have one of those riding outfits?"

"No." She didn't have the means to buy one either, even if the mercantile had a ready-made one. "I can make do with this."

She was an expert at making do. Running was the new twist on her life. But the fate that awaited her should she get caught was all the incentive necessary to propel her to do what she must to carve a life for herself.

"If you say so." He nodded to the little black horse. "This mare is even tempered and sure footed. She ought to be a good fit for you."

Ought to be . . . Maggie forced a smile, not about to complain now. That might be enough incentive for him to go off without her.

Though a part of her preferred traveling alone, she surely understood she'd be an easy target for the bounty hunter if she did. She had to keep up the pretense of being Dade's sister, though that would likely run its course too. Then what?

She refused to consider playing the part of his wife. That would be a cruel taunt, for her dreams had put her in his strong arms far too often of late.

Maggie wasn't about to open herself up to more rejection and heartache. She wasn't going to yearn for something—or someone—she couldn't have.

Besides, right now she had to subdue her choking fear of horses and concentrate on learning how to ride one without breaking her own neck. She stared at the big western saddle and frowned. No wonder he'd asked if she had a riding skirt.

"That isn't a lady's saddle," she said.

"Tenfeather doesn't have a used one, and I can't afford to buy a new sidesaddle for you."

Heavens, she surely didn't expect him to. But she couldn't afford to buy a saddle either, so she was stuck riding astride like a man.

"What do I do?" she asked, resigned to seeing this through to the end, whatever end that might be.

At this point breaking her neck was almost preferable to trying to conquer her fear of horses.

"Get a grip on the saddle horn and swing your leg over the back of the horse. I'll give you a leg-up." He moved to the black horse's side, twined his fingers together to create a step, and fixed her with a look that dared her to refuse.

For a heartbeat she was sorely tempted to turn around and run like hell in the other direction. Other considerations were playing into this scheme of Dade's.

She'd surely show a good deal of leg riding like a man. It couldn't be comfortable for a woman either. But squaring off against him would get her nowhere. And God help her she wanted to get far, far from here.

Buck up, Maggie girl. This man is your only ticket to freedom.

She grabbed the saddle with one shaky hand and lifted her hem with the other. A cool breeze played with the hem of her drawers, reminding her she was about to shuck modesty.

The way his shoulders tensed sent heat coursing through her and awakened a different urge in her, one that she'd heard whispers about among the servants. This was that pull that a woman felt for a man she was attracted to. And God help her, Dade Logan was just the most virile man she'd ever met.

Without a doubt she was fixing to ride into danger in more than one way. She took a deep breath, ready to live life for once.

She placed her foot in his cupped hands and got a grip on the saddle though she really wanted to hold onto Dade.

"Up with you," he said, and matched action to words.

Maggie's heart was in her throat as she shot into the air. Her skirt caught on the saddle, riding up farther than she'd feared. Not that she realized that right off.

She was too busy getting a stranglehold on the saddle horn and willing the river of anxiety flowing through her to ebb. When it did, she noticed her state of dress. But short of dismounting, she couldn't figure out any way to right her skirt, which was now bunched beneath her.

That wasn't a problem for Dade. He slid his hands on both sides of her bottom and grabbed her skirt, partly freeing it in a matter of moments. She couldn't have been more quivery with energy if she'd stuck a finger in one of Mr. Edison's new light sockets that Harlan Nowell had bragged about having throughout his mansion.

"Put your feet in the stirrups and lift yourself up a bit," he said, the warmth of his breath fanning her thigh, which was covered in thin muslin and so close to his mouth.

Good grief, her face would surely burst into flames any second. Still she did as he asked and managed to ease up enough for him to jerk her skirt into place.

Maggie held herself still and drank in these very odd feelings. She'd never had a man handle her skirt before. Never felt his breath fan her thigh. Never had the yen for him to press his mouth to her skin, right there on her thigh.

This settled it. She could not tolerate this every time she gained the saddle. She had to get a riding skirt before they left on their journey.

He left her shaking inside and out and strode to his chestnut gelding, mounting with an economy of movement and masculine strength that made her mouth go dry. Why hadn't she realized before how very strong he was?

"Now then, get a grip on the reins," he said, bringing his horse up beside hers. "Give your mare just enough line so as not to choke her."

He reached over and adjusted the reins that she had a death grip on. "Relax, Maggie."

"I'm trying."

Truly she was, but she simply couldn't feel at ease. Not only was she quaking with fear over being on a horse but she was achingly aware of Dade Logan as a man.

"You'll get the hang of it," he said. "Come on. Nudge your horse with your heels—not hard, just a gentle squeeze."

He rode off, and she fought down the panic of being on a horse all alone. If she didn't get her anxiety under control, she'd find herself being Whit Ramsey's wife.

That was the reminder she needed. She gave the black mare a gentle tap of her heels. The horse started toward the stable door that Dade had just opened.

Maggie clung to the saddle horn, reins trapped between it and her palm. Every nightmare she'd had of the accident galloped before her eyes. The thunder of hooves, the screams, the accusations all swirling in a black morass of her own guilt and fear.

The accident wasn't her fault, yet she'd felt that her presence was what goaded Becka to toss caution to the wind. How could she possibly think to ride out of here pretty as you please?

"Let go of the saddle horn," he said.

She couldn't. She simply was afraid.

He grabbed her horse's lines and stopped the animal, and she wanted to cry with relief. "Squeeze the horse's sides with your knees. You'll be able to keep your seat and ease up on the reins."

Absolutely not. She wasn't about to let go of the saddle horn. "I can't."

"Yes, you can," he said, and laid his big hand on her thigh.

Her nearly bared thigh.

A new energy licked up her leg to the juncture of her

thighs. The oddest sensations expanded in vibrating waves and left her restive. Edgy. Aware of Dade as a man and herself as a woman.

"That's it," he said.

Oh, that was definitely it.

She and Caroline had struck up a friendship with a Bohemian woman on their last jaunt to Manitou Springs. That bold lady had been a proponent of women's equality in all things, especially the sensual pleasures to be savored between a man and woman.

She'd explained all about the sensations a woman felt when gripped with desire, shocking Maggie and Caroline. That lecture opened their innocent eyes too.

She insisted it was perfectly natural and that a woman should embrace her passions. It was the direct opposite of what both girls had been taught by their straitlaced tutor.

In fact Maggie was having great difficulty bringing to mind that stern woman's dictums. Desire was weaving ribbons around her and Dade right now. Staring into his warm brown eyes made it so easy to look at him as a possible lover.

Pretend they were married? Yes, that possibility held enormous appeal.

"Maggie." His voice was a low rumble of sound that rippled over her skin like a warm breeze.

Her heart was beating far too fast again. The darkening of his eyes and wicked curl of his lips told her he felt this sensual connection too. What would it be like to kiss him?

"Am I doing it correctly?" She caught herself from leaning into him and shifted one hand so it rested over his.

He jerked his hand from her thigh. The mouth that had curved in invitation a moment ago was now pressed in a grim line. "You're getting there. Let's head out."

With a click of his tongue, both horses took off at a

sedate walk. The feel of the big animal moving beneath her snapped those gossamer ribbons of desire.

Maggie's hands flew back to the saddle horn, her grip tight but not as urgent as before. Her face surely was red as the bandana tied around Dade's strong neck.

Heavenly days, had she misread Dade's intent? She was mortified to have let herself surrender to those urges. Why, she'd all but thrown herself on him. And what had he done?

He'd turned away from her. He'd rejected her advances.

How much plainer could he make it?

They were pretending to be brother and sister. She'd do well to remember that fact for the next month that she was in his company.

The mare trailed his big gelding to the narrow valley outside town. Mountains rose around them to give the elusion they were protected but Maggie knew safety was a rare commodity. Anything could lurk behind rocks and in the dense cover of trees that reached toward the heavens.

The grandeur around her was mesmerizing, leaving her feeling small and insignificant. But the magnificence around her paled in comparison to the power emanating from the tall man riding ahead of her.

It didn't seem to matter that she didn't want to want him. When she was in his company, she simply couldn't ignore him. When they were apart, he commanded far too much of her thoughts.

She didn't want to feel these deeply sensual urges for him, but she couldn't seem to stop it either. So she might as well give up trying to remain unaffected by his nearness and surreptitiously admire him.

If nothing else, it took her mind off her choking fear. It made riding for nearly an hour less like a chore and more like a treat.

Even being on a horse wasn't as horrible now as it'd

been, but she was still eons away from being relaxed. But if they stayed at this pace, at least she'd be able to manage their journey.

As for her dealings with Dade? Well, that was another matter entirely, and one she wasn't quite sure how to handle.

He reined up, and her horse stopped as well, a fact she was grateful for. "Now that you're used to sitting a saddle some we'll start with trotting toward that ridge of boulders up ahead." He swung from the saddle and hooked a rope onto her horse's halter. "This will remind your horse not to run off with you."

So soon? That old fear set her insides tumbling. "Shouldn't we practice walking them longer?"

"No time. We need to get you used to running with a horse."

It wasn't necessary for him to add that their lives might depend on their outrunning the bounty hunter. She was well aware of the danger. But still, she wasn't ready for this.

He swung back into the saddle and tied the lead to her mare around his saddle horn. "Ready?"

She'd never be ready. "As much as I'll ever be."

His gelding started off at a faster walk, urging hers to follow. Tension sped through her unchecked in a nauseating wave, forcing her stomach up to her throat.

Just when she was getting her balance, his big gelding broke into a trot. The mare did likewise.

Maggie swallowed a squeak and clung to the saddle so tightly she was sure her fingernails scored the leather. She'd never felt so jarred in her life. Each time her bottom left the saddle, she feared it wouldn't return. But somehow she stayed on the horse, and they made it to the boulders without incident.

Knowing she'd accomplished this insane feat didn't stop the tremors or the threatening roll of her stomach.

Though she wasn't prone to tears or hysterics, she knew that the light lunch she'd eaten was on its way back up.

"Help me down," she said.

Dade stared at her. "We're just getting started."

"I'm going to be sick."

She'd never seen a man move so fast in her life. One moment she was leaning over the saddle sucking in air in a vain attempt to keep from heaving, the next Dade plucked her from the saddle and carried her to the boulders. If her stomach hadn't been rebelling she'd have thanked him.

After the heaving stopped, she leaned against the cool boulder and wondered how in the world she'd ever be able to escape on horseback with Dade. How in the world could she conquer her fear?

"I can't do it." She just couldn't get back on that horse.

"Never figured you to be a quitter," he said, and that got her back up.

"I'm not, but you don't understand—" Her words faded into nothing, because she couldn't understand either how one incident in her life could still debilitate her so.

"You going to tell me what brought this on?" he asked.

"I have a fear of being thrown to my death from a horse," she said.

He was quiet for the longest time. "You ever been tossed from the saddle?"

She shook her head, knowing he'd hound her if she insisted on keeping her secret. But sharing her past with a stranger was totally foreign to her.

"No, but my foster sister was," she said at last.

"Nowell's daughter?"

She shook her head. "The daughter of the first family who adopted me. It was a horrible accident, and I've never forgotten it."

"Reckon you never got back on a horse again, unless you were forced to."

"There was no reason for me ever to ride," she said.

No opportunity for her to either, even if she'd wanted to. She surely had no desire to get on a horse again.

He shook his head as he strode to the horses and grabbed their lines, his back as straight as the towering pines.

Either he didn't believe her or he had trouble imagining that anyone could get around sans horseback. The simple truth was that Harlan Nowell had vehicles and matching teams for his family to use.

His wife was a delicate creature who spent her days in lavish gowns and being doted on hand and foot. Caroline Nowell was too crippled to even think of horseback riding.

As for Harlan Nowell, Maggie could count the times she'd seen him ride a horse.

Not so for Whit Ramsey.

The first time she'd seen him he'd ridden up to the mansion dressed in black like a dark knight challenging the fortress. Looking back that's just what he'd done.

His horse was just as dark and restive. He'd controlled the animal with a strong hand, adding to her fear of the beast and him. But she'd also learned a valuable lesson that day from two chambermaids.

"I wager he's one that takes what he wants," one of the maids had said.

"He wouldn't take no for an answer," the other had remarked.

Maggie had put their opinions from her mind. But a few days later, she had learned firsthand that the maids were right. That's when she realized the only way to avoid her fate was to run away.

She buried her face in her hands and pinched her eyes shut, well aware that her fear of horses worked to Whit's advantage. She had to surmount that debilitating feeling and soon, and the only way she knew to conquer a fear was to face it head on.

The question remained: would she exhaust Dade's patience before they had to run for their lives?

She lifted her head and met his steady gaze. To her surprise there was no condemnation or disgust in his eyes.

"Only one way you can beat your panic," he said. "Get back on the horse."

"What if terror overcomes me again?"

"You puke it out of your system and start all over." He stared at her, not with rancor but with concern. "You keep doing it until you conquer your fear."

She shook her head. "Is that experience talking?"

He rolled one broad shoulder, the movement casual, yet there was something in his eyes that belied his ease. "It's just common sense. You either control the fear or it controls you."

Easy for him to say. But he was right. She straightened and eyed the black mare again.

"How badly do you want to get to St. Louis and learn this nursing stuff?" he asked.

"Badly enough to get back on that horse," she said.

The animal did have gentle eyes, and hadn't done one thing to warrant her irrational fear. No, the memory of what could happen was doing that. She was letting the past get a stranglehold on her future.

"Okay, let's try it again," she said.

He dipped his chin smartly and shifted to the mare's side, cupping his hands together again. She appreciated that he hadn't ridiculed or tried to browbeat her. Actually, now he didn't even look at her. He just silently waited for her to make the next move.

She thought back to his earlier instructions on gaining the seat. Grab the saddle. Swing her right leg over the saddle and ease down. The first time, she'd managed everything but the easing down part.

She'd dropped like a stone on the saddle the first time, so she vowed to do a better job now. The black mare whickered softly, as if telling her it would be all right.

That was Maggie's fondest wish too. She just hoped Dade couldn't hear her knees knocking as she forced her legs to carry her toward him. She grabbed onto the saddle, having to do it twice because she simply missed the first time.

If Dade noticed that, he gave no outward indication. But she doubted much got past this man. He possessed an uncanny alertness that could well save both their lives down the road.

It was getting down the road that worried her most. They were taking off on horseback. Good heavens, she was going to do this. She refused to cave in to her own fears.

Dade gave her a boost up immediately, and she focused on swinging her leg over the saddle. She landed easier than the first time too. Why, the mare took no more than one sidestep.

Still she grasped the reins with one hand and reached for the saddle horn with the other. Out of the corner of her eye she was simply awestruck by the ease with which Dade swung into the saddle.

Concentrate on what he told you the first time, she ordered herself over the too rapid pounding of her heart. First thing was righting her skirt, which had gotten bunched under her again.

She managed that the best she could and simply ignored the fact that her stockinged legs were exposed. Acquiring a split skirt was the only means to surmount that obstacle.

Right now her mode of dress was the least of her worries. She had to cope with her debilitating fear of riding and become comfortable on this horse.

Dade glanced back at her, his captivating gaze probing hers. "Ready?"

She huffed out a shaky breath and nodded. God help her. "Ready."

They started out at a walk, but she had the feeling it was more for the horses' benefit than hers. He still held the line to her mare, which relieved her more than she wished to admit.

"Let's ease into a trot," he said and matched action to words effortlessly.

Her little mare followed his gelding's lead, and though they weren't moving fast, the gait was torture. Her bottom slammed the saddle, and her teeth were sure to shake from their sockets.

"Relax," he said.

Was he joking? "I can't."

He brought both horses back to a walk so quickly she nearly cried out in relief. "Plant your feet in the stirrups, sit back in the saddle, and move with the horse, not against her."

Easier said than done with yards of petticoat, a small bustle, and a corset that was suddenly choking her. Those restrictions would have to be severely modified before they embarked on their jaunt. But she wasn't about to explain that to him.

For now she'd just make do. Oddly enough, getting a good footing in the stirrups did ease the ache that had begun in her lower back.

Dade urged both horses into a trot again. "Stop holding your breath, Maggie."

How could he tell she'd been doing that when she wasn't even aware of it? She exhaled heavily and tried to breathe normally.

"Let out a little more rein," he said.

Then he went on to explain that each shift she made in

the saddle and on the reins gave the horse an order. Some were self-explanatory.

Four were crucial to master. The commands to walk, trot, gallop, and stop.

"You lead this time," he said. "Break into a trot when we reach that stand of aspens to your right."

She followed his instructions, so intent on doing everything he'd said that she hadn't realized they'd trotted across the clearing until he brought both horses to a stop near the tree line. It hadn't been the most comfortable jaunt, but she'd done it.

"How do you feel?" he asked.

"A bit jarred, but not as afraid."

"Good."

He thumbed his hat back and smiled, and Maggie simply forgot to breathe again. Without a doubt Dade Logan was the most handsome man she'd had the pleasure of meeting in a long time. Why, his mouth had the most inviting bow to it.

Shaken by that admission, she fixed her attention on the little mare whose ears were perked as if taking in everything. She really was a pretty horse.

"You said you got this mare at the livery?"

"Yep, bought her from Tenfeather," he said. "He'd had her for a year and rarely rented her out because of her size."

She stared at him, scarce believing what he'd done for her. "You bought her for this journey? For me?"

He dipped his chin. "I rode her once, and she had a good steady gait for a greenhorn. No offense, Maggie."

Again that arresting smile that did odd things to her insides, warming her and leaving her tingling all over. Her experience with men was so minimal it was laughable, but she'd seen others flirt. She'd heard the change in a woman's laugh when she was smitten with a man.

Those were things she'd have to guard against now, for she was surely smitten with Dade Logan.

"Best we walk the horses for a spell and get you used to leading your mare," he said.

He swung from the saddle. Surely she could manage dismounting from her mare.

Putting action to words was a whole other thing. Through no fault of her own, the smart little heel on her halfboot got caught in her skirt.

She clung precariously to the saddle horn and tried to kick her foot free but couldn't with her weight on one stirrup. So she swung her leg back to gain the saddle. That must have given the mare a signal because the horse suddenly moved.

Maggie felt suspended in midair, as one foot remained caught in her skirt and the other slipped from the stirrup. She yelped as she fell.

Only she slammed into Dade instead of the hard ground. His arms banded around her and crushed her against the solid wall of his chest.

"You should have waited for me to help you down," he said, though there was no heat in his words as he untangled her skirt from her heel.

"I didn't want to be a burden." But she'd become one anyway, and my, didn't it feel wonderful to be in his arms.

Before she could extract herself from a position that was far too cozy and too comfortable, he turned her to face him. She looked up at him, expecting a lecture on being impetuous to follow.

He cupped the side of her face in one palm, and the glide of his thumb over her hot cheek sent a delicious shiver coursing through her.

"Beautiful, independent Maggie," he said. "What am I going to do with you?"

"What do you want to do?" she asked, a bit shocked by her own boldness.

A low sound rumbled from his chest, but she scarcely heard it over the hammering of her heart. And then he did just what she'd dreamed he'd do.

He lowered his head and captured her lips with his. This wasn't the tentative peck that she'd expected.

He kissed her with bold intent. He kissed her as if he wanted only her.

She felt safe, desired. She felt his need in his touch and the change in his body, and an answering want zinged along her nerves. She was startled by her own electrifying response.

All the reasons she should avoid an intimacy with the man she'd be traveling with for one month drifted to the back of her mind. She just wanted him to go on kissing her. She wanted to pretend she could have a romance with a man without looking over her shoulder for Whit.

Bringing that man to mind was all the impetus she needed to tear her mouth from Dade Logan's.

"Don't ever take such liberties again," she said, hoping she sounded affronted and not breathy with passion.

The mouth that had moved so powerfully over her own pulled into a grim line. "Sorry to have offended you, Miss Sutten."

She offered a pained smile, but he'd already turned away from her and didn't notice. His cold dismissal was like a northerly blast off the Rockies.

His broad shoulders were impossibly stiff and unyielding. "We need to get back to town. I'll give you a leg-up."

"Thank you."

He boosted her onto the saddle and swung astride his gelding. She'd hurt his feelings and felt absolutely miserable about doing so.

But it was for the best.

Whit wouldn't stop looking for her. He'd track her down if only to punish her. If there was a man in her life then, she knew Whit would kill him just to hurt her.

No, she couldn't risk getting close to anybody, especially Dade Logan.

Chapter 10

Dade had to get his damned head out of his ass. There was no other explanation for kissing Maggie Sutten like there was no tomorrow. None other than that he'd thought about it since the day he met her.

He slid her a glance and noted the stiff way she sat the saddle. She hadn't expected him to kiss her. That was evident in that shocked moment when their lips touched and she went still as death.

Even when she did kiss him back, there was a hesitancy there. Once her shock wore off, she pulled away like he was a rattler she'd ventured too close to.

Now the little lady had her back up and for good reason.

For one thing, he'd had no right to kiss her. For another, he'd grabbed her like she was a saloon girl and laid one on her—never mind they were alone out here.

He'd taken what he'd wanted without respecting her wishes. Mind you, he wasn't sorry he had done it. Nope, he wouldn't trade the memory of her sweet lips moving beneath his for anything.

But now he had to deal with the consequences.

She'd likely not want to travel with him. Hell, he was lucky she was willing to ride back to town with him. But four weeks was a long time to be in the company of a man she couldn't trust. And she surely wouldn't trust him after that stunt.

Oh, he could tell her it wouldn't happen again. But he wouldn't place that bet on himself.

Nope, the best thing to do was to stick to their plans. Allis Carson was far more dangerous to her than Dade. Surely she could see that.

"You did good today," he said, breaking the silence that had been roaring around them.

"I feel awkward on a horse."

"You'll get used to it."

"When do we leave?"

"Tomorrow."

"So soon?"

He heard the panic in her voice and grimaced. He surely didn't have time to coddle a woman with cold feet.

"Duane Tenfeather is fitting right into the job of deputy and is prepared to take over as sheriff," he said. "I want to be gone before Allis Carson returns."

She was quiet a good long time, and he suspected she was weighing her options. "I don't know if I'll be ready to ride all day this soon."

"You'll be fine, Maggie," he said.

"I'm afraid," she said, and the troubled look she cast him proved she was telling the truth.

Damn, he should've figured she'd be green in the saddle. But even if he'd had another day to teach her, he couldn't see where it would make that much difference.

"I know I'm asking a lot in asking you to trust me, but I just have a feeling we'd best get going while the getting is good."

This time she hauled back on the reins and stared at him. Her eyes said it all. Behind the very real fear she was likely questioning if he'd decided to hustle her off quickly so he could get her alone and have his way with her.

Damn tempting, but he'd only do it if she was game. Even then it didn't set well with him to take her as a lover when he had no intentions of marrying her.

"Trust is something one earns," she said. "As yet you have failed to do that."

"You've got every right to doubt me. Make up your own mind. Stay here and risk getting caught by Allis Carson or leave with me tomorrow."

"You make it sound so simple."

"It is, Maggie. Help me find Daisy, and I'll see that you're safely delivered to that nursing school."

She looked away from him, her gloved fingers tightening around the saddle horn. "All right. I'll go with you, but if you force yourself on me again, I'll run away."

"I kissed you, Maggie. That was all."

"Kissing can lead to other things."

"I'd never go farther than you wanted me to," he said.

He was many things, but he'd never force himself on a woman like she was thinking. It was the one thing he could remember his ma telling him over and over again. It was the one thing he feared would raise its ugly head in him some day.

Don't abuse a woman in word or deed, boy, she'd said.

As far as he could recall, he'd had the misfortune of seeing his pa wallop his ma far too many times. He guessed at least one of his uncles was just as disrespectful, for his uncle Brice had been there the last time his ma took a beating and didn't do a damned thing to help her.

He'd just stood there while Dade's pa knocked his ma to the ground, her belly swollen with child, her split lip bleeding.

Yep, there was bad blood in the Logans, and he couldn't promise he'd stay civil the rest of his life. He didn't aim to marry for that reason. If he ever did cross that line, it'd be with a woman who could protect herself from him if necessary.

History wouldn't repeat itself with him.

He wouldn't pass on that vicious streak to his sons, and if he ever harmed a woman—if he hurt Maggie—well, he hoped to hell she shot him dead.

They rode in silence to the boardinghouse. Dade jumped off his gelding and helped her down, careful to keep his touch proper. He wished to hell he could keep his thoughts the same, but feeling the tremors in her had him longing to pull her close.

As soon as her feet hit the ground, she moved out of his grasp. "Thank you for the lessons."

He suspected she meant more than riding a horse. "I'll let you know when we'll leave at supper."

"All right. I'll pack and be ready to go."

Yep, he imagined she would be in more ways than one.

He led the horses to the livery, going over what needed to be done after he finished rubbing down the horses. He'd need to secure a packhorse and supplies, but not too many provisions as they needed to move as quickly as possible from here.

That meant traveling light with just the bare essentials. He dreaded thinking how a woman would complain over that news.

"You the sheriff?" a man asked, stepping into Dade's path after he'd corralled the horses and stepped from the livery.

"I am." He faced the man and carefully freed his gun hand, taking the man's measure and sensing no threat. "You are?"

"Adam Tavish, U.S. Marshal," he said. "I need a word with you when you can spare the time."

Dade turned back to the mare and picked up the brush he'd dropped. "Talk away, Marshal."

"Received a wire from Lionel Payne saying his bank had been robbed yesterday," Tavish said.

He swore under his breath, guessing the reason for the marshal's visit to town. "Yep, but if you're looking for particulars, you'd best ask Payne or the mayor. I wasn't in town at the time."

"That's what I heard," Tavish said. "What I found interesting is that the Logan Gang was responsible, and you just happen to be a Logan."

Dade faced the marshal again, and this time there was no mistaking the cool regard on the lawman's face. "I've done told Mayor Willis and Payne that I had nothing to do with the hold up or the gang that did it."

"Even though you're Clete Logan's son?"

"I haven't laid eyes on my pa or my uncles since I was eight years old," he said. "Don't rightly care if I ever do again."

Tavish stared at him, as if deciding what to believe. "Heard you were orphaned and taken in by Kirby Morris."

"Who told you that?"

"Reid Barclay."

Now there was another sore spot, but this one he didn't aim to discuss with Tavish or anyone. "My deputy and me found out that the Logan Gang had been holed up in a mine north of here all winter."

Tavish folded his arms over his chest and rocked back on his heels, his features closed. "Then you must know a bounty hunter caught up with them. One dead and one close to it."

Dade stared at the man, willing him to give their names. But Tavish just met his gaze without blinking. He was forcing Dade to ask for details, and damned if he'd give the lawman the satisfaction.

He'd find out sooner or later.

"Seth Logan died," Tavish said. "Brice will be locked up, but between you and me he'll likely die from his wounds before he goes to trial."

One uncle dead. One dying. He didn't attempt to drum up sympathy he didn't feel. If the marshal thought him heartless, so be it. Like Kirby had taught him, you reap what you sow.

"Allis Carson will make a haul off their rewards," Dade said. "What about Clete Logan?"

"He got away, but Carson vowed to bring your pa in," Tavish said.

That was a given. So was the fact that his pa would vow to take down the bounty hunter for killing his brothers. The Logan Gang didn't give a damn about their women and children, but they were fiercely loyal to each other.

"Carson thinks you're the key to finding him," Tavish said.

Dade figured as much. "Because I happen to be the sheriff in the town the Logan Gang robbed?"

Tavish nodded. "That and the fact that they wintered in a mine not far from here."

Damn. If Allis Carson was convinced Dade could lead him to Clete Logan, he'd never be free of him.

"That was a surprise to me. Course I didn't venture any further than I had to last winter."

"It was a brutal one. I spent the winter in Maverick, Wyoming," Tavish said, and Dade went as cold as ice inside. "There was talk in town that you and Trey March had rustled cattle off the Crown Seven the year before."

"Bullshit! They were our cattle."

Tavish nodded. "That's what Barclay claimed."

Dade stared at him, unable to believe the brother who'd sold him out had also backed up his claim. Had Reid had a change of heart?

He had trouble believing that. It'd been late last summer when he'd gotten word that Reid was back at the Crown.

It'd been the first time that he'd heard they all had until Christmas to claim their shares. He hadn't been surprised that Reid had gotten there first.

"Was Trey March there too?" Dade asked.

Tavish shook his head. "Nope. Just Barclay."

So Reid owned the Crown now. "What took you up north?"

"Tracking a horse rustler."

"Reid's thoroughbreds would be a temptation to a rustler," he said. "He running cattle on the Crown again too?"

Tavish shrugged. "Right before I headed out of town I heard he sold the ranch."

"Makes no never mind to me," Dade said, which was a damned lie.

Anger speared through Dade, as hot and fresh as the day he'd heard that Reid had sold them out to Kirby's cousin and gained majority shares. Kirby hadn't been cold in his grave before his cousin ordered Trey and Dade to pay up or lose their shares.

Only way they could do that was to sell off their share of the herd. It was worth it to keep the land—the only home they'd ever known.

But when they went to sell the stock, the sheriff informed them they'd been charged with rustling. Didn't matter that it was their own cattle because nobody believed them. They'd been double-crossed by Kirby's cousin and Reid.

They lost their shares of the ranch and the cattle and the last of their family. They lost faith in their brother.

Trey hired on with a rancher he'd met at the stockyards. Dade decided it was past time that he find his sister. They'd promised to keep in touch, but Dade hadn't heard from Trey since then. Hell, he didn't even know where he was at.

He shook off his ire the best he could. That was part of his past, and he had no intentions of going back down that rocky road. If and when he did, it'd be to have it out with Reid.

"For what it's worth, most folks I talked to in town are pleased with the job you've done here," Tavish said. "That includes your deputy who speaks mighty highly of you."

"Duane's a good man from a good family."

"He seemed worried about this woman Allis Carson is looking for," Tavish said. "Swore that his description of her was nigh identical to a good many women in these parts, your sister being one of them."

"That it is," Dade said, and debated whether to show part of his hand now or not. "You hear why he's after this woman?"

Tavish nodded. "Said she stole a hundred dollars or so off the lady of the house as well as a broach that's a Nowell family heirloom."

"Seems that piece of jewelry would be the easiest way to find her then," Dade said.

"Unless she's hocked it by now." Tavish scrubbed a hand over his nape. "Seems a lot of fuss to go to for so little."

"I thought the same." And he still did.

It was the part of Maggie's story that he found questionable. He hadn't pressed her for answers before but he would once they left town.

That had to be soon. And it had to be done with forethought.

The plan he had in mind could backfire and have the marshal thinking that he and Maggie intended to meet up with Clete Logan all along, that the robbery had been set up with the Logan siblings conveniently gone from town that day. But if the marshal was as smart as Dade suspected, he'd see that notion was just too cut and dried.

Doc would back up what had taken them away—that

Maggie had stayed on to help the Orshlin family and Dade had simply ridden out to check on his sister. The hold up was as much a shock to them as it'd been to the townsfolk.

Two events cast doubt on Dade's story. He had ridden into town on the heels of a fracas that had taken the former sheriff's life. About the same time, the Logan Gang set up camp in Myron Zule's mine before Zule was cold in his grave.

There's no way in hell Dade could convince Allis Carson that he wasn't in cahoots with the gang. The truth could be interpreted two ways, and Dade had no proof to back up his claim.

He'd be on their trail unless Dade created a false one.

"You like being sheriff?" Tavish asked.

This time Dade spoke the truth. "Not particularly. All I ever wanted to do was raise cattle. Been thinking of heading back to Maverick with Daisy. She'd like it up there."

So would he, now that Reid had sold the ranch and was gone.

"It's a nice town," Tavish said. "Reckon you're homesick."

Sick that he'd been swindled out of his home was more like it, but he kept that to himself.

Dade hoped that was enough to send the bounty hunter in that direction. By the time he realized his mistake, Dade and Maggie would be heading east to the settlement where Daisy was adopted off the train.

"You say Allis Carson is heading back here?" Dade asked.

The marshal nodded. "Likely tomorrow. Can't see how he could get out of Denver any sooner."

The bounty hunter could if he took the train.

If Allis Carson arrived before Dade could leave, he'd never shake the bastard. Hell, he stood a chance of losing Maggie if he failed to convince the man she was his sister.

That meant they'd best leave town before dawn. Even then they'd risk crossing paths with the bounty hunter.

"When are you and your sister planning to leave?" Tavish asked.

"In the morning."

They'd have to take the north road out of town to look convincing. Somehow they'd have to cut off through the hills far enough north of town that nobody would notice.

From there it'd be a rough ride across trails best fit for wild game. And the whole damned time he'd have to hope that the bounty hunter hadn't picked up their trail and wasn't following them.

Dade knew it'd be like the man to lie in wait until they least expected trouble. Then he'd swoop in and grab Maggie. He wouldn't hesitate to put a bullet through Dade's heart in the process.

"I take it you haven't told Mayor Willis you're leaving," Tavish said.

"Nope, but when I hired on I told them all it was just temporary until I found my sister."

Tavish's rugged features softened. "You been separated from her long?"

"Twenty years or so."

Dade shook his head, finding it mighty peculiar that he still felt that sting of abandonment so keenly after all this time.

"That's a lifetime for some," Tavish said, and Dade nodded agreement, knowing that was true.

If only they hadn't separated him from his sister in the orphanage. If they'd just kept the family together and not sent her off on a damned orphan train.

"You planning on sticking around?" Dade asked.

"Nope. I'm being sent down to Pueblo. From what I saw, your deputy is going to do just fine."

Dade surely hoped so. At least his fear that the Logan Gang would return to cause trouble was gone.

"Guess I'll look up Mayor Willis and turn in my badge," Dade said, and felt a weight lift off him at the thought.

He wasn't an outlaw by any stretch, but he wasn't cut out to be a lawman either. Nope, he was a sodbuster at heart.

Maybe one day he'd own a small spread. Farm a bit. Run some cattle.

Alone?

His thoughts turned to a beguiling woman with lips like honey and blue eyes a man could drown in.

Maggie Sutten was all wrong for him. She had plans for her life, and they surely didn't include him. But that didn't stop the wanting.

Nope, the next month was going to test his patience and the promise he had made her to keep his hands to himself.

The ride tomorrow was going to kill her.

Maggie pressed a hand to the small of her back and straightened from packing her satchel. Muscles she hadn't known she had were aching something fierce. What she wouldn't give to soak in the mineral waters in Manitou Springs about now.

Of course that wasn't a possibility since they were headed east. To Kansas, of all places.

She folded another day dress as best she could and tucked it into her satchel. Thankfully she hadn't taken much with her when she fled Harlan Nowell's house. Escapes in the night tended to require that one pack lightly.

But she had to add one item to her wardrobe—if it could be found in town, that is. She had to buy more suitable riding attire. The dress and petticoats just wouldn't do for a journey on horseback.

Unfortunately she had very little money, barely enough to pay for necessities once she reached St. Louis. But since she couldn't sew a stitch, she had no choice but to buy ready wear.

"Are you still down in the back?" Mrs. Gant asked from the doorway.

"Some." An understatement. "Do you suppose they sell riding skirts at the mercantile?"

"I'd be surprised if they did." Mrs. Gant folded her arms over her generous bosom. "You're still planning to leave on a horse?"

"Dade insists, and I agree it is the wisest course." Though certainly not the most practical.

She had gone a long way toward learning how to tamp down her terror and control the horse, but she was still by no means ready to ride on her own. Yet she suspected that was exactly the picture Dade would present tomorrow when they left town.

"I may have just what you need," Mrs. Gant said. "I'll need your help finding it."

The older woman turned and hurried down the hall to the far door, her limp more pronounced today than usual. Maggie wondered if the woman was beset by arthritis or if her infirmity was the result of an accident.

They mounted the stairs to the attic. Crescent windows in both gables let light in, but the years of dust coupled with an unusual assortment of trunks and the like absorbed the light.

Thankfully, Mrs. Gant made her way to a large trunk standing near the south windows. A swath of light played over the colorful stickers pasted haphazardly on the trunk.

"This has certainly journeyed far and wide," Maggie said, fascinated by the places this trunk had been. "My, even Paris."

Mrs. Gant's smile was wistful as she ran a finger over

that particular stamp. "That was a wondrous summer. Our troupe drew a goodly crowd every night."

"Troupe?" Maggie asked.

"Bender's Wild West Extravaganza. We traveled all over the world performing for ten years."

"Did you sing?"

"Oh, yes."

Maggie waited for her to go on, intrigued by the life this woman must have led. But Mrs. Gant fell silent as she fussed with the old clasp.

"There we go," she said as the trunk finally creaked open.

One side of the trunk held garments on wooden hangers. The brilliant hues of the fabrics proved they were costumes.

"These were yours?" Maggie asked, fingering the rich velvets and silks.

"Most of them."

Clearly the woman was closing the door on what had to have been an exciting past. If the costumes could talk, Maggie was sure she'd hear about a fascinating life in a world that few ladies knew anything about.

Mrs. Gant opened the middle drawer on the other side of the trunk and removed a dark blue garment. "Some years back a married couple arrived in town on horseback," she said as she held the garment by the waistband and let it unfold.

"A riding skirt," Maggie said, not quite believing her eyes or her luck.

"She called it a split skirt, and the quality of it told me she had come from money and from an area where such garments were necessary."

Maggie agreed with that assessment. Whoever owned this garment had had it specially made.

"She left it here. You're welcome to it," Mrs. Gant said, and passed it into Maggie's hands.

She clutched it close and resisted the urge to run to her room and try it on. It wasn't just worry over Mrs. Gant getting to her feet and managing the stairs again.

No, there was a sadness pulsing in the attic as Mrs. Gant fingered a red lace shawl visible in the drawer.

"That's truly beautiful," Maggie said.

"Jack bought it for me when we were in Paris."

Maggie smiled, hearing the affection in the older woman's voice. She wanted to ask who Jack was. She wanted to know if Paris was the city of romance as she'd often heard it was.

But she wasn't one to pry, for she knew the value of secrets more than anyone. So she stood patiently in the stuffy attic and waited for Mrs. Gant to say more if she wished to share a bit of her past with a stranger.

"Have I shocked you into silence?" she asked.

Maggie actually laughed at that, a bit of nerves and also appreciation for Mrs. Gant's frankness. "I am simply waiting for the story to unfold, if you deem me a worthy audience."

Mrs. Gant's mouth twitched in what could only be a sly smile, and Maggie knew she'd given the correct reply.

The older woman pushed the drawer shut and stared into the opened trunk a long time, as if watching a slice of her life play out in its depths.

"Jack was my lover," she said at last, her face wreathed in a smile so filled with love that Maggie felt a pang of jealousy for never having experienced such a deep affection. "He was married, and so was I, but neither of us lived with our spouses."

"Because you were both performers?" Maggie guessed.

"No, that had nothing to do with it," she said. "Jack's wife lost her mind when their child was born dead. He placed her in an insane asylum and saw that she was well cared for, but he couldn't divorce her."

Her respect for the man grew.

"My husband was brutal." She looked Maggie dead in the eyes. "I ran away from him after the last beating. Jack found me and took me in. When he asked me to leave with him on a European tour, I agreed and never looked back."

"Did you ever regret it?"

"Never." She sighed and shook her head. "It just ended far too soon."

This time Maggie couldn't contain her curiosity. "What happened?"

"He came down with pneumonia. We were on our way to San Francisco, but he was so ill we got off the train so he could see a doctor." She lowered her head, and her fingers tightened on the trunk lid again. "Two days later he was dead."

"I'm so sorry for your loss," she said.

"Without Jack, I didn't want to perform anymore. I just wanted to find a place to hide from the world and grow old."

Maggie looked around the attic, guessing this was the ideal place for that. It seemed such a waste.

Mrs. Gant laid a hand over Maggie's. "You're wise to get out of town with Dade, but don't lock yourself away from life. Don't turn away from a good man just because of what one bad one has done to you."

Sage words of advice, no doubt. But for Maggie, it wasn't that simple. Mrs. Gant didn't know just how much was at stake between Harlan Nowell and Whit Ramsey.

"I'll bear that in mind," she said.

"Good. Now go try on that skirt." She stood before the trunk, seeming in no hurry to return to the living quarters.

Maggie hesitated a moment, then left Mrs. Gant standing in front of the trunk that held a lifetime of beautiful memories. What would it be like to experience such love just once?

She had the chance to find out, she reasoned, as she slipped into her room. One month of traveling with Dade.

It was wrong. It was risky. But she wanted him to take her in his arms again. She wanted his kisses and more.

The longing only grew as she exchanged her day skirt for the split one. It fit perfectly. It felt wickedly freeing.

She'd not be encumbered with petticoats and the like with this skirt. Perhaps she should rid herself of the mores that weighed her down as well.

She went to the window and gazed out on the town where she'd found refuge. She'd had a taste of an innocent affection with Lester Emery.

There was nothing innocent about the emotions she felt for the present man behind the badge.

A reflection from below caught her eye. She looked down at Dade Logan.

He shifted his stance and light bounced off the star pinned on his vest. He stood on the walk, looking up at her room. Looking up at her.

Though she couldn't see his eyes, a bolt of awareness went through her. There was no denying they were drawn to one another.

She rested her hands on the windowsill, unable—or was it unwilling—to break eye contact. Surely she was being bold staring at him so. But hearing Mrs. Gant's story made her realize how short life could be.

Maggie had pushed Dade away earlier out of fear—not because of what he'd do, but of what she ached to have him do.

The next time Dade Logan reached for her, she'd not pull away from him. She'd welcome him into her life and her bed.

Chapter 11

Dade strode into the house and up the stairs, taking each one slowly and deliberately. In the six months he'd lived here he'd never veered from taking a direct path from the door to the dining room to his own room.

Not today.

He paused at the landing and splayed his fingers on the smooth banister. Besides the grandfather clock ticking away the seconds in the foyer, there wasn't another sound to be heard.

Good. He'd just as soon nobody was around when he spoke with Maggie.

He climbed the stairs with the same unhurried gait, the worn carpet runner muffling his steps. At the top, he turned left toward the front of the house. Toward Maggie's room.

Her door, and the one to the empty room beside it, were closed. But he knew she was in there.

Dade rapped his knuckles on her door once, then reached for the knob. To his surprise it opened.

Maggie stood by the window bathed in afternoon light that shot gold through her honey-colored hair. She returned his perusal with the same openness as she had before.

His throat felt suddenly dry. He swallowed anyway and proceeded to inform her of the news.

"The U.S. Marshal arrived this afternoon by way of Colorado Springs," he said. "Claims Lionel Payne sent a telegram to him for help, seeing as an outlaw's son was the sheriff here."

"How dare he make such a derogatory assumption," she said, her fervor surprising and pleasing him.

He smiled, feeling oddly warm inside. It'd been a long while since anyone had stood up for him.

"It's Payne's right to believe what he will," he said. "As for the marshal, he's just doing his job."

She rubbed her arms and stepped away from the window. For the first time he noticed she wore one of the straight plain skirts he'd seen ranch women wear of late. Noticed too the way it nipped in at her waist, flared over her womanly hips, and fell in gentle folds to her feet.

"So what is the marshal going to do?" she asked, drawing his attention back to why he'd come up here.

"Nothing he can do," he said. "He did impart news about Allis Carson. Seems he was hauling my uncles to Denver for the reward."

"But he'll return to Placid," she said.

He nodded. "Marshal figures Allis Carson will head back here tomorrow. I'm thinking he'll do it sooner if he can."

The color left her face. "We have to get out of here."

"Before dawn."

She took a shaky breath, no doubt fretting about setting off riding when she'd only been on a horse once. "I'm nearly packed."

"Good. One other thing. You know how to handle a gun?"

He hadn't thought she could get any paler, but right now her face looked colorless. He took a step toward her, fearing she was about to swoon.

"No," she said, her voice so small he barely heard.

Damn! "Don't tell me you're afraid of guns too."

"All right, I won't."

Just what he didn't want to hear. He didn't have time to teach her how to shoot, and he couldn't trust her to keep a sidearm on her for fear she'd shoot herself, her horse, or him.

"We'll get you used to one in a day or so."

The tight set of her narrow shoulders relaxed a smidgen. "How long will it take us to get to Kansas?"

"Longer than usual," he said. "I told the marshal I was taking my sister to Maverick, Wyoming. So we'll head north out of here until we find a trail that we can take east."

The lips he longed to possess again parted. "We're riding toward Denver? Toward Allis Carson who is on his way here?"

"Folks will see us head that way, and when the marshal tells Carson I'm taking you to Wyoming, he will be obliged to follow."

She rubbed her arms and paced to the other window, and he took a step toward her before bringing himself up short. Now wasn't the time to try to comfort her.

"We stand a chance of riding right into the bounty hunter," she said.

No hysterics or pleading, just rational fact. He damn sure appreciated that about her.

"That's why we're leaving before dawn. By the time the sun is up, we'll be on the trail that'll angle us east again."

"Why can't we leave now?" she asked, her eyes sparking with fear.

"You need your rest tonight," he said.

She crossed to him and stared him down. "I can't afford

the leisure of rest, not when I need to get away from here before that bounty hunter returns."

Dammit, she was right, and he'd already seen that their provisions were at the livery, ready to stow on the pack-horse. They could reach the trail and find a spot to camp for the night well before darkness fell. But they'd have to move soon.

"I have to meet with Mayor Willis before we leave." He fingered the tin star and felt a moment's hesitation over handing it and the safety of this town into the hands of such a young man.

"How long will that take?" she asked.

"Thirty minutes at the most." He'd already stowed what he owned in his saddlebags.

"I'll ask Mrs. Gant to prepare us a basket dinner and meet you at the livery."

He pointed to her satchel. "If you're done packing I'll take it now."

She gave her clothes a critical look, and he hoped she wasn't one to spend hours deciding what to wear. They'd not have that luxury traveling the routes he aimed to take. Hell, there'd likely be days when she'd be obliged to wear the same clothes night and day.

"This will do," she said at last.

Still she went around the room opening drawers and the wardrobe, likely checking to ensure she hadn't left any-thing behind. She made to close her satchel.

"Take a wrap," he said. "Soon as the sun sets the tem-perature will drop. I don't aim to unpack our provisions until we set up camp for the night."

Maggie nodded and dug through the satchel again. She pulled out a short jacket that looked more fashionable than serviceable, but it was clear the lady didn't own anything suitable for rough traveling. Nothing, that is, except the riding skirt that hugged her behind when she bent just so.

Yep, that wasn't bustle or padding of any sort. Just firm, rounded womanly flesh.

He took the satchel she'd secured again and backed to her door. The tightness that settled below his belt was a distraction he couldn't afford.

"I'll meet you at the livery," he said, and hightailed it before his discomfort became obvious.

Focusing on what he had to do in short order doused any lingering desire. He fetched his saddlebags and bounded down the steps.

But instead of heading out the door, he ducked into the kitchen. As expected Mrs. Gant was at the stove.

He set down his bundle, reached into his vest pocket for the money he'd counted out earlier, and handed it to her. "Much obliged for all you did for me over the winter."

Mrs. Gant fingered the wad of greenbacks. "There's more here than needed."

"Keep it. We're leaving today."

She stared at him a good long time. "You're a good man, Dade Logan. Take care of yourself and your sister. See that your past doesn't ruin your future."

He smiled at that. "Maybe it isn't my past that's casting a pall over things."

"I think you both have ghosts," she said. "Most folks do."

It was what a person did with them that made the difference. He brushed two fingers over his hat brim and left the boardinghouse.

He squinted up at the sun that was dipping toward the horizon. It shouldn't take more than thirty minutes to get things squared away with Mayor Willis.

If they could get on the road then, they'd have three hours of good light left before they had to make camp. That'd get them far enough off the trail so they could find a place to hole up for the night.

Just him and Maggie.

He blew out a rough breath. It could be one helluva long night for him.

Twenty minutes later, Dade stood in the jail with his arms crossed and his temper simmering at a slow boil. Mayor Willis had wasted no time coming to the jail to relieve Dade of his duty, give him his severance pay, and swear in the deputy under the watchful eye of Marshal Tavish.

The whole thing shouldn't have taken more than ten minutes to complete. But somehow Payne got wind that a new sheriff was about to get sworn in and barged in to give his two cents, which with a banker's inflation cost twice as much time and wasn't worth the air it took for Payne to spew it out.

In short, Lionel Payne was an obnoxious son of a bitch.

"I maintain it is highly suspicious that Logan chooses now to leave town," Payne said.

"What in blazes are you getting at?" the mayor asked.

"The robbery. Logan is curiously absent the one day outlaws ride into town. Why, for all we know he intends to meet up with his father as planned and divide his take of the money."

"Be careful what you accuse a man of," Dade said.

Payne took a step back from Dade, his gaze slewing to the marshal's in what looked like mock fear. "Did you hear that? He threatened me."

"Didn't sound that way to me," Tavish said. "But then I'm not the one trying to make a mountain out of a molehill."

Payne's florid face purpled. "His father is an outlaw. The same outlaw who rode into town and robbed my bank. Had I caught the connection in his name six months ago, I would have refused to accept him as our sheriff."

"It wasn't your sole decision to make," the mayor said.

Shit, at the rate they were going, they'd argue the night away. Dade had had more than enough.

He tossed his tin star on the desktop. "Do what you wish with it. I'm moving on."

"You can't let him just ride off," Payne told the marshal.

"There's no reason to hold the man," Marshal Tavish said, which made Payne grump all the more.

"He's a Logan!"

"He's done nothing wrong," the marshal said.

"We knew from the start that Dade would leave once he found his sister," Mayor Willis said as he handed Dade an envelope. "Now that he and Daisy have been reunited, that day has come."

Dade stared at his last pay as sheriff, then did a quick thumb through the greenbacks to ensure it was all here. It was, plus a few dollars more.

He folded the envelope in half and stuffed it in his pocket. "Thank you, mayor."

Dade crossed to the gun rack and grabbed his rifle. The banker fumbled in his coat pocket and produced a Derringer.

"Come closer, and I'll shoot," Payne said, sweat beading on his brow.

"Put the gun down," Tavish said, but the banker seemed frozen to the spot.

So was Dade. Last thing he wanted was to get shot. But he wasn't about to waste time here either at the whim of the banker.

Out of the corner of his eye, Dade caught a blur of movement. A heartbeat later the banker's Derringer clattered to the floor.

Duane leveled his rifle on the banker, who'd gone white around the gills. "I won't hold with trouble in my town, Mr. Payne. You, sir, are causing trouble."

"If I'm right—" Payne began.

"You're not," Dade finished, and gained a nod of agreement from the mayor. He scooped up the Derringer and handed it to the marshal. "Swear in the deputy. He'll serve this town right."

The ghost of a smile played over Tavish's face. He nodded to Willis. The mayor wasted no time making Duane the new sheriff of Placid, Colorado.

Dade gave the room one last glance and walked out the door. A mountain of worry lifted off his shoulders then and there.

He was Dade Logan again, and the only thing he'd sworn to do was find Daisy. And keep Maggie Sutten safe.

The last could take every bit of cunning he possessed. He settled his hat on and started down the boardwalk with his senses tuned to trouble, just like he had every time he'd made his rounds the past six months.

Nothing seemed off. Folks went about their business like they always had. A few paused to nod at him. Some just stared. He wondered if the town was divided in their loyalties with some backing the banker and some firmly on Mayor Willis's side.

Not that it mattered now. When the bounty hunter arrived tomorrow or the next day, he'd no doubt get an earful from Lionel Payne.

But he'd also get a sane version of why Dade had left town and his destination. He just hoped to hell that the man believed it and set out for Maverick.

The time it would take Allis Carson to get there and realize he'd been had would put that much more distance between them. It wouldn't be easy picking up their trail then.

Yep, only one person knew that wasn't so. Doc surely wouldn't do or say anything to jeopardize Maggie's safety. He couldn't see Mrs. Gant sharing her suspicions with Carson.

But then, he'd been wrong before about the brother he'd trusted with his life. Even Trey hadn't bothered to look Dade up in well over a year. Sad to say he wouldn't know where to begin looking for Trey March.

He strode past the saloon and lifted his gaze to the livery at the edge of town. Maggie stood right outside the big doors talking with the blacksmith, giving her full attention to the man who likely reeked of sweat and hot steel.

She was as composed and fetching as ever. A hat that was more stylish than practical covered her wealth of hair and barely—just barely—shaded her face.

He wanted to kick his ass right here and now for not thinking of what the sun would do to that delicate skin after riding all day. Now that he had, there was only one recourse left to him.

Dade backtracked to the general store and pushed open the door to the tinkling of a bell. The owner perked up at the sound and came toward Dade, a smile wreathing his face.

"Afternoon, sheriff," he said. "What can I do for you?"

Time was just too valuable to waste explaining he wasn't the sheriff any longer. He had jingle in his pocket and an item to purchase as quickly as possible.

"I need a hat for Ma—, my sister," he said.

The old man scratched his mutton chop whiskers. "The missus usually sees to the women's frippery and such." He glanced at the feminine side of the store with what Dade could only call repulsion. "You know what your sister wants?"

Long gone out of here, he reckoned. "She needs a wide brimmed hat that'll shade her face."

"Let's see what we got." He ambled into the ladies' section of the store and led Dade straight to the hats. "See anything there you want?"

Yep, his gaze fell on a sassy little hat that had a wide blue ribbon band that would match her eyes and bit of a brim that tipped up like her nose. He'd surely give a second look to any woman he passed wearing such a hat. But it was as impractical as all get out.

He pointed to a wide brimmed straw hat that would do a farm wife proud. "Let me see that one."

The storekeeper fetched it from its hook and handed it to Dade. "The missus sells a lot of these each year."

That was all he needed to know. Women would spend their meager stipend on the things that served them well. Those who minded their pennies couldn't worry about what was fashionable or just plain pretty.

"I'll take this one," he said, and pressed his fist against the low crown to test if it was sturdy.

His gaze flicked back to the jaunty hat with the wide blue band that hung on the peg. He could damned near see Maggie wearing it at a jaunty angle with a kiss-me-quick look on her face.

But would she wear it? Would she offer up a kiss?

He wouldn't know unless he bought it for her.

It was an extravagance for sure and one he could ill afford. But he wanted to buy something nice just for her. For the first time in his life he wanted to buy a lady a gift.

"Toss in that straw hat with the blue band and wrap it up good," Dade said, pointing to it so there'd be no mistake which one he had his eye on. "What do I owe you?"

"A dollar for the garden hat." The old man lifted the fancy hat off the peg and whistled. "Tag here says it costs three bucks, but don't seem right to pay so much for this circle of straw and hank of ribbon."

"Reckon there's a good reason why it costs more." Dade dug bills from his pocket, but had to dig deeper to come up with the cost for both hats.

"This one's been here a spell," the old man said. "Give me two bucks for the pair, and we'll call it even."

Dade eyed him. "You sure about that?"

"It's my store, ain't it? I set the price, and I say these two hats are worth two bucks."

He wasn't about to argue, not when he needed every cent he could scrape up to pay for provisions along the way. He handed over the money, then waited while the merchant wrapped the fancy hat in brown paper.

Dade stopped him before he did the same to the garden hat. "I'll take that one as is."

Maggie needed to wear it today. The other . . . Well, he'd give it to her later on, and she could don it whenever it damned well suited her.

He took the garden hat and the parcel and headed back to the livery. She was still standing there, only this time she was alone.

As always, a swift punch of awareness of her as a desirable woman jabbed him square in the gut. She looked neither afraid nor confident, just anxious.

That was something they shared. He had a month of Maggie's help to find Daisy. Four weeks of just the two of them traveling together.

The whole while they'd worry about the bounty hunter tracking them. What the hell had she done to Harlan Nowell?

It had to be more than stealing money and a broach that was hers to begin with. There was more to it than that, but Maggie was still hiding the whole truth.

He doubted Carson knew any more than that she was a thief he'd been hired to bring back. He suspected Doc knew part of it, but he had refused to divulge the particulars to him, saying it was up to Maggie to tell him why she'd fled Harlan Nowell's mansion.

Dade hated to speculate because the two reasons that

came to mind fired his rage. Orphans weren't supposed to be taken in as indentured servants, yet he wouldn't put it past Nowell to have wrangled a contract from her.

Orphans weren't supposed to be abused either, but Dade had heard of rich men taking advantage of their young charges. He'd worried for years that such a fate had befallen Daisy.

He didn't want to think Maggie had been the victim of such a horrific fate either. Though she kissed like an innocent, Harlan still could have had his way with her.

The crack of fine straw penetrated Dade's rage. He eased his punishing hold on the farmer's hat, annoyed with himself for bending the brim on it.

The shame of it all would keep Maggie from divulging such a dark secret. But if he found out Harlan had abused her, he'd be tempted to go after him.

Yep, he could see her reasons for keeping her past secret. He understood her reluctance to put much confidence in a stranger.

Sooner or later Maggie was going to have to confide in him. He'd have to know what he was up against if he was to keep her safe and see her to that nursing school in St. Louis.

After that, he'd likely never see her again.

He'd come back west, hopefully with his sister, and settle down to farm. Maybe in Kansas. Maybe somewhere he passed through that called to him to stay a while. A place he could call home.

Once again he thought about heading back to Wyoming, but there was nothing there for him now. The Crown Seven was sold.

He had no home. No family other than Daisy and two foster brothers who had drifted apart. Everything he owned was packed in a pannier or stuffed in his saddlebags.

Maggie offered him a smile when he drew near, and for a heartbeat he pictured her doing that when they were both old and gray. That'd never happen, not if they both followed their dreams.

"I started to worry when you didn't arrive on time," she said.

That admission warmed the constant chill that lived deep in him. *Don't go reading more into what she said.*

She had every right to be worried that he wouldn't show up, but it wasn't because of tender feelings for him. Nope, she was thinking of the hell she'd endure if Allis Carson caught her.

"It took longer than expected, thanks to Payne's interference." He handed her the wide brimmed garden hat. "That hat you're wearing won't protect you from the sun, so I bought this one."

"Oh!" She took it, looking as excited as a kid just given a bag of penny candy.

Why, just watching her quickly remove her hat and don this new one filled him with a sense of pure pleasure. He'd never imagined something so simple could make him feel so good.

"I know it is vanity, but I will admit to being concerned about the sun," she said, adjusting the wide brim just so and casting her pretty face in shadow.

His finger lightly brushed her flushed cheek, and he stayed the urge to trail it across the lips he ached to taste again. "It would burn your fair soft skin to a turn."

Her lips parted, and her eyes went wide, but instead of leaning into him like he wanted, she stepped back.

He let his hand drop and stared at her while silence thundered around them. Damn, now why did he say and do that?

Talk about an awkward moment. He should be trying to

gain her confidence, not fill her with doubt about what he'd do when they were off on a trail alone.

Just thinking of them being cozy made the hunger to explore Maggie Sutten's hidden secrets more intense. But she had warned him not to steal another kiss, and her pulling away now made it clear she didn't want to get cozy with him.

"Let me give you a leg-up so we can get going." He strode to her mare, already saddled and waiting for them, and made a stirrup with his fingers, hoping to hell she wouldn't back out.

Her cheeks darkened to a dusty rose, and she looked away, as if debating what to do. To his relief she turned to the horse and accepted his help gaining the saddle.

He gave her a boost up and drew her sweet flowery scent into his lungs. "You're likely to attract bees with that perfume." She was surely attracting him with it.

"It's not perfume," she said and blushed a deeper red. "It's just lavender soap."

He didn't need to know that; he was tormented by the image of her running a sudsy cloth over her body. He swung into the saddle and hooked the lead line for her mare to his saddle horn. A good hard ride would drag his thoughts above his belt again.

The packhorse line was secured to her saddle, keeping her black mare in the middle. Her horse would be less likely to bolt in a trail line.

"Ready?" he asked, glancing back at her.

She nodded, her kid gloves strained from her tight grip on the saddle horn. "Ready."

Dade started them off slowly through town. A few folks came out to wave good-bye. Some wished them luck.

Even Doc Franklin had stepped outside his house to watch them leave. He read the concern in the older man's eyes and nodded in silent understanding.

They were riding into the unknown, with no clear sense of where they were going. Didn't help they'd have a bounty hunter on their trail.

Even if he kept his hands to himself, this jaunt would surely taint Maggie's reputation if anyone found out she'd taken off alone with a man. Yep, she'd do well to pass herself off as his sister. Or as his wife?

That notion held a whole lot more appeal than it should. Dammit, he was supposed to protect her from the bounty hunter and other men who'd lust after her—himself included.

But the memory of that kiss threatened to erode his good intentions.

Yep, this promised to be a long month.

Chapter 12

Maggie's back felt as if it would break in two any second. She'd tried to do as Dade had instructed and move with the horse instead of against the little black mare. She really had tried hard, and it had worked for the first hour.

But after they left the main road for this path that wound through the wooded, jagged terrain, her endurance began to lag. By the third hour of steady riding, her muscles began protesting from sitting astride for so long.

Now her legs were growing numb. The last thing she was prepared to do was sit the trot again, but the moment they emerged from the foothills they did just that.

The mountains were to her back now, and she caught glimpses of the railroad tracks that snaked east. She needed to get off this horse and rest, but Dade didn't seem ready to stop yet, and she surely didn't want to complain.

After all she'd assured him she could travel this way, and she would even if it killed her. Right now that was a strong possibility.

"When will we stop for the night?" she asked when Dade slowed the horses from the backbreaking trot they'd been doing for the longest time.

He thumbed his hat back and frowned at the sky.

"Another hour will put us on the other side of Walsenburg. I hope to make it and find cover before that storm moves in."

She peered up at the sky and saw nothing but blue—until she glanced back in the direction they'd come. She cringed at the dark clouds creeping over the mountains. Dade was right. The storm would hit in an hour or so.

She faced east and scanned the undulating plains. Ahead of them she saw the watery shapes of a town hugging the horizon. But another grueling hour passed before she was sure that this wasn't a mirage.

Still, Dade headed them north so they skirted the town and the few farms nestled in the valley. They crossed the railroad tracks, and he picked up their pace again. Beyond her she saw nothing but dwarfed trees and scrub covering the high plains.

"What kind of shelter do you hope to find out there?" she asked.

"See that line of trees off in the distance?"

"Barely," she said.

"Don't see that many trees grouped together unless there's a stream nearby. Since this was all open range years back, I'd bet there's a line shack around there."

And if he was wrong? Maggie gave the darkening sky behind her another look. More riding held no appeal to her and riding hard sounded like torture. But she didn't want to get caught out here in a downpour either.

"Then I suggest we get there as quickly as possible," she said, earning her a quick grin from Dade.

"Hold on, Maggie."

She did, though her back screamed from the jostling and she couldn't feel her extremities. Rest. She dreamed of rest.

Unfortunately she supposed that wouldn't be the comfort she needed either. She held no illusions that the shelter he sought would have a soft bed, if it had one at all.

There was a bedroll behind Dade's saddle and another behind her own. That would have to suffice as a bed.

And if he didn't find shelter?

She grimaced at the thought as the horses galloped toward the crop of trees. Without a doubt this was the longest trek yet, made more stressful by the distant thunder and lightning that zigzagged from the ground to the dark clouds.

The storm was moving fast. Faster than they were.

"There it is," Dade shouted.

She scanned the plains for a cabin but only saw a small shack tucked amongst the trees. Surely he didn't mean that.

But as he continued to head straight toward it, she realized he hadn't been exaggerating when he called it a shack.

Even that might be a generous description. Why the gardening shed at Nowell's mansion was twice this size.

The memory of being trapped in there with Whit made her heart race, and not in a good way. She swallowed hard and pushed that memory from her mind.

This was Dade, not Whit. Never mind that both had stolen a kiss from her. She'd felt dominance and anger in Whit's touch. But with Dade, her entire body had hummed with pleasure.

As they neared the shack, those amorous feelings faded. At one time she would have called this shelter cozy. Intimate.

Two words she didn't want to associate with any man just yet, especially with Dade Logan. She surely didn't fear what he'd do. He was a gentleman at heart. No, in truth she doubted her own ability to keep a respectable distance from him.

He reined up before the shack and swung from the

saddle, looking no worse for the wear. She made a feeble attempt to get off the horse, but couldn't make her left foot support her weight.

"I'll give you a hand down then see to the horses," he said, matching words to deed.

Maggie held onto his shoulders as he set her on her feet, but when he let go of her, her legs refused to hold her up. "I'm sorry," she said, clinging to him so she wouldn't fall.

He swung her into his arms and strode to the shack. "I'm the one that's sorry. You're not used to the hard riding we did today."

She wanted to hate being held so tightly, but the sensations that arced through her cracked like lightning on the plains. Just like when he'd kissed her, she didn't want this moment to end. She wanted more.

Dade kicked the door open and strode into the shack. He gave it a quick scan and headed toward a makeshift stool.

It didn't look sturdy enough to support her, but the only other choice was a bunk nailed to the wall.

She didn't care to sit on what served as a filthy bed.

Dade released her, and she found her balance by grabbing on to the bunk post. "I'll be back as soon as I get the horses settled."

Then he was gone, and she could draw a deep breath again.

Maggie cradled her face in her hands, more frightened over these feelings toward Dade than she was about being alone with him. It wasn't terribly difficult to pretend she was Dade's sister in public. But all pretenses fell away when they were alone.

But her situation demanded that they avoid people as much as possible. That meant they'd remain together day in and day out until they found Daisy, or until her month was up and she could find sanctuary in the nursing school.

Her only other choice was to strike out on her own. But the thought of being on the run and alone sent a chill through her that had nothing to do with the drop in temperature. Even if she used a false name, there was a chance the bounty hunter would figure out where she'd gone and come after her.

If she could enroll in the school immediately, she wouldn't hesitate. But she'd be on her own for a month.

She had no place to stay there. No place to hide from the bounty hunter. And her funds were sparse to begin with.

No, staying with Dade was the only choice she had. She simply hoped they'd find Daisy before she surrendered to temptation and threw herself into Dade's strong arms.

Dade flicked a glance at the darkening sky as he finished shoring up the rail fence on the pen. The horses had huddled beneath the lean-to that was better suited to two horses, but they sensed the storm was nearly upon them and didn't balk at being cramped up.

His thoughts turned to the woman inside the shack. Huddling up with her held a whole helluva lot of appeal, but he didn't dare do what he wanted with her.

She wasn't a loose woman by any means and to treat her as less than a lady just wasn't right. Didn't matter how much he wished otherwise.

Maggie was here for her protection and to help him find Daisy. That was all.

Dade tested the gate and deemed it'd hold if the horses put their weight against it. He removed the pannier and their bags, and carried their provisions inside first, sparing Maggie a glance before going back to fetch their tack.

The first splats of cold rain hit him as he hefted both saddles and hustled back to the cabin. Maggie was sitting where he'd left her, likely not by choice.

He dumped their gear by the door and secured the old hook and pin latch, secluding them against the elements. Secreting them together in a room that suddenly felt way too small.

"Your legs getting the pins and needles feeling now?" he asked.

"Yes," she said, looking absolutely miserable slumped on that hard stump of a stool that some cowboy had likely made one winter so he'd have something besides that poor excuse of a bunk to rest on. "How'd you know?"

"Of all the things I remember about learning to cowboy, that one never left me," he said.

She smiled, and he wondered how he could get her to do that more often. "And here I thought you were born in the saddle."

He laughed. "Far from it."

"Tell me."

He wasn't much inclined to talk about his past. When he was a scared, angry eight-year-old dumped in the Guardian Angel's Orphan Asylum, it'd taken him nigh on a year before he confided about his past to Reid and Trey, the two boys he'd become buddies with.

"I was born on a dirt farm in West Virginia. My pa was a sharecropper when he wasn't working the coal mines." That was another memory that had stuck with him—his pa reeking of coal dust.

"If Daisy remembered that, she never mentioned it," she said. "She'd been told her folks had died."

"That's a damned lie. Ma died birthing our baby brother, who died as well, but before she did, she had me lift Daisy on the bed so she could kiss her." His throat felt thick and dry as he remembered her doing the same to him and gaining his promise to always look out for Daisy.

An odd expression played over her face. "That must have been horrible for you."

"It was."

"Where was your pa?"

"Off with his brothers in the mine." Though looking back he wondered if that was true.

He took his hat off and fiddled with the brim, needing something cherished to hold onto when he longed to drive a fist through a wall. You'd think he'd have forgotten the pain and fear and resignation in his ma's voice, but it was clear as day.

That woman had trusted that her husband would come home like always and know what to do. He'd fetch the doctor or the midwife. Either would have known what to do.

"I shouldn't have waited for Pa to come home." He shook his head and eased up his punishing hold on his hat. "I should've fetched the doctor myself."

She stared at him, and he had the feeling she was looking clear to his soul. "You were just a boy."

But he'd felt much older with the responsibility foisted off on him. He flung the hat on the bunk to avoid destroying it and strode to the tiny morning stove with a clap of thunder dogging his steps.

"I promised Ma I'd take care of Daisy. I failed her."

"How can you say that? You were put in an orphanage. They're the ones who separated you and Daisy."

He hung his head and listened to the rain pounding down on the tin roof like he had thousands of times. It'd rained like this the day they took Daisy away, yet he'd heard her screaming for him over the sound of the storm.

Some memories didn't leave. They just turned into nightmares, riding through the mind like mavericks.

"I was nine when they sent Daisy west. I begged them not to. I promised I'd get a job or apprentice or anything they wanted of me if they'd just keep her there at the orphanage." When they had refused to listen to him, he'd tried to go after her, and he'd ended up getting the beating of his life.

"You can't blame yourself because they put your sister on an orphan train," she said.

"Yeah, I can. I couldn't stop them from hauling Daisy off, but if I'd escaped right then instead of six months later, maybe I'd have found her."

He could have convinced Reid and Trey to run away sooner. But he hadn't tried. Just like his pa hadn't tried to keep his family together, preferring to raise hell instead of raising his children.

"You have to know the chances of finding Daisy are slim," Maggie said, voicing the fear he dreaded facing.

"I know."

Six months ago he'd thought he was closer to finding her. But except for Maggie's recollection of the last place she'd seen Daisy, he was right back to searching in vain for her.

Dade checked the small stove for wood. The fact it'd already been banked told him this shack had been used recently. Another traveler looking for shelter? An outlaw?

Whoever had stayed here hadn't been gone too long.

He lit the kindling, and the dry wood caught in no time. It might be summer, but they'd need the fire to keep the chill off and cook a meal.

He needed the chore to get a grip on himself too. He'd said more than he'd intended, but at least she wasn't pressing him for more. Nope, Maggie Sutten was curiously quiet.

With a low fire going, he rose and turned to her. She still looked miserable sitting there on that hard stool.

He took in the shack and grimaced at the dust coating everything. The bunk had a straw mattress that'd seen better days. He wouldn't be surprised if field mice had made a home there.

Carefully as he could, he scooped up the filthy mattress and the rags that served as blankets. He tossed it all in the corner away from where he aimed to bunk, then paused a moment to look out the small window.

The black clouds that had swept down from the mountains were now north of here. They'd missed the worst of the storm, but the rain that was still coming down would have made riding miserable.

Make that more miserable for Maggie.

He closed the window shutter and faced her. "What hurts the worst?"

"I'm not sure." She offered up a pained smile. "My legs ache, but so does my back."

He figured as much and knew that a good rubbing down with liniment would go a long way toward relaxing tight muscles. Problem was he'd have to do the rubbing in. The notion of touching her bare backside and legs got his temperature, and more, up.

"You took a good jarring, what with this being your first time spending hours in the saddle." He grabbed her bedroll and made short work spreading it out on the bunk. "It's not the softest bed, but stretching out will ease your backache."

"Where will you sleep?"

He heard the note of panic in her voice and grimaced. Damn, did she fear he'd pounce on her now that they were alone?

He wouldn't, even though the notion of sleeping with her in his arms had been on his mind far too long. What a helluva fix to be in.

"Thought I'd bunk down in front of the door," he said, turning his attention to the provisions he'd brought in. "That way we won't have unwanted visitors walk in on us."

"Oh. That's a good idea." Out of the corner of his eye he

caught her squirming on the rough stool. "If the rain has let up, I need to step outside for a moment of privacy."

Her flushed cheeks told him her need was pressing. "I'll take a look around the shed first, then leave you to it while I put on supper."

"Thank you."

The rain had lessened to a sprinkle, and the temperature had dropped, but neither helped to cool him down. Nothing would as long as he was confined in that shack with Maggie.

Why the hell hadn't he thought of this before setting off? What made him think that he could ignore her allure as a woman?

As the old saw went, he'd made his bed and now he could lie in it. Problem was he wanted to do just that with her.

He checked the area around the shack and found a natural shelter that butted up to the lean-to for the stock. It'd do for now and afford her as much privacy as one could expect out here on the Colorado plains.

She was waiting at the door when he returned. "Head around the back," he said.

She pushed past him and scampered around the corner of the shack, leaving her faint lavender scent in her wake. He shook his head and strode inside, determined to be noble if it killed him.

He'd packed canned tomatoes, tinned meat, and beans. Not elegant by any stretch but it'd keep body and soul together.

First though he needed coffee. He filled the old tin pot with water from his canteen and set it on the flat stove to heat, but his thoughts strayed to Maggie.

He should've staked out a place for her comfort on the trail, but he hadn't thought about her needs at all. Nope, his soul concern was putting miles between them and Placid. Then he had wanted to find shelter before the storm.

Traveling with a woman was a whole new experience. He'd have to consider her needs as they traveled.

Hell, there were probably a slew of other things that she'd need that he hadn't thought of. Problem was that he hadn't spent much time alone with a woman—except when he was paying for a lady's company.

They'd had Mrs. Leach at the Crown Seven, but she was a crusty old gal who'd worked in a brothel when she was young. She knew how to deal with men of any age and could handle herself in any situation that he'd seen thrown her way. She surely didn't need a man's help around the house or in getting to town.

Maggie was totally different. From what Doc had told him and what little he'd gleaned from her, she'd spent her life cooped up in Harlan Nowell's mansion with his crippled daughter.

She didn't know how to ride a horse. He doubted she could handle a team either. On the forays she'd made with Nowell's daughter to Manitou Springs, they'd taken the train. As far as he knew they'd only ventured off the straight route the few times she'd visited Placid.

In short, Maggie Sutten was helpless when it came to fending for herself. She was used to folks doing for her.

The door opened, and she stepped inside, walking like an old woman instead of a young vibrant one who had clipped down the boardwalk like one of Reid's spirited fillies. She made it to the bunk and eased down, but moaned softly doing it.

Yep, she was hurting now, and she'd continue to be miserable until she got used to riding astride. He didn't have time to go slow with her either. As long as Allis Carson was dead-set on finding her, they had to keep moving as fast as they could.

"Coffee?" he asked.

"Yes, please."

He poured the steaming brew into a tin cup and handed it to her, debating if he should question her now about Harlan Nowell. If she'd tell him why the Silver King was going to such lengths to find her.

Maggie hadn't told him all of it. He was sure of it.

For now they both needed food and rest, in that order. He'd get the truth out of her eventually.

Tomorrow they'd reach La Junta, but they couldn't take the train east. That would leave a trail a blind man could follow.

Their only course was to head northeast to Kansas and Wakeeney. If the cattle pens Maggie recalled weren't there, they'd simply follow the tracks east until they found them.

After that, it was anyone's guess how long it'd take to find Daisy. This journey to find his sister took Maggie farther away from Colorado and Allis Carson. It kept her with him for a month, forcing him to mind his manners and ignore his baser needs. That alone wouldn't be easy.

But he'd promised her and Doc that he'd take her to St. Louis, the place where his own life had changed one cold wintry night. The place where the defiant boy he'd been gave up searching for his sister to become one of Kirby Morris's foster sons.

Now he was coming full circle. Even living on the Crown Seven, he'd felt like a part of his life was missing. He was sure he'd feel complete when he found Daisy.

Maybe, just maybe, he'd find himself.

Maggie had never eaten such poor fare in her life, but even if it'd been a fine steak with all the trimmings, she doubted she would've appreciated it. She was just spent.

All the worries she'd had about being alone with Dade

faded under the strain of her exhaustion. She wanted to curl in a ball and sleep, which she did as soon as her belly was marginally filled.

But peace eluded her in sleep.

She woke in the dead of night, gripped with terror from her very real nightmare of Whit dragging her into the shed. She inhaled the musty scent of earth and his spicy cologne that was branded on her memory, still troubled that he'd planned to have his way with her.

She sat up, buried her face in her hands and stifled a moan. By sheer dint of will she'd fought him off and escaped, but the memory of what almost happened still tormented her.

"Hurting?" Dade's voice came out of the secret-laden darkness to startle her more.

"I had—" A nightmare, she nearly said, then thought better of it. "A cramp in my legs. It came and went like lightning."

That wasn't a total lie.

She'd fallen asleep, plagued by intermittent cramps and twinges, but none had awakened her. She stretched and just felt sore, which wasn't as draining as the pain.

The fear gripping her was another thing all together. Would she ever be free of it? She didn't know.

"That's it," he said. "Just muscle spasms?"

"Yes," she said. "I'm fine now."

Or she would be once she pushed those memories from her mind again. Talking about that dark day in her past would serve no purpose other than to satisfy Dade's curiosity.

He was silent for too long, and she worried that he'd press her for details. Details he deserved to know.

"Get some sleep," he said at last.

She tried to, but the night crawled by. Guilt over using Dade seemed to grow with each passing minute.

She was very much aware of each breath Dade took. If she called out to him, she knew he'd come to her.

Before she did, she had to tell him why she'd run away. He had to know that just by helping her escape, he'd made enemies of two powerful men.

She had to give him the choice to get out while he could, or fall deeper into her nightmare with her.

Chapter 13

Sometime after she'd finally dozed off, a muffled thump outside brought her wide-awake again. She lay still as death, listening. It came again, louder. Closer.

The door shook but held.

She bolted upright and lunged from the bunk, desperate to run. To hide. Someone was trying to get in. The bounty hunter?

With only one door leading into the shack, they were trapped. She backed toward the corner, her gaze locked before the door where Dade had spread his bedroll. The old fears bubbled up in her until she was shaking.

"Shh," Dade said, slipping an arm around her waist and pulling her back against his chest so he could whisper in her ear. "Get behind the door and don't make a sound."

She shook her head, not wanting to venture that close to the unknown. But Dade carried her there anyway and set her down.

He pressed a kiss to her cheek, and she wanted to cry at the tenderness in that brief gesture. Then he stepped into the shadows again, and she pressed her back to the wall and hugged herself.

The door to her right rattled again, and she bit back a startled cry.

"State your business," Dade said, his voice crackling like a whip in the darkness.

The rattling stopped. "My business? Hell's bells, you're in my cabin, and I want you to get out of it."

Dade chewed out a low curse and strode to the door. Surely he didn't believe this man who sounded older than time. It could be the bounty hunter tossing out a lie just to get them to open the door.

And Dade was about to do just that.

She stepped in front of him and pushed his hand from the catch. "Don't. It might be a trap."

"More likely it's the truth." He pushed her hand aside and lifted the catch.

Maggie held her breath as the door swung open. A swath of light stretched across the shack's floor. It didn't seem possible that dawn was breaking already.

She heard a shuffle at the door, but she couldn't see anything more than Dade's back through the crack in the door.

"You alone?" a man asked, his voice sounding scratchier this close.

"Nope," Dade said. "You?"

The old man snorted. "I've been alone for nigh on ten years now. That coffee I smell?"

"Not much more than dregs now," Dade said.

"That's more than I've had the past week. You gonna let me in my shack?"

To her surprise, Dade stepped back and granted the man silent admittance. The old man hobbled straight to the stove and the promise of coffee, reeking of sweat and a musty odor that was similar to the one she'd first smelled when she entered this shack.

That alone convinced her that the old man called this

hovel home. She took in the place in a whole new light. The bunk she'd thought hard and dirty was all he had to rest his tired bones on. The makeshift stool served as his only chair. And his mattress . . . Her gaze lowered to the heap of cloth and stuffing that Dade had tossed aside so she wouldn't have to sit on it.

She stepped out from behind the door just as Dade un-hooked the shutter and flipped it open. More light filtered through the grimy window, enough to see details now.

The old man was about her height, but the sack coat and baggy trousers he wore kept her from telling if he was fat or lean. His slouch hat had seen better days too.

He set the coffeepot down and faced them. "She your missus?"

"Sister," Dade said.

The old man nodded and took a sip of coffee. "Figured as much since you ain't sleeping with her."

So the old man was more observant than she'd thought. What other attributes could he be hiding?

He bore watching, and judging from Dade's rigid stance he was doing just that. "You put your horse in the pen?"

The old man shook his head. "Ain't got one."

"How'd you get here then?"

"Rode shank's mare," the old man said, and slapped a hand on his thigh and laughed.

He walked here? From where?

"You been in Walsenburg?" Dade asked.

"Pueblo." The old man finished off the coffee and set the cup down, his gaze flicking from her to Dade. "I head up there once a month or so to see a friend, if you know what I mean."

Dade coughed, or was that a muffled laugh? "You lived around here long?"

"Since they laid the tracks from Atchison to Santa Fe," the old man said.

"Were you a railroad roustabout?" Dade asked.

"Nope, a bridge monkey before I fell and hurt my leg," the old man said. "Railroad ain't got any jobs for a cripple."

She watched him hobble to the lone stool with renewed empathy and wished there was something she could do to ease his affliction now. But she had hoped for the same for Caroline and learned at a young age that nothing could be done to stop the ill effects of arthritis or similar pain born from injury.

"How's your memory of the race to lay rails west across Kansas?" Dade asked.

The old man smiled, revealing gaps in his teeth. "Like it was yesterday. Hell, I worked on every damn bridge on that line."

"You recollect any cattle pens built along the Kansas Central that were similar to what they had in Abilene?" Dade asked, and she realized he was trying to narrow their search for the place where Daisy had been taken off the train.

The old man scratched his nape. "Nothing near that big, though I recollect there were several good-sized ones here and there."

Dade turned to her. "Tell him what you recall of the place where you last saw your friend. See if he recalls it."

She did, going into as much detail as she could remember. But there simply hadn't been much there besides the cattle pens, cows, a trading post, and the big white house.

"I know this place wasn't a town," she said. "The house sat on a hill and a wide lane crossed the tracks right in front of it." At least it had looked big to an eight-year-old girl.

"You remember it?" Dade asked the old man.

"Remember it!" The old man slapped his game leg and

laughed. "I tell you, boy, men from six counties around here saved up their money so they could visit the Crossroads."

"Why?" she asked, earning a frown from Dade.

The old man shuffled his feet, looking uncomfortable. "It was a sporting house, ma'am, and a mighty highfalutin one at that."

He didn't have to explain more. But knowing what it was filled her with dread.

That explained why Maggie had always felt they'd stopped in the middle of nowhere, because in reality they had. Nothing but cattle pens and a brothel.

She'd seen the man who'd taken Daisy go up to his house. Why would the gentleman who'd adopted Daisy take her to a brothel?

The worry in Dade's eyes told her the same question had crossed his mind. "This brothel still there?"

"Don't know," the old man said. "Ain't heard of anyone who's visited Miss Jennean's in many a year."

"How far is this place from here?"

The old man gave that some thought. "Reckon a good two days' ride if you angle northeast out of La Junta."

Maggie didn't have to ask if they'd be heading that way today. The determined glint in Dade's eyes confirmed it.

The old man turned to her. "You fixing to put breakfast on directly, ma'am?"

All she knew how to make was flapjacks, if she had a stove and griddle and the proper ingredients. "I-I can't."

"If that don't beat all," the old man mumbled.

She refused to look at Dade. Mercy, she'd never felt so inadequate as a woman.

"I've got salt pork and spuds to fry," Dade said, and the old man rubbed his hands together and smiled.

She envied Dade the ability to put food on the table— even poor fare. Why, all she was really adept at was making herself a cup of tea.

Her culinary experience ended shortly after it had begun. Mrs. Nowell had caught Maggie in the kitchen, making flapjacks for herself and Caroline, with the cook's supervision.

The lady had ordered both girls to their room, then threatened to fire any member of the staff who dared to allow such a thing to happen again.

After that, those few trips Maggie made to the kitchen were to fetch or filch something that Caroline or she desired, like a tart, fruit, or a cookie. She never even made her own tea.

So here she was, twenty-seven years old and having no clue how to take care of herself, much less a family. But even in her exhausted state last night, she'd been fascinated by the ease with which Dade had built a fire and prepared coffee.

He'd done the same just now, passing her a cup of coffee that was as strong and bracing as he was. She took it, not having the heart to tell him she rarely drank coffee, and when she did, she preferred cream and sugar in it.

Those commodities weren't on hand, and while the coffee wasn't to her liking, it would surely give her a jolt of energy. God knew she'd need stamina today to endure another long hard ride in the saddle.

So she forced down her coffee and watched Dade. The old man had offered the use of his big skillet and now seemed equally as interested in every move he made—or rather in the fact that a meal would be forthcoming.

Yes, she wouldn't have had any idea where to start to prepare breakfast. But she intended to learn. A good part of her fight for independence depended on her being able to take care of herself.

Surely in the weeks she'd be in Dade's company she could learn a lot from him. She wouldn't be so helpless.

The enticing aroma of sizzling bacon woke her appetite.

Her gaze strayed to Dade again. She hadn't thought that something as simple as peeling a potato and slicing it into a skillet would test his muscles. But his shirt strained across his back with each metered movement.

Maggie smoothed her hands down her skirt, well remembering the feel of those hard muscles shifting beneath her palms. He was strong and unpretentious.

He was nothing like Whit. Nothing at all.

That had to be why she hadn't shied away when he'd stolen a kiss. When he touched her, even doing something as simple as helping her on her horse, she didn't feel fear. She felt desire.

Dade passed a tin plate and fork into her hands. "It's not much but it'll fill the void."

"Looks damned good to me," the old man said, helping himself to a generous portion of fried potatoes and bacon.

She took a bite and sighed her pleasure. "This is delicious."

He flicked her another of those questioning looks, but clearly didn't feel like sharing his thoughts. In short order, he filled his own plate and then dropped down on the bunk beside her to eat.

Maggie forced her mind back on the food before her instead of the man sitting far too close. It wasn't easy, but she had begun to learn how to hide the turmoil that went on within her whenever he was near.

She credited that ability to her having learned to hide her revulsion for Whit, as well as her plan to flee him.

With Dade she had to be more careful. While folks in Placid would expect a certain hesitancy between the estranged siblings, strangers that they'd meet on their journey would question those odd looks and telling flinches when they ventured too close or touched each other. That's one thing they wanted to avoid, for that would generate talk. The bounty hunter would be sure to pick up on that oddity.

They had to blend in as brother and sister, not draw attention. That meant she had to control this awareness that arced through her whenever Dade was close.

But mercy did it have to seem as insurmountable as holding back a flood?

Dade finished first and set about stowing their provisions. She took another bite of potato, but simply couldn't force down the rest. Her appetite was gone, replaced by a wad of nerves over longing and cold hard reality.

She simply couldn't afford to be a free woman right now.

"It was delicious, but I've had enough." Instead of dumping the food, she offered the old man her plate.

He took her leftovers without hesitation and scraped them into what little remained in the skillet. She was certain he intended to enjoy it later.

Though she hadn't realized it before, she did now. Dade had prepared far too much food. On purpose? She'd bet on it.

"No sense in wasting good victuals," the old man said.

He passed the empty plate back to her. The action caught her by surprise, for nobody had ever handed her an empty plate before. But this was Dade's tin plate. The old man was likely many things, but he wasn't a thief.

She flicked a glance at Dade, but he'd already carried their saddles outside. All that remained was the straw pannier holding their provisions.

Her dirty plate and the rag he'd used to clean up were the only things of his not packed. She grabbed the rag and wiped the plate, surprised how quickly the food had adhered to it.

That small thing reminded her of the trays loaded with plates and bowls that the servants had brought to Caroline's room. How the two of them had picked and fussed and wasted far too much of the fare.

Whoever was in charge of cleaning the utensils and dishes—and it embarrassed her now that she had never bothered to know their names—had scrubbed the remains of their meals off time after time.

She applied rag to plate and scrubbed and wiped until it was clean. Until she'd be willing to eat off it again. Only then did she rise with intention of packing it in the pannier.

Dade stood there watching her, his eyes dark and unreadable. If he appreciated her help, he kept it to himself.

She fidgeted and debated whether to pack the plate or hand it to him. This was his plate. His provisions. His journey to make.

She was just the hanger on. The one person he had agreed to take to St. Louis because she could help him reach his goal of finding Daisy first.

Maggie handed him the plate. "I need to—" She broke off and motioned toward the door, praying he understood.

"Make it quick as you can," he said. "Sun's up now."

She'd had privacy to attend to her needs before, but the light of day dispelled that. "I won't dawdle."

Maggie wasted no time hustling out the door. A crimson glow brightened the horizon, and she hoped that meant fair weather for today's ride.

By the time she'd finished, Dade had the horses saddled and the packs secured. The old man was sitting on his stump chair right outside the door, looking relaxed.

"You're welcome to stay longer if you want," the old man said.

"Appreciate it, but we have to get going," Dade said.

He gave Maggie a boost up onto the saddle, and she smothered a wince as her sore muscles protested being back on a horse. She gripped the saddle horn with one hand and took the reins Dade handed her with the other.

He flicked her a questioning look, and she managed a smile. He must have taken it to mean she was settled in the best she could, for he swung onto his gelding without a word.

"If Miss Jennean is still running the Crossroads, you tell her that Omar Orley said hey," the old man said.

"If I ever get over that way, I'll pass the word on," Dade said, surprising Maggie.

But only for a moment. She realized he wouldn't admit their destination in case the bounty hunter trailed them here.

"Thanks for the hospitality," Dade said.

"Come back any time," Orley said.

Dade headed them east over the rolling plains, breaking into a ground-eating trot far too soon for her liking. Again she concentrated on riding with the horse rather than against the mare. She tried not to think too much about the cowboy leading her into the unknown.

A refreshing breeze swept down from the west, but the bright sun in a cloudless sky promised that the day could turn torturous. She was doubly grateful for the wide brimmed straw hat he'd bought her.

But she wasn't sure she could continue at this pace. Just as she was about to voice a protest, Dade slowed the horses to a walk.

She thought their chances were slim of finding anyone at the Crossroads who'd remember Daisy. The fact that Daisy had been taken to the house of ill repute didn't sit well with her. What had become of Daisy? Would they ever know? Had her fate been kinder than Maggie's?

She stared at the set line of Dade's shoulders. He blamed himself for losing his sister to the orphan train. If a baser fate had befallen her, she feared he'd never forgive himself.

They topped a rise, and Dade brought them to a stop. "This looks like a good place to rest."

She stared out at the undulating plains, noting sparse clumps of trees in the distance in any direction she looked.

He took a drink from his canteen, his throat working as he drank. He swiped a hand across his mouth and handed her the canteen.

She took a sip from it, giving in to a shiver as her mouth settled over the place his had just been. It seemed so intimate to drink after a man.

"I don't doubt the old man is right about it taking two days of hard riding to get to the Crossroads," Dade said. "When you get too weary to ride or need to stop, speak up."

"I will. Do you think we'll find shelter along the way?"

"We'll be damned lucky if we do."

She had been afraid he'd say that.

Chapter 14

After a grueling day of riding northeast, they headed east, staying within sight of the railroad tracks. Dade knew Maggie was ready to drop from the saddle, but he didn't dare venture into any of the towns they'd passed. So they camped on the plains that night, and sleeping beside her without touching her was damned near impossible.

Near the end of the second day, Dade heard the lowing of cattle and caught the unmistakable smell of manure long before the cattle pens came into view. It sure as hell wasn't anything near the size of the stockyards he'd seen in Cheyenne, Laramie, or Denver. But then this was pretty much still the middle of nowhere.

The barbed wire fence barring them from riding straight toward the pens confirmed that this land was privately owned now. Hard to guess how many acres stretched south over the Kansas prairie, but the glint of wire as far as he could see had him thinking it was a section at least.

A large red barn stood to the west of the pens. Farther west still was a two-story white house with a large yard enclosed with a white picket fence.

"Is that the Crossroads?" Maggie asked, sounding more tired than she had last night.

"You tell me."

The snake of railroad tracks extended as far west and east as he could see. A worn trail, smaller than the road that had taken them on an easterly route since noon, stretched from the house to beyond the tracks.

That had to be the lane to the property. A fair-sized building near the tracks and the water tower likely served as the depot. If there was a trading post there too, he'd be surprised.

"I don't know. There wasn't a depot back then," she said. "We stood on a platform near the pens."

"The auction block," he said, and she flushed.

How many similar places had Daisy and Maggie stood waiting for someone to claim them? Too many.

Just thinking about what those children went through got his dander up. The orphan train was supposed to be a better fate than indenture, but through his eyes it hadn't looked much different.

He'd never forgotten how the factory owners had visited Guardian Angel's Orphan Asylum, looking for stout boys to apprentice in a variety of trades, from steelworkers to wheelwrights. Or how businessmen and the like came every few months looking for strong healthy boys to work the fields or labor in their shops for room and board.

The guardians at the home told them over and over that it was a better fate than ending up on the street. Dade hadn't been convinced.

For one thing he didn't want to be a steelworker or hired hand. He wanted to own a little piece of land. A farm where he could provide for his sister like he'd promised his ma.

Instead his sister had been chosen by the man who'd taken her to the big white house—the Crossroads, one of the most elite brothels of its time. There was no good reason why a gentleman would do that. None at all.

"The white house looked different," she said. "But it's right where I remembered it would be."

He squinted as sun reflected off the glass windows, his heart pounding faster at the thought of finally finding Daisy. "Let's pay it a visit, and see if anyone recalls Daisy."

They skirted the barbed wire to their west. Yep, this was clearly a working ranch now and a prosperous one to boot.

Nearly fifteen minutes passed before they reached the lane leading up to the house. The road here was wider and worn.

The area saw a lot of traffic, and the reason was obvious when they reached the depot. Tucked behind it was a long low building boasting a sign that read LARK'S TRADING POST.

"I saw this place when the train pulled in," Maggie said.

Dade reined up in front of the trading post and dismounted. "Let's see what we can find out."

He secured the horses to the hitching post, then helped Maggie down. Her hands gripped his shoulders, while his bracketed her waist. Their eyes caught and held, and he felt a frisson of energy pass from her into him.

The baser part of him ached to pull her close and kiss her and taste those sweet lips pressed against his once again. He set her aside and stepped back, cursing his abruptness when she swayed before steadying herself.

To hell with her fevered denial the other day. The high color on her cheeks told him she was equally affected.

"Dade," she began, her expression troubled.

"Later, Maggie." He didn't care to get a lecture on holding her just now. "After you."

She strode to the trading post with him right behind her.

He reached around her and opened the door, and his arm brushed her shoulder. A soft gasp escaped her, just loud enough for his ears.

Maggie hurried inside. A wiry man with a beard and thick spectacles perched on his beak of a nose smiled at them.

"Afternoon, folks. How can I help you?"

Dade wasted no time explaining. "You lived around here long?"

"Close to twenty-five years," he said, his gaze narrowing. "You looking for someone?"

"That I am." He nodded toward Maggie. "Our sister was on an orphan train that passed through here some twenty years back. A gentleman took her to that white house up on the rise."

"I remember the train, but don't recall the man or the girl he took," he said. "But Miss Jennean would. Why, she can remember everyone who's passed through her doors."

Dade's insides tightened. While he had higher hopes now that she'd remember Daisy, there was the fear that his sister had never left the brothel.

"Heard that house was once called the Crossroads," Dade said.

The shopkeeper nodded. "Still is by those who know."

But was it still a brothel? Before Dade could ask, Maggie posed a question of her own.

"Does Miss Jennean have children?" she asked.

"A daughter," the man said. "Miss Isabella Reed is back east getting an education."

Miss Isabella. Not Miss Daisy.

His first thought was relief that his sister hadn't ended up being a prostitute's daughter. Then a darker thought seeped into his mind that Daisy might have become one of the Crossroads doves.

Dade didn't want to think along those lines. "Thanks for your time. Believe we will pay the lady a call."

"You tell Miss Jennean that Charlie sent you up to the house," he said.

"I'll do that."

He guided Maggie out the door and to the horses. In moments they were riding down the graveled road that ran parallel to the railroad tracks.

"It's a beautiful place," Maggie commented.

"That it is."

If it had been built and maintained with the profits from the brothel, then this business had been a thriving one. His gaze flicked from the massive herd of Black Angus to the stock pens.

This entire setup bellowed money and good planning. If they'd suffered during the hellish blizzard of '86, it didn't show now.

As they drew near the house, a cowboy stepped from an outbuilding and strode toward the house. He was waiting for them when they pulled up.

Dade had a feeling this was the man's job. "Afternoon," he said. "I'm looking for Miss Jennean. Was told she lived here back when the orphan train passed through in '74."

"Why are you asking?"

"My sister was taken off that train here," Dade said. "If the lady can shed any light on that day and the man who took my sister, I'd be most appreciative."

The cowboy relaxed. "Come on in, then. Miss Jennean will likely want to talk to you."

Dade tried not to read anything into that statement. He helped Maggie off her mare then motioned her to precede him again. The cowboy had already reached the door and had it open, a welcoming gesture that wasn't lost on him either.

Since this had been—or still was—a bawdy house, he'd expected the place to be dressed in garish elegance. He was sorely mistaken.

There was a quiet grandeur to the house, with an attention to detail in everything. Quality came to mind.

It had a homey feel that he hadn't expected either. A matronly lady greeted them, her smile as warm as the sun.

"Miss Jennean?" he asked, and the woman shook her head.

The rustle of skirts on the balcony drew his attention. "I'm Jennean Reed."

He looked up at the mistress of the house. She was dressed in a style that he'd expect to see worn by someone high up the social ladder.

The lady didn't smile, but she didn't seem annoyed to have a visitor or two either. She just stared at him like she was trying to place his face.

"This fellow is looking for a girl who was adopted off the train back in '74. Says he's her brother."

"Thank you, Jerome," the lady said, and he promptly dipped his chin and left. "Mrs. Wray, do show my guests into the parlor and see to their comfort. I will join them directly."

"This way," the housekeeper said.

Dade and Maggie followed the lady into a brightly lit parlor furnished with a rich brocade settee, plush armless chairs, and artfully arranged knickknacks on the table.

There was no clutter or extravagance. Like everything here, it bespoke of money and good taste.

"Would you care for tea, coffee, or a more bracing libation?" the housekeeper asked.

"I'd enjoy a cup of tea," Maggie said.

Dade could've used a cold beer, but he didn't want to dull his senses. "Coffee, ma'am, black and strong, if you have it."

She smiled. "That, sir, is a requirement in the west. Do make yourselves at home."

Mrs. Wray bustled out the door. Maggie settled onto an armless chair angled out from the front bow window. Dade moseyed to the fireplace where several framed photos resided on the mantel.

The women were all elegant and young. They couldn't all be family. Prostitutes? If so, then this place's reputation for high dollar was warranted.

This wasn't your ordinary brothel. This was a trip to heaven for a man.

He studied the photos carefully and felt a monumental relief when he didn't recognize anyone with Daisy's features. Maybe, if his sister hadn't been taken in to work, Miss Jennean had adopted her and changed her name.

"Dade," Maggie said. "Come look at this."

He turned to find Maggie holding a framed photo. His gut clenched as he crossed the room to where she sat. Had she found Daisy after all?

The young woman smiled back at him, and he just plain forgot to breathe for a moment. He'd seen many pretty women in his day and a few truly beautiful ones, but this lady had a quality he'd never seen in another woman. She was a strange mixture of innocence and cunning.

Though her hair was pale as wheat and her eyes were wide, she didn't favor anyone in his family.

"That's not Daisy," he said.

"I thought the same until I noticed this." She tapped the picture, or more specifically, the broach the young beauty wore at her throat. "Look familiar?"

No, it couldn't be. "That's Ma's."

"I found the one Daisy was wearing, remember? This has to be a duplicate."

He studied the picture more closely. "You think that's her?"

"It could be. Daisy might have realized she'd lost her broach long after we'd moved on," she said, toying with the locket at her throat. "If Miss Jennean adopted her, perhaps she had a new one created as close to this one as possible."

If Miss Jennean adopted her. Changed her name to Isabella.

It was possible that Daisy hadn't lost her broach. There hadn't been any photos inside it.

He only had Maggie's word that the inscription he recalled was on the locket she wore. Why hadn't he demanded to see it?

She could have talked Nowell into buying a similar broach for her. She could've planned it that way all along so she could go on pretending to be Daisy Logan.

He flicked a glance at the broach pinned at her throat and tried to remember if the stones in his ma's had glistened so. Too many years had passed since then.

Allis Carson had told him that Maggie Sutten had stolen a family heirloom worth a pretty penny. Dade was mighty sure the one his pa had given his ma was nothing more than tinned jewelry. But it was all she'd had, and she'd cherished it.

Dade had thought his pa had buried it with her until that day he left him and Daisy at the orphanage. Clete had pinned it on Daisy then and reminded her it was her ma's—reminded Daisy that he'd given it to her ma when Daisy was born.

Damn, who was he to believe?

"Isn't she stunning?"

Dade jerked around to face the newcomer. Miss Jennean stood in the parlor doorway, as elegant as any well-to-do lady that he could imagine.

"Who is she?" he asked, knowing he was being rude but just not giving a damn right now.

"Isabella, my daughter."

Isabella. But names could be changed—he'd learned that much from his foster brother Reid who'd come back from England with a new surname.

He booted that memory aside, not willing to waste time

on the past. If this lady had adopted his sister, he damn sure wanted to know about it. Or had she taken her in to fatten her stable?

It was all he could do not to grit his teeth over that very real possibility. Respect for the fairer sex was all that kept him from demanding if she'd taken children in and raised them to earn their keep on their backs.

"Did you name her?" he asked.

"Yes, after my mother," Miss Jennean said, which told him nothing. "And you are?"

"Dade Logan, ma'am."

She turned to Maggie. "Are you Mrs. Logan?"

Maggie's chin came up. "I'm Maggie Sutten, his sister's childhood friend."

"I see." She stared at him and looked more than a bit unnerved. "Are you any kin to the Logan Gang?"

"Yep, Clete is my pa." Though he surely wasn't a caring father, even before their ma passed over. "You know him?"

She gave a throaty laugh. "Our paths have never crossed, but I've learned that an outlaw's notoriety is the only thing greater than a madam's."

"I'm not so sure about that," he said, but he didn't argue the point either.

"As you've likely surmised, I'm the proprietress of the Crossroads. A discreet gentlemen's parlor." The madam sent him an assured smile. "I'm also the owner of the Cedar Hill Ranch."

"Mighty fine place," he said.

"Thank you." She took a seat across from Maggie, sparing her a smile before facing Dade again. "Now, what's this about you looking for a girl who was taken off the orphan train?"

"My sister Daisy was the only orphan taken off it here back in '74," he said, removing his hat when she pointedly frowned at it in clear disapproval.

"That was the only time the orphan train stopped here," she said. "It was prearranged."

"By you?"

Miss Jennean laughed. "Hardly. I had one daughter and had no desire for another."

"If there's a grain of truth to that," Maggie said with heat in her voice, "then how did your daughter end up wearing Daisy's broach?"

"I can assure you that the locket you see in that photograph was given to me by a tinker from Ohio years before Isabella was born," she said, smiling as if the memory was a fond one.

"Was it inscribed?" Maggie asked.

"Why, yes, it was," she said. "Before you ask, it read, 'Love endures.' Isabella fancied the broach and thought that was a good creed to live by, so I gave it to her."

He believed her. It wasn't his ma's broach after all, just one that looked like it. Admitting that affirmed his belief in Maggie's story. But his trust might've come too late, if that cold look Maggie pinned on him was any indication.

"Whatever gave you the idea that I had taken an orphan in?" Miss Jennean asked.

"Because I was there and saw it," Maggie said, and Dade knew from the glint in Maggie's eyes that there was no holding her back this time. "I was there, Miss Jennean, when they herded us off the train onto that platform down by the cattle pens. I saw the man take Daisy. She put up a fuss the likes I'd never seen before, but when she broke free of him, she fell off the platform and knocked herself out. He picked her up, put her in his fancy buggy anyway, and drove here. He went in like he owned the place."

"Ah, that explains it." Miss Jennean pressed her fingers against her mouth, her expressive eyes wide. "You have a remarkable memory."

"Does that mean you remember Daisy now?" Maggie asked.

"I've never forgotten that poor child, though I didn't know her name," Miss Jennean said.

"How could you not know that?" Dade asked.

Miss Jennean sighed. "When she finally woke up, I asked the child her name. She just stared at me and cried and said she didn't know."

Again, Maggie's story held water. She'd told him Daisy had taken a bad fall—so bad she'd feared she was dead.

Maggie faced Dade with what could only be genuine worry. "She'd known who she was up until then, even if she couldn't recall much else. Gracious, this is worse than I expected."

He silently agreed. He just hoped she'd gotten her memory back at some point. But even as the thought crossed his mind, he reasoned that had never happened.

It explained why Daisy had never attempted to find him. Why the only news he'd heard of Daisy Logan was traceable to those times when Maggie Sutten had assumed her name.

"Please tell me what you recall," Dade said to the madam.

Miss Jennean fussed with her skirts, her frown carving deep lines that showed her age in her elegant face. "As your lady friend stated, the child was brought here late one afternoon, limp as a dishrag and pale as death except for the large red knot forming on her forehead."

"Why did the man bring her here?" Dade asked.

"Back then, there was just the trading post and the Crossroads," Miss Jennean said. "Bringing her here to seek my help was the best choice."

A new thought struck him, as sharp and unwelcome as a punch to his gut. "Did she recover?"

"Eventually," she said. "At the time, I thought she

would die. When she finally did wake up, I tried to reason with her, calm her, but all she did was cry."

"Poor Daisy! She must have been scared to death," Maggie said, voicing the thought going through his mind.

"That she was, and I could do nothing to console her." Miss Jennean's smooth brow pulled into a disapproving frown again. "I surely don't know what broke my heart more. Hearing that child wail when she first woke up, or watching her cower and just stare at us."

Dade swore under his breath. Daisy had always been a fearful child. He could imagine the terror she suffered when a man took her away from Maggie. It had to have been even more horrifying for her to have lost her memory and find herself around strangers, not even knowing who she was.

"This man who adopted her. Surely the custodians on the orphan train told him Daisy's name," he said.

Miss Jennean shrugged. "If he knew it, he didn't share it with me. I can only guess that he intended to change the child's name. He was an austere man."

The idea of gentle Daisy under the control of a strict man got Dade pacing, needling him with the same old guilt for not being there for her. By damn that would change.

"Did he scold her? Hurt her?" Dade asked.

"He did absolutely nothing, which was what terrified the child more," Miss Jennean said. "I suggested that he comfort the little girl and gain her trust. He informed me that that task was up to his wife."

So Daisy had been taken in by a family. Oddly enough Dade didn't feel relieved knowing that.

"What's his name? Where can I find him?" he asked.

"Vance Jarrett," Miss Jennean said. "He owned a freighting firm in Dodge City."

That was all Dade needed to know. "Thank you for your time, ma'am."

He rose, and Maggie did too. He didn't look forward to another long ride tomorrow, but now that he knew who'd taken Daisy, he wanted to get there as soon as possible.

"Vance didn't keep your sister," Miss Jennean said.

Those five words froze Dade to the spot. He turned back to the madam, noting Maggie looked as worried as he felt.

"Why not?" he asked.

Miss Jennean shook her head and sighed. "Vance and his wife lost their only child—a daughter—six months before he took your sister into his home. At the time, his wife was nearly out of her mind with grief. He thought bringing another child into the home to replace their daughter would snap her out of it."

"But it didn't," Dade guessed.

"No," Miss Jennean said. "When Vance passed through here a few months later, he told me that his wife had gotten worse after he'd brought the little girl home. He said his wife wouldn't even look at the child."

"Poor Daisy, stuck in a home where she wasn't wanted," Maggie said.

Dade knew Maggie was also thinking of her own fate when she made that statement. While he believed she'd been truly unhappy with Nowell, he wasn't convinced yet that she'd been abused. Not that it mattered now . . .

"What happened to my sister?"

"Vance told me he found someone to give her a home," she said.

"You know this person's name?"

She shook her head. "I asked, but he refused to speak of Louise again. That's what he named your sister."

"This Jarrett still in Dodge City?" he asked.

"You won't get any help from him."

"I can be mighty persuasive, ma'am." He'd pound the answers from the man if he had to.

Miss Jennean laughed at that, and he knew she understood what he meant. But her humor died as quickly as it started.

"I have no doubt of your ability to wrest the truth from anyone," she said, "but Vance Jarrett came down with the ague and died a year ago."

"What about his wife?" he asked.

Miss Jennean gave the barest shrug. "You can ask her, but I doubt she knew where Louise went."

He threaded his fingers through his hair and swore to himself. Damn, he hoped somebody in Dodge City remembered the girl Jarrett gave up. How else would he find out who the hell took her in?

"Thank you for your help, ma'am." Dade settled his hat on and waited for Maggie to take her leave.

Before she got to her feet, Miss Jennean said, "I realize you are eager to find your sister, but you won't get far today before you have to stop for the night. There aren't many places to rent a room between here and Dodge City."

"We came prepared to camp out," he said.

"I assumed as much, judging by the state of your attire. But considering the time of day and the distance you likely rode getting here, you'd do well to spend the night and start fresh." Miss Jennean smiled at Maggie. "I'm sure your traveling companion would appreciate a bath and the comfort of a bed."

Put that way it was hard to refuse. But he'd leave it up to Maggie to decide whether to spend a night with him alone on the prairie or here in a notorious brothel.

"Your decision, Maggie," he said.

"Well, Miss Sutten?"

Maggie smoothed her hands over her soiled skirt, and

Dade knew that she'd prefer comfort over haste. "We'd be grateful to spend the night."

"Excellent. Mrs. Wray will show you to your rooms," Miss Jennean said. "You'll have sufficient time to bathe and rest before dinner is served at six."

"Thank you, ma'am."

Chapter 15

It took every ounce of poise and determination that Maggie could summon up to walk up the wide horseshoe shaped staircase. She hoped the room given her was one of those at the top of the stairs. But the housekeeper struck off down a hall, passing door after door.

Were they all occupied? Would Miss Jennean's girls entertain men tonight? Would Dade be one of them?

Her stomach rebelled at the last question, which was a stupid reaction. He wasn't her man and wasn't about to be hers. But last night, as she slept in her bedroll beside him under the stars, she'd dreamed of remaining his for the rest of her days.

Whenever she thought of Dade, her entire body tingled with the memory of that one stolen kiss. Then there were those accidental brushes of his arm against her bottom or his hand grazing her bosom when he helped her on and off her mare.

Or this morning when she awoke to find they'd rolled together in sleep, and he'd slipped an arm around her waist. She'd been so awash in heat that she felt as if she'd touched the sun.

She certainly hadn't wanted that moment to end, but

before she could find the courage to lift her face to his in shameless invitation of a kiss, he had pulled away from her and gotten to his feet. And she was left with a longing so keen she ached.

The housekeeper finally stopped at a door and threw it open. "This is your room, Mr. Logan."

Maggie hid her disappointment. Surely her room must be one of the two left at the end of this hall.

"Thank you, ma'am, but please call me Dade."

"As you wish, sir," the housekeeper said, but Maggie doubted the woman would be informal around a guest.

Certainly none of those in Harlan Nowell's employ would have been so bold, even if invited to be.

The housekeeper continued down the hall, and Maggie struck out after her. She was so tired she feared she'd drop in her tracks, and then Dade would be obliged to carry her to her room.

Oh, how tempting.

The housekeeper opened the last door on the same side of the hall as Dade's. "Here you go, Miss Sutten. Would you like me to turn down your bed?"

"No, I can manage." Mercy, if she took to bed now she'd sleep clear through 'til morning.

"There's a bathing chamber across the hall," the house-keeper said. "Miss Jennean stocks an array of salts and oils for your pleasure. Shall I draw you a bath now?"

How deliciously decadent. "Yes, please."

Maggie wanted to rid herself of trail dust and soak her weary body. "I'll need to have my satchel brought up."

"I'm sure Miss Jennean has sent one of the men to do that."

The housekeeper bustled around the room, pulling back the drapes so light flooded the elegant space. And oh, my, it was a grand room.

Why, Maggie had never seen such a massive bed. As for

the way the room itself was dressed, well there was nothing subtle about it.

A gossamer fabric the color of the darkest forest served as an intimate veil for the bed. The rich chintz bedcover bloomed with flowers in mauve and pink on a background of varying green leaves. The same colors appeared in pillows mounded against the carved headboard.

She walked across the darker burgundy carpet that was plush underfoot to the dresser. Bottles of perfume graced one side while a mirrored tray held a gilded comb and brush.

"There are gowns and the like in the wardrobe and an array of unmentionables and sleepwear in the dresser. Feel free to avail yourself of anything until your baggage is delivered to your room."

"Thank you," she said as the housekeeper closed the door in her wake.

Maggie stood there a moment then crossed to the wardrobe. The housekeeper hadn't exaggerated. There were several elegant dresses and a confection of dressing gowns—all had daring necklines.

She pressed a hand to her bosom and felt her cheeks burn at the idea of exposing so much flesh. The Nowells idea of a daring neckline was exposing the pale skin at her throat, and even then Mrs. Nowell had remarked that it was unseemly.

"Mother is a prude, and father is a prig," Caroline had remarked more times than Maggie could recall. "One day I shall toss convention to the winds and embrace my free spirit and truly shame them."

"And I will join you," Maggie had vowed.

They'd both laughed like children and recounted memories of the day they'd met a true Bohemian woman on their last jaunt to Manitou Springs.

The woman had been bold in appearance and speech.

She'd worn her hair long, tied back from her face with a bright scarf. Instead of a day dress, she had on striped satin trousers and a lacy chemise, leaving her pale arms bare whenever her shawl slipped, which was often.

It was her view on equality for women in and out of the bedroom that shocked Caroline and Maggie. Why, the Bohemian woman had even dared to take the waters with the men, and heavens only knew what went on in those pools.

Surely none of the men had complained.

She and Caroline declared the Bohemian woman their idol at that moment and vowed to be just that bold the next time Caroline was sent there to take the waters. They hadn't realized there would be no more forays to the springs.

Maggie opened a dresser drawer and fingered the silky trousers and a chemise. If she closed her eyes, she could almost imagine how that fabric would feel gliding over her skin.

"You going to stare it to death or wear it?"

Dade? She whipped around to find him standing in the connecting doorway leading to his room. How dare Miss Jennean put them in adjoining rooms! How dare he barge in here uninvited. How dare her body tingle and come alive at his nearness.

He braced a shoulder against the doorjamb and smiled at her, one dark eyebrow winging up in a devilish arch. "Well, are you going to put them on?"

"No." She stuffed them back in the drawer and slammed it shut. "I was looking for a wrapper."

A lie, but she'd rather burn to a crisp in hell than admit she was imaging herself flaunting about in that risqué getup.

Since her satchel hadn't been brought up yet, she strode back to the wardrobe and rifled through the gowns and wrappers again. She hadn't been mistaken before. Every one of them would show a good deal of bosom. But that was preferable to the filmy trousers and chemise that would leave absolutely nothing of her form to the imagination.

She slipped a dressing gown off the hanger and moved toward the door. God, but she could feel his eyes on her back, as intimate as a caress.

"Going somewhere?" he asked.

"Yes, the bathing chamber."

"Need help washing your back?"

"No!" Maggie cringed, hating that needy tone that escaped her when she intended a firm refusal.

If her knees weren't on the verge of buckling, she'd have turned around and put Mr. Dade Logan in his place. But seeing him would surely sap the starch holding her upright.

She fumbled with the knob and all but stumbled into the hall. Thankfully nobody was around to see her lapse of control, but she expected Dade to follow if for no other reason than to taunt her again.

Damn him for planting that suggestion in her head, and damn herself for actually considering it for one wild moment. She hurried into the bathing chamber.

Maggie closed the door and secured the catch. The heady scent of lavender and exotic spices hung in the air, but she was too nervous to appreciate that Mrs. Wray had drawn her bath and added the calming scents.

She slumped against the door, her heart hammering and her throat suddenly dry. What had possessed him to pose such an outrageous suggestion?

Maybe being in the brothel had tempted him to cross the line of propriety. God knew she'd nearly succumbed to the lure of being risqué just because she had those clothes at her disposal.

Those clothes.

She glanced down at the dressing gown clutched to her bosom. Though daring, it would suffice until she could return to her room and her own clothes.

But what was she to do about that connecting door and Dade?

Leave it open tonight.

That notion pulsed in her veins as she stripped off her filthy clothes and sank into the warm water.

Whit would kill Dade for taking Maggie away with him, whether they slept together or not. In fact Whit would never believe that she and Dade hadn't been intimate.

She had nothing to lose by holding to propriety. Nothing at all.

Dade mounted the stairs to his room, his saddlebags slung over one shoulder and Maggie's satchel in his hand. The housekeeper had let him use the hip tub off the kitchen.

He'd scrubbed the trail dust and sweat off himself, and he'd put distance between himself and Maggie. But he hadn't gotten her out of his mind.

She'd likely finished soaking in the tub and returned to her room. She'd be wearing that silky dressing gown she'd had in her hand. Or would she relent and put on those silky trousers she'd been holding when he'd walked in.

That's the image he couldn't get out of his head. The split skirt she'd been wearing showed a good deal of her shape, namely her firm bottom. But imagining how the trousers would drape her curves got his blood pumping below the belt.

A cool bath hadn't helped his condition at all.

Yep, he shouldn't have barged into her room earlier. Seeing her with that silky dressing gown in her hand only had him dreaming of what she'd look like fresh from her bath, smelling of lavender and desire.

This time he'd knock on her door first. If she wasn't back yet, he'd set her satchel in the room and vamoose.

He'd just passed the door to his room when the one across the hall opened. Maggie stepped from the bathing chamber and started toward her door. The silky dressing gown she wore showed off the creamy upper swells of her bosom, nipped in at her waist, and hugged her hips and bottom like he longed to do.

The long hard talking he'd given himself had been a waste of breath. "My, but you do look fetching."

Her gaze swung to his. She was innocent curiosity and bold invitation wrapped up in one enticing package.

He wanted to unwrap her slowly and savor each prize he revealed. He wanted to kiss her long and deep. Hell, he just wanted her.

This woman had had him tied in knots since the day he'd met her. They'd shared a similar past, both shuffled to orphanages. Like him, she kept that part of her life secreted away.

He understood that, because other than owning up to the fact he had a sister, he rarely spoke of the family he'd lost. Maggie was the first person he'd talked with about that dark time in his past.

She'd taken it all in and commiserated with him. He'd sensed her hurt when she'd admitted to being Caroline Nowell's companion and not a member of that family. But she'd not revealed anything of her life before Harlan Nowell took her in.

Damn, had she spent all of her life up until then in an orphanage? He'd surely met plenty of children who'd never known their family—his foster brother Trey being one of them.

But he sensed that Maggie remembered her family, and

not necessarily fondly. Maybe that explained why she'd never mentioned them.

"Your hair is wet," she said.

"I treated myself to a hip bath."

Her cheeks turned apple red. "I'm sorry I took so long."

"Don't be."

He stopped in front of her and nudged her chin up with his finger, his head spinning from the mix of spice and sweet flowers. He saw her pulse warble in her neck. Noted the rapid rise and fall of her bosom. He warmed inside as open desire burned in her eyes.

"Unless you tell me no, I'm going to kiss you, Maggie."

She opened her mouth, but nothing came out but a breathy sigh.

It was answer enough for him. He damned sure wasn't going to give her a second chance to refuse him.

He lowered his head to hers, and the first brush of his lips on hers sent a bolt of lightning zinging through him. He felt a shiver tear through her.

Knowing that he affected her as much as she did him stirred a tenderness in him that he'd never felt with another woman. He dropped her satchel, slid an arm around her waist and pulled her flush against him.

She moaned into his mouth, but instead of pushing him away like he half feared she would, she slid her arms around his neck and held on. Her lips trembled beneath his, then firmed as they moved with his in the most hungry kiss he'd ever had the pleasure of sharing with a lady.

Hands down he couldn't recall getting near as worked up with any woman as he did with Maggie. But then he'd never spent any time with a lady either—never with an innocent one.

He was going to be the first Logan of his generation to walk the straight and narrow. He wasn't going to steal from others. He sure as hell wasn't going to love and leave a good woman, stealing her heart and hopes for a better life.

Yet here he was, fumbling behind her back to open the door, too caught up in the kiss to see reason. She didn't raise a fuss when he backed her into her room and kicked the door shut.

She didn't stop him when his hands took to wandering down her curves, gliding over her full hips, measuring her waist with the span of his hands, skimming up her middle before settling over her full breasts.

Nope, she didn't protest when his kisses went from teasing to ravenous. Hell, she kissed him back with equal hunger until his only thought was to have her now.

Her breathing had grown as labored as his. Her womanly curves pressed against his hard hot body as if she was trying to worm under his skin, the desperation he sensed in her telling him it was an invitation and not a taunt.

A part of his brain warned that he was fast on his way to getting in too deep with Maggie Sutten. She wasn't a light-skirt he could dally with at whim.

He tore his mouth from hers and pressed his forehead against hers. What the hell was wrong with him?

Maggie Sutten was a lady. Thanks to Doc Franklin she had a future lined up in St. Louis. Though right now she sure wasn't acting prim and proper. Nope, she was firing his blood more by dropping hot little kisses along his neck.

Those impatient sounds coming from the back of her throat damn sure weren't for show either. But all that proved was that even a lady had needs.

It didn't mean that her head was any clearer than his right now. Like him, she was following the path that desire led her on. Regrets would come later, and he was sure she'd have them.

Maggie Sutten was his sister's childhood friend for a few months at an orphanage and during one long train trip west. Even if he wanted her in his life on a permanent basis, she surely didn't want to tie her wagon to a drifter who didn't have a home to call his own.

Sure, he aimed to buy a small spread and farm one day. He wanted a wife and children. He hoped to include his sister in his life again.

But all that was in the future, and right now it didn't look good for him. The going would be rough for him for a long time.

He was in no position to ask a lady to be a part of his life on a permanent basis—at least on the permanent basis a lady had to be imagining. Marriage.

Nope, he couldn't give her that. So she was off limits.

He wasn't a love 'em and leave 'em man.

"My apologies for letting things get out of hand," he said, using every ounce of willpower he possessed to push her away from him.

Now if he could just tear his gaze from her heaving bosom, which was spilling out of that silky gown and daring his hands to catch it. But that left him staring at her too pale face, and he was hard-pressed to ignore the hurt that popped into her eyes and darkened to something he knew all too well. The feeling of rejection.

He scrubbed a hand over his face and swore. He was damned if he did and damned if he didn't.

"I'm not about to apologize for doing something we both wanted and enjoyed," he said.

She snapped her gaping gown shut. "Is that your excuse for breaking your word?"

"Reckon it is."

"Fine. You got what you wanted, now leave."

"There you're wrong, Maggie. All I got was another taste that left me wanting more."

"Then why did you stop?"

"Because I won't be accused of defiling a lady when I have no intentions of doing right by her."

He strode to the door and stepped out, snagging her satchel with one hand. He turned to find her dogging his steps.

"Reckon you'll want this," he said, and set the satchel inside her door.

She fussed with the opening on her gown again. "Thank you for bringing it up."

"You're going to thank me one day for stopping when I did."

The eyes that had burned with desire now snapped with anger and hurt. "Will I?"

Dade swore, well aware that he was fighting a losing battle. Maggie hadn't come to grips yet with her own needs, and his reminding her of it wasn't winning him any points.

He backed into the hall. "I'll escort you downstairs for supper in an hour."

"I can find my own way." The door slammed in his face, and the telltale click of the lock echoed in the hall.

Women! He stalked into his room and deposited his saddlebags on the floor. She could deny it all she wanted. If he hadn't pulled away, they'd still be tongue dueling.

A click echoed from the connecting door.

He stared at it, finding that insulting for all of a minute. Locking that door did them both a favor.

Tonight he needed to think through this ride to Dodge City.

Vance Jarrett was dead, and the only person who could tell him what had happened to Daisy was his widow. Depending on how much she remembered or even knew, he'd likely be starting over trying to find a lead on Daisy.

All he had was a vague description of his sister, the fact

Jarrett had taken her into his home for a spell, and "Louise"—the name the man had given her.

That alone could make the difference in finding her. But only if whoever had taken her in was from around Dodge City as well. Surely somebody there would remember.

Dade stowed his gear, then settled down at the fancy writing desk to study the map he'd gotten from the foreman here. The route from the Crossroads to Dodge City was a fairly straightforward one.

Still, it was a hard day's ride or more from here. There wasn't much choice when it came to towns that had hotels. He wouldn't know if the ones the foreman had pointed out had rooms to let until he got there.

That left camping on the range again.

Just him and Maggie and a passel of desire raging between them. How long could they deny what they both wanted?

He pinched the bridge of his nose as he heard her moving around in her room. The occasional snap of cloth and mutter of sound had him guessing she was removing her clothes from her satchel.

It'd likely take her an hour to decide what to wear to dinner. He couldn't see the fuss as all the clothes she owned were much the same—fitted, bustled, and revealing not one bit of skin.

The clang of metal wheels rattling the tracks invaded his ruminations a moment before the train whistle let out a squawk of steam. He pulled the curtain back and saw the westbound train pull into the depot.

Nobody got on, but three men got off. From here they appeared to be well-dressed and completely out of their element standing on the loading platform.

Not that they stood there long. The trio climbed into a waiting surrey and started up the road.

Understanding slapped Dade upside the head as the surrey turned down the lane to the Crossroads. He suspected few cowboys and sodbusters in the area could afford the favors of Miss Jennean's girls. Yet she appeared still to offer feminine entertainment.

The question of who could afford it was answered. The train allowed gents to take a short trip either east or west to the Crossroads, spend the evening on business, and catch the train the next day back to their homes.

Damned clever way to stay in business.

He turned his attention back to the map. As the foreman had noted, Dade would be obliged to go out of his way around the sections of open prairie that were now fenced. That left him the choice of two possible routes that would take him through small towns.

Heading southeasterly was the logical choice. The last person he wanted to meet on the trail was Allis Carson.

The outer door to Maggie's room opened and heels clicked on the hardwood floor. He lent an ear, not to eavesdrop on any conversation but to determine if she was leaving her room.

"Everything is covered in dust," Maggie said, and he guessed she was referring to the contents of her satchel.

The fancy cloth bag was fine if it was contained in a baggage car or boot. But strapped on a saddle? Why she would've done just as well draping her dresses over her lap.

"Would you prefer I have a maid beat it out or launder the pieces?" the housekeeper asked.

"Launder them." Maggie heaved a sigh that likely stirred the window curtains. "But then I won't have anything to wear to supper."

The idea of her in those daring unmentionables sent a bolt of heat spearing through Dade. He was on his feet and pacing, the map forgotten.

"With the proper undergarments, the gown you have on now would suffice for supper," the housekeeper said.

Dade closed his eyes with a groan, but couldn't blot out the memory of Maggie's creamy breasts spilling out the deep vee of that gown.

"I couldn't wear this in public," Maggie said.

The housekeeper clucked her tongue. "Now, now. You and your friend are dining in Miss Jennean's private room. They are the only people you'll see, besides the serving girl and myself."

"You're sure?" Maggie asked, and he went dead still when he realized she was considering it.

"Positive," the housekeeper replied, then all was quiet except for the glide of drawers opening and a few murmurs between the women.

What the hell was Maggie thinking to agree to wear that gown to supper?

"I'll see if I can find a dust cover for your satchel," the housekeeper said.

"Thank you again."

There was a rustle of fabric, then the door to Maggie's chamber opened and closed. Footsteps beat a rapid retreat in the hall and faded.

Dade forced himself to swallow. The idea of sitting across the table from Maggie while she was wearing that revealing gown had his heart pumping like an oil rig. Had his blood thumping to a fare-thee-well below the belt too.

Yep, it promised to be a tense evening and an even longer night of wanting what he couldn't have.

Chapter 16

Maggie gave herself a critical look in the cheval mirror and flushed. She'd pinned the low bodice together, but the cut of the neckline still showed an unseemly amount of flesh.

The housekeeper's promise that she'd be dining alone with Miss Jennean and Dade didn't reassure her. She knew where his gaze would roam, and the memory of his hands cupping her bosom was not one she could dismiss.

That experience should've angered her. Instead it had left her awash with need and cold humiliation that she hadn't been the one to pull away. She feared if he hadn't stopped, she'd have gladly let him have his way with her.

That should humiliate her into taking more care around Dade Logan. It shouldn't leave her dreaming of the next time he took her in his arms. But it did.

A firm knock sounded at her door, and she jumped. "Yes?"

"You about ready to go down for dinner?" Dade asked.

"Not quite."

She went hot all over again just thinking of walking beside him down the stairs. This giddy fascination she had with him had gotten way out of hand.

It was what she'd expected to feel toward the man she'd one day marry. It was exciting and a bit naughty and so enticing that she never wanted the feeling to end.

But it must for exactly the reason Dade had stated.

She shouldn't feel annoyed with him for having a level head, but she did. She should be glad he was an honorable man instead of smarting from his rejection.

She shouldn't still want to make love with him, but she did.

They had a month of travel together, if he held to the promise he'd made Doc. She was sure Dade was a man of his word.

They'd be together day and night. This guise of traveling as brother and sister would only fool some folks.

Those who were savvy would see straight through it. Talk about Dade traveling with a woman would eventually reach the bounty hunter. Allis Carson would waste no time wiring that information to Whit.

Then all hell would break loose.

Oh, Whit wouldn't want her as his wife after that. But he wouldn't wipe his hands of her until he'd made her pay for humiliating him.

From what she'd heard, Whit Ramsey lived and breathed revenge. He was, as Dade would say, one mean son of a bitch.

Her becoming Dade's lover wouldn't stop Whit from extracting his vengeance. Quite the opposite, in fact. He'd have Dade shot dead just for encroaching on what he deemed was his, and then he'd make her life hell for her defiance.

She pressed her hand over her heart, which was pounding too fast again. If Dade died because of her, she'd surely wish herself dead.

The admission brought her up short, for it was more

than empathy for an innocent man. No, what she felt for Dade Logan went beyond friendship.

She couldn't love him. Could she?

Is this what that emotion felt like, being nervous and bold, hot and cold, quiet and giddy in turn?

"Maggie? You all right in there?"

"I'm fine. Really, I just need a moment or two."

Maggie closed her eyes and saw him clear as day, a crooked smile, brown curls grazing his forehead and nape, and warm brown eyes that looked clean to her soul. It hadn't taken Dade long to chisel away all the lies and half-truths and uncertainties that made up her world.

She wanted to run from him, and she wanted to crawl into bed with him and know him in the age-old way a woman learned about her man.

They couldn't have a future, but they could have the here and now. They could love the night away, and she'd know the gentle needy touch of one good man in her life.

A man who wanted her as his lover. Not to dominate. No, to share that bond that she'd only dreamt of.

No matter this noble front he'd put up, his kisses told her he felt the same. He wanted her. But he was being the gentleman.

She had pulled away from him before.

She couldn't do it again.

They'd have tonight in a safe comfortable bed, in a place that was designed for lovers. Somehow she had to get him to stop fighting these urges.

After that . . . Well, they'd pose as husband and wife until they found Daisy. They'd take what they could now. They'd enjoy each other to the fullest.

Then he could leave her at the nursing school in St. Louis and go on with his life. Yes, she would become Dade's lover.

He'd made an enemy of Whit already. The punishment couldn't be worse if Dade availed himself of her.

Dade wanted her.

And she wanted him.

The question was, who was going to make the first move? She toyed with a curl that had slipped loose of her bun again. She had a feeling it would have to be her. Sadly she knew absolutely nothing about the art of seduction.

But she knew where to find the answers.

"Dammit, Maggie. What's taking so long?"

"I'm ready." Bother her hair and propriety! "Coming." She paused a second to steady her breathing. Yes, she was ready to turn a new page on her life.

Miss Jennean had told her if there was anything she wanted she had only to ask. Well, she intended to ask.

Maggie gave her reflection one last glance and carefully unpinned the blue cameo holding her bodice tightly together. This was her chance to woo Dade Logan. She was going all out to see her dream become a reality.

She crossed to the door and opened it wide. Dade stood there scowling but not for long. His brown eyes bugged and lifted no higher than her bosom. The firm brown column of his throat worked.

"I thought you'd changed clothes," he said, his voice oddly strained.

"I wanted to, but there was more trail dust on my dresses than there was on the trail." She smiled and smoothed her palms over her hips, surprised when his gaze followed the movement. "So I'm resigned to wearing this while my garments are being cleaned."

He nodded, looking back toward the big staircase and frowning. "The Crossroads just got a trio of visitors, so we'd best take the back stairs to the dining room."

She went ice cold inside, her plan for seduction faltering. "Allis Carson?"

"He wasn't one of them, but we'd best keep out of sight all the same. No sense advertising that we're here." His gaze finally lifted from her bosom to meet her eyes. "Besides, you're bound to be remembered wearing that gown."

Maggie didn't know if that was a complaint or a compliment, but she wasn't about to argue that point. They wanted to avoid the attention of strangers—not draw it.

Anyway, her plan to tempt a man began and ended with Dade. She didn't want any other man seeing her in something this revealing.

"Come on," he said. "Sounds like one of the men and his lady for the evening are headed upstairs."

His big palm closed over her bent elbow and guided her toward the door at the end of the hall. Before ducking through the door, she glanced back down the hall.

When had that heavy velvet rope been hung at the start of the hall? It had to have been recently, likely to serve as a gentle reminder that this hallway was private.

The man's laugh joined a woman's, getting closer to the hall. She slipped into the stairwell with Dade at her side.

The closing of the door closeted her in and gave rise to her fears. These stairs were narrower and closed in and for a tense moment she had trouble drawing a decent breath.

When she finally did, Dade's scent of castile, shaving soap, and fresh air wrapped around her like welcoming arms. It was vastly different from being trapped in a shed with Whit and the heavily spiced scent he favored.

They emerged into the far end of the kitchen. A plump gentleman worked at the stove and barely spared them a glance. The housekeeper greeted them with a smile.

"Miss Jennean is waiting for you in the dining room," she said and motioned to a door to their right.

"Thank you, ma'am." Dade gave Maggie a nudge that direction.

She balked a moment, reminded that the Crossroads had other visitors now. "You're sure nobody else is joining us?"

"Positive," Mrs. Wray said. "Miss Jennean always guards her visitors' privacy whether they are simply taking a meal here or availing themselves of other pleasures."

Now that was surely an interesting way to put it. If Maggie had her way tonight, she'd avail herself of the same pleasures with the handsome man at her side. But first she'd have a few moments alone with Miss Jennean.

They stepped into a dining room that was small and cozy and not the least bit pretentious. Miss Jennean sat at the head of the table, looking more like royalty than the queen of a prairie brothel.

"Just in time," she said, smiling at Maggie and then Dade.

A pearl pendant the size of a robin's egg rested between her breasts, which were nearly as luminous as the stone. Her deep blue gown gave her almond-shaped eyes a knowing, sultry look that the curve of her ruby lips mirrored.

No wonder the woman had made a good living from her trade. She oozed sensuality—something Maggie was certain that she lacked.

Dade held the chair for her, and she quickly slid onto it. She thought nothing of him seating her until she heard his breath catch.

She was baffled at what had captured his interest until she heard Miss Jennean's throaty laugh. The lady smiled and slid a finger across her own bare bosom to toy with the pearl.

And then she knew what Dade had been staring at.

Maggie dropped her gaze to her neckline and felt her cheeks burn. Sure enough he could see the valley of her bosom clearly. Why, she might as well be naked.

"I trust your bath was satisfactory?" Miss Jennean asked her.

"It was heavenly," she said as she spread her napkin on

her lap and surreptitiously adjusted her neckline. "Thank you for the loan of the gown."

"It fits you well." Miss Jennean took a sip of her wine and looked across the table at Dade. "Don't you think so, Mr. Logan?"

Dade stared at Maggie's bosom and smiled, his gaze lifting slowly to her eyes. "Yes, ma'am, the gown does fit her like a glove in places."

"Really, Dade." Maggie fidgeted with her neckline and fought off a wave of self-consciousness. "Forgive me, Miss Jennean, but I'm not used to wearing anything this revealing."

"I can see that," she said. "I dare say you've never showed that much skin to another person, let alone a man."

Maggie managed a weak nod and knew her cheeks had turned an unbecoming pink. Could this conversation get more uncomfortable for her?

Out of the corner of her eye, she noticed Dade shift in his chair. Instead of looking at him, she reached for her wine and hoped the spirits would dull her embarrassment.

Miss Jennean rubbed her thumb over her wineglass and looked from Maggie to Dade. "I thought you two were old family friends, but I can see that I was mistaken."

Maggie nearly choked on her wine. "We've only known each other a few weeks."

That earned her a scowl from Dade, but really, what was the point in lying to Miss Jennean? If they weren't posing as a married couple, and if they weren't lovers, then what did that leave but traveling companions?

"Like Maggie told you," he said, "Maggie was my sister's friend on the orphan train."

Miss Jennean leaned back in her chair as if considering that. "A very devoted one, I'd say. But I sense there's another reason why Maggie has tossed convention and mores aside and set off on a journey with a man."

"Suffice it to say I am fleeing from a situation that was being forced on me," Maggie said.

"By your parents?" she asked.

Maggie stared into her knowing blue eyes and recognized a kindred spirit there. "By the couple who took me in."

She hoped the woman wouldn't ask about her parents. She had no idea who her father was. As for the Suttens, she barely remembered the tense woman—her aunt, she believed—who'd placed her in the orphanage because she couldn't be bothered with another mouth to feed.

"It's best if nobody recalls us being here," Dade said.

"My staff have very poor memories." Miss Jennean smiled as a young woman brought platters of steaming food to the table then left. "Help yourself."

"Believe I will," Dade said and went straight for the platter heaped with roast beef.

Miss Jennean took a portion of potatoes and onions before passing them on. "I hope you don't mind eating family style. It's one thing I enjoy doing when I have company."

"Not at all. It looks scrumptious," Maggie said, and realized she was starving.

"Isabella maintains that dining informally makes everyone feel like family." Miss Jennean's smile was a touch sad, and Maggie guessed the woman missed her daughter.

"How often is your daughter able to visit?" Maggie asked as she took a small portion of roast that smelled divine.

"She comes home a couple of times during her school year," Miss Jennean said, taking the platter from her.

Maggie couldn't imagine having a home to return to, even one that still operated quietly as a brothel. She couldn't imagine having the love of a parent. Her gaze flicked to Dade. Or anyone's love for that matter.

"Isabella will spend the summer here, then return for her last year at the university," Miss Jennean said, pride ringing in her voice.

"What is she studying?" Maggie asked.

Miss Jennean smiled. "Law. Isabella feels that the best way to support the suffrage movement is by becoming a lawyer, which will enable her to see women are justly served."

"She's got her work cut out for her," Dade said. "But she's right. It's past time that women and children had a voice."

His remark brought a smile to Maggie's face. "Well said."

The rest of the meal passed with little said. But Maggie caught Dade's gaze on her more times than not. She'd at least snared his attention. Now if she could just fully capture his desire tonight.

"This is fine eating," Dade said and shoveled in another forkful of meat and roasted potatoes.

Miss Jennean swallowed her food and nodded. "I am fortunate to employ such a talented chef."

"Only meals I ever ate that a man fixed was on the ranch I grew up on," Dade said. "What our cook threw together in that cook shack couldn't compare to this."

The two laughed, and Maggie joined in, though a bit late.

Maggie had suffered years of rigid meals with the Nowells. Conversation was always minimal, with them holding to the belief that children were rarely to be seen and never heard.

Since she was nothing more than Caroline's companion, she learned at a young age that she wasn't to say a word unless spoken to. That rarely happened.

"Is the food to your liking?" Miss Jennean asked.

"Oh, yes," Maggie said, and in an effort to be part of the conversation, she asked Dade, "Tell us about the ranch where you grew up."

"Yes, please do," Miss Jennean said.

A smile teased Dade's mouth, and she knew right then that he held a special place in his heart for the ranch he'd grown up on. But she also sensed a melancholy in him about the place and those he'd known there.

Good and bad memories. She'd had few of the first and far too many of the latter.

"The Crown Seven was a fine spread up north of Maverick, Wyoming," he said at last, leaning back in his chair with a sigh. "The man who owned it—Kirby Morris—was from England. He came here with a dream to run a cattle ranch, and he nearly didn't make it past the Mississippi."

"What happened?" Miss Jennean asked.

"He was set upon by thugs one night and nearly beat to death." A troubled look came over Dade, and she knew that event must have been far worse than he let on. "Reid and Trey, the two orphans I'd run away with, and myself happened on them. We ran them off. Kirby was so grateful he asked us to go west with him."

"Was he looking for stout workers for his ranch?" Maggie asked.

"No, but that's what we thought at first. He took us into his house and treated us no differently than he would have if we were his own," he said. "Hell, he treated us a damn sight better than our kin had."

Miss Jennean toyed with her wineglass. "I heard something about that ranch and Mr. Morris a few months ago."

"I'd be mighty interested to hear about it," Dade said.

At first, she didn't think Miss Jennean would divulge a thing. She poured more wine in her glass and leaned back in her chair as if mimicking Dade's relaxed demeanor.

To Maggie's way of thinking, both of them seemed tied tight with anxiety.

"The information I received was from a gentleman visitor," she said. "I can't divulge his name, but suffice it to say he's a reputable lawyer from Cheyenne. The owner of the ranch hired him to dispose of it and the stock."

Dade snorted. "That'd be Reid Barclay."

Miss Jennean shook her head, frowning. "No, that wasn't the name, but I can't recall it now. Anyway, there was some discrepancy about the way the other shareholders—the original owner's foster sons—were dispersed. I assume you are one of the shareholders?"

"Yes, ma'am, I was," he said, his jaw set so hard and tight Maggie wondered how he could talk at all. "The way it was explained to me, my brothers and I had to come to Maverick and claim our shares by the end of December or default on them."

"You didn't meet the deadline," Maggie guessed.

He snorted and gave a jerky shake of his head. "I was in Placid when I heard about this deadline. But I stayed there too late in the season and got snowed in."

A deafening silence pulsed in the room and set Maggie's teeth on edge. The image she had of Dade as a drifter had just popped like a carnival balloon.

She was sure he'd been swindled out of his shares. "That was cruel of your foster father to set such strict limits."

"Wasn't Kirby's doing," he said, clearly defensive of the man. "He trusted Reid, the eldest of us boys. Hell, we all trusted him to manage the ranch. Instead he got himself in a fix and had to put up our shares to get out of it. Last I heard he ended up selling the Crown Seven."

"Yes, that's what I heard," Miss Jennean said. "But there was some oddity about the sale. Something that pertained to the original stockholders being granted an extension."

"Then Dade might still own part of the ranch," Maggie said.

Miss Jennean took a sip of her wine, then smiled. "It's certainly worth looking into if you're interested."

Maggie knew he definitely was interested, but she also knew he wouldn't stop his search for Daisy right now. Not when he was finally close to finding out what became of her.

"I've been through Maverick before, long ago when the Union Pacific was being laid," Miss Jennean said.

Maggie wondered if the madam had been a track follower going from one hell on wheels town to the next, or if she'd had a different life back then. It certainly wasn't a question she felt she could ask.

"It's prime cattle country," Dade said. "Kirby imported Durham cattle. Had quite a big spread for many a year."

Maggie couldn't imagine living on a ranch surrounded by livestock and cowboys. The isolation had to be horrendous in the winter when they had nobody but themselves to generate entertainment.

Then again the idea of being alone with Dade for that long had her squirming. Would they tire of each other? Would they wish the winter would never end?

"How many head of cattle survived after the blizzard of '86?" Miss Jennean asked.

Dade's expression turned troubled again. "Damn few. Like most ranchers in the west, that winter wiped us out."

Miss Jennean studied him. "But you didn't lose the ranch."

"Not then. We were able to barely hang on until after Kirby passed on," Dade said. "After that it was Reid's dealing that we could not weather."

The way he turned to finishing his meal told her the subject was closed. Except it wasn't closed. What had happened between him and his foster brothers still troubled him. He hadn't spoken of them except in chance remarks, but the anger she sensed in him told her the parting hadn't been pleasant.

Now she guessed why. Dade Logan wasn't a drifter at all. He was a cowboy at heart without a place to hang his hat, thanks to a foster brother who robbed him of his shares of the ranch he'd spoken of with affection.

He was a man without a family who gave a damn.

Her heart went out to him then and there. Yes, they had more in common than she'd imagined.

They'd both had family who'd turned them out, both blood kin and those they'd trusted. The hurt and anger and hesitancy to trust that she sensed in him was as strong as her own.

Only he might still have a stake in his home. But she wondered if he'd ever go there and make peace.

"You've lost touch with your foster brothers then?" Miss Jennean asked.

"Yes, ma'am. I've no idea where Trey got off to, and I'm not inclined to visit Reid anytime soon." Dade pushed his plate aside, his expression remote. "That's all in my past now. Time to move on."

Miss Jennean bowed her head in agreement. "You won't rest until you are reunited with your sister. I applaud that decision, but know that she might not have met with a kind fate."

"That's more reason why I need to find her," Dade said.

"I wish you luck," Miss Jennean said.

The maid cleared the empty plates and served custard topped with fresh wild blackberries. Maggie restrained herself from digging in until Miss Jennean took the first bite. Some habits were just too engrained to ignore, even when a sweet tooth begged to be satisfied.

"Now then, Miss Sutten. I need to know who you are running from if I'm to keep your stay here secret," Miss

Jennean said to her as she spooned up a dainty portion of the dessert.

Maggie hesitated for a moment, torn between distrusting this woman and divulging the whole truth right now. Dade's nod encouraged her to be honest. Dare she?

"Harlan Nowell," she said.

Miss Jennean's smile vanished, replaced by a brittle expression that startled her. "I know him. He doesn't do anyone a good turn unless it benefits him."

"Exactly. He took me in to his home to serve as the companion for his crippled daughter," she said.

"How old were you?" Miss Jennean asked.

"Eight."

The elegant madam shook her head. "You were just a child yourself in need of a home."

But that fate had eluded her. She was granted room and board in a clean nice house and was only required to be a rich girl's playmate. For years she hadn't viewed it as a horrid fate because she and Caroline had bonded as closely as sisters.

Then last winter she had realized Nowell had a far more permanent duty awaiting her. "I tired of living under his dominance and ran away. So he hired a bounty hunter to find me."

"The man's about as cold-blooded as a rattler," Dade said. "Just last week he gunned down two of the Logan Gang while he was supposedly looking for Maggie."

Miss Jennean put her spoon down. "Your family?"

"Two of my uncles," he said. "I let it be known that we've headed up to Maverick."

"This is a very troubling situation." Miss Jennean stared at her. "Why did Nowell hire a bounty hunter?"

"He claims I stole jewelry and money, but I didn't," Maggie said. "All I took was what little belonged to me."

Miss Jennean leaned toward Maggie and stared at her

with dark knowing eyes. "There is more to it than that. If I'm to help you, you must be honest with me."

Maggie hung her head, knowing there was no good reason to keep her secret any longer. No reason except that Dade would think less of her for lying to him for so long.

"I'm not entirely sure of all the particulars," Maggie began. "But Whit Ramsey's father kept Harlan Nowell from going bankrupt during the panic of '73. They made a bargain then that Ramsey's son Whit and Nowell's daughter would marry, thereby joining the two major mines in the west."

"The crippled girl?" Miss Jennean asked.

"Yes, but apparently the severity of her condition wasn't known at the time." She felt Dade's gaze boring into her and knew he was debating whether to believe this story. "When Whit found out, he demanded Nowell amend the deal, or he'd call in his markers immediately."

"Amend it how?" Dade asked.

"Whit wanted the contract to involve Nowell's adopted daughter instead of his natural one," she said.

"You?" Miss Jennean said, and Maggie nodded. "I didn't realize he'd formally adopted you."

Maggie laughed, remembering the disgust on the Nowells' faces when they were faced with this dilemma of legally giving Maggie their exalted name. "He hadn't, but he knew if Whit found out he'd been bamboozled, his contract would be null. He'd also be the target of Whit's wrath."

"I didn't know he could adopt a grown woman," Dade said.

Miss Jennean answered for her. "He couldn't, not unless she agreed. Did you?"

"No. When I refused, I was locked in my room." Maggie wadded her napkin in her fist. "I overheard the

Nowells discussing who they could approach about backdating the adoption."

"It must have fallen through," Dade said. "The bounty hunter is looking for Margaret Sutten, not Margaret Nowell."

She shook her head, wishing that were so. But she knew the way the wealthy operated. Discretion was key here.

"He's trying to avoid publicity," Maggie said, earning a darker frown from Dade that left her fearing the train of his thoughts. "A runaway servant won't draw any attention. A runaway heiress would."

Miss Jennean drummed her fingernails on the table. "He won't give up looking for you until he's exhausted all possibilities."

"Even then Nowell and Whit will burn for vengeance."

"You've made powerful enemies of them," Miss Jennean said. "If it was anyone else, I'd suggest you marry and put an end to this nonsense. But I know that won't stop Nowell from exacting his pound of flesh."

Maggie flicked a glance at Dade and felt her heart stutter when he continued scowling. Now that he realized the danger he was in, he was probably thinking of a way to sever all ties with her. She didn't blame him one bit.

"What are your plans?" Miss Jennean asked.

"A friend secured a position for me in a nursing school in St. Louis in a month," Maggie said. "I agreed to help Dade find his sister during that time."

"Staying one step ahead of a bounty hunter won't be easy." Miss Jennean reached over and laid a hand atop Maggie's trembling one. "You are welcome to stay here for the next month. Nobody will find you, and when the time comes, you can take the train directly to St. Louis."

Maggie bit her lip, seriously thinking over the generous offer. Dade would be free of his obligation, and she'd be on her own again.

But would he see it that way?

Chapter 17

Dade watched the play of emotions cross Maggie's face and knew in his gut that she was going to accept Miss Jennean's offer. He should be glad that the madam was lifting the burden of responsibility off his shoulders.

He knew where Daisy had been taken by Vance Jarrett and then been given up shortly after that. It shouldn't be hard to find out who'd taken in a shy, pretty little girl.

Yep, he likely wouldn't need Maggie to point out his sister to him. No reason for them to stay together. No reason other than he wanted her in his life for more than a few weeks.

"I don't like it," Dade said, annoyed that he'd been dutifully shuffled out of this decision.

Both women turned to stare at him. Maggie appeared stunned but not shocked, and he was mighty pleased with himself that he could tell the difference.

She was likely going to agree to do what she felt was the right thing to do. But that flicker of hope he caught in her eyes hinted that she was glad he'd spoken up, yet wasn't about to admit it.

He wasn't about to try to understand why.

Miss Jennean? Well, a smile wreathed her beautiful

face and lit her warm blue eyes with pleasure, as if she had expected he'd object to leaving Maggie behind all along.

"What's wrong with my staying here?" Maggie asked.

She would ask that. He pushed aside the personal reasons that seemed to be stacking up and reasoned out an answer.

"Allis Carson will find out we came here sooner than we both want him to, perhaps by piecing together what the old man tells him," he said. "He'll find you, Maggie."

"Pray tell who is Allis Carson?" Miss Jennean asked.

"The bounty hunter," Maggie and Dade said at the same time.

Dade leaned forward, his gaze locked on Maggie. "Miss Jennean's men will keep him off this ranch, but he'll be waiting for you when you board that train. He'll follow you, Maggie."

Maggie paled. "You can't be sure of that."

He shrugged. "You said yourself that Ramsey and Nowell won't give up trying to find you. If Carson can't wait you out, they'll hire another man who will."

"Dade has a valid point that we must consider," Miss Jennean said. "You're safe as long as you're here, but I can't protect you once you leave the Crossroads."

"I can," Dade said.

Maggie lowered her head and sighed, and he knew she was fixing to balk about going with him. "I'll just bring trouble on you."

"Sweetheart, you did that when you took on Daisy's name," he said. "If Carson can't find you, he'll come after me."

Her head snapped up, wide eyes searching his. "I'm so sorry."

He reached over and took her hand in his. "Don't be. We're in this together."

"You're baiting the bear," she said, and he knew she was softening.

"Been doing that since I was a kid." Their only chance to beat the Silver King was to stick together. "What'll it be, Maggie?"

He leaned back and braced both arms on the table when what he really wanted to do was take her in his arms. He wanted to hold her and tell her everything was going to be all right.

"Miss Jennean has been nothing but kind to us. Least we can do is draw trouble away from her," he said.

All that answered him was the metered tick of the clock in the hall. Damn, had he misjudged her? Was she going to turn him down anyway?

"All right," Maggie said at last. "I'll go with you."

Dade drew in a breath, more relieved than he ought to be. Right or wrong he'd convinced her to stick to their original plan. Now if he could just honor all his promises.

"When will you leave?" Miss Jennean asked.

"Before dawn," Dade said.

"I'll see that you have provisions to last you for your journey." Miss Jennean gracefully rose and crossed to the glass-topped liquor cabinet, removing something small from inside.

"Thanks for your generosity," he said and got to his feet.

He was too anxious to sit here at the table much longer. With Miss Jennean having callers tonight, he didn't dare venture beyond the private quarters. He knew their horses were being cared for, so there was nothing to do outside.

So that pretty much left returning to his room. If he was lucky, he'd be able to sleep instead of lying awake like he had most of last night, pondering if Maggie's skin was as silken as it appeared.

Now that he knew that it was, he'd likely spend the night thinking about running his hands over her bare form.

"An old friend of mine owns the Iago Theater in Dodge City. She's a bit eccentric, but you'd be safe there." Miss Jennean returned to Dade and handed him an old nickel voucher that was stamped with "The Ruby Slipper" on one side, and "Good for one hour" on the other. "Go to the back door. Give Gwyneth this. She'll know I sent you."

"I'll do that, ma'am." He pocketed the voucher and turned to Maggie. "Ready to go up?"

She fidgeted on her chair. "I need to see about my clothes and have a word with Miss Jennean. You go on."

He didn't want to leave her here, but he didn't have much choice if Maggie was fixing to discuss women issues with the madam. "Don't stay up too late."

"I intend to be in bed within the hour," Maggie said, her cheeks kissed with pink.

He nodded and left the women to talk, but he still hadn't gotten the picture of Maggie lying in bed from his mind by the time he returned to his room. Hell, it was going to be another long night.

Maggie waited to speak until she heard Dade's footsteps reach the upper floor. "I need your advice."

Miss Jennean didn't seem the least bit surprised. "I gather this has nothing to do with your clothes."

"No, ma'am. Mrs. Wray assured me she'd have everything cleaned and packed by morning," she said. "I have a problem."

"A female problem?"

"No, a man problem." She took a sip of her coffee though it had gone cold and tried to decide how to broach the subject.

"Dade?"

"Yes. He's a good man." She bit her lower lip, unsure

how to voice her problem. "He's too good at times, if you know what I mean."

A knowing smile lifted the corners of Miss Jennean's mouth. "Too good in that he hasn't taken advantage of you?"

"Yes, that's it. I hoped you'd understand the problem."

"I've made a comfortable living being able to read men."

And Maggie had no doubt in her mind that Miss Jennean wasn't making an idle boast. Whereas she herself was sorely lacking in experience with men.

Miss Jennean rose and crossed to a sideboard where several bottles of liquor resided. She chose two brandy snifters and poured a spot of amber brew in each.

"Take a sip, let it settle and warm your stomach, then tell me what's bothering you," Miss Jennean said.

Maggie did as told and felt fire spread from the back of her tongue to her stomach. Once the initial shock of the liquor faded, she felt oddly relaxed.

"The next time Dade kisses me and things get heated up, I don't want him to stop," Maggie said. "But I know he will."

Miss Jennean cradled the snifter in her hands, her expression thoughtful. "He's done this before?"

"Yes. It's as if he realizes I'm a lady and pulls away."

"That's understandable," Miss Jennean said. "He's a good man, and you are a lady."

And that, Maggie thought as she took another sip of brandy, was the problem. "I don't want to be a lady with him."

Miss Jennean was quiet for the longest time, leaving Maggie to wonder if she'd insulted the madam. She surely hadn't meant to. She simple wanted sage advice on the art of loving a man.

Another troubling thought occurred to her. Heavens, did Miss Jennean think Maggie didn't stand a chance of seducing Dade? Was she searching for a gentle way to tell her she was wasting her time?

"Are you absolutely sure that's what you want?" Miss Jennean said at last. "Because once you've taken that step, there is no going back."

"I'm sure," Maggie said, and knew in her heart it was true.

"Very well. I assume you are aware of the consequences."

Only one crossed Maggie's mind. A child. "Once I attain my nursing license, I can support myself and a baby."

"Before then?"

She pressed two fingers to her lips as that fate loomed before her, but the thought didn't terrify her as she'd half expected it would. "If that happens, I'll manage somehow."

"That is the reason why some women have entered my profession," Miss Jennean said, seeming a bit perturbed.

"I know," Maggie said. She suspected that she had been an unplanned, unwanted child born from a tryst. "I'm willing to take that chance with Dade."

"You love him."

Did she? She wasn't sure what that emotion felt like. She only knew that she didn't want to be apart from Dade.

In his arms she fell into a world that embraced her with warm tomorrows and blocked out the ugly reality that was her future if the bounty hunter found her.

But could she love Dade?

"I think I might," she admitted.

"He has a good heart," Miss Jennean said. "He'd never desert you or his baby."

She smiled as she imagined a future with Dade and a cluster of children. But it was nothing but a dream for her.

"Harlan Nowell might wash his hands of me if that did happen," she said. "But I doubt Whit would let me live in peace. He wants me, if only to break me to his will. If I deny him that, he'll burn with a desire for vengeance."

Miss Jennean laced her fingers together and stared at the table, the odd quake that shook her body hinting she'd either known of or suffered a similar fate. "If he can't have you, he'll make damn sure nobody else does either."

"Yes. Even now I feel Dade is risking his life by staying with me."

"He won't desert you," Miss Jennean said again.

"I know." Maggie swallowed hard. "I'll have to be the one who walks away."

A companionable silence wove around them, invisible ribbons of understanding that bound two women together. She'd felt the beginnings of this feminine connection with Daisy for that brief time in the orphanage and the journey west. She'd had the same connection with Caroline Nowell, coming close to understanding the bond between sisters or close friends.

Now it had happened again with a kind madam who she admired and respected for carving a niche for herself in this world and providing well for her own daughter. But like all the others, the tie was destined to be short-lived.

"Maybe fate will be kinder to you than you think," Miss Jennean said.

"I can only hope." But she knew that'd only happen if Whit and Nowell gave up on seeking retribution and let her be.

The madam reached over and patted her arm, the gesture so maternal that Maggie felt her eyes burn with unshed tears. This was another thing she'd missed all her life. That connection with a mother.

Mrs. Nowell certainly hadn't paid her the time of day.

But here at the Crossroads, sitting with Miss Jennean, she felt that closeness to another woman. She sensed the madam truly cared. It was the most uplifting experience she'd ever had in her life.

"If you get with child and can't take care of yourself

properly, come back here," Miss Jennean said. "You'll have a home at the Crossroads for as long as you'd like."

"Thank you, Miss Jennean."

"My pleasure. Let's see about making you irresistible to a certain cowboy tonight."

Maggie was more than willing to do anything as she trailed Miss Jennean up to her exquisite suite. She'd seen expansive wardrobes before, but this was the first time she'd been in a room devoted to nothing but a lady's wardrobe.

Lavish gowns hung on wooden rods. Bandboxes were neatly stacked on shelves. A wall of drawers spilled with lacy confections that had to be the most daring undergarments Maggie had ever seen. Why some of the corselets were so brief and transparent that one might as well be naked.

"That's the idea," Miss Jennean said in answer to Maggie's spoken worry. It was likely an unnecessary one by the madam's standards.

"You want me to wear that in front of Dade?" she asked, and an odd little thrill of excitement zinged through her at the idea of being so bold.

Miss Jennean lifted one delicately arched eyebrow at her protest. "If you can't imagine letting the man you intend to have sex with see you in this, then why attempt to seduce him at all?"

Why indeed? Insecurity. Inadequacy. The fear of rejection.

Maggie fingered the sheer black garment and gulped, for the last was her greatest fear. Nobody had ever wanted her. Not her real family. Not the first couple who brought her into their home and got rid of her for bringing tragedy into their lives. Certainly not the Nowells who took her in but who never opened their arms or hearts to her.

The madam was right. Maggie needed to tuck all her

timidity, self-doubt, and rocky sense of self-worth into the small recesses of her mind and go into this seduction of Dade Logan with her eyes wide open.

"All right. I'll wear it."

"That's the spirit." Miss Jennean perched on a plush chair and made no move to grant her privacy. "I know you'll be breathtaking in this confection."

"You can't think I'd put this on with you watching?"

"I don't know why not," Miss Jennean said. "The body isn't something to be ashamed of. They come in all shapes and sizes, and I dare say I've seen them all."

She didn't doubt that for a second, but it didn't make revealing her own inadequacies any easier. "Very well, but I'll warn you now that there is nothing remarkable about me."

God knows Mrs. Nowell had told her that all too often as Maggie went from a tall and sturdy child to a gangly young woman. When Caroline had needed a back brace, Mrs. Nowell had insisted Maggie wear one too so she'd learn proper posture.

With an economy of movement, she stepped from the dressing gown and removed her short corset. She felt naked standing there wearing only her modest shift.

"That goes too," Miss Jennean said.

Maggie groaned, sure her face was red as a beet. But she whisked it off and stood there stone-faced, reminded of the times she'd had to suffer an inspection for lice at the orphanage. She also remembered later times when Mrs. Nowell had rudely interrupted Maggie's bath and found fault with her long legs, narrow hips, and full bosom.

She reached for the black garment Miss Jennean held, fighting the urge to attempt to cover herself with her hands.

"You, my dear, are your own worst enemy." Miss Jennean leaned back and gave Maggie a long critical assessment that made her want to run and hide. "Black is too severe for you. Your pale skin needs the heat of color."

She'd rather have a nice warm wrapper, but a glance at the frothy unmentionables in here showed that each was all but transparent. What had she gotten herself into?

Miss Jennean rummaged in a drawer and held up a minuscule red corset cover and matching red drawers trimmed in lace. Though wide, the red lace straps just barely made purchase on her shoulders. The plain sheer bodice slid over her bare skin like silk.

Maggie fingered the fine fabric. She had never owned anything red in her life. Red drew too much attention, Mrs. Nowell said. So she had dressed Caroline and Maggie in drab greens and blues all their lives.

Well, Caroline had been allowed to wear pink on occasion. But Maggie never had, which was likely why she was most comfortable blending in to her surroundings like a chameleon.

She certainly couldn't be missed wearing red. She didn't look like herself. She looked a bit decadent, daring and womanly.

But Miss Jennean was right about the color warming her skin. Instead of looking stark, her pale skin took on a warm honey hue.

"Now for the crowning touch." Miss Jennean made short work of adjusting the corselet to mold over Maggie's form, tightening it just enough at the waist to make her hips look womanly.

Maggie wet her dry lips, which trembled slightly. The corselet gathered the drawers just enough to shadow the hair between her legs. But it tightened the silk over her bosom and clearly delineated her nipples.

"Dade will not be able to resist you in this," Miss Jennean said.

"If you say so." For if he rejected her after she'd

blatantly offered herself to him, she'd be too shamed to leave with him in the morning.

And maybe that was for the best too. Better to know it now than later.

"What do I do?"

Miss Jennean laughed and gave her a gentle hug. "Just go into his room and smile. Nature will guide you the rest of the way."

Maggie shook her head. "I can't just walk into his room for no reason." Never mind that her reason was seduction.

"You won't be," Miss Jennean said. "He asked for something earlier, and I told him I'd have it brought to his room tonight. I want you to take it to him."

Well, that would certainly get her into his room, but the flaw in that plan was just too obvious. "He'll know this was set up to tempt him."

"He likely will assume that, but he'll have difficulty remaining annoyed."

Maggie wasn't so sure, but she'd gone this far. She might as well go all the way.

Tonight she'd either have what she'd wanted or be heartbroken. She was well acquainted with that feeling.

"All right. I'm ready."

Miss Jennean smiled and got to her feet. "If I may give you one more piece of advice. Don't hold back. Let your emotions guide you with Dade."

Right now her emotions were wound tight, telling her to run like hell. And she just might do that if Dade turned away from her.

"I will try my best," Maggie said. "Just give me whatever you were sending to his room, and I'll be on my way." To sensual bliss or disaster.

Maggie knew it could easily go either way. In fact, considering her case of nerves, she'd likely be the worst lover he'd ever had. If they even got that far.

Miss Jennean extracted a small vial from her pocket and handed it to Maggie. "Give him this."

She took the vial filled with powder. "What is it?"

"Saltpeter." Miss Jennean snorted. "Do you know what it is used for?"

Maggie's cheeks burned. "They used it at the orphanage on the bigger boys to diminish their urges."

"How sad to use this on children," Miss Jennean said. "There are few reasons to give this to a man unaware."

But Dade wasn't unaware. "Dade asked for this?"

"Yes, he did." She smiled. "I knew why. He's smitten with you, Maggie. He's afraid he won't be able to control himself."

Maggie looked from the vial clutched in her hand to her decadent outfit. "And you still think I should be the one to deliver this to him?"

"Without a doubt. He's vulnerable, and you are simply irresistible tonight."

That remained to be seen. "Well, I suppose time will tell."

"Think positively, Maggie."

She smiled, having given up hopeless dreams long ago. "Good night."

She crossed to her own room with a world of uncertainty riding her shoulders. A lamp burned low on the dresser and cast a welcoming glow on the room, and the bed had been turned down.

Miss Jennean must have sent her housekeeper in, for she seemed to think it was a given that Dade would pounce on her the moment he saw her. Maggie wasn't convinced.

He'd asked for a powder to suppress his sexual tendencies. He didn't want to make love with her—nothing could be plainer. Yet here she was, ready to tempt him to do just that.

Except she was afraid to take the chance.

She should just take the powder to him and leave.

But she didn't want to spend the rest of this night in her bed alone.

With a bolstering indrawn breath, Maggie crossed to the connecting door and pounded on the wooden panel before she could change her mind. The silence that answered her took the starch from her spine.

In the event he'd dosed off, she gave the door another hard knock. Again, nothing but silence.

Either he wasn't in his room or he wasn't going to answer her. She turned to cross to her bed. The best she could hope for this night was rest.

She was halfway to the bed when the connecting door opened behind her. A strange mix of nerves and bravado seized her just knowing that Dade had caught her in this outrageous getup.

"Maggie?"

She forced a composed smile and turned to him. And she promptly forgot how to breathe. He was bare to the waist and barefoot, and she thought he was the most gorgeous man she'd ever seen in her life.

"I thought you were asleep," she said at last.

"Couldn't sleep."

He was staring at her with a hunger that made her limbs feel like jelly. Had his breathing become more erratic as well?

She made to clutch her own trembling hands together and realized she had a death grip on the vial of saltpeter. Good grief she was making a muck of this.

Maggie crossed to him on shaky legs and held out the vial. "Miss Jennean asked me to give you this."

"Did she now?" He took it and rolled the vial over and over in his palm. "She tell you why?"

She shook her head. "She only told me what it was."

Dade scratched his chest, the movement of skin shifting

over taut muscle so intriguing she couldn't tear her gaze away. "What are you doing?"

"Nothing," she said and hoped she sounded flippant.

He crossed his arms over his chest and leaned against the doorjamb. "You trying to tell me you was wearing that under your gown at dinner?"

"Of course not."

This was her chance to seduce him, and they were on the verge of an argument. That couldn't be a good thing.

"Then why are you dressed like that?"

Nothing could make her confess the truth. "My clothes are being cleaned, so Miss Jennean let me borrow these."

One dark eyebrow winged up. "At this time of night?"

"We're leaving before dawn," she said, and he nodded.

My, but that was a shaky gesture. Interesting that he seemed to be staring at her bosom again.

Miss Jennean swore he wouldn't be able to resist her. Could it be true?

She drew in a deep breath, and his throat worked. She took a step toward him, and his breathing hitched.

"These are a bit risqué," she said, her hands fluttering at her bodice with the intention of undoing the top hooks of her corselet. "Miss Jennean said this color was perfect for me."

"Perfect," he repeated, staring at her with open hunger now.

She gave the hooks another tug, but they wouldn't budge. Not once, not twice, but three times they remained firm.

Genuine panic set in. She'd be miserable if she had to spend the night in this.

"Something wrong?" he asked.

She looked up to see he'd straightened. "The hooks are stuck."

"You sure?"

"I'm sure I can't get out of this without help," she said.

He groaned, and she was certain he wouldn't volunteer to undress her. But he closed the distance between them and slid his thumb between the corselet and her skin.

She surrendered to a telling shiver and pressed her palms against his warm firm chest. A moan escaped her lips as he freed one hook then another.

"Damn," he said, though it was barely a whisper of sound.

She slid her palms up his chest, marveling at the muscles shifting beneath her palms. This is what she'd craved, to touch him as he'd touched her before.

"You make me feel things I've never felt before," she said.

"You're doing a fair job on me too." The corselet fell away and his palms cupped her bosom. "Maggie, you might as well be naked."

Just what she'd said to Miss Jennean. "Good idea for both of us."

She dragged her palms down to his waist and skimmed her fingers beneath the belt. He stiffened and hissed a breath, but he didn't back off. He didn't stop caressing her through the scrap of silk either.

The most intense need she'd ever felt seized her. She leaned into him, hoping Miss Jennean was right. Hoping he'd take the initiative and make love to her.

She lifted her face to his. Instead of the sweet kisses he'd treated her to before, his mouth came down on hers with a hunger that robbed her of breath.

That first dart of his tongue in her mouth shocked her. But the shock wore off quickly, replaced with an explosive raw need.

She clung to him and mimicked his hot kisses, wanting more, giving herself to him fully. He didn't disappoint.

But he didn't make any move to go beyond torrid kisses

and bold caresses. The fear of rejection taunted her and robbed her of the pleasure she felt in his arms.

She couldn't let history repeat itself, not after she'd opened herself up to him. Her fingers fumbled with the buttons on his jeans, but the damn things held tight.

And then the thing she feared most happened. He broke off the kiss and stood back, eyes pinched shut and chest heaving.

"No," she protested.

"It's too soon," he said.

"You can't mean that," she said and stroked the hot skin below his belt. "You can't stop now."

He jerked and moaned, and his eyes blazed into hers. "Maggie mine, if I don't stop now there will be no turning back."

"I know." She ran her palms up his corded arms since he wouldn't let her get closer. "I know," she repeated, hoping her voice was softer and inviting.

He muttered something and dropped his hands from her. She winced and bit back a sob as her seduction seemed doomed to fail.

Before she crumbled into that cold reality, his hands skimmed up her torso and swept the corset cover from her. She was too startled by his change of heart to feel embarrassed by standing here with her breasts bared.

She stared into his eyes that had gone dark with passion. His hands paused at the ties at her waist.

"Last chance to back out, Maggie."

"I'm not taking it," she said. "Kiss me, Dade."

He did, sending her transparent drawers sliding down her legs with one quick tug. This kiss dominated her, stripping away any lingering inhibitions.

She battled another moment of panic that this was moving too fast. Stupid really, since she feared if he didn't get on with it he might change his mind again.

He scooped her up in his arms, and that first crush of bare breasts to chest sent a jolt of electricity arching through her. Before that delicious charge ended, he laid her on the bed and followed her down.

The solid weight of him covering her felt good and natural and so arousing that she couldn't remain still. She pressed against the solid heat of his body, clinging to him like she'd never clung to anyone in her life.

She'd never felt so vulnerable, so afraid of rejection. But with Dade she was willing to risk her pride and offer herself, body and soul, to him.

He tucked her against him, his hands as greedy as her own. One thickly muscled leg slid between hers, and she tangled her legs with his too, arching her back to get closer.

She relished running her hands up his back, testing the power in his shoulders, and sweeping down his spine to glide over his firm butt. She loved being close to him, feeling his heart pounding against her own.

The fact that he was still wearing his pants gave her cause to worry. He still could stop. He could leave her aching and wanting him so badly she'd die.

He could still reject her.

His mouth pulled from hers to skim down her neck, then her bosom. She was drowning in the new sensations each bold kiss and caress evoked. She trembled in his arms, desperate for his total possession. But he seemed in no hurry.

So she did as Miss Jennean had suggested and let her emotions guide her. "Please," she said, reaching down to release the buttons on his trousers and feeling empowered when his manhood sprang free on a guttural groan—slick, hot, and oh, so long. "I can't wait any longer. Please."

Chapter 18

Dade slipped his arms around Maggie, buried his face in the valley between her breasts, and tried to slow down. His heart slammed hard and fast with the urge to pound into her.

But this wasn't some whore he'd paid for a night's pleasure. This was Maggie Sutten. Sweet innocent Maggie who'd decked herself out tonight to tempt him to take her.

This was why she'd wanted a word in private with Miss Jennean. That lady of the evening had obliged Maggie and hopefully told her what to expect.

But she'd given her some pointers on seducing a man too, and that had him trembling like a boy again. Still he wouldn't claim her innocence this quickly. He wanted her as much as she wanted him, but he was determined to give her pleasure first.

That damn sure wasn't going to happen if he didn't control the lust pounding through him. The way her sweet little hands explored his cock wasn't making this any easier for him to be a generous lover.

Hell, he couldn't recall ever being this horny before. Couldn't remember a time when a woman commanded so many of his thoughts.

"Maggie, what the hell are you doing to me?"

"I could ask the same of you," she said, her voice breathy, one hand sweeping up his back in long caresses that fired him up more while her fingers played his cock like a flute. "I've had so few choices in my life. I want this tonight. That's all."

"First time will be a bit rocky," he said, tugging her hand from between them with a wince. "So let's go slow and enjoy each other."

"I don't want slow." Her eyes were huge and glittering like deep blue pools in the lamplight.

If he hadn't been full to busting he'd have taken his time fondling her, but he was fast losing control. Still he slipped a hand between her thighs, a play of fingers on smooth warm skin. Her legs trembled apart, and that slight hesitation was a reminder for him to temper his lust.

It'd be easier to stop a stampede, but he clenched his jaw and fought the urge to thrust into her. This was going too damned fast. Hell, she was likely dry as the desert with nerves.

He ran a hand down her belly, taking in the shivers and tightening of young, strong muscles. She was long and lean and pale and felt like heaven beneath him.

She deserved a slow lover. A man who'd take his time bringing her to pleasure before slaking his own needs. But that sure as hell wasn't going to be him tonight.

He'd wanted her too long to hold back much longer. Still he fingered the moist cleft at the juncture of her thighs and heaved a breath of relief that she was ready for him.

Easy, he thought. But he couldn't swear if he was or not as he kneed her thighs apart more and settled between them, capturing her mouth in another long, drugging kiss that sang through his veins. God, she was sweetness and hot desire all wrapped up in sheer red silk that he'd loved ridding her of.

"I can't wait any longer," he whispered against her lips.

"Neither can I."

He braced on his elbows and cradled her face in his palms, thinking he could drown in those big blue eyes of hers. His lips captured hers as he rocked forward hard and fast.

She flinched and dug her fingers into his back, and he softened his kiss and went still. He'd never hurt a woman in his life and to think he had now made him feel like shit.

"I'm sorry, Maggie mine," he said, meaning it and unsure how to make her feel better.

Her fingers eased the punishing grip he surely deserved and made one slow sweep down the deep valley of his back. That gentle touch made him weak in the knees.

"It's all right," she whispered against his skin.

And then she did the thing that made him come undone. She pressed a warm kiss to the pulse in his throat.

"Thank you," she said.

He groaned and captured her lips, sinking into her more. Somehow he managed to go slow so she could adjust to being joined to a man, then he found a rhythm that she seemed to understand, moving with him as if they were truly one mind, one soul, one desire.

That alone nearly goaded him to take what he wanted and be done with it. He hadn't given of himself in too long and never like this with a woman.

Damn, but this was the most exquisite torture he'd ever endured in his life. And sweet Maggie—

She'd dropped all the barriers and given freely of herself.

He could count the gifts he'd gotten on one hand, and this was better than any of them. This touched him deep inside and scared the hell out of him.

In so many ways this was a first time for both of them. First for her being with a man. First for him having a sweet young woman who'd wanted him to be her first lover.

Who'd be the second man?

He faltered over that, hating the image that formed in his mind of her lying beneath another man with affection glowing in her eyes. His thrusts grew more forceful, as if he were trying to stake his claim to her—mark her as his own.

His woman. He liked the sound of that. But it couldn't be so, at least not now. Would it ever?

Dade shook off the uncertainty nagging at him and stared down into Maggie's luminous eyes. She deserved the best of him. He aimed to please her for as long as he had her.

Somehow she found the frantic tempo he'd set and met him thrust for thrust. They clung to each other and still strained to get closer, as if this was the last moment they'd be together, as if each was trying to crawl beneath the other's skin.

As if he wouldn't take her again later after they'd rested.

He would, because once would never be enough of Maggie.

She quivered in his arms, eyelids fluttering and the most pleased look on her face that he'd ever seen on a woman. Then she arched, her muscles tightening around him as she exhaled the breathiest sigh he'd ever heard in his life.

Masculine pride swelled his chest because he'd done this to her. He'd brought her to completion and nearly waited too long to withdraw.

With a hoarse shout he eased from her and followed her over, holding her fast as he spilled his seed into a linen. He rolled off her and sprawled on his back, chest heaving and body humming with pleasure.

He couldn't believe what had just happened.

At long last a woman had chosen Dade Logan.

When they were growing up, Reid tended to attract the ladies with his dark swarthy looks and devil-may-care attitude. Trey never lost that boyish charm that women seemed to think signaled he needed mothering—and more.

Dade?

He was the middle man. He'd had a family and lost it. He wasn't one to be conned by the promise of a home and family because he knew it was a damned lie. Yet he'd agreed with the majority rule when Kirby offered to take them in.

He'd gone with Kirby Morris, Reid, and Trey to Wyoming, not balking when Kirby made him his foster son too. But all along he'd known one day it'd all fall apart. And it had.

Then Maggie had barged into his life with her lies and bravado. She was the best thing to come his way in years. But he couldn't offer her a damn thing but hard work and uncertainty. That'd crush her. Crush her dream.

Maybe one day she could be his. But not now.

All he could give her was a brief affair. Four weeks at the most, and then he'd deliver her safely to St. Louis and this school she had her heart set on.

Her fingers skimmed down his arm, lighter than down. Charges of energy quivered over his skin.

Her fingers slid over his and slipped between them, not holding on. Just tangling with his. Like their limbs had done earlier. Like lovers basking in the afterglow.

Dade turned his head and stared into her eyes. There was wonder there as well as pleasure. But he caught that shadow of doubt lurking there too, and that tempered the joy of the moment for both of them.

"Regrets?" he asked, turning his hand palm up so her smaller fingers rested more naturally between his larger ones.

She laced her fingers with his, and he felt that quiver of desperation pass from her into him. "None. Is it wrong of me to want more than just this one time?"

He smiled at that, for the same thought had crossed his mind. "Nope. Way I see it we have one month together. We can do damn near anything we want in that time."

"I know that." A faint flush stained her cheeks. "I meant can we do this again tonight."

He'd surely die if they didn't. "If you're willing, I'm more than ready to oblige."

And with a wink, he pulled her atop him and kissed her with all the longing pounding away in his soul. She could set the pace this time, and the slower the better would suit him just fine.

Maggie had still been lolling in the wonderment of lovemaking as well as bleary from lack of sleep when they left the Crossroads at dawn. She enjoyed just sharing the quiet morning alone with Dade, but by noon that pleasure had faded.

She hurt. There was no other way to put it. Her back ached, the muscles in her thighs kept trying to cramp, and her woman's place felt raw. Bouncing in the saddle for several hours had her ready to scream with pain.

But she didn't complain. She'd been the one to initiate their lovemaking last night, and had asked to partake of the pleasures of the flesh not once but four times.

Now she was paying dearly for her wanton streak.

"You about ready to stop for lunch?" Dade asked as they neared a stream.

She had been ready three hours ago. "I'd enjoy that."

Or at least she hoped to.

Just getting off the horse for a while would be a relief. In fact, she'd almost prefer walking for an hour. Anything but straddling this horse again.

He reined up near a thicket of trees that clung to the banks of the creek. She envied his stamina as he swung from the saddle and strode to her, giving no indication that the ride had left him any worse for wear.

In fact the amorous gleam in his eyes hinted he would enjoy a bit of diversion with his lunch. If she hadn't been hurting in more places than she could name, she'd laugh at the irony of it.

"Let me give you a hand," he said.

She planted her hands on his shoulders and tried not to cringe when she swung off the horse, but the movement needled her legs with pain.

"You're hurting," he said.

"A bit."

"A helluva lot," he said. "What hurts you the most?"

"It'd be easier to list what doesn't hurt."

Dade set her on her feet but didn't drop his hands from her waist. "Why didn't you tell me?"

She sighed, seeing no sense in putting up a brave front now. "Because we couldn't afford to waste a day while I rested."

"I should've known better." He stepped away from her and scanned the area. "Damn, I don't like the idea of making camp out here in the open."

Neither did she. "How much farther till the next town?"

"Hard to tell," he said. "Since we forded the Pawnee River some time back, I'd guess we're a little better than an hour's ride from Ravanna."

Hopefully it had a hotel or boardinghouse, though as tired as she was she'd settle for a hayloft. "Then I say we set off for Ravanna as soon as we've eaten our lunch."

The look he gave her said he wasn't sure she could hold up to more riding. But Maggie was serious about moving on.

"I feel vulnerable here," she said.

"You're not alone."

There was nothing around for miles but unbroken prairie. They'd be able to see for miles while they had light, but at night their campfire would be a beacon. She didn't wish to make it easy for the bounty hunter or some other outlaw to find them.

Maggie washed up in the stream and returned to find Dade had spread a blanket and set out their lunch. Though this was all done out of necessity, she allowed herself to daydream that this was what it'd be like if Dade were courting her and they'd taken off for a picnic.

She settled down across from him and bit back a wince when her muscles protested this position too. He handed her one of the sandwiches Miss Jennean's cook had prepared.

"How did you and your foster brothers manage to survive when you ran away?"

"We scrounged for food and begged for handouts," he said. "Nighttime was the worst because we had to sleep on the street. We took turns sleeping so if a sodomite happened on us, we stood a chance of fighting him off."

She couldn't imagine the fear they'd felt. "It's a wonder you all survived."

He snorted. "Things were mighty bad right before we crossed paths with Kirby Morris. It was getting on winter and mighty cold. We'd taken to walking the alleys, looking for discarded food."

She stopped chewing, stunned to realize he'd been reduced to fighting rats for his meals. It was a wonder the three boys hadn't frozen to death.

"That's when you happened on Kirby Morris?" she guessed.

He nodded and finished off his sandwich. "Kirby was

a damned good man. When he passed on, I cried, and the last time I'd done that was the day Ma died."

"Were you happy on the Crown Seven?" she asked.

He smiled, revealing a bit of the easygoing youth he'd likely been. "More than I'd ever been in my life. The second year we lived there, Kirby surprised us by giving us each one-sixth of the ranch, with the promise we'd each gain another sixth when he passed over."

"That was generous of him."

"That was Kirby Morris. The Crown Seven was my home, and I'd have been content to stay right there and raise cattle." His expression hardened. "You know the rest of it now."

He stared at the ground, his expression somewhere between furious and troubled. She reached over and laid a hand on his arm; his tightly coiled muscles filled her with concern.

"Will you go back?" she asked, knowing she was prying but believing he needed to get this pent up rage out of him.

"I don't know." He stared off across the plains, his mouth set in a grim line.

"So that's it?"

He shifted restlessly, that hand fisting again and again. "It's over and done with now."

"But Miss Jennean heard there was a dispute about your shares," she said. "You could still own part of that ranch."

"Maybe. Tavish said that the Crown Seven sold, but he never mentioned anything about a title dispute."

"He might not have known about it." She laid a hand on his forearm. "You should go back to the ranch, if for no other reason than to settle this bad blood between you and Reid."

"I don't rightly give a shit if I ever see him again."

She knew that was a lie.

Dade wasn't a chameleon who changed his feelings at whim. He was hurting inside over the betrayal. She just wasn't sure how to help him deal with the pain.

Maggie sensed the abrupt change in him before he got to his feet. His right hand curled around his sidearm so instinctively that she doubted he realized just how lethal he looked.

"Rider coming," he said. "Pack up."

Her heart hammered with the force of a sledge striking a blacksmith's anvil. *Please don't let it be Carson.*

This far away she couldn't tell who was approaching. She ignored the aches and twinges as she hurried to gather up their provisions.

"I'm betting he's on one side of the law or the other," Dade said as the lone rider drew closer.

Maggie agreed. The man sat the horse with military precision, his hat low to shadow his face, his left hand holding the reins while his right hand rested on his thigh.

A rifle barrel extended from the scabbard. But it was the sun glinting off the sidearm strapped to his hip that caught her attention. The rider could likely pull his gun in the blink of an eye.

"What do we do?" she asked, her throat parched despite the sweet tea Miss Jennean had furnished for their lunch.

"Say no more than you have to."

Maggie would gladly adhere to that advice. She was comfortable playing whatever role Dade deemed necessary, trusting him as she hadn't trusted anyone in so long.

The cowboy was doing his best to protect her reputation and would likely palm her off as his sister. In public. In private was a whole different thing. Just thinking of what they'd done last night made her ravenous for more of the same.

She dabbed at a trickle of sweat that took a meandering

trail down her throat and disappeared beneath her collar. A shiver played over her skin as a snippet from last night returned to tease her.

Somewhere in the wee hours of the morning she'd complained about being hot. Dade had dribbled cool water over her bare skin, helping a lady out, he'd said. Then he'd proceeded to lap it off her skin.

She closed her eyes and smiled, having loved every deliciously wicked second of what had transpired after that. This man certainly knew how to make a woman feel adored.

The loud splash brought her eyes popping open. The intruder crossed the creek and stopped less than twenty feet from them.

"Dammit to hell," Dade said, his voice no more than a breath of sound.

Her gaze flicked from Dade's rigid form to the rider. A shaft of cold passed through her as his pale, glacial eyes skewered her to the spot.

She'd never seen such emotionless eyes. As for his face, she couldn't tell if he was as old as he seemed or if he'd simply led a hellish life.

"Well, now," he said in a gruff voice that abraded her nerves. "Who you got there, boy?"

"A man ought to remember his children." Conviction rang clear and loud in Dade's voice, and for one heartbeat Maggie almost believed that she was Daisy Logan.

So this was the infamous outlaw who'd taken his children to the orphanage. She had absolutely no respect for anyone who turned their children out, and looking into his cold gray eyes didn't change that opinion. But the fate they'd been dealt at the orphanage was far better than what they'd have had living with their outlaw father.

She held her breath as the outlaw's steely eyes flicked from Dade to her. "Daisy?"

The man was smart to question that, for she looked nothing like Daisy. Still, she wasn't about to reveal Dade's lie. He had reason to hide the truth, and she'd given her word that she'd go along with whatever ruse he wanted.

"Who are you?" She forced her chin up, attempting a brave front though her knees were knocking something fierce.

"Clete Logan," he said, his chest puffed with the false pride only an outlaw could have. "Your pa."

She turned to Dade, positive that Daisy wouldn't remember this man either. "Is he?"

"Yep," Dade said. "Except he gave up that right when he left us standing on the steps of an orphanage in the dead of winter."

"You got a good memory, boy," Clete said. "I did what had to be done."

"You did what you damned well wanted, and that was ridding yourself of the responsibility of a family."

Clete Logan went still, his hand poised at his sidearm. She feared he'd pull it in a spurt of anger. "You still wearing a tin star, boy?"

"Nope," Dade said, clearly keeping to his word now and saying no more than necessary.

Not that it mattered. They'd both riled Clete Logan, and a man who'd deserted his family would likely have no qualms about shooting either or both of them dead right now.

The old man thumbed up his hat, revealing a face that looked as if it'd been chiseled from bedrock and baked in hell's inferno. "That holdup in Placid have anything to do with you turning in your star?"

"Not one damned thing."

Animosity arced between the two men like sheet lightning, the energy so strong it raised the fine hair on her nape.

"Reckon you heard about Seth and Brice," the old man said.

Dade nodded. "Allis Carson made a sizable reward off them."

Saddle leather creaked as the old man shifted his position. "Carson made an enemy too, one who will track him to hell."

Maggie caught the quick set of the old man's jaw and angry curl to his upper lip and knew he was in pain. But it was the flash of awareness in his cold eyes that stole her breath.

Clearly the outlaw was after the bounty hunter hired to find her. Did that mean Carson was in this area as well?

"You on his trail now?" Dade asked, as if reading her thoughts and fears.

"Not sure. I lost his trail outside La Junta a day back. But I heard he was heading to Eminence to round up a horse thief." Clete Logan stared at Dade for a long uncomfortable moment, as if silently challenging him. "I need your help cornering him, boy."

"I want nothing to do with him or you."

Dade turned his back on the outlaw and stowed the provisions in the pannier that Maggie had gathered up. Clete Logan's eyes went so black and angry they looked like flint, and for one moment she feared he'd draw his gun on Dade just for the hell of it.

With a curse, the outlaw kicked his horse's flanks and rode off. But Maggie had the uneasy feeling they hadn't seen the last of Clete Logan or the bounty hunter he'd vowed to kill.

Chapter 19

They reached the outskirts of Ravanna late that afternoon, and Dade was mighty grateful that they hadn't met up with anyone else on the road. Still, he kept his eyes peeled and his senses honed for any sign of Allis Carson or Clete Logan.

With his old man dead set on finding the bounty hunter and extracting his brand of vengeance, Dade was more determined than ever to keep Maggie hidden. That meant keeping her name secret.

He reined up and looked her over. Her shoulders tended to droop and her mouth was pursed, but her eyes were alert. Likely her worries ran alongside his own.

"I'd planned for us to pass ourselves off as brother and sister," he began, "but with Allis Carson this close to us, we'd best change plans."

"Yes, I've used that identity too much now for it to still work as a disguise," she said. "Do you have any suggestions?"

He shook his head. "Pick a name that don't stand out."

"Ann," she said. "It's my middle name, though I doubt many folks know it."

"Ann Morris it is."

Her big blue eyes sparkled with mischief. "And what is your alias, dear brother?"

He gave her mare's line a tug to bring her alongside him, then leaned over and stole a kiss, no more than a quick peck, but one he felt sizzle through his veins all the same.

"As in my wife," he said, and had the satisfaction of seeing desire flare in her eyes. "I'm not leaving you alone at night and the one decent place here won't rent a room to a couple who aren't married."

That stole the color from her cheeks. "There's no need to explain."

Damn, did she think he was using that as an excuse to bed her? "I won't force you, Maggie."

"I know," she said, color returning to kiss her cheeks and nubbin nose. "It's all right, Dade."

He hoped to hell she felt that way when their time together ended and he delivered her to St. Louis. He sure didn't want her pining for him or worse, to leave her with a baby swelling her belly.

That meant he either had to leave her alone or use utmost care each time he took her. For damn sure he couldn't be with her without having her again. So he had to keep a clear head around her.

That wasn't easy to do. He'd never given up control of his thoughts and body before, but it had nearly happened twice last night. Both times he'd just barely remembered to pull out of her before spilling his seed.

"Is something wrong?" she asked.

Yep, he'd surely lost himself in this woman. "Nope. Just getting a feel for the place."

He forced his gaze from her questioning one and took another gander at Ravanna. The drawback of a small town was that most folks would remember them. But their only other choice was bunking down on the plains, and that would leave them sitting ducks for anyone who happened by.

"Miss Jennean's foreman said they have a hotel. Nothing fancy, but it'll do for the night." He picked it out among the structures and resumed his perusal of the other buildings.

There were several shops, churches, a bank, a livery, and a big courthouse. Houses ranged from small shacks to fine homes. The whole town was laid out well.

It looked peaceful and welcoming. But Allis Carson could already be here.

He could be inside a shop jawing with whomever would pay him the time of day. He could be hiding in the livery, just waiting for the unsuspecting to pass by.

Dade wouldn't know until they rode in—until it was too late. But he couldn't stay out here on the plains either. Nope, they had to take the chance.

Clete Logan seemed to think the bounty hunter was headed to Eminence, a rival town some miles from here. He believed his old man about as far as he could throw him. But the fact that the outlaw seemed to be headed to Eminence cinched Dade's decision to ride to this town.

He hoped he didn't live to regret it. "Let's get a room and treat ourselves to a meal tonight."

They reached the town in short order, and Dade headed straight for the hotel. Once he got Maggie settled, he'd see to their horses and make sure they were safe.

So far the only attention they had drawn was from the pair of old men sitting outside the general store. That would generate enough talk. Who else was watching?

He was so attuned to looking for trouble that he almost missed her wince as he lifted her from her mare. He set her on her feet but didn't let go of her.

"Can you walk?" he asked.

"Just give me a moment," she said, and when she wouldn't look at him he knew.

Dade called himself ten kinds of an ass. He'd loved her long and hard last night then put her astride a horse and forced her to ride all day.

She needed to soak out the kinks and soreness. She needed rest. She needed him to keep his damned pecker in his britches tonight.

"I'll see if the owner can draw you a hot bath," he said.

She nodded. "That'd be very nice."

"Come on." He escorted her into the hotel.

A cherry-cheeked matron stood behind the counter. "Good day to you."

Dade brushed two fingers over his hat brim. "Same to you, ma'am. Me and the missus would like a room. A bath too, if you can provide it."

"That can be arranged." She opened a book and angled the pen his way. "If you'd just sign here, Mr.—"

"Morris," he supplied.

He caught himself from scrawling just his name and wrote Mr. and Mrs. Daniel Morris instead. A strange feeling of rightness settled in his soul as he put the pen back in the holder.

It didn't matter that he liked seeing his name teamed to a lady's. Didn't change anything that he felt good being the other half to Maggie Sutten.

Like everything else in his life, this couldn't last. He'd do well to keep that in mind.

The smiling woman handed him a key. "Room four at the end of the hall. It's much quieter and private."

Her innuendo wasn't lost on him. "Thank you, ma'am. I'll see my wife to our room then fetch our bags."

"My son will see to those bags," the woman said. "You just set them inside the door, and he'll take them up for you."

"Much obliged," Dade said and took Maggie's elbow.

This was a woman he'd never tire of touching. She wouldn't bore him with chatter either.

Nope, she'd been through the hell of being shuffled off to an orphanage. She understood how being unwanted tore at a person's soul.

He didn't know all of her past yet—she'd not offered, and he hadn't pushed. But he knew how secrets kept hidden could fester like a sore.

He still felt off balance from meeting his pa today. So many years since he'd laid eyes on him, but the pain of rejection was as fresh as if it'd just happened.

It was clear the old man hadn't wasted any energy worrying about his children. Hell, he'd believed Maggie was Daisy. The man didn't even know his own daughter.

"I am looking forward to the day when I can stay in one place for an entire week without ever getting on a horse," Maggie said.

She moved slowly up the stairs. Anyone who didn't know her would have thought she was just taking a ladylike stroll. But Dade caught the slight wince when she bent just so and the unnatural stiffness to her back. She was hurting, and he wasn't sure that a hot bath would ease all her discomfort.

That could pose a problem tomorrow, for they had just as long a ride into Dodge City. She'd do far better in a well-sprung buggy, but he doubted he'd find anything besides farm wagons and buckboards in this town.

He unlocked the door and let her enter first. She made straightaway to the armless chair by the window and eased onto it.

"Finally something to sit on that isn't moving," she said.

Guilt took a bite out of him again. Yep, it was mighty clear that not all of her discomfort stemmed from sitting a saddle all day. A good part of her misery could be laid at his feet for loving her long into the night.

She needed rest from the saddle and him.

"You aren't going to be in any shape to ride again tomorrow."

She hiked her chin up, her lips pursed in that way that told him she was getting her back up again. "Is it wise to spend more than a day here?"

"With Allis Carson close by? Nope," he said. "The sooner we get to Dodge City and the Iago Theater, the better off we'll be."

"Then we ride again tomorrow."

"You need rest, Maggie," he said. "I'll fetch our bags so we can settle in."

"Don't take a foolish risk because of me. I'd rather suffer a little inconvenience now than risk getting caught here by Allis Carson."

"All right. I'll arrange for a bath to be brought up to you while I'm seeing to the horses and getting a feel for the town."

Dade slipped from the room before she could protest any further. It took no time at all to remove her satchel and his saddlebags from the horses.

A request to make his wife's stay comfortable was easily procured as well. "I'll have your things taken to your room first, then set up her bath," the matron assured him.

"Thank you, ma'am."

He left the hotel and stood on the wide porch a moment, getting a feel for the town. While it didn't look to be in decline, it didn't seem to be growing either.

It was a sleepy Western burg where nobody seemed to be in any hurry. Still he took care riding to the livery.

The liveryman met him at the wide open doors. "Afternoon. What can I do for you?"

"Need to board my horses overnight."

"You're passing through?"

"On our way to Dodge City."

"You got kin there?" the liveryman asked as he stabled the horses.

To Dade's way of thinking, he'd said more than enough about his destination. Folks in small towns tended to have long memories. Time to cover their trail.

"My wife has family in Santa Fe," Dade said. "We plan to catch the train in Dodge City."

The lie wouldn't fool the bounty hunter for long, but it might give Dade and Maggie enough time in Dodge to find out who'd adopted Daisy. After that they could disappear.

"Guess you plan to leave early in the morning then," the liveryman said.

That had been Dade's intent, but he was worried about Maggie's condition. "Depends on how my wife feels. The journey has been hard on her."

"Where'd you come from?"

Again, Dade didn't dare tell the truth. "We had a small place in Nebraska."

"Times are hard everywhere."

Dade nodded, and let the man think what he would. He knew as time went on, the story would become embellished.

"Just send word down in the morning, and I'll have your horses ready," the liveryman said.

He'd do just that if Maggie was up for the ride.

He gave the town another cautious glance and returned to the hotel. Maggie should've finished her bath by now.

His gut grumbled in protest of the small meal he'd had today. Didn't help that the most appetizing smells were wafting from the hotel dining room. He was tempted to escort Maggie down here for the evening meal, but fear that the bounty hunter would walk in on them changed his mind.

He'd have their meals brought up to their room, he decided as he entered the hotel. The owner was most obliging.

"I'll have trays sent up in an hour," she said.

Dade thanked her for her trouble and doled out what he owed. "Any chance you have a bathing chamber downstairs?"

"We certainly do," she said. "Many of the men folk partake of it while their ladies are indisposed."

She led him to a small room just off the kitchen. "There might not be much hot water left by now."

"That's fine." He was used to taking a dip in a creek when the need arose.

Half an hour later, he bounded up the stairs in his same duds that had most of the dust beaten out of them. The sound of feminine laughter inside his room brought him up short. One woman was Maggie, but the other was a stranger.

"Do tell me more, Maggie," a woman asked.

He set his teeth, annoyed with his traveling companion. After all the fuss of coming up with a new identity for her, she went and told some woman her real name.

His knuckles wrapped the door a bit more loudly than necessary, and the laughter inside instantly died. Talk about feeling like a killjoy. But damn, what if the bounty hunter had overheard them instead of him?

"It's me," he said.

To his relief, Maggie replied, "Come in. You won't believe who I ran into."

Someone she knew? Is that why the other woman called her by name?

It seemed impossible, but as he stepped into the room it was obvious that the two women knew each other by the relaxed way they were with each other. It was just as clear that Maggie trusted the other woman.

"Afternoon," he said.

The welcoming smile and fitted dress Maggie wore caught him off guard. A vagrant thought crossed his mind that she'd greet him this way every time he came home.

As for the other woman, he'd seen her in the dining room when they'd first arrived. He doubted she worked here since she was great with child.

"Maggie and I have been catching up on old times," the woman said.

"You won't believe this," Maggie told him, eyes bright with excitement, "but Rita was on the orphan train with me and Daisy. Just last year she married Faron Owens, the hotel owner's son."

Well now he damn sure hadn't expected Maggie to meet another soul from that train here. More than anyone, Dade understood the bond of orphans. But he had learned the hard way that trust among brothers could be shattered by betrayal.

"Small world," he said.

"You'll wish that were so after you hear this," Maggie said, her expression serious as she turned to Rita. "Tell him about Daisy."

The woman's smile faded. That's all it took to drive a prod in his worry, because that look told him that whatever she knew about Daisy was bad.

"The McCray's—that's the family that adopted me— were visiting family in Hays when the orphan train passed through. But they lived in Dodge City," she said. "I came down sick on the way back there, and they took me to the doctor. There were maybe a half dozen rough looking cowboys outside on horses. Two of them were inside with a little girl. That's when I realized she was Daisy."

Again, that followed from what Maggie and Miss Jennean

had said about his sister being out of sorts after her fall.
But his gut clenched with fear that Daisy had worsened
enough to need a doctor's help.

"At least if she was ailing, Mrs. Jarrett got help for her,"
he said, remembering the name of the family who'd taken
in Daisy only to give her up shortly after.

Rita shook her head. "But that's just it. There wasn't any
woman there except Mrs. McCray."

He had a real bad feeling he knew the answer, but he
asked anyway. "Who the hell brought in Daisy?"

"The cowboys, or rather the one who seemed to be in
charge," Rita said and shivered, leaving him to wonder if
that reaction was born out of revulsion or fear or a combination of the two. "He was so tall and big and gruff that he
scared the dickens out of me. And Daisy . . . Poor girl just
stood beside him with tears streaming down her cheeks."

Dade flung his hat on the bed and drove his fingers
through his hair. Pacing was a waste of shoe leather, and
he lacked Trey's explosive temper that would have had him
driving a fist through a wall. He hadn't inherited his pa's
inclination to shoot somebody just for the hell of it either.

But dammit all he sure had the urge to do something to
vent the anger boiling inside him.

"You have any idea what was wrong with her?" he asked.

Rita's eyes held a world of apology. "Not really, though
afterward my mama, Mrs. McCray that is, said that the
child was suffering from headaches."

"You're sure she didn't know who she was?" Maggie
asked, her blue eyes swimming with moisture.

"Positive. She didn't remember me either," Rita said,
and in a small voice added, "She didn't even know her
own name."

That was a gut punch he hadn't braced himself for.
Never mind that it followed with what Maggie and Miss

Jennean had said all along. A part of him had hoped that they were embellishing the facts.

Hell, maybe they all were. Could he trust that Rita was telling him the truth? Was she backing up a friend's story?

"You sure that Daisy was with these cowboys?"

She bobbed her head. "Without a doubt. When they left, they took her with them."

Half a dozen men and one little girl who didn't know her name. He didn't like the direction his thoughts were taking him on this one damned little bit.

"Any idea who this big cowboy was?" he asked.

"None," Rita said. "But after they left, I recall Mama and the doctor expressing concern about a child being in the company of cowboys for so long."

That sounded like they were planning a longer trip. He hoped it was to a good family.

"Can you describe him?"

She did, and the description matched half the cowpokes he'd met in his life save one thing.

"I've never seen a man that big before. And his voice." Rita hugged herself. "He spoke softly and with a deep drawl, but there was thunder in his tone."

Sounded like he was a man to be reckoned with. A man's man by most standards. So why was he taking on the care of a little girl?

He wanted to believe the cowboy was a family man. A rancher maybe who took in a pretty little girl out of the goodness of his heart. God knew the idea of his sister being handed over to cowboys, especially in a rough town like Dodge City that saw hundreds of men pass through each season, didn't set well with him.

He strode to the window and stared out at the quiet street. Though Maggie saw no harm in drawing a childhood friend into their confidence, he wasn't so quick to trust.

From his own experience, women tended to gossip.

Men said only what needed to be said, and even then the truth had to be pried out of them.

He faced Rita again and caught the worried look that passed between her and Maggie. "This doctor who treated you and Daisy. You recall his name?"

"Of course. Dr. Pike," Rita said, brightening a bit at being able to supply that. "I haven't seen him since I married last year and moved to Ravanna, but I know he's still in Dodge City."

It was more than he had known before setting out from the Crossroads. If Mrs. Jarrett couldn't or wouldn't tell him who'd taken Daisy, maybe this doctor would recall treating his sister.

And if he hit a dead end?

Dade didn't want to think on that. "Thank you for telling us about my sister, ma'am."

"I wish there was more I could do to help," she said.

There was, if she'd do it. "I'd appreciate it if you didn't tell anyone we'd passed through here."

"Oh. Of course," Rita said.

But Dade wondered if the woman could keep that promise. Hell, he and Maggie might as well wear bells, for it wouldn't be hard for Carson to find out where they were headed. They'd be easy pickings.

"It seems logical that this big cowboy must live near Dodge City." Maggie fidgeted with a handkerchief, folding it up a smidgen then ironing it out with her hand. "He surely wouldn't assume the care of a child over a long journey, especially one who was ailing."

Dade wished that were so. "A cowboy views miles a damn sight differently than most folks. I doubt this cowboy gave a second thought to heading out with Daisy, be it twenty miles or two hundred."

Hell, that was likely the reason he'd sought the advice

of a doctor—to see that Daisy was trail worthy. They could've ridden in any direction from Dodge City.

The pain of loss sank into him again. Unless he could find somebody who knew where the man was headed, he could wander in circles looking for his sister for years. He could be within miles of her and not know it.

She could be lost to him forever.

Chapter 20

Maggie saw worry dim the hope in Dade's eyes, and her heart went out to him. Since the first day she'd met him he'd projected an aura of confidence that he'd find his sister. He had been so sure that she would recognize Daisy when his own memory failed him.

But for the first time she saw his assurance falter.

She allowed that Rita's memory of that day in the doctor's office might not be entirely clear. For one thing, she couldn't see a doctor standing by and letting a couple of rough cowboys ride off with a terrified little girl who didn't even know her own name.

Daisy had needed care, not jostling around on a horse. Thanks to her own recent painful experience, she knew how such a journey taxed a person. She didn't want to think how horrible it would've been for Daisy to endure.

"This cowboy must have been a rancher in the area," Maggie said, drawing Dade's and Rita's attention. "Maybe he owned a ranch in the next county."

"It's possible," Dade said, though his flat tone screamed doubt. "Just as likely he drove cattle up from Texas or Indian territory."

She hated that he was right. But then she'd never thought finding Daisy would be easy.

Knowing what she did now made it harder to remain positive. Dark thoughts of why those men had taken Daisy eroded her peace.

Their only chance of finding the man's identity was to visit the doctor and hope his memory was clear. Surely he'd remember a little girl in the company of cowboys.

"Do you think her memory ever returned?" Rita asked, her soft inquiry shattering the tense quiet.

Maggie didn't have to think about that answer. Daisy had lost her memory shortly before Maggie met her, and she had been relearning who she was and where she was in the months they were together in the foundling home. The fall Daisy had taken at the Crossroads erased all she'd learned and then some.

But one thing Maggie was certain of now. Daisy had to have been as devoted to her brother as Dade was to her.

"I doubt it," Maggie said. "If Daisy's memory came back to her, she'd have tried to find Dade."

"She might not have been able to," he said, and she hated the terrible reasons that sprang to mind.

To her dismay, his expression remained remote. It was like he'd shut down a part of himself and had ceased to feel.

Two hard raps hit the door, and she jumped. "Got your supper."

"Coming." Dade moved to the door.

Maggie supposed it wasn't so much his clipped tone but the hard glint in his eyes that startled her friend.

Dade opened the door a crack with his left hand while his right rested on the butt of his revolver. He visibly relaxed and threw the door open.

"Thank you for your trouble," he said.

"Not a problem." The older man strode in bearing a

large tray and set it down on a side table that Rita had rushed to clear.

The enticing aroma of a home-cooked meal filled the room. Sadly Maggie's appetite had deserted her.

"Faron just got back and is looking for you," the old man said to Rita.

A warm glow spread over Rita's face, leaving Maggie to believe her friend loved her husband Faron with all her heart. She couldn't imagine being that devoted to someone.

Rita paused to give Maggie a hug before hurrying from the room. "If I don't see you before you leave in the morning, have a safe and productive journey. Write a letter if you have the time."

"I will."

Maggie watched her friend all but run from the room. The old man shuffled out after her, leaving Maggie and Dade alone.

An uneasy silence crackled in the air, similar to the tension she'd sensed the first day she'd met Dade. She wasn't sure what to say, for they'd pretty much expressed their concerns earlier.

"Let's eat," he said and dropped onto one of the chairs.

"Go on. I'm not that hungry."

He slid her that dubious look that she was beginning to hate. "Eat anyway. We have a long day ahead of us."

At least he wasn't planning to leave her behind. She took the other chair and made a show of picking up her utensils.

The sliced beef, roasted potatoes, and snap beans looked and smelled luscious. But her stomach simply refused to tolerate a heavy meal.

She played at eating while Dade finished off his supper. The only thing more nerve-wracking than what lay in store for them was the distance she felt growing between her and Dade.

"What time will we leave in the morning?" she asked, draping her napkin over her nearly full plate.

"Before dawn. The liveryman will bring the horses around so we can head right out."

Just as she'd thought. "Who do you plan to question first?"

He snorted and leaned back in his chair, cradling his cup of coffee. "It's a toss up between calling on Mrs. Jarrett or going straight to Dr. Pike. I know you have an opinion."

Oddly enough that remark eased some of the tension arcing between them. "I think you'll learn more from the doctor. He'll be impartial and just may want to help us."

He sipped his coffee, his expression thoughtful. Seeing him like this reminded her of just how handsome he was. If he'd only relax more often.

"You're right," he said. "But I still aim to call on Mrs. Jarrett."

"Let me guess why. You want her to tell you why she turned out your sister."

"Damn right I do." He rocked forward and rested his arms on the table, but she barely noticed anything besides the heat of anger in his eyes. "She was sick, Maggie. My sister had lost her memory and God knows what else was wrong with her. Yet that woman tossed her out like garbage and her husband let her do it."

She had nothing to say to that, for the same anger over the injustice of it all burned in her soul as well. She doubted if the Jarretts had considered Daisy's feelings when they rejected her.

The orphan girl was just a commodity to them. But Maggie knew firsthand the hurt of being passed over by people looking for a child to adopt and the pain of being taken into a family's home, only to have them change their minds.

But then she'd done something unforgivable, while Daisy had simply needed someone to care for her while she was recuperating from her accident.

He got to his feet and stretched, and she caught herself staring at the play of muscles across his body.

Maggie rose and crossed to the window, surprised it was dusk already. It would be totally dark in an hour.

They'd need to get much needed sleep soon, and with only one bed—

She chaffed her arms, certain Dade would make love with her again tonight. Though she was still tender from their journey today, she longed to lie in his arms and feel the thunder of his heart beneath her ear. She wanted to relive that special excitement that surged through her when their lovemaking reached its zenith.

The muffled thump on the door had her whirling around. Dade was in the process of spreading his bedroll against the wall.

"What are you doing?" she asked.

"Getting ready for bed." He tugged one boot off then the other and set them neatly to one side.

Unlike last night, he seemed in no hurry to undress. He didn't even look at her.

"Surely you don't intend to sleep on the floor," she said when he rolled up a blanket and carefully positioned it at one end of the bedroll to serve as a pillow.

"You need your rest and so do I."

That was certainly true, and she was grateful he didn't mention that she was too tender from sitting a saddle all day. But just because they weren't going to indulge in passion didn't mean they couldn't share the bed. They were adults, capable of controlling their urges for one night.

Never mind that her body was humming with the promise of his touch, his kiss. She'd actually looked forward to cuddling with him, to feeling his solid weight beside her in the bed. She wanted to know she wasn't alone.

"This is ridiculous. You'd rest better in the bed," she said.

He snorted, and that curt sound was a slap of reality she hadn't expected. "Hardly. Quit dawdling, Maggie. Morning is going to come mighty early."

She stared at his long feet incased in worn stockings and gave in to a shiver. Last night his long bare legs and feet had tangled with hers. The rasp of his crisp hair against her skin had been an erotic thrill that had heightened her senses.

It was clear she wouldn't feel anything but cool sheets against her skin tonight.

He flicked a glance her way, then proceeded to remove his shirt. His gun belt followed. The entire process was smoothly done. She knew it was routine, that he'd done it countless times before.

But she'd bet he'd never slept on the floor while the woman he'd bedded the night before snoozed in the bed. This was done by choice, and it hurt. He'd dismissed her from his mind just like that.

She swallowed the bitter taste of reality. He was rejecting her. He was saying that if he couldn't have sex with her, he didn't want to sleep with her either.

Maggie slipped behind the dressing screen and went through the motions of changing into her nightdress. Fool that she was, she'd chosen a frilly one that buttoned from her neck to well below her waist because she'd been thinking of seduction again—not sleep.

She crawled into the bed and tugged the covers to her chin. "Good night."

"Night."

She saw him douse the light, and the room faded into a velvet darkness. But she didn't need light to know Dade Logan was in the room.

She was attuned to his every movement, the breath he

took, the shift of his body on the pallet. She'd done what she had sworn she wouldn't do. She'd lost her heart to him.

He didn't even know she was alive. Wanting him. Hurting for his touch.

Pride wouldn't let her reveal it. She'd gone to him once and initiated their lovemaking. The next time—if there was a next time—it would have to come from him.

For the last ten miles guilt plied the whip to Dade's conscience over his decision to ride into Dodge City today. Maggie was ready to drop from the saddle, and there was no place that he deemed safe enough to bunk down.

Their only option was to keep moving.

Because of her tender condition from riding too much on the mare and on him the night before last, he held them to a snail's pace. It was mighty clear that even that was a form of torture for her.

So they arrived at dusk. The Iago Theater was easy enough to find though, thanks to the fact that a play was going on at the time.

He rode past the two-story brick building and the two that butted next to it. Both were shops that were closed for the night.

"Miss Jennean said we should go to the back door and ask for Gwyneth," Maggie said.

Just where he was heading. "I remember."

"Do you still have the token?"

"In my breast pocket." He patted his chest where the small disk rested, but with the diminished light of dusk he doubted she noticed.

He reined up their horses at the mouth of a narrow alley that reeked of piss and rotting vegetables. He could guess what caused the first. The last had an obvious source thanks to a restaurant that backed up to the theater.

"Not a very inviting place," Maggie said.

Downright dangerous in his estimation. "I don't much care to leave the horses tied up out here in the alley while I get you settled inside."

In fact, he wasn't partial to leaving her alone while he saw to their horses. But his only other choice was for them to head to the livery and then hire a buggy to return with their provisions and bags.

She surely wouldn't be able to walk that far. Even if she could, they'd attract attention.

"I'm sure I'll be fine," Maggie said. "After all, the owner is a friend of Miss Jennean's."

He didn't miss the weary tone in her voice. Like it or not, he'd have to see her settled, then stable the horses.

"Let's see if we can raise someone then," he said.

Dade guided the horses down the alley with care, disliking the pile of crates where anyone could hide. A couple of cats darted from one stack and raced down the alley.

His gelding shied, but thankfully Maggie's mare paid the cats no mind. He scanned the shadows again before dismounting.

Steps led up to the rear door of the theater. He rapped on the solid door and hoped it wouldn't take long for someone to answer.

"Maybe they can't hear you with the show going on," Maggie said.

No doubt she was right. He heard piano music, then the clapping of hands that seemed to go on and on.

Dade waited until the applause died then pounded on the door again. If they didn't raise somebody this time, he was moving on.

After too long a wait, the door creaked open, and a

strange little man stared back at him. He glanced from Dade to Maggie and back again.

"If you're looking for a job, look elsewhere," the man said in a voice that sounded pinched. "I've got all the actors and actresses I need, and when they aren't working, they do the repairs on the theater."

"Not looking for work, sir." Dade held up the token and felt marginally better when the little man smiled. "I'm looking for Gwyneth."

"Ah, yes, yes. This does change things," the man said, his voice taking on a feminine edge. "I am Mrs. DeMare."

Why would a woman dress in masculine clothes and kohl her eyes? "Sorry, ma'am."

"No need for apologies. One of my actors left me in the lurch, so I was obliged to play his part tonight." Mrs. DeMare snagged the token from his hands with lightning speed. "Where did you get this?"

"From Miss Jennean," he said. "She sent us here."

Mrs. DeMare stared at Maggie again. "Who's the woman running from? A jealous husband? The law?"

Dade sure as hell didn't want to talk about this on the back stoop of the theater, but Mrs. DeMare didn't appear anxious to let them in without knowing.

"The family she worked for wants to marry her off to a man she fears," he said. "They hired a bounty hunter to bring her back."

"Trouble," Mrs. DeMare hissed.

That was putting it mildly. He wasn't about to own up to being an outlaw's son.

Instead of slamming the door in his face as he half expected, Mrs. DeMare opened it wide. "Bring her in. Your bags too."

Dade didn't wait to be asked twice. He lifted Maggie off the mare and held her until he felt the worst of her tremors leave.

"You able to walk?" he asked.

"I think so." But one faltering step convinced him she wasn't as steady as she claimed.

Dade scooped her up in his arms and carried her inside the theater. He spied a wooden bench and eased her down on it.

"I'll be back with our bags."

Mrs. DeMare waved him on and set to fussing over Maggie. He returned to the packhorse and made quick work getting their belongings inside.

"I need to stable the horses," he said.

"Westin Livery is four blocks south," Mrs. DeMare said. "He takes good care of your stock and doesn't ask questions."

Just what he wanted. "I'll be back soon as I can."

"I'll be all right." Maggie got to her feet and held on to the high back of the wooden bench. "Be careful."

Dade nodded, then stood there like a dolt when what he wanted to do was take her in his arms and kiss her. All the reasons why he shouldn't trotted before him, and the wary manner in which Mrs. DeMare eyed him cinched it.

So without a word, he slipped out the door and crossed to the horses. The back door of the theater closed with a final-sounding click.

Maggie was safe now. He could see to their mounts without fretting over her. But he worried just the same as he headed back the way he'd come.

There was something damned odd about Mrs. DeMare that went beyond her dressing like a man. First off was the fact that there wasn't a livery four blocks down.

He excused it as the lady not knowing her directions. But the feeling he'd been sent on a wild goose chase ballooned when he rode north the same distance and found nothing but houses.

Dade motioned for the approaching buggy to stop. The

man driving it did, but he looked mighty uneasy about doing so.

"Pardon, sir," Dade said, "but would you direct me to the Westin Livery?"

"I'd be happy to. Go three blocks east and turn to your left. The stable is halfway down the block."

"Much obliged," Dade said.

He backtracked again and found the place right off. Interesting that he was less than two blocks from the theater. In fact, he could see the top of that building from the front of the livery.

"Need to stable my horses for a few days or so," Dade told the liveryman, who looked big enough to wrestle a bear and was just as wooly.

"Two bits a day per horse. You fail to pay, I keep the horses."

"Fair enough." Dade swung from the saddle and dug out the right coin.

With the horses settled in, he walked the surprisingly short distance to the theater. Darkness had fully fallen by the time he rapped on the rear door again.

Like before, his first knock wasn't answered. He pounded on the door again, but a minute turned into five.

That uneasy feeling settled into his gut as he thumped his fist on the door a third time. No answer.

Dade trudged to the front of the theater. The folks that had been standing there were gone.

"Ticket?" asked the pretty girl sitting behind the window.

He shook his head, his impatience getting a stranglehold on him. "Mrs. DeMare told me to meet her around back, but nobody answered the door."

The girl blinked. "Mrs. DeMare? You must be mistaken, sir. There's nobody here by that name."

"That's a damn lie," he said, his patience exploding into anger. "I just talked with her thirty minutes ago."

The girl wasn't moved. "There's nobody here by that name."

Shit, this would get him nowhere. The only way to find out if Maggie was still here was to search the damned place.

"Does the name Miss Jennean mean anything to you?" he asked.

"Oh yes! She's a patron of the theater." The girl's burst of excitement instantly dimmed. "Why do you ask?"

"Miss Jennean sent me and my friend here."

The girl looked around and frowned. "Friend?"

"Maggie is already inside," he said. "Miss Jennean told us to go to the rear door and ask for Gwyneth."

The girl nodded and for a moment he thought he was getting somewhere. "Do you have a token?"

"I gave it to Mrs. DeMare."

Her eyebrows lifted in twin dubious arches over her pale eyes. "There's nobody here by that name."

Dammit. He was done trying to reason with this girl. He tried the door, but it was locked.

"Let me in."

"Not without a ticket," the girl said.

Fine, he'd buy a damned ticket. He dug in his pocket and came up with a handful of change.

"How much?"

"The evening performance is three dollars," the girl said.

He had two silver dollars on him, and the rest of his money was stowed in his saddlebag that was somewhere in this goddamned theater.

He flipped the girl the Morgans. "I'm short a buck, but if you'll let me fetch my saddlebag, which is inside the theater with Maggie, I'll gladly pay you the rest."

"Sorry, sir." She handed the money back to him. "The manager doesn't allow us to extend credit to patrons."

If Dade had thought he stood a snowball's chance in hell of kicking down the door he would have. He was surely getting nowhere trying to reason with the girl.

"Fetch your boss," he told her. "I want answers, and I damned sure want them now."

The girl gave an indignant huff that rankled him even more. But the slap in the kisser was when she closed the window and pulled the shade, blocking his view of her and the theater lobby.

If he had thought she'd gone to fetch her boss or someone in charge, he wouldn't have gotten so steamed. But he had a hunch she'd just flat-ass ignored him.

Dade pushed away from the window and paced the front of the theater, pissed off and filled with the nagging fear that Maggie was in trouble. It made no sense that the person who'd let them in earlier no longer existed.

Dammit, he'd talked with Mrs. DeMare or whoever the hell she was. That woman had let him and Maggie into this theater. By damn he'd find a way to get in again.

Chapter 21

Maggie lounged on the tufted chaise, too tired to fully appreciate the elegant room she'd been given. The warm bath had been divine. The soothing tea relaxed her even more.

Though she was sorely tempted to crawl onto the bed and fall asleep, she refrained. She was too worried about Dade.

He should have stabled the horses and returned long before she stepped from her bath. So what was keeping him? Had he decided to pay Mrs. Jarrett a visit without her company? Was he simply increasing his distance from Maggie now that they'd reached Dodge City?

She stared at his saddlebags resting beside the pannier. If he hadn't left his possessions here, she would've feared that he wasn't coming back.

The thought of never seeing him again filled her with a cold hollow ache. But that fate was inevitable.

How strange that when Doc Franklin had first suggested Dade deliver her to St. Louis in a month, she'd dreaded being in his company that long. Now one week had ended, and they were a step closer to finding Daisy.

When that happened, the closeness she shared with Dade would have to end. Or was it already over?

Last night she had feared that could be the case when

he refused to share the bed with her. He'd not made any move to be amorous or even jocular today.

Yes, something was definitely wrong.

A soft knock sounded at her door and she sat up, hoping it was him. "Come in."

An elegant woman swept into the room in a lavish flurry of skirts. "How are you feeling now?"

"Much better." She stared at the woman, certain she'd seen her before. "Have we met?"

"Indeed we have, but I was in costume." She closed the door and crossed to the window.

No, it couldn't be. "Mrs. DeMare?"

The petite beauty released a throaty laugh. "Mrs. DeMare is a nom de plume I've used when caution is advised. I'm Gwyneth Vale, the owner of the Iago Theater. You're safe from the man who brought you here."

"What? Why would you think that I needed protection from Dade?"

Gwyneth parted the curtain and looked out, and from her position on the chaise Maggie could tell that night had fallen. "The token Miss Jennean gave him was a signal to me that you are in danger. It's in your best interest and mine to discover if you are traveling with him against your will."

How to answer. Telling the truth would put an end to Gwyneth's doubts about Dade. But if Maggie lied, would she save Dade from a deadly confrontation with Allis Carson?

"You are taking an awfully long time answering a simple question," Gwyneth said.

That was because she wasn't accustomed to making decisions on her own. "Dade and I struck an agreement. I vowed to help him find his sister, and he promised to see me safely delivered to St. Louis in a month."

"Did that arrangement stipulate that you were to become his lover?"

Maggie couldn't stop her face from flushing, but the cause was annoyance that this stranger had asked something so personal. "That was my choice."

Gwyneth let the curtain fall and crossed the room to her again. "It still is, because if you wish I can arrange for you to leave here without his being the wiser."

Put that way, it was a tempting choice and probably the one she should make for Dade's sake. She finished the last of her tea and set the delicate cup aside.

It was likely that Dade would find Daisy soon. Surely the doctor or Mrs. Jarrett would remember the man's name.

Dade wouldn't need Maggie much longer. So if she took Gwyneth Vale's offer, he would be free of his obligation to take her to St. Louis. He could go on with his life, and she with hers.

But Maggie couldn't do it.

The simple fact was that she loved Dade Logan. By damn she selfishly wanted to spend what remained of this month and more with him if possible.

If he wanted her.

She felt tight and anxious about the rejection that surely loomed in her future. He'd want to protect his sister, and that would mean he'd want to get rid of the woman who was more trouble than she was worth.

But even that didn't stop her from wanting him.

"When I leave here, it'll be with Dade."

A slow smile played over Gwyneth's refined features. "As you wish. I'll send word down to admit Mr. Logan."

"Thank you. I was worried what was keeping him so long."

"Oh, he has been outside for quite some time, no doubt trying to figure out a way to break in." Gwyneth sighed, seeming not the least bit repentant over locking Dade out.

"I'll have some explaining to do to Mr. Logan, but if he's as worthy a man as you deem him to be, he'll understand my concerns."

Maggie wasn't so sure he'd see it that way. She swayed as she got to her feet or was the room spinning a bit?

"Perhaps I'd better go down with you."

"No. You should rest. I have an evening show that's scheduled to begin in half an hour," Gwyneth said as she laid her hands on Maggie's shoulders and eased her back down on the chaise lounge. "I'll speak with Mr. Logan then send him up to you. We would prefer that guests stay upstairs during a performance."

She wanted to protest over being verbally locked in a room again, but she was simply too tired. It was getting increasingly difficult to keep her eyes open. Even carrying on a conversation was just too taxing.

"Of course," Maggie said. "I'll wait here for Dade."

Gwyneth stepped out the door and paused. "We hold to a rather odd timetable here and partake of dinner after the last performance. If you prefer, I can have a meal brought up to your room now."

"In all honesty, I'm too tired to think about food."

"As I thought. Rest."

As soon as the door closed, Maggie lounged back on the chaise and fought the urge to surrender to the sleep that lured her. She didn't want to nod off now. She needed to talk with Dade when he came up about the plans made for her.

She wrinkled her nose at that annoying fact.

All her life she'd done as others had told her to do. At the foundling home, she'd been a model orphan, never crying for attention, never disobeying in the years she'd been there.

When Becka's family took her in, she'd tried to be just as dutiful. Living in a home was a whole new experience, as was having a sister. But Becka's death ended her dream of family, and the guilt that she'd carried for failing to be a good daughter haunted her upon her return to the foundling home.

Still, she did what she was told while she remained there. She'd smiled when folks came around, hoping. In vain, it turned out. She didn't fuss when she was put on the orphan train, because it was a chance for her to start over. To find a good family.

She squirmed and shifted uneasily, mindful of that long train ride that had brought her westward. There were so many children. Some crying. All scared for various reasons.

Maggie had known this was likely her last chance to find a family who'd take her because they wanted a daughter. And she knew her chances weren't good, because she wasn't small or dainty. A sturdy girl, the matron had remarked.

So she prayed hard that somebody would finally want her because she was a little girl who needed a family. Needed love.

But stop after stop she was looked over. She never found a place to call home. What was wrong with her?

She licked her lips and tried to force her muzzy mind to reason out her fate. Doc's solution, his way for her to escape a forced marriage sounded more and more like a prison sentence. She'd have to hide while taking her schooling and then what? Would she spend the rest of her life looking over her shoulder?

She didn't want that at all. She wanted freedom. She wanted to be wanted just for her. She refused to be a pawn.

She yawned and snuggled down on the chaise, simply unable to keep her eyes open any longer. Unable to think anymore.

Tomorrow. That's when she'd make her stand.

She'd confront Whit Ramsey. She'd make him understand that she wasn't going to marry him—by choice or force.

But she didn't want to wait until she returned to Colorado. She wanted him to know now. She wanted him to call off the bounty hunter.

Dade would help her. Dade . . . What was keeping him?

Maggie stretched, and that effort was nearly too much for her. She'd never had a bath drain her of energy before.

No, that wasn't quite true. She'd had the devil's time staying awake after drinking the tea.

She turned her head to the table and tried to bring the cup into focus. What was in it?

She reached for it, her eyelids too heavy to keep open. She heard the shatter of china, then nothing but blessed silence.

The Iago Theater was the craziest damned place Dade had ever stepped foot in. Nobody claimed to know Mrs. DeMare, which had to be a lie. But he wasn't going to argue the point.

After pounding on the rear door until his fists were sore, a dapper gentleman had opened it and let him in. He'd showed Dade straight up to Maggie's room, apologizing profusely for the mix-up.

"It was the token, you see," he said in a refined English accent that reminded him of Kirby Morris. "One can't be too careful."

"What do you mean?" The only token he knew of was the one Miss Jennean had pressed into his hand, claiming that it would be the key to grant them a safe place to stay in Dodge City.

The lanky man fidgeted with his hands. "I spoke out of turn, sir. Madam Vale will explain it all."

"Who's she?"

His boney chin lifted in a regal angle. "The owner of the Iago Theater."

They'd reached the room by then, and Dade gave up trying to make sense of this farcical story.

The room was set off so he just barely heard the actors on stage. It was large and fancy, and he was glad to see the pannier and his saddlebags were there.

Though he wanted to check to see that his money hadn't disappeared, Maggie commanded all his attention. She reclined on an elegant chaise, sleeping like an angel.

Dade finally allowed himself to take a deep breath. She was all right.

"One more thing you should be aware of," the gentleman said. "A sleeping draught was delivered here by mistake. The lady drank it all before the error was discovered."

He didn't believe that for a minute. Maggie had been drugged on purpose.

"How long ago?"

"Soon after her bath, I believe. I'm sure she will awaken in the morning completely refreshed," the gent said as he backed from the room and shut the door.

She might, but Dade was sure he wouldn't be able to close his eyes in this place. *Safe my ass!*

He checked the door and was surprised to find it unlocked. He closed and locked it from the inside, though he didn't want to bet that it would keep out intruders.

The windows opened, but there was nothing below them but a two-story drop. They were in effect trapped here.

Dade pulled the plush chair to the window and eased down onto it. He had a good view of the street, the door, and Maggie from here.

Seeing her vulnerable in sleep gave him that odd pull in his gut again. Though she'd been taken into a fine home, she'd been alone all her life.

If she recalled her family, she'd never mentioned them.

Maybe that was for the best—not remembering, that is. Too much of the past had stayed in his mind.

The arguments. The raised voices. The slap of skin on skin, and his ma crying afterward.

He'd hated his pa for that. He'd vowed he'd never lay an angry hand on the gentler sex, and he hadn't.

Hell, if he'd ever had the inclination to do so it would've been with Maggie. God knew she'd given him plenty of reasons to fume.

But now all he wanted to do was hold her. Keep her safe. Make love to her.

As folks left the theater and the streets grew deserted, he was beset by a feeling of protectiveness the likes of which he'd never felt before. Sure, he'd vowed to see that she arrived safely in St. Louis.

He was willing to guard her with his life on the trail.

But this feeling went beyond that.

The emotions bottled up inside him were akin to possessiveness. He wondered if being her first lover had triggered those feelings in him. He wondered if it was love.

He'd never been with an innocent woman before. Never been with a woman who needed a man as much as Maggie did.

He'd never needed a woman as badly as he did her. He didn't want to let her go, but he didn't see any way around it.

She'd spend the next year or so in St. Louis getting her nurse's training. After that he had no idea where she'd go.

He didn't know where he'd be a month from now, much less a year. So much depended on him finding Daisy.

If that fell apart on him again, he wasn't sure what he'd do. Maybe he would return to the Crown Seven.

If he did still own a share of it, he'd consider selling it. That way he could buy what he wanted. It'd be all his. No partners. No shares to haggle over.

He'd have a place to call home. But would he have anyone to share it with?

Dade rubbed his palms over his thighs, the chafe of his skin on his dungarees seeming loud in the quiet. Everyone in the theater must be in bed now. Everyone but he and Maggie, though she was dosing.

Dade crossed to the chaise and scooped her up in his arms as gently as he could. He laid her down on the bed just as carefully.

She didn't rouse. Didn't seem to know that he'd moved her.

His hands shook as he removed her dress and laid it on the chaise. He made quick work of stripping down to his undergarments.

The bed barely dipped as he stretched out beside her. He gathered her close, smiling that she snuggled against him even in sleep. "What am I going to do with you, Maggie mine?"

The tension that had gripped him all day began easing. They were safe for tonight. Tomorrow would likely bring its own set of troubles.

But tonight he'd do what he'd wanted to do last night. He'd hold her close to his heart and pretend that she was his not just for now, but forever.

Maggie came awake slowly, her senses humming with pleasure, and her body deliciously warm. She drew in a deep breath and recognized Dade's slightly spicy scent.

That triggered other sensations as well, each unfolding like a rosebud kissed by the sun. A masculine hand rested on her hip. Legs tangled together and the press of his bare skin hot against hers.

She wondered if waking in his arms was just a dream. Wondered if it would pop like a soap bubble if she moved.

Maggie uncurled the hand trapped between their bodies and skimmed her fingers over his taut belly. Muscles rippled beneath her touch, and his groan rumbled in her ear.

She smiled. This was very much real and very much wanted.

"Morning," he said, his voice rough from sleep.

She nuzzled her face against his broad chest, the heartbeat strong and sure. "Good morning."

"How do you feel?" he asked, the hand on her hip making a slow sweep up her back.

Safe. Desired. Suddenly hungry for more of his touch. But she kept those thoughts to herself, for this moment was too new and fragile, and she was too afraid she'd say the wrong thing and it would shatter.

"I'm sorry I fell asleep last night before you got back." She frowned as scattered memories flitted through her mind. "Gwyneth Vale shouldn't have locked you out."

"Who's she?"

"The owner," she said. "Gwyneth thought she had to protect me from you. Something about the token from Miss Jennean being a sign that I was in danger."

He snorted and rested his chin on her head, seeming in no hurry to get up. Not that she was complaining. She just regretted that she'd slept like the dead and hadn't enjoyed the comfort of his touch until she'd awakened.

"I damned sure didn't know what was going on," he said, and she caught the edge of annoyance in his voice. "I pounded on the back door but nobody answered. Then the girl in the ticket window swore she'd never heard of Mrs. DeMare."

What a bizarre chain of events. It all left her feeling a bit unsettled and less sure of their safety here.

"Apparently DeMare is a persona Gwyneth Vale adopts when the mood strikes." She pulled back then and stared into his eyes. "I waffled between worry that you'd abandoned me, and fear that something had happened to you."

His mouth hitched into a crooked smile that coaxed an answering one from her. "Here I thought I'd screwed up real bad and you were in trouble." His smile faded. "Guess you were, in a way. The butler told me you'd been given a sleeping draught by mistake."

That explained her inability to stay awake and the mild headache this morning. "No wonder I didn't hear you come in last night."

He pressed a kiss to her forehead, the gesture so soft that it brought tears to her eyes. "Got to tell you, Maggie, I don't care to stay here any longer than necessary."

He'd get no argument from her. "I assume we'll visit Mrs. Jarrett this morning?"

"As soon as we get out of here."

He rolled to his feet and padded across the room. Though she admired the shift of his thin undergarments, she disliked being denied another look at his naked form.

Seeing him begin dressing reminded her he was serious about leaving soon. She eased from the bed and donned her corselet.

"Will we return here tonight?" she asked as she slipped into her blue dress and buttoned up the bodice, looking like a lady for a change instead of a vagrant fresh off the trail.

"Nope. If we have to spend another night in Dodge City, I'd just as soon take my chances in a hotel."

That was a relief. Though she believed that Gwyneth Vale's actions were those of a woman who erred on the side of caution, she couldn't find a solid reason for her drugging her tea.

She made short work of pinning her hair up in a loose bun. "Then we'd best make sure we have everything of ours packed."

A quick check showed that nothing of hers was missing, but the brim on her straw shade hat was ruined. That left the wide brimmed farmer's hat as her only protection against the sun.

It was perfectly fine on the trail, but she dreaded wearing it with her dress.

"Nothing's missing," he said as he slung his saddlebags over his shoulder. "You going to wear that or not?"

"I don't have a choice." Maggie put on the farmer's hat and cringed at the picture she presented.

Dade appeared beside her, his mouth pulled into that crooked smile that made her heart skip a beat. "Here. I aimed to give you this when we reached St. Louis, but it appears you could use it now."

Maggie took the package he handed her and tore into it with all the enthusiasm of a child at Christmas. The new leghorn shade hat was just beautiful.

"Where did you get this?" she asked.

"Bought it the same day I got that farmer's hat for you." He downed his head, seeming a bit nervous.

She ran her fingers over the sassy brim and fingered the wide blue ribbon that matched her dress. "It's perfect."

The gift touched her like nothing else had in a long time. It was rare for her to have new clothes, since Caroline's mother saw that her daughter always wore the latest fashions. Maggie ended up with the castoffs, which were perfectly lovely gowns. Some had only been worn once.

But this . . . Well, nobody had ever bought her one new hat, let alone two.

She slipped the hat on and adjusted it so the brim dipped at a jaunty angle over her one eye. After securing it with a pin, she was ready to get this day started.

"Ready."

"Then let's get out of here," he said.

The theater was quiet as a tomb as they descended the

stairs to the first floor. They didn't see or hear anyone until they neared the rear door.

Maggie smelled bread baking, and her stomach grumbled as if to remind her she'd missed dinner last night. But after the drugging incident, she didn't want to test her luck with any food or drink.

Dade seemed to be of the same mind, because he hustled her out the door without bothering to drink his usual morning coffee. They walked up the alley to the street. She was relieved to leave this odd place.

"The livery is about three blocks this way." Dade adjusted his packs and headed off with her right beside him.

"I could carry my satchel," she said.

"I've got it."

And she knew that was that. "I thought Mrs. DeMare directed you the other way last night."

"She did. Took me a good spell to backtrack and find the livery."

Another oddity about that place.

Few people were out this early, and maybe that's why Maggie felt so vulnerable. She was glad when they reached the livery.

She stood just inside the wide double doors while Dade talked with the owner. From what she overheard, Mrs. Jarrett lived on the other side of town.

When he hired a buggy, she nearly cried out with relief. She wasn't the least bit sore this morning, but she wasn't anxious to strain her muscles again. That would come soon enough when they set off in search of Daisy.

Dade stowed their gear in the livery and helped her up. She settled onto the seat and adjusted her skirts.

"You want to eat first?" he asked.

She was hungry, but she sensed time was of the essence here. "Let's visit Mrs. Jarrett first."

It would likely be a very short visit. She just doubted

that the woman would welcome them, especially once she discovered why they were there.

With a flick of the lines, Dade had the buggy moving smoothly forward. The canopy kept the sun from bearing down on them and provided a bit of privacy as well.

"What will we do if Mrs. Jarrett proves uncooperative?" Maggie asked as they left this side of town behind them.

"Heckle her until I find out all she knows about Daisy."

Dade had no difficulty finding Mrs. Jarrett's house. Not only had the liveryman given excellent directions, the Victorian house with twin turrets would be hard to miss.

He parked the buggy at the curb and set the brake, but he didn't make a move to get out. Instead he just stared at the big house.

"Penny for your thoughts," she said.

That earned him a quick grin. "I was just wondering what Daisy's life would've been like if they'd raised her as their own. She'd have been one of them debutantes."

"Don't think that money can buy happiness," she said. "Caroline had everything a girl could ask for except freedom. She was expected to live her life a certain way, and would have if she hadn't taken ill."

He shook his head and climbed from the buggy, extending a hand to help her down. "Let's pay the lady a visit."

Everything about the house was tidy, from the urns overflowing with ivy to the doormat that was positioned just so in front of the oval glass door. Dade gave the acorn knocker three smart raps, then stood beside her and silently waited for a reply.

They didn't have a long wait.

A woman opened the door, her hair white as cotton and her face as deeply wrinkled as a raisin. If her starched white apron hadn't proclaimed her position in the household, the small silver salver she held certainly would.

"Who may I say is calling?" the woman asked.

"Sheriff Logan," he said, and Maggie bit back a smile. "It's important that I speak with Mrs. Jarrett."

The housekeeper was already pushing open the door. "Come right in, sheriff. Have a seat in the parlor while I announce your arrival to Mrs. Jarrett."

Dade escorted Maggie into a fussy room dominated by an intricate étagère laden with all manner of prize possessions. The furniture consisted of a deep claret brocade sofa, and a gentleman's and a lady's chair. Pastoral landscape and still life paintings hung on the wall.

A life-size portrait of a girl roughly four years old filled the space above the mantel. Her black hair was done in curls held with pink bows that matched the trim on her frilly dress.

She was neither beautiful nor homely. Just an average child who seemed far too stern for one that age.

The scuff near the door had Dade and Maggie turning around. This painfully thin woman had to be Mrs. Jarrett.

She walked into the room with the aid of a cane. Her steel gray hair was scraped back off a face that didn't appear to have smiled in ages, if ever.

"That's my daughter Melanie," Mrs. Jarrett said. "Tomorrow will mark the twenty-first anniversary of her death."

"My condolences, ma'am," Dade said, and Maggie murmured her sympathy as well.

Mrs. Jarrett eased down on the lady's chair that faced the mantel, but turned a bit to stare at Maggie. "Who are you?"

"My wife," Dade said.

Maggie promptly clacked her teeth together to keep from gaping and dropped onto the sofa a bit harder than she'd intended. But Mrs. Jarrett wouldn't have noticed for she'd turned to fix her full attention on Dade, who'd taken the place beside Maggie.

"What brings a sheriff to my door?" Mrs. Jarrett asked.

"I'm looking for my sister," he said.

Mrs. Jarrett regarded him with cold gray eyes. "If she was a domestic I hired once, I suggest you speak with my housekeeper. She would know the staff that has come and gone over the years."

"She wasn't a servant, ma'am."

"Then what was she?"

"A child," Dade said. "Your late husband claimed her off the orphan train back in '74. But I heard she didn't stay with you long."

Mrs. Jarrett's mouth puckered into an unbecoming knot. "Orphan train, indeed. I refused to raise his bastard when my own precious daughter was barely cold in her grave."

Maggie felt the tension roll off Dade in waves and marveled that he could keep a civil tongue. "She wasn't a bastard, ma'am. She is my sister, and I'd surely like to know who took her in after you turned her out."

The old woman glared at him as she got to her feet, and Maggie was sure she wouldn't answer. "Barton was his name. He owned a cattle ranch in Colorado. That's all I know, so leave me be."

Dade rose, and Maggie did too. "Thank you for your time, ma'am."

Mrs. Jarrett turned her back on them and stared at the portrait of her daughter. Maggie was certain she'd never seen such a bitter woman. If only she'd had the heart long ago to channel the affection she'd had for her daughter to a lonely orphan girl.

"What do we do now?" Maggie asked once they returned to the buggy.

"Hard to say. A lot of ranchers back then owned a helluva lot of cattle but damned little land." Dade set the buggy in motion, the hard set of his features betraying more tension than she recalled seeing in some time. "I'll head down to the stockyards. Hopefully somebody there will remember him."

And if they didn't? Well, they had a name to go by this time. That was far more than they'd started with.

The lowing of cattle reached her long before they arrived at the depot. But though wooden pens extended as far as she could see, there were few cattle waiting to be loaded onto the train.

"Damn, I don't like leaving you here," Dade said. "But it could take a spell and a good deal of walking and talking to find anyone who remembers Barton. They may not feel inclined to talk if a woman's around."

She certainly understood the need for prudence. "I'll wait inside the depot."

At first she thought he'd balk, but he gave a curt nod and got out. He flicked the railroad agent some change. "Keep an eye on my buggy."

"Yes, sir."

Dade guided Maggie to the depot and stuck his head inside first, likely checking to see if Allis Carson was lurking. But instead of hustling her inside, he took her by the arms and stared into her eyes.

"I'll be back as soon as I can," he said.

She smiled, nervous about what the future would hold now. "Take your time."

Dade hesitated as if he wanted to say more, then he dipped his hat brim and was gone.

Maggie crossed to one of the windows and watched him cross the railroad tracks. In moments he'd disappeared amid the warren of pens and cowboys.

If Mrs. Jarrett was right and Barton was a Colorado rancher, dare Maggie return there with Dade?

Nervous energy expanded within her and kept her on edge. Yes, she was worried that Dade wouldn't find Daisy. She worried that Allis Carson would find her and drag her back to Burland. Back to Harlan Nowell and a forced marriage to Whit Ramsey.

The notion of confronting Whit face to face crossed her mind. It'd come to her last night but had gotten muddled with everything else that had happened this morning.

Now she looked at it anew. He was surely due a piece of her mind for hiring a bounty hunter to track her down like she was a criminal. And just maybe she could convince him that she wasn't about to marry him either.

She walked to the ticket window, determined to make a stand for once.

"How can I help you, ma'am?" the ticket agent asked.

She blew out a heavy breath. "I need to send a telegram to Burland, Colorado."

Chapter 22

After an hour of asking around the stockyards about Barton, Dade found an old man who claimed to have known him.

"Yep, Barton drove his cattle up the old Santa Fe trail until they put the train through," the old man said. "Ain't seen or heard from him since."

"Anything you recollect about him?" Dade asked.

"Well, he was a Texan and one big mean sonofabitch. Fought in the War of Rebellion, and he didn't hold with no truck from nobody."

Not the kind of man Dade would have wished Daisy to end up with. "Was he a family man?"

"Never mentioned having a wife or young'ns, but then I ain't one to pry." The narrow-eyed glare the old man gave him said he thought Dade was doing just that. "Why are you asking, boy?"

Dade saw no use in lying. "I was told that Barton adopted my sister when her first adoptive family gave her up."

"Can't help you there."

He wondered if the old man would, even if he knew. So

many of the old-timers were close-mouthed about their pasts, and many had good reason.

"Where's Barton's ranch?" he asked.

The old man scowled and kicked at a red rock, and Dade knew he was debating about being honest or clamming up on him. "He had a spread in Las Animas near the Purgatoire River."

"Much obliged," Dade said.

He took his leave of the old man and trudged back to the depot, having enough information now to set out west. West.

Dammit all, he hated to haul Maggie back to Colorado. But what could he do with her in the meantime?

Maybe it'd be best to just head east and stick around St. Louis until Maggie was accepted in the nursing school. He'd waited twenty years to find Daisy. Another few weeks shouldn't make any difference.

He'd promised to watch over Maggie, and he was honor bound to do just that. Only he knew deep inside that his reasons for staying with her went far beyond that.

She'd nested in his heart. Thinking of her made him smile. Being with her eased the turmoil that lived deep in his soul. Making love with her was the best thing that had ever happened to him.

He could see himself waking up beside her for the rest of his life and feeling fulfilled. He could see her flitting around a nice house, the mistress of her own home. Their house.

That's all it took to pop the image.

He'd lost his shares in the ranch. He had no place to call home. No money to buy a place, and no job to support a wife.

He had nothing but three horses, saddlebags, and a pannier that held his few possessions. Even if the gossip Miss Jennean had passed on to him held merit, he wouldn't be able to offer Maggie a home like she was accustomed to off his share of the Crown Seven.

She greeted him with a smile when he stepped into the depot, and all his noble ideas of letting her go threatened to crumble. He had to hold to his promise. He had a few weeks left to enjoy her company, and he damn sure was going to savor every second.

"Barton runs a ranch near Las Animas," he said.

"Is that far from here?"

He shook his head. "It's halfway between here and Pueblo."

She paled, and he knew she'd just realized they'd be uncomfortably close to the area she'd escaped. "We've come close to going full circle in a week."

"Yep." He jammed his thumbs under his gun belt to keep from reaching for her, torn between doing what he ached to do and doing the right thing. "If you want, we'll head to St. Louis—"

"No. I'm going with you."

That suffocating fear that she'd want to leave him vanished like smoke. They'd come this far together. They might as well ride it out to the end now.

He took her elbow and smiled at the feeling of rightness that came over him. "Let's head back to the livery."

"I hope that the liveryman has a place where I can change into my trail clothes," she said.

Damn, he hated putting her through another long ride. "I'll be right back."

He strode to the ticket counter. "When's the train leave for Santa Fe?"

"In an hour and twenty minutes."

That'd give them time to eat breakfast before pulling out. "I need passage to Las Animas for two passengers plus space for three horses and tack."

The ticket agent tallied up the cost. It'd take a chunk out of his savings, but he wanted to get there before nightfall.

Dade doled out the money and pocketed the tickets and stockcar vouchers. He returned to Maggie and escorted her out the door.

"We're taking the train to Las Animas," he said.

"We are?"

"I want to get there before dark." And he wanted her rested for a change. "Let's return the buggy, get our horses and gear, and head back here. Once the horses are in line to be loaded on, we'll find a diner."

"It sounds wonderful." Too wonderful. Too right.

Maggie let her hand rest in his a bit longer than necessary, desperate to steal a caress, relieved beyond words that she wouldn't have to ride a horse all day again.

Her pleasure was tinged with guilt. She wasn't sorry she'd sent a telegram to Whit, but she should tell Dade what she'd done.

But throughout their meal, she never could find the right time to tell him. She'd wait until they were on the train headed west.

The ride to Las Animas was enjoyable, partly because it was uneventful and partly because Maggie had the pleasure of Dade's company. More than once she'd seen young ladies cast longing looks his way, but he never gave them one bit of encouragement.

He'd be a faithful husband, she thought.

But she feared he wouldn't be hers.

Even if her telegram dissuaded Whit from his pursuit of her, she knew Dade wouldn't make that type of commitment when his own future was so questionable.

And always, his drive to find Daisy overshadowed his own wants—whatever they may be.

"What are your plans once you are reunited with Daisy?" she asked.

"That depends on her," he said. "I'd be happy to live close to her home and be a part of her life again, if she wanted me to."

Those last five words held a wealth of longing and fear. He'd been denied his family for too long, but would Daisy welcome the brother she hadn't seen in twenty years? Would she be content to have him suddenly live on the fringe of her life?

The whistle screamed, and the train slowed. They were here, and she still hadn't told him what she'd done.

Later. She'd find the right time to tell him later when they were alone.

Dade was convinced he'd been lied to about Barton when day turned to night and he still hadn't found anyone in Las Animas who'd heard of him. He wouldn't be surprised if the old man at the stockyards had sent him on a wild goose chase out of spite.

The death of Mrs. Jarrett's daughter had soured her on life. But he'd believed the old-timer in Dodge City when he'd told Dade about Barton. Now he wasn't sure.

He'd started asking if anyone knew the Texan shortly after he and Maggie ate dinner in the hotel restaurant. With her safely tucked away in the room resting, he tramped the streets asking damned near everyone he passed if they knew Barton.

So far none had.

He was about to give up for the day and head back to the hotel and Maggie when a wrangler of advanced age who'd been leaning against the corner of the dry goods store straightened as Dade approached. Something about the man triggered a warning in him.

That feeling turned to alarm when the man stepped in his path. "You still looking for Barton?"

"I am," Dade said. "You know where I can find him?"

"Yep. Got him a spread near the Purgatoire River, not far from La Junta, which is why folks around here don't much know him."

"But you do," Dade said, not entirely convinced.

"Worked for Barton for ten years back in the day when money could be made rounding up mustangs," the wrangler said. "If you want, I can draw you a map showing you how to get there."

Dade was torn. If he'd have found just one other person who'd known Barton, he'd have believed this man.

He had doubts, but not enough of them to refuse a map to the ranch. "I'd be mighty grateful for directions. What's the name of his spread?"

"Circle DB," the wrangler said as he thumbed a cigarette paper from a pack. "Named it after his daughter."

Daisy Barton? Dade went hot and cold inside watching the wrangler sketch a crude map with the stub of a pencil, willing this to be the time he finally found his sister.

"How big a place is it?" Dade asked, taking the map and studying the faint lines and squiggles.

"Not much to talk about now. Barton ran cattle on thousands of acres, but only held title to a squatter's portion."

That would explain why the wrangler didn't work for Barton anymore. His ranch, cattle, and hired hands had been severely reduced. He just hoped the place hadn't fallen into squalor.

"Much obliged for the map," Dade said, and tossed the man two bits.

It wasn't much by any standards. But he had to watch his pennies after splurging on the train ride.

He crossed the alley and passed an adobe building that turned a rich brown in the setting sun. The shop next to it was a modern glass-front style that housed an assay office and an attorney.

Dade glanced back at the wrangler, but he was long gone. He poked his head inside the office door to find the clerk donning his bowler hat, likely about to leave for the day.

"You ever hear of a Circle DB ranch down around the Purgatoire River?" Dade asked.

The clerk mumbled the name over and over. "Sure. Was a time when they ran more cattle than anyone else in these parts."

"Thanks for your time."

Dade picked up his pace, anxious to get back to the hotel and tell Maggie the good news. They'd head out tomorrow morning, but tonight would be theirs to savor.

She was sitting by the window when he walked into their room. For a moment he just drank in the sight of her. She was on his mind more times than not. She was in his heart too. How was he going to be able to let her go?

He locked the door before crossing to her. "The ranch is half a day's ride from here."

She met him halfway, her arms open and her smile welcoming. "I'm going with you."

He drew her into his arms and kissed her, drinking in her passion like a man parched for water. Refusing her never crossed his mind.

As long as they were together, she was his. He damn sure didn't want to think beyond that point right now.

The guilt that had been nagging at Maggie drifted from her mind as Dade's hands made bold sweeps up and down her body. She never knew a caress could bring every nerve in her body to life. She hadn't believed that touching a man could give her so much pleasure.

But then she'd never met a man like Dade before.

She glided her palms up his muscled arms and curved her fingers over his shoulders, bowing into him. "Mmm."

"That's it." As she hoped he'd do, his arms came around her and held her tight. "Move with me."

The unease and hesitation that she'd honed from a young age to keep people from getting too close to her drifted away, replaced by a sense of safety that she'd only felt with him. Yes, he'd vowed to keep her safe, but his protectiveness went beyond duty.

In his arms she not only felt protected, she felt wanted. She felt loved, and that was something she'd never experienced before.

Nobody had ever loved Margaret Ann Sutten. At least nobody that she could remember.

She sensed each rise and fall and matched him.

Her clothes fell away slowly with him pausing to kiss the skin he'd bared. He ripped his clothes off quickly, which was fine by her because she longed to run her hands over his skin, marveling at the muscles that flexed at her touch.

He kissed her so deeply her head reeled and her knees went weak. If he hadn't been holding her, she would have crumbled at his feet.

She realized she trusted him to give her pleasure too, and oh, how he could pleasure her. He rocked against her in a slow, sultry tempo that she fell into naturally. She let her head loll back as sensation after sensation pounded through her, thinking she was decadent for letting him do the seducing while she enjoyed every second of the sensual adoration.

"That's it, Maggie mine," he said, backing to the bed.

She smiled against his lips, touched by the endearment, touched by his patience in this.

Yes, he might not love her with his heart, but he acted as if he cherished her as a lover. He made the moment special. Made her feel special.

They fell onto the bed with her on top of him, straddling

his lean hips. His caresses grew bolder and more frenzied, but then so were the odd sounds bubbling up from her.

"You're ready," he said, his finger slipping into her.

Desire rippled through her in hot waves. She pressed against him on a hum of pleasure. "For you. Only for you."

He groaned, shifting again as she came down on him. She threw her head back as she took him into her, holding him there as tightly as he'd held her against him.

"Yes," he groaned, grasping her hips and guiding her through this new way to love him.

She rode him hard, moving with him yet feeling bold and in charge. She wasn't naïve about lovemaking now. She realized that each time when she trembled and reached for that final thrum of pleasure, he'd withdrawn from her. She understood he did it to guard against pregnancy.

But to her it smacked of rejection. Just when they were as close as a man and woman could be, he'd denied her that final intimacy.

No more. This time she wanted all of him. This time she wouldn't be denied. This time she was willing to do anything to achieve that goal.

They strained together, their bodies slick with sweat. She felt the change in his rhythm, the urgency in his touch. Desire began splintering off in brilliant strokes that left every nerve throbbing, every muscle quivering with the force that was bearing down on them locked together.

"Stay with me," she said, clinging to him.

"Maggie mine," he groaned, teeth clenched as he tried to hold back what she wanted most.

"Please," she said, her legs locked on his hips and her eyes begging him to give her this. "Please."

She tightened around him, and streaks of energy exploded within her. She heard his groan. Felt him plunge deeper into her. Marveled at the hot seed spurting into her that chased away the chill that had persisted in tormenting her.

Before the last tremors shook his big body, she collapsed upon him. She thrilled at the strong heart pounding beneath her ear. She gloried in the knowledge that this moment sang of the freedom she'd been denied all her life.

"We took a helluva risk then," he said.

"I know, but some things in life are worth the risk." With her pleasure ebbing, guilt nipped at her again.

Tell him. Tell him now while he'd mellowed. Tell him before he finds out on his own.

"I sent Whit Ramsey a telegram today."

Eyes that had been drowsy with desire sharpened. "What?"

She swallowed the trepidation stealing over her, leaving her cold and trembling. "I'm tired of running. I want a normal life. I want him to leave me be."

"And you think he's going to back off just because you begged him to?"

"Maybe," she said, and hated the childish note that crept into her voice. "Whit won't want me if there's a chance I could be carrying another man's child."

She didn't think his eyes could get any harder or darker, but she was wrong. "You used me to turn Ramsey against you?"

"Yes, but I wanted to make love with you, too. I wanted to feel closer to you. Why can't you understand?"

He rolled away from her and gave her his back. "Go to sleep, Maggie. We've got a long day ahead of us tomorrow."

She curled in a ball and refused to cry. Had she gotten what she wanted only to lose the man she loved?

After four hours in the saddle, Dade could see why nobody in Las Animas knew about Barton. He'd followed the river to where the grassland began to give way to deep arroyos.

If the old wrangler had drawn this map correctly, then they were less than five miles from the Circle DB ranch. He stood in the saddle and took another long careful look at the area.

He saw nothing that would alert him that they were being followed. They were alone. Just him and Maggie and thousands of acres of waist-deep grasslands.

Cattle would get mighty damned fat off this prairie grass. Yet he hadn't seen evidence of a cow in twenty miles or so.

The old wrangler said Barton had fallen on hard times. Shit, had he nearly lost the ranch? Were they hard-scrap farmers just trying to hold on to what they had?

"We're almost there," he said. "You need to take a rest?"

She shook her head, still sitting straight in the saddle and still not meeting his eyes. "I'm fine."

That was bullshit. She might be tolerating the ride, but she wasn't fine at all.

They'd had the best damned sex he'd ever had in his life, then she had fessed up what she'd done and ruined it all. Fine time for her to decide to bait the bear.

Not that he blamed her for standing her ground. What annoyed him was that she'd made the decision on her own. She'd cut him out, not even bothering to get his opinion.

"Dade? Did you hear that?" she asked.

He slammed the door on those musings and forced his attention to the here and now. Bells. He heard the distinct clang of a dinner bell.

"What is it?" she asked.

He smiled at his pretty orphan who had all the smarts of a rich girl and none of the glory. "That's the dinner bell on the nearest ranch. Let's head that way."

He held to an easy canter when every nerve in his body

screamed at him to ride like thunder to the Circle DB. He damn sure knew better.

Riding onto a spread like that could get him shot. But the main reason was Maggie. He wasn't about to make her life hell so he'd get to the ranch a few minutes sooner.

They topped a rise, and he reined up as the ranch came into view. It was worse than he'd thought.

There were plenty of pens and corrals, but he only saw a handful of stock. The outbuildings were frame and in serious need of repair.

The adobe house sat low to the ground and blended into the landscape. It looked deserted, yet the dinner bell continued to clang—a discordant sound that echoed for miles and chafed his nerves raw.

"If this is a cattle ranch, where are the cattle?" Maggie asked.

Damned if he knew. "The wrangler I talked to said that Barton had fallen on hard times."

"Poor Daisy."

He didn't want to think how she'd been living. Without a word, he heeled his mount to head out, knowing Maggie's and the packhorse would follow.

The place didn't look any more welcoming up close. But the pair of horses in the corral looked well tended. They looked out of place to boot.

He dismounted, his thoughts on his sister. As soon as his boots hit the ground he thought better of it. But Maggie—his sweet Maggie—chose this time to get off her little black mare on her own.

"Where is everyone?" she asked.

Dade stepped between the two horses and hemmed her between them. Not ideal cover, but it was the best he could do.

"Damned if I know," he said, his voice barely above a whisper.

She rested one small hand on his back, her fingers flexing like she wanted to crawl under his skin. He wished to hell he could burrow into a hole and drag her in with him.

The unmistakable click of a trigger being hammered back broke the silence. Sonofabitch—he'd walked into a trap.

"Nice of you to bring her to me," came a voice that scorched his soul like hot coals.

Dade yanked Maggie in front of him and pulled leather as he whirled. But the restive horses' rumps bumped together and blocked his view of and aim at Allis Carson.

That didn't stop the bounty hunter. He fired two shots.

Dade's gelding screamed and took off. Maggie's mare followed at a gallop. Dade grabbed Maggie's hand and ran to the house, his revolver barking lead to give them a minute. But Carson had taken cover behind a dilapidated buckboard and just kept firing.

Dade yanked on the door, but it was locked. Panic welled inside him as he threw his shoulder against the panel. Once. Twice. It shuddered but held tight.

"Kiss your ass good-bye, lawman," Carson said.

Dade pushed Maggie behind him as he spun around and stared down the barrel of Allis Carson's six-shooter. Anger and regret collided in a heartbeat.

He was trapped. Dade could get off one shot, but he'd likely take a bullet too.

Carson strode toward him, his gait cocky, his eyes wild with the promise of a kill and the spoils of victory. "Before I kill her, I'm going to enjoy taking her over your dead carcass."

Damn the bastard to hell and back! He took aim and fired just as he caught movement out of the corner of his eye. His Peacemaker clicked. Helluva time for his gun to jam.

Carson spun toward the shadow of movement and emptied his gun, then dropped and rolled. A shotgun boomed to his right, once, then again.

The bounty hunter bowed backward and clutched his thigh, then made a jerky movement forward. Dade knew Carson had been hit, but the bounty hunter still tried to crawl behind the buckboard. He had nearly made it when he suddenly stopped.

Dade stared at him for the longest time, waiting for some sign that confirmed he was still alive. But Carson didn't move.

An unnatural quiet settled over them, the air thick and acrid from the cloud of gunpowder and spent lead.

Dade tore his eyes off Carson and stared at the shooter. He waited for some emotion to bubble up in him.

Nothing came as he stared at his pa, sprawled on the ground in a pool of his own blood.

"Are they dead?" Maggie whispered behind him, her small hands gripping his sides.

"Don't know." He almost said he didn't care either, but he did care.

Dammit all, this was his pa. A rattlesnake mean outlaw who'd turned his back on Dade years ago.

Countless nights Dade had hoped his pa would return, that he'd apologize for making the biggest mistake of his life. That he'd take Dade and Daisy out of the orphanage and go home.

It never happened. It never would have either.

Yet Clete Logan had put his life before Dade's today.

Dade ejected the jammed cartridge from his six-shooter and automatically slipped a new one into the chamber, his fingers surprisingly sure.

"Stay here," he told Maggie.

He slipped off the porch and eased toward the buckboard, his heartbeat striking an erratic beat as he faced the unknown. Allis Carson lay facedown on the ground, blood pooling from the gaping hole in his thigh. Another wound soaked the ground beneath his head.

Dade kicked the bounty hunter's revolver aside and toed his shoulder. His hat fell to the side and exposed what remained of the man's head.

Slowly, Dade holstered his gun and walked over to Clete Logan. Judging from the blood soaking his pa's shirtfront, he expected he'd given up the ghost.

Pale glassy eyes fixed on his. His pa's mouth moved and Dade was obliged to go down on a knee to hear him.

"Is he dead?" Clete asked.

"Yep."

Clete swallowed with effort, his gaunt face twisting in a grimace as he did so. "Good. Now I can rest in peace."

Dade doubted there'd be any peace for the outlaw who'd gunned down innocent men. He stared at the man who'd come here for one revenge and tried to feel something besides pity and disgust. But he couldn't.

His pa had been tracking Allis Carson for one reason—he'd vowed to kill the man who'd done the same to his outlaw brothers. He'd have done the same no matter who Carson had cornered.

The outlaw let out a choked cough, his eyes an unnatural white now. "Haul my ass into the U.S. Marshal. You might as well collect the reward."

"Don't want blood money."

"Fool. I owe you that and more."

His pa still didn't understand that he'd just wanted a parent who gave a damn. No amount of reward money could make up for those lost years.

"Why'd you do it?" he asked. "Why'd you give up your family?"

Clete Logan's upper lip curled in a mockery of a smile. "Never wanted the responsibility."

His chest heaved once, then the outlaw went dead still.

Maggie's hands rested on Dade's shoulders. "Are you all right?"

He nodded, feeling numb inside. That's all the emotion he could muster for his pa.

Dade got to his feet and drew Maggie into his arms. He scanned the ranch again and this time hoped it was truly deserted.

"Let's take a look around," he said. "I have to make sure Daisy isn't here."

She wasn't. Dade found a back window busted out and crawled inside the house. There wasn't a stick of furniture or any indication that anyone had lived here in years. Where had Barton gone? How long back? Was Daisy still with him?

"What are you going to do about the dead?" Maggie asked.

"Haul them into the marshal."

He'd put the reward money to good use, even though it chaffed him to collect it. And the only way those wanted posters would come down was to turn the outlaw in.

"I'm sorry," Maggie said.

"So am I." He slid his arm around her shoulders and squinted at the sky. "We'll head out as soon as I round up our horses and heft Carson and Pa over their saddles."

"Back to La Junta?" she asked.

He shook his head. "Pueblo. Tavish is working out of there. I trust him to see that Clete Logan is finally put to rest. We'll stay there overnight, then take the eastbound train to St. Louis."

She stiffened in his arms. "What about your search for Daisy?"

"It could take months for me to find out what happened to Barton." If he was lucky. "I promised I'd see you to St. Louis—"

"I'm going back to Placid." She slipped out of his arms and he felt the distance yawn between them. "I have to make Whit understand that I won't be the pawn in his dealings with Harlan Nowell. If I don't, I'll be looking over my shoulder the rest of my life, wondering if either man has hired another bounty hunter to haul me back to Burland."

He didn't like the idea of her confronting Ramsey, but she was right. Neither of them could look to the future until they'd buried the ghosts of their pasts.

"All right," he said. "But I'm going with you."

She smiled, and something warm expanded in his chest to thaw the ice surrounding his heart. "I hoped you'd say that."

Yep, the death of the Logan Gang freed him from being linked to outlaws. In time their names would be forgotten.

Then there was Daisy to fret over. Somewhere out there he had a sister who didn't even remember him. A sister that he feared he would have the devil's time finding.

But if Miss Jennean was right, he still had unfinished business with Reid Barclay. He had to settle that before he could forge a future.

With Maggie?

God knew he wanted her. He couldn't think of living without her. But he didn't know if she felt the same, and now wasn't the time to ask.

Chapter 23

A hanging was the only thing that drew a bigger crowd than the arrival of a man leading horses with lifeless forms draped over their saddles. Folks knew the dead had to be outlaws, and speculation ran wild about who'd finally met his fate and who'd gunned them down.

Dade was mighty glad that a deputy was on hand to watch over the dead. He ushered Maggie into the U.S. Marshal's Office and straight into Tavish's path.

"Who'd you bring in?" Tavish asked.

"Clete Logan and Allis Carson." Dade went on to explain what had happened on the Circle DB, leaving nothing out.

"I figured it was just a matter of time before the two of them drew on each other." Tavish crossed to his desk, wrote out a voucher and handed it to Dade. "On behalf of the United States Marshal's Service, I thank you for upholding the law and bringing in a criminal. You can claim your reward at the bank."

Dade folded the voucher and slipped it into his vest pocket. He had enough money now to buy a nice spread and settle down.

For the first time in his life he'd found a woman he

wanted to spend the rest of his life loving. But he hesitated to ask for her hand.

Oh, she'd told him she loved him. But could a city girl be content to be a rancher's wife? Would she one day resent that she'd given up her dream to follow his?

Those doubts were more than enough to keep him from proposing to her. He'd waited this long to find her. He could wait a bit longer until he was sure their dreams would mesh and not collide.

Maggie flicked a glance at Dade as the train rattled over the tracks toward Placid. He'd been withdrawn ever since the shootout.

Then when they'd made love last night at the hotel, he'd held her long into the night, as if he did not want to let her go. If she just knew what was on his mind . . .

Though she longed to comfort him, she sensed he wouldn't accept it readily. So she left him alone to come to grips with his grief and silently fretted about what today would bring.

The train pulled in to Placid thirty minutes late, and Dade and Maggie were the only ones to get off. While he saw to the horses and their bags, she crossed to the window to see if Whit had responded to her telegram.

"Nothing came over the wire," the railroad agent said. "But a gentleman left this letter here for you."

She tore it open with trembling fingers and quickly read the message.

We need to talk. I've taken a room at Gant's boardinghouse. Respectfully, W. R.

Maggie closed her eyes and gave in to a shiver of pure fear. Dear God, Whit was here waiting for her.

"You all right, Miss Logan?" the agent asked.

"Yes, I'm fine." She looked out the window at Dade who was waiting impatiently for the horses to be unloaded. "Tell Dade I went to Mrs. Gant's."

"Sure thing."

The walk there had never seemed longer to her. Perhaps she should have waited for Dade to join her, but this wasn't his battle. And down deep she still worried that Whit would turn on Dade in anger.

She stepped into the house she'd considered her refuge to find Whit Ramsey sitting in the parlor. The stern expression he'd always worn was gone, replaced by an easy smile that she didn't recognize.

"Thank God you came back," Caroline said, rising from her chair and crossing to Maggie with just the aid of a cane.

"What are you doing here with him?" Maggie asked.

Caroline beamed. "We are on our honeymoon."

The look of adoration her foster sister gave Whit left Maggie thunderstruck. She looked fit and happy. With Whit.

"I don't understand. This man didn't want you as his wife," Maggie said.

"Actually that wasn't true," Caroline said. "Father had told Whit that my health had taken a downward turn and that I'd likely not survive the winter. He compounded that lie by telling Whit that you'd agreed to take my place as his wife with my blessing."

"Why would he say such a thing?" Maggie asked.

"I can answer that one," Whit said. "If I married Nowell's daughter, I acquired her shares of Nowell Mining and gained control of his holdings. If I wed you instead, I'd only become his equal partner."

"But after you escaped Burland and Father's clutches, he

feared that Whit would insist on marrying me," Caroline said. "So Father sent me to a sanitarium in Manitou Springs."

Whit patted Caroline's hand and smiled at his wife. "It took me awhile to find Caroline. When I finally did, I asked her to be my wife."

"We married at the Springs, much to Father's outrage," Caroline said.

Maggie took that in and realized that Harlan Nowell had carefully manipulated them to do his bidding. "No wonder he hired a bounty hunter to bring me back to Burland."

Caroline grasped Maggie's forearm with trembling hands. "Oh, God, Maggie. If it were only that simple. You're in grave danger."

"What are you talking about?" she asked, trembling now too.

"Father held you to blame for losing control of his empire," Caroline said. "Because if you hadn't run away, Whit wouldn't have visited me in the sanitarium in hopes that I knew where you'd gone. We wouldn't have realized we'd been lied to from the start, and we surely wouldn't have had the chance to form an affection for each other."

Whit nodded in agreement with his wife. "Your telegram made me realize that something quite foul was afoot. So we confronted Harlan. He admitted he hired a bounty hunter to find you. But after our marriage, Harlan wired Carson and ordered him to kill you."

Maggie pinched her eyes shut, reminded of a similar story that Mrs. Gant had told to her. At the deserted Circle DB ranch, Allis Carson had come terrifyingly close to murdering her as he'd been hired to do.

"You need to come with us," Caroline said, drawing Maggie's attention back to her. "You'll be safe in our house until Whit can figure out a way to diffuse this situation."

"There's no need for Maggie to hide," Dade said, his voice strong. "Allis Carson is dead."

Whit tensed. "Are you absolutely certain?"

Dade gave one curt nod. "Saw him gunned down myself. What about Nowell? What's to stop him from hiring another gun?"

Maggie's knees threatened to buckle, for she'd not thought of that very real threat. How could one man be so vindictive?

"Father was so enraged over it all that he suffered a fit of apoplexy. He can't move, talk, write, or care for himself," Caroline said.

"The doctor told us he's failing quickly," Whit added.

Maggie couldn't feel any sympathy for the man. Just relief that she was truly free now.

"Then it's finally over. I don't have to hide," she said, turning to Dade with the intention of rushing into his arms.

The remote look in his eyes froze her in place. "You're safe. I'll be back in two weeks to escort you to St. Louis."

And with that he was gone.

She knew he was headed to the Crown Seven to confront his brother Reid. She knew, even if he didn't, that he needed her by his side. But that old fear of rejection kept her from running after him.

So she blinked back tears and tried like hell to put on a brave front. But Caroline, the woman who knew her better than herself at times, saw right through her ruse.

"Oh, for heaven's sake," Caroline said. "Don't just stand there like a lack wit. Follow your heart."

The chance of his turning her away scared her, but the fear of losing him forever terrified her. She threw her arms around Caroline. "Thank you."

"Go with him, Maggie, and be happy," Caroline said.

Maggie needed no further urgings. She lifted her hem

and raced out the door, hoping she wasn't too late to catch Dade.

The second Dade guided the buggy over the rise, he was hit with that odd sense of coming home that he'd felt the very first time he'd laid eyes on the Crown Seven Ranch. He let his gaze meander over the plains where a herd of fat Durham cattle grazed.

A dozen or so horses roamed with the cattle. The mix of calicos, buckskins, grays, and screwbalds told him these were the hands' cow ponies.

His gaze shifted beyond the barn to the stable and the stout corral built on a protected rise. There were horses there too, and though he was too far away to get a good look at them, he knew they were Reid's thoroughbreds. His foster brother's pride and joy.

Beyond the corral rose a brand new house, not near as grand as the one Kirby had built. But a fine place all the same. Who lived in it? The new owner? Reid?

"It just takes your breath away," Maggie said.

He eyed her and smiled, thinking she did the same to him. He'd surely burn in hell for leading a lady astray, but he didn't regret spending the last two days and nights with her either.

"Let's get this over with." He flicked the line and guided the buggy down the lane to the house he'd called home.

He parked in front of the house and damned the case of nerves that gripped him. A few cowboys looked his way.

One hand ambled toward him, his limp the only visible change Dade could see in the foreman.

"As I live and breathe," Booth Howard said. "About time you showed your face."

Dade laughed though it sounded a bit strained to his ears. "Heard the place sold."

Howard turned somber. "Just the shares Kirby and his cousin held."

That meant Reid still owned part of the Crown Seven. Was Miss Jennean right? Did he and Trey still own shares as well?

"Reid around?"

"He left two days ago with Mr. Charlton, bound for Kentucky. Don't expect them back for a month." Howard thumbed his hat back and smiled at Maggie. "How do, miss?"

"Hello to you." She extended a gloved hand to him. "Maggie Sutten."

"Pleasure," Howard said, giving her fingers the barest squeeze.

Before Dade could figure out how to explain his relationship with Maggie, the front door opened and a lady stepped onto the porch. A moment later a young woman joined her, and there was no mistaking she was with child.

"Welcome," the older woman said, her accent reminding him of Kirby Morris. "What brings you to the Crown Seven?"

Howard spoke for him. "This here is Dade Logan."

"Oh, my! Well, don't just stand there, Mr. Howard," the older woman said, suddenly seeming flustered. "See to their bags."

"Yes'm," Howard said and limped to the rear of the buggy.

Of all the scenes that'd played over in Dade's head, a hearty welcome home hadn't been one of them. He wasn't sure what to make of it as he climbed down and lent Maggie a hand. And damn if she hadn't been right—he did feel a helluva lot better with her by his side.

The older woman met them at the steps leading to the front porch. "Forgive my rudeness. I'm Gertrude Charlton. Oh, my, I've heard so much about you."

Dade was surely at a disadvantage here. "Pleased to meet you, ma'am."

Mrs. Charlton grasped Maggie's hand. "And you are?"

Maggie blushed. "Maggie Sutten, childhood friend of Dade's sister."

If Mrs. Charlton thought it indecent for Maggie to be traveling with Dade, she hid it well. "Welcome. Please, come inside and make yourselves at home. After all, it is Dade's home."

Dade was still reeling from that pronouncement as they trailed into the parlor where he'd spent many an evening playing chess or cards. A woman's touch was clearly evident, and he found himself liking the change.

"A pot of tea is in order," Mrs. Charlton said to the stoop-shouldered butler.

"I'll alert Mrs. Leach," Hubert said, then looked at Dade and added, "Welcome home, sir."

"Good to see you, Hubert."

"Have you heard from your younger brother?" Mrs. Charlton asked Dade as they took seats.

"No, ma'am. I lost track of Trey well over a year ago."

"Oh, dear." She tugged a lacy kerchief from her sleeve, dabbed at her eyes, and shared a worried look with the mother-to-be. "I'm beginning to lose hope."

"Reid feared something dreadful had happened to Dade," the younger woman said, "yet here he is. We have to believe that Trey is fine and possibly unaware of what's happened here."

He wasn't the only one, Dade thought.

"Forgive me for not catching your name," Maggie said to the young woman.

She laughed, a light sound that lifted the somber mood Dade was close to slipping into. "We've certainly made a muddle of this homecoming. I'm Ellie Jo, Reid's wife."

Dade scratched his head, more confused than if he'd

stepped into the middle of a drama. "Suppose somebody start at the beginning and tell me how you all came to be here."

"Excellent notion. Explain it to him, Ellie," Mrs. Charlton said.

For the next hour, Dade listened to a story that shocked him, and enraged him. All this time he'd been led to believe Reid had betrayed him. But that wasn't the case at all.

He'd been blackmailed to do the bidding of Kirby's cousin or risk seeing his foster brothers hang for rustling. But what really stunned him was this tiny Englishwoman who believed that Trey could be the son stolen from her at birth.

Because of that small chance, she and her husband had stepped in and saved the Crown Seven for Reid, Dade, and Trey.

Their shares were here if and when they wanted them. Reid had already built his house beyond the stables. There was plenty of land for Dade and Trey to do the same.

"I don't suppose you remember if Trey had a birthmark?" Mrs. Charlton asked.

"If he had one, I never saw it," Dade said, and wished he could say otherwise when the lady's shoulders slumped.

That evening Dade and Maggie sat on the front porch alone. His head was still reeling from all he'd learned.

"I hope I can find Daisy," he said, troubled that he hadn't picked up his sister's trail, worried that she could be dead.

"Have you thought of hiring a Pinkerton man?"

"Nope, but I could afford to now." He reached over and took Maggie's hand in his. "Thank you, Maggie mine, for insisting I come back here."

She smiled, and he knew he'd never tire of sharing moments like this with her. "I can see why you hated to leave here. Why it angered you so to think you'd been betrayed by your brother and robbed of your home."

"It's a good place to grow up, and grow old," he said.

She laughed softly. Intimately. "I've only been here a day, and I don't want to leave the Crown Seven."

He entwined his fingers with hers, feeling the beat of her heart thudding in time with his. "Don't tell me you're thinking of giving up the idea of going to nurses' school."

She didn't say a thing for the longest time, just sat beside him, holding his hand, unknowingly holding his heart in her hands.

"Nurses' school was a means to an end," she said at last. "I like helping people, but I don't want to spend the rest of my life taking care of strangers."

She looked at him then, and pale moonlight kissed her nose and mouth like he longed to do. "What are you getting at, Maggie?"

"I want to spend my life taking care of my own family," she said, her voice small and shy, as if she was afraid to admit her deepest longing.

"You sure you'd be content to be a wife and mother?"

"If the right man asked me," she said with a smile.

"Interesting," he said, allowing a smile of his own. "What's your idea of the right man?"

"He's honest. Generous. Brave. I'd love him, of course." She lowered her head, and he'd bet she was blushing. "And he'd have to love me."

He wet his lips and swallowed hard, gazing at the land that he owned and then back at the woman he longed to make his. He'd thought he just might love her the first time he'd stolen a kiss. The notion had grown stronger when he made love with her.

Now? Now he knew he loved her and didn't want to think about living without her in his life.

He leaned close and brushed her lips with his. "The right man is asking, Maggie mine."

He heard her breath catch. "Truly?"

"Truly," he said, this time kissing her long and deep. "I love you, Maggie. I have for some time."

"You know I love you," she whispered against his lips. "That I want you."

He rested his forehead against hers, stunned by the contentment washing over him. Any doubts he'd had about this ranch or this woman were long gone now.

"Marry me, Maggie mine. Say yes, and we'll pay the preacher a visit tomorrow."

"Yes," she said, turning just so to nuzzle his neck and nip his chin. "About tonight . . ."

"You got something in mind?"

He felt her smile against his throat and drank in her sigh. "Stay with me."

"You can count on it." Tonight, and every night for the rest of their lives.